BUILD
UNIVERS

Ken Wilson

The Duke's Portrait

Lynette!
I hope you enjoy
my little story!

Ken

europe books

© 2021 **Europe Books**| London
www.europebooks.co.uk | info@europebooks.co.uk

ISBN 979-12-201-1430-1

First edition: October 2021
Distribution for the United Kingdom: **Vine House
Distribution ltd**

Printed for Italy by *Rotomail Italia S.p.A. - Vignate (MI)*
Stampato presso *Rotomail Italia S.p.A. - Vignate (MI)*

The Duke's Portrait

February 1937

In The Times, *Charles discovered that Lord Halifax was on his way to Germany to negotiate with Chancellor Adolf Hitler. After the announcement in parliament, which according to* The Times *was met with almost universal approval, Winston Churchill made a speech warning of the dangers of appeasement, saying that the Germans were developing missiles that could be launched in their own country and rain destruction on London. Churchill was shouted down by members of his own party.*

On another page, Charles read that MPs had also voted to fund the building of air raid shelters in London and other cities.

Staying at Great Park suddenly seemed like a pretty good idea...

Dramatis personae

Diana Bagshot, 30s, Viscountess Grimbledon, widow of Eustace Bagshot

Bert Branch, age unknown, chauffeur to Godfrey Krumnagel

Rupert Burgess, 54, assistant manager, Krumnagel's Bank

Betty Burton, 20s, barmaid at The Flask pub, Hampstead

Leonora Capstan/Goodgame, 40s, novelist, second wife of Horace Goodgame and mother of Polly Capstan

Polly Capstan, 20, secretary to the Duke of Burfaughtonleigh

Ronnie Capstan, age unknown, first husband of Leonora Goodgame and father of Polly Capstan

Sergeant Conway, age unknown, Cheltenham police officer

Henry Dumont, age unknown, former racing driver

Wilfred Flockton, 18, under butler at Great Park

Charles Goodgame, 23, portrait painter

Ernest Goodgame, 50s, entrepreneur, bon viveur

Horace Goodgame, 50s, amateur watercolourist, father of Charles Goodgame and brother of Ernest Goodgame

Martha Goodgame/Donkin, age unknown, first wife of Horace Goodgame

Lawrence Kimberley-Waugh, 20s, Sotheby's watercolours expert

Sebastian Kugelhorn, age unknown, solicitor

Godfrey Krumnagel, 38, executive manager, Krumnagel's Bank

Gisèle Lemarchand, 60s, maid to Veronica Stoodley

Alexander Malleson, age unknown, doctor

Arnold McGurk, age unknown, Stanford Saint Mary stationmaster

Edna Normington, age unknown, housekeeper for Horace Goodgame

Carlos Petworth, age unknown, Argentinian business partner of Ronnie Capstan

Montmorency Pickles, age unknown, butler at Great Park

Constable Prodgers, age unknown, Cheltenham police officer

Garth Prodgers, age unknown, gardener at Great Park and brother of Constable Prodgers

Emily Roebuck, age unknown, friend of Martha Goodgame

Inspector Gordon Sparrow, age unknown, police inspector

Veronica Stoodley, 80s, neighbour of Ernest Goodgame

Turnbull, age unknown, Cornelia Wickham-Thynne's chauffeur

Walter Washbrook, 60s, artist

Arthur Wickham-Thynne, age unknown, entrepreneur and theatre impresario

Cornelia Wickham-Thynne, age unknown, wife of Arthur Wickham-Thynne

Eric Winstanley, age unknown, the Duke of Burfaughtonleigh's chauffeur

Gilbert Woolnough, 20s, Marquis of Stanford, son of Tarquin Woolnough

Tarquin Woolnough, age unknown, fourteenth Duke of Burfaughtonleigh

Chapter 1
It's pronounced Burley, actually
Monday 15th February 1937, Stanford Saint Mary -
overcast and chilly

Travelling third class on the Paddington to Cheltenham
stopping train, Charles Goodgame drifted off to sleep
somewhere near Reading. When he woke up, the train
was rattling past farmland and rain was spattering
against the windows. A couple of pasty-faced old
people, a vicar and a woman, were in the seats next to
the door on the opposite side of the compartment. The
vicar's head was drooped over his chest, and he was
snoring loudly. Charles smiled at the woman but when
he opened his mouth to speak, she looked away.

"Excuse me?" said Charles. The woman continued to
look out of the window. "Excuse me?" he repeated, a
little louder. Reluctantly, the woman turned to look at
him. "Would you happen to know what time it is?" he
asked.

The woman leaned forward and tapped the vicar on
the shoulder. "Cedric!" she hissed. This failed to wake
him up, so she kicked him firmly on the shin.

"Uuf!" he said, opening his eyes. He rubbed his shin,
then glared at the woman. "Did you just kick me?" She
jerked her head to indicate Charles. The vicar turned and
glared at him instead.

"Sorry to be a problem," said Charles. "Would you
know the time? I'm getting off at Stanford Saint Mary.
Train should get there about ten to three. I wanted to
make sure I haven't missed the stop."

The vicar took out his pocket watch and looked at it.
"It's five and twenty to three," he said.

"Oh marvellous, thank you," said Charles. "Better get my things together."

The couple turned and stared out of the window again. Charles wondered why they were so unfriendly. They were dressed top to toe in black and their general demeanour suggested they were on their way to or from a funeral. Charles was wearing a cream suit with a bright green pullover over a white shirt, a long red scarf and scuffed brown boots. His mustard-coloured fedora was on the seat next to him and his sandy hair was sticking out at angles. Were his clothes too bright for them? Too untidy?

Maybe they were alarmed by the broad smile on his face. He couldn't help it. He was excited at the prospect of seeing his stepsister Polly for the first time since Christmas, knowing that he would finally be able to spend time with her away from the rich young men in London who clustered round her like moths. The thought that he would have her all to himself made him chuckle out loud. The vicar and his wife looked at him again, alarmed.

The train whistled and slowed as it approached Stanford Saint Mary station. Charles took his suitcase and a wooden box down from the luggage rack, forgetting that his portfolio was under the suitcase. The door to the platform was on the side of the train where the couple were sitting. He tried not to stand on their feet as he moved towards the door, but the wooden box he was carrying struck the vicar on the side of his head.

"Uuuuf!" said the vicar for a second time.

"Sorry," said Charles. The vicar said something under his breath that he would probably have to apologise for the next time he prayed. Charles pushed open the door and stepped onto the platform. "Awfully nice to have met you," he said with a smile, and slammed the door. He put the suitcase and the box down and promptly fell over them. A tall man wearing a hat with STATIONMASTER written on a metal label marched down the platform, grabbed one of his arms and tugged him to his feet.

"Ouch! Um... thank you," said Charles. "Oh, bugger!" he added, when he realised that his portfolio and hat were still on the train. "Hold on a sec." He turned to get back into the compartment, but the stationmaster continued to hold his arm in an iron grip.

"I say, can you let go?" said Charles. "I need to get back on the train."

"The train is about to depart," said the stationmaster, and blew his whistle. Charles pulled away from him, opened the compartment door and leapt inside. The stationmaster slammed the door and blew his whistle again. When the train started moving, Charles had no choice but to lean up and pull the communication cord. The train braked, and he fell and landed heavily in the vicar's lap.

"Uuuuuuuf!" said the vicar, much louder than the previous two times.

"Awfully sorry," replied Charles. He pulled himself to his feet, the train lurched again, and he fell the other way onto the vicar's wife.

"Oooh!" she said.

"Many apologies."

"Don't mention it," she said, with a fleeting smile.

Charles put on his hat, pulled the portfolio down from the luggage rack and opened the door. He quickly stepped back onto the platform, where the stationmaster grabbed him by the shoulder. "I arrest you for a railway-related misdemeanour," he said.

"Really?" said Charles. "Can you actually do that?"

Instead of answering, the man emitted a loud yelp and collapsed in a heap on the platform. Charles looked down at him, puzzled. When he looked up again, he saw Polly standing behind the fallen giant.

"Hello, Chas!" she said, brightly.

"Hello, Pol. Er ... did you do that?"

"Knock out our friend here? Yes."

"How?"

"Yoko Geri," said Polly.

"What?"

"Yoko Geri. It's a karate kick. I've been taking lessons." She leaned back and jabbed her right foot in front of Charles's face, missing his nose by inches.

"Steady on!" Charles looked down at the large motionless man. "Is he still alive?"

"I imagine so. Yoko Geri is only fatal in about ten per cent of cases."

"Good ... what???"

The vicar pulled down the window and put his head out. "Is this train leaving or not?" he asked. He looked down and saw the stationmaster lying on the platform. "I say, is that chap all right?"

"He's fine, he just fainted," said Polly. "A touch of sunstroke."

"Sunstroke?" repeated the vicar, looking up at the dark skies. "In February?"

Polly bent down and took the whistle from the unconscious man's hand and blew it hard. The engine whistled a reply and the train moved slowly away. "We'd better make ourselves scarce," she said, pocketing the whistle. She picked up the wooden box and hurried towards the exit. Charles grabbed his suitcase and portfolio and ran after her out of the station, where an

14

open-topped two-seater sports car was parked. Polly opened the boot and threw the box into it.

"Be careful," said Charles. "Those are my oils."

"Just put your things in and get in the car," said Polly.

"What about that chap you just knocked out? Shouldn't we ---?"

"Get *in*, will you?"

Polly was already in the driving seat, revving the engine. Charles put his suitcase and portfolio in the boot, closed it and jumped into the passenger seat. She pressed her foot hard on the accelerator and the car roared away from the station. Charles's hat flew off, but he caught it in time and jammed it between his knees. The road was lined with trees that loomed above their heads. Charles ducked as the car weaved its way under them.

He gazed at his stepsister, as she gripped the huge steering wheel, her teeth biting her bottom lip, her blonde hair flying wildly behind her. She was wearing a brown leather flying jacket, tight riding breeches and long black boots. A white scarf caught in the wind and waved madly over her shoulder. As always, he felt an urgent desire for her.

"Is this car yours?" he asked.

"No, it belongs to Gilbert."

"Who's Gilbert?"

"A friend. This is his jacket, too. Leather's awfully good when you're driving in winter. You should get one."

"Very amusing. I can afford neither a car nor a leather jacket."

The needle on the large round speedometer passed sixty miles an hour. The noise of the engine increased, making it almost impossible to have a conversation.

"It's awfully fancy," said Charles. "What is it?"

"SORRY?"

"WHAT KIND OF CAR IS IT?"

"Oh. It's an Alfa Romeo. Latest design, brand new. It has an inline six engine."

"What does that mean?"

"Six cylinders, in a straight line. Revolutionary."

"I'll take your word for it."

"Don't you know anything about cars?"

"Not a thing," said Charles. "By the way, I didn't know you'd passed your driving test."

"I haven't."

"What?"

"Well, you don't really need a licence out here in the sticks. I don't imagine you'd get asked for one unless you were in town."

"I'm sure that's not actually true, Polly."

"Relax, Chas! Driving this thing is a piece of cake. Oh heck..." She swerved to the left to avoid a small furry creature and the car careered towards a tall thorny hedgerow.

"Look out!" yelled Charles.

The car slammed into the hedgerow and sped along, shaking from side to side. Sharp hawthorns rat-tat-tatted against the windscreen. He wasn't quick enough to pull his arm away, and a spike tore a hole in the sleeve of his jacket. Polly turned sharply to the right and the car accelerated across the road and scraped along the hedgerow on the other side.

"For Christ's sake, Pol, will you slow down? You're going to kill us both!"

"Chas, you're such a worry-widget, just relax."

"Relax? You nearly ripped my bally arm off! And you've torn my jacket!"

16

She turned the wheel to the left, then to the right, then left again. The car zigzagged down the narrow lane until she got it back in control and continued more or less in a straight line.

"I'm so glad you're here," said Polly. "I've missed you."

Despite fearing for his life, Charles felt a glow of delight when he heard these words. He had known Polly for less than a year and since then, the only time his life felt remotely exciting was when he was with her. He smiled and gripped the sides of the leather seat.

"So," she said, taking a quick sidelong look at him. "Are you pleased you made the effort to get out here?"

"Of course, I am." Polly had written two weeks before, inviting Charles to come out to Stanford Saint Mary to paint a portrait of her employer. "Imagine!" he said. "Me getting the chance to paint the Duke of Burfaughtonleigh!"

"It's pronounced Burley, actually," said Polly. At a crossroads, she raced to the left round the corner, causing an old man on a bicycle to swerve across the road and into a ditch to avoid her. Charles looked back, watching the man curse and shake his fist as he disappeared.

The road was now wide and straight, so Polly drove even faster. "OK, first of all, I need to clear something up," she said. "The Duke is actually expecting Walter Washbrook to paint his portrait."

"What?"

"The Duke is ---"

"I heard what you said. He's expecting Walter Washbrook to paint his portrait?"

"Yes."

"The chap who paints royalty?"

"The very same."

"So what am I doing here?"

"You're going to pretend to be Walter Washbrook."

"Is this some kind of joke?"

"No, I'm deadly serious."

"But Walter Washbrook is about sixty!"

Walter Washbrook was one of the most successful portrait painters in the country, having been commissioned to paint not only the late King George but also his wife and all six of their children. His success was the result of an immense stroke of luck. In 1877, when he was twelve years old, he had been sent by his parents to work on HMS Britannia, a cadet training ship in Plymouth. The young Prince George, who was the same age, was also on the ship. At the time, no one expected George to become king, he was after all the second son, and he was generally thought to be a bit of a waste of space, so his parents hoped he might at least be able to serve in the navy. Washbrook's parents were similarly disappointed in their son. The two boys hit it off immediately and had remained close friends until George's death the previous year.

"Sixty, is he?" repeated Polly. "In that case, it isn't going to be easy."

"Polly!"

"Don't worry, I was only joking."

"Thank goodness."

"I mean I was only joking about not knowing how old Washbrook is. I saw a photograph of him in a magazine. Fear not. I will make you look just like a sixty-year-old buffer who paints portraits of kings and queens."

"What are you talking about?"

"Chas, do try to keep up. Before we meet the Duke, I'm going to disguise you to look like Walter Washbrook."

"But why are we doing this?"

"Relax. Polly has a plan. All will be revealed."

Charles thought for a moment. "Look here," he said. "You told me that the Duke had asked for me personally to paint his portrait. You've brought me here under false pretences."

"I didn't, and I haven't," replied Polly, as the car zoomed over a limping hedgehog. "When he said he wanted his portrait painted, I told him you'd be the ideal person to do it, but he was very keen on this Washbrook chap, so of course I said I knew him, too."

"Do you?"

"Do I what?"

"Know Walter Washbrook?"

"Well, I know who he *is*," said Polly. "So I wasn't actually telling fibs."

Charles sighed and shook his head. "He'll know I'm not Walter Washbrook," he said. "I'm a hundred per cent certain of that."

"No he won't," said Polly. "Tarquin's never met him. He's never even seen a photo of him. I checked."

"Tarquin? The Duke?"

"Yes."

"Right. What do you do for him, anyway?"

"I'm his secretary."

Charles burst out laughing. "You? A secretary? You can't even type! Never mind type, you can't even *spell*!"

Polly's face clouded over for a moment. "Well, maybe Tarquin has seen some hidden talent of mine that you haven't."

I bet he has, thought Charles. "So, how did you get the job?"

"Gilbert told me about it."

"Gilbert. The chap who owns this car?"

"Yes."

"Who is he?"

"Gilbert Woolnough, the Marquis of Stanford. He's Tarquin's son."

"How do you know him?"

"I met him at a party in Chelsea and ..."

"And...?

"... we got chatting."

"You got chatting with a Marquis."

"Yes. You know how much I enjoy meeting rich young men." She laughed. "That was a joke," she added.

Charles knew it wasn't a joke. Not only did Polly enjoy meeting rich young men, but she also made a habit of getting engaged to them. She was only twenty, but she had already been engaged three times that Charles knew about, and there were possibly more. The only one of her fiancés he had actually met was a good-looking but rather dim man in his thirties called Humphrey Fotheringay, the heir to the Fotheringay's Sausages empire. He had met Polly when he was still in shock after his first wife had divorced him before they'd even been married for a year. The engagement lasted for about a month. Fotheringay was now thinking of becoming a monk.

Polly called off her engagements as soon as she took possession of a ring, which she then sold. Charles presumed that selling engagement rings was one of the ways she made a living.

"Hold onto your hat, we're nearly there."

There was a wall along the road lined with leafless trees and now the trees were taller, evergreen and framed the entrance to an estate. The car passed a small gatehouse and Polly turned left up a muddy track. Charles saw a dilapidated sign behind the wall that had been ravaged by the weather over the years and the writing on it was faded. He could only see the letters EAT ARK.

"What's the name of this place?" he asked.

"Great Park."

"Ah," said Charles. He thought for a moment and then said: "Look, Pol, I don't think I can go through with this."

"You can and you will."

"The thing is ... "

Polly put her foot down hard on the brake and the car lurched to a stop in the mud, half in and half out of the gate. Charles had to put his hands on the dashboard to prevent his head from hitting the windscreen. Polly turned and grabbed his chin with her left hand. He was alarmed by the fierce look in her eyes.

"The thing *is*, brother dear ..." she said, holding his face in a tight grip which really hurt, "I have a plan which is going to make us a lot of money."

"You said I'd get thirty pounds for painting the old boy's phizog. That *is* a lot of money."

"Painting the Duke's portrait is just a way to get you into the house. My plan involves doing something that will make us *heaps* more than that."

"What? Doing what?" Charles had visions of wearing a mask and a striped pullover, carrying a sack bulging with the family silver and being chased by dogs. "Look, Pol, whatever it is, leave me out of it. I'm not the criminal type."

She let go of his jaw. "Not the criminal type? Really?"

"Really."

"Shall we talk about that painting you sold to my mother's best friend?"

Charles stared at her. "You wouldn't."

"Try me."

21

Of course, Polly knew about the painting. It had all been a terrible misunderstanding, but if she ever did tell anyone what she knew, it would be curtains for his chances of continuing to make a living in the art world.

"You're a funny one," he said. "On the one hand, you tell me you trust me more than anyone you know, and on the other, you blackmail me."

"It's for your own good," she replied. "We're going to make a small fortune out of this."

"What is it you want me to do?"

"I want you to paint the Duke's portrait."

"I know that. What's the big money-making plan?"

"Let me finish," she said. "Tarquin has some extremely valuable paintings hanging around the place, and one of them is a Van Gogh."

"Seriously?" said Charles. "What is it?"

"A portrait of Robert Louis Stevenson."

"The chap who wrote *Treasure Island*?"

"Yes."

Charles had studied Van Gogh as part of his course at the Royal College of Art, he had even visited the Rijksmuseum in Amsterdam, but he had never heard of a Van Gogh portrait of Robert Louis Stevenson. "Are you sure it's genuine?" he asked.

"Absolutely. A chap came up from that art place in London last month to have a look at Tarquin's collection."

"Art place? You mean Sotheby's?"

"The other one."

"Christie's?"

"That's it."

Charles thought for a moment, fearing that what he was about to ask would get an affirmative answer. "You aren't planning to steal the painting, are you?"

"Of course not."

"Thank goodness. "

"You're going to paint a copy of it."

"What?"

"And then we're going to steal it."

"What? That's ... it's ---"

"Clever?"

"Completely mad!"

"Not really," said Polly. "I know you can do it. You once told me you could copy anybody's style except that Spanish cove. What's his name - Picossi?"

"Picasso," said Charles. "Pablo Picasso."

"That's the chap. I'm sure copying a Van Gogh will be a piece of cake to an expert forger like you."

"Listen. I wish you wouldn't ---"

"Oh do pipe down, Charles. You might as well acknowledge what you're good at."

Charles now understood why she'd asked him to bring more than one canvas. She told him there might be other paintings he could do while he was there. She'd even specified the size of the canvases. It had never occurred to Charles to ask her why.

She started the engine and drove through the gate and, after a hundred yards, turned left down a muddy track. The car passed through a small copse of willow trees and came to a halt outside a cottage.

"Where are we?" asked Charles. "I mean, I presume this isn't Great Park."

"Well done, Sherlock, right first time," said Polly. "This is Willow Cottage."

"Do you live here?"

"No, I don't. My friend Garth lives here. He's the Duke's gardener."

"So why are we here?"

"I have to turn you into Walter Washbrook before we go to the main house."

"But this Garth chap, how does he fit into all this?"

"This Garth chap, as you call him, is our accomplice."

"Can we trust him?"

"To the ends of the earth and beyond. Get out of the car."

When Charles opened the door of the two-seater and put his foot down, his boot almost disappeared into the mud. He pulled himself up and out of the car, took a step forward, then slipped and fell flat on his back. He tried to leap up, fell sideways and onto his face. When he stood up, he was covered in mud from his sandy hair to his brown boots. Polly burst out laughing.

"This is NOT FUNNY!" he shouted, "and to be honest, I'm A BIT ANGRY now!"

Polly got out and walked to the other side of the car and stood in front of him. "Oh Charles," she said, looking him straight in the eyes, "I do love it when you're a bit angry." He started to say something else, but she put her arms round his neck and kissed him firmly on his muddy lips.

"What a pity we just missed Valentine's Day," she said, and kissed him again.

Chapter 2
Charles, take off your clothes

Monday, Willow Cottage, early evening - turning chilly

The walls of Willow Cottage had clearly not seen a coat of paint for a while, and the windows were caked in dirt. Polly knocked on the black wooden door and waited. There was no sound from inside.

"There's no one here," said Charles. "I need to ---"

"Just be patient," said Polly.

Eventually, an upstairs window creaked open, and a large head covered in tangled black hair appeared, slowly followed by an equally enormous face, most of which was concealed behind a bushy beard. The face had clearly been asleep, and the eyes blinked slowly two or three times and then opened wide to focus.

"Wakey wakey, Garth, you have visitors," shouted Polly.

Garth said not a word. He looked at Polly, then at her mud-stained companion, withdrew from view and closed the window. Charles heard heavy footsteps coming downstairs and across the floor. The door creaked open, and the occupant had to bend his enormous frame to get out.

Garth was well over six feet tall and broad shouldered, with muscular arms protruding from the rolled-up sleeves of a brown woollen shirt. He was wearing army issue khaki trousers held up by a pair of black braces. He had no shoes and the thick brown sock on his right foot had a hole in it, out of which protruded a long, big toe. The left foot was covered by a grey sock, free from holes.

25

The gardener pushed back his long straggly hair and revealed a pale forehead of Neanderthal proportions. He looked Charles up and down, and his features darkened. Charles smiled weakly, his knees turning to jelly. He felt sure that Garth could, if he wished, knock the wind out of him with even an accidental blow from one of those enormous hands.

Polly stood on tiptoe and kissed Garth on the cheek, an action which caused a brief smile to flicker across his face, visible in his eyes despite his mouth being camouflaged by facial hair. "Garth, this is my brother Charles," she said. "You two are going to get on like a house on fire."

Charles wasn't sure that Garth agreed, but he put out his right hand. The gardener stared at the hand for a moment, then held it in a tight grip which made Charles's eyes water.

"Sooooo pleased to meet you," he said, his face screwed up in pain.

"Come in," said Garth. He sounded like a juvenile whose voice was breaking. Having expected the large man to have a voice that rattled the eaves, Charles had to bite his lip to avoid chortling out loud at this unexpected sound. He didn't feel quite so intimidated any more.

The giant gardener turned and walked into the cottage, the downstairs of which was one large dark room with a door at the back and a staircase off to the right. There was a threadbare sofa, a high-backed leather armchair, another wooden chair with a straw seat and a table, on which there was a candlestick, a single plate and a large mug. Charles could dimly see a black wood-burning stove against the back wall and a shelf with a water bowl next to it. On the right was a fireplace with the embers of a fire, and there was a large clock on the wall above it. All round the room were piles of old books.

"Garth, poppet," said Polly. "Charles needs to clean up a bit. What do you suggest?"

Garth looked at Charles's mud-stained clothes and walked to the back of the cottage and opened the door. "There," he said. Charles looked outside and saw a well surrounded by trees.

"Perfect," said Polly. "Charles, take off your clothes."

"What?"

"Take off your clothes."

"But----"

"Charles, please just do as I say. We need to get up to the house." She looked at the clock. "I have to turn you into Walter Washbrook as fast as I can." She took off his jacket, throwing it onto the sofa. She then began to unbutton his white shirt, which had mud stains on the collar.

"I say, do you mind?" said Charles. "I'm perfectly capable of undressing myself."

"Then do it!" said Polly. "We have to press on. Do you have another shirt?"

"Yes, in my suitcase."

"OK, I'll go and get it while you're getting washed. By the way, I'm going to call you Walter from now on, so you can get used to your new identity."

Charles took off his trousers and gave them to Polly. She glanced at his flannel vest and long johns and laughed. "I see you don't buy your underwear at Harrods," she said. Charles quickly made his way out of the cottage to avoid the embarrassment of being seen in a state of arousal.

Charles had never seen a well before. There was a pulley across the top with a rope coiled round it and a

27

handle to the side. He peered down and saw a bucket attached to a hook on the rope. He turned the handle and winched the bucket up. It was empty. He winched it down again and heard it splash into the water. It was harder to bring back up when it was full, and the pulley squeaked as he struggled to get it back to the top. When the bucket was visible, he let go of the handle and leaned forward to unhook it, but the rope uncoiled rapidly, and he heard the bucket hit the water again.

Charles cursed loudly. "How in God's name is anyone supposed to *live* in a place like this?" he shouted. Eventually, he managed to get a full bucket out of the well and onto the muddy ground. He plunged his hands into the icy water, rubbed them together and then washed his face and hair. By the time he had finished, he was shivering, and his teeth were chattering.

When he went back into the cottage, Polly and Garth were standing in front of the fireplace talking quietly to each other. Charles felt a pang of jealousy but tried to comfort himself with the thought that Polly couldn't really be interested in a huge muscular gardener. Could she?

"I'm afraid your jacket is split down the back as well, Charles ... I mean Walter," she said. "It must have happened when you fell in the mud."

"What am I going to do?" asked Charles. "It's the only jacket I have. I can't turn up in my shirtsleeves. It's February, for goodness sake."

"Don't you have an overcoat or something?"

"No. I was going to buy some new clothes when I got the money for painting the portrait."

"I'm sure Garth has something," said Polly. "Anyway, sit down, I have to turn you into Walter Washbrook."

Half an hour later, Charles walked out of the cottage a transformed man. Polly had glued white hair onto his cheeks and chin and stuck some more over his eyebrows, and his red hair was covered with a luxurious grey wig. Garth's black overcoat stretched down almost to his feet. The sleeves were rolled up so that his hands were visible. His eyes were hidden behind a pair of black-rimmed dark glasses, and he was walking with a stick.

"I must look like a bally blind person," he said.

Polly ignored his complaints. "Walter! Come on, do try to walk like a sixty-year-old," she said.

"How do sixty-year-olds walk?" he asked.

"Well, they're at death's door, aren't they?" she replied. "I expect they huff and groan a lot. Try huffing and groaning any time you move."

They got into the Alfa Romeo and Polly drove up the lane, turned left and accelerated along the wide driveway towards the house. When the line of trees ended, a massive area of parkland appeared and a large neo-Gothic building came into view, elevated from the surrounding land. Seeing Great Park for the first time through his dark glasses, Charles thought it looked like the castle in the film *Dracula*. There was a tower in one corner, and a smaller turret in another, and a line of tall narrow chimney pots down the middle of the roof.

"When we arrive, we'll be met by the butler," said Polly. "His name is Pickles. And the under-butler, his name's Flockton, will take your suitcase to your room. I'll tell them you're feeling dead as a dodo after your trip and you need some rest, so you can disappear for a bit and make yourself at home."

Charles felt a rising sense of anxiety as the car sped along. They pulled up at the front door and parked behind a black car. Polly looked at it, puzzled. "I wonder who that belongs to," she said.

Charles stared up at the giant mansion, which looked even more dark and forbidding close to. It was four floors high, and there were five or six windows on either side of the massive double doors. The original grey stonework was black in places and in need of a thorough clean. On the right, there was a smaller newer wall, which presumably hid some kind of garden or courtyard.

One of the doors opened with a loud creaking sound, and Charles braced himself to see someone resembling Bela Lugosi emerge. In fact, a short thin man wearing a black suit appeared and walked down the steps towards them. He had a pale face and a long thin nose, the top of his head was egg bald and at the sides there was thin wavy hair which was dyed black. He had the build and demeanour of an ancient ballet dancer and looked as if the merest puff of wind would knock him over. It was Montmorency Pickles, the Great Park butler.

"Hello, Monty!" said Polly. "Meet Walter Washbrook."

Pickles glanced at Charles, raising his eyebrows slightly. "Welcome to Great Park, Mister Washbrook," he said. "I trust you had a pleasant journey."

Before Charles could reply, the butler turned to Polly. "We have a small problem," he said. "The duke has some visitors and I'm afraid you need to meet them too. Both of you."

"Oh, I say," said Polly, "can't Walter have a moment to snooze? He's had a long journey, and he's positively pooped. Aren't you, poppet?" she added in a loud voice.

Charles nodded and felt the wig shift. He made a mental note not to do that again. "Yes," he said, and was horrified to hear that his first attempt at a sixty-year-old voice came out falsetto.

"I really must insist that you attend the duke forthwith," said Pickles. "He's in the blue drawing room. I'm most awfully sorry, Mr Washbrook!" he shouted in Charles's face, making him jump. "Please follow me."

Pickles turned and walked elegantly up the steps to the front door. Polly tripped lightly after him, and Charles leaned on the stick and huffed and groaned as he followed them. They walked into the dark interior of Great Park and down a central hallway. The butler knocked on a door and opened it, indicating that Polly and Charles should go in before him.

"Hello all!" said Polly. "Let me introduce the incredibly famous portrait painter, Walter Washbrook!"

"Hello!" said Charles, smiling, which stretched the glue on his beard. "Awfully nice to be here."

He looked around the room and the smile disappeared from his face. There were two police officers standing in the middle of the room and another man sitting in an armchair. It was the Stanford Saint Mary stationmaster.

Chapter 3
I think Pickles has a past
Monday evening, Great Park - getting colder

Charles peered through his dark glasses, first of all at the man in the armchair, the stationmaster that Polly had knocked out. He was looking Charles up and down, taking in everything about his appearance. Charles was convinced that he was staring at the two inches of cream trouser that were visible below the hem of Garth's long overcoat, and that he might remember the colour of his suit after their brief skirmish on the station platform. He was relieved that he had at least left his brown hat in the car, in case the man recognised that.

The two police officers walked forward and stood in front of Charles and Polly. The older man was wearing an officer's peaked cap and the younger one was wearing a constable's helmet. Like the stationmaster and Garth the gardener, the constable was a vast human being. Charles thought there must be something in the Gloucestershire water that created such giants.

The sergeant took off his peaked cap and cleared his throat before speaking. "Good evening, Mr Washbrook, Miss Capstan," he said. "I'm Sergeant Conway from the Cheltenham Constabulary, and this is Constable Prodgers, who mans the police station at Stanford Saint Mary. This afternoon, we received a phone call indicating that there had been an assault and robbery."

"Good heavens," said Polly. "Who's been assaulted and robbed? Not the Duke, I hope?"

"No, not me, darling," said someone with a deep baritone voice. There was a high-backed red leather armchair facing a coffee table in front of the fireplace, and the man who was sitting in it stood up and approached them. He was about the same height as Pickles, but twice as wide.

Giants and dwarves, thought Charles, the place is populated by giants and dwarves.

The Duke of Burfaughtonleigh waddled elegantly towards the new arrivals. An ancient fat black Labrador that had been sitting next to his chair got up and plodded uncomfortably after him, wagging his tail like a slow metronome.

"Sergeant, dear," said the man, "could you wait just a moment while I welcome my distinguished guest?"

Sergeant Conway bowed slightly, stepped back and replaced his cap. The Duke held out his hand and Charles extended his own, which was immediately clasped between the other man's pudgy sweaty palms. Charles felt as if his hand had been consumed by a toothless lizard.

"Mister Washbrook, it's the most profound honour and pleasure to welcome you to Great Park," said the Duke, a broad smile spreading across his jowly face, causing his luxuriant head of brown curly hair to shift slightly. Charles looked at the mobile wig and resolved not to smile in case his false head of hair moved, too.

"Charmed, I'm sure," replied Charles, experimenting with a less squeaky voice. He glanced at Pickles, the only member of the Great Park household who had heard his original misjudged falsetto delivery. Pickles was staring fondly at the Duke.

"We've met before, haven't we?" said the Duke.

Charles froze, alarm rising from his gut to his throat. His hand was still trapped inside the mouth of the lizard. But in the midst of his fear, he remembered Polly saying that the Duke had never even seen a photo of Walter Washbrook. He hoped to goodness that she was right.

"Yes, of course we have!" said Charles. "Buffy Snodgrass's fiftieth birthday party, wasn't it? Back in '35."

"Yes, indeed!" replied the Duke enthusiastically, looking around the room to make sure that everyone was aware of the fact that a world-famous artist remembered meeting him.

Sergeant Conway coughed loudly. The Duke turned to face him. "What is it, sergeant?" he asked.

"Your Grace," said the sergeant, "with your permission, I feel we must press on with our investigation. I have to ask Mr Washbrook and Miss Capstan a few questions."

The Duke sighed. "If you must," he said. "But I hardly think Mr Washbrook needs to be questioned about a case of common assault. I mean, he's a world-renowned *artiste*."

The sergeant addressed the new arrivals. "This afternoon, someone arrived at Stanford Saint Mary station on the train from London," he said, "and at approximately the same time, there was an assault on the person of Mister Arnold McGurk, the stationmaster." He made a dramatic sweep of his arm to indicate the victim of the crime, who was still seated. "The assailant also stole Mister McGurk's whistle, which is the property of the Great Western Railway Company. We have reason to believe that the perpetrator of the crime was the person who disembarked from the train, who was described by a witness as a young man with red hair."

Sergeant Conway paused to see what effect his words were having.

"What an extraordinary story," said Polly. "Do go on. We're all ears."

"After the assault, the man was observed leaving the station in a sports car in the company of a young woman with blonde hair." The sergeant paused and looked at Polly, and then looked up at her hair. "The witness said they'd seen the car before, leaving the Great Park estate."

"I say! What jolly bad news," said Polly. "Sorry we can't help you, but we haven't been anywhere near Stanford Saint Mary station. I picked Walter up in Oxford."

"Oxford?" repeated the sergeant.

"Yes, Oxford. He missed the Cheltenham train at Paddington and caught the Oxford Express instead, so I had to go and pick him up in Oxford. Didn't you, Washy?" she added more loudly.

"Oh yes indeed," said Charles. "Missed the bally thing by a whisker. Slow on the old pins these days. Getting on, what?" And getting better at behaving like an old person, he thought to himself.

"I see," said the sergeant. "Miss Capstan, how did you know Mister Washbrook had missed the Cheltenham train?"

"Um..." began Polly.

"He sent a telegram from the station." Charles was surprised to hear the source of this alibi. It was Pickles.

"Absolutely right," said Polly. "Pickles came racing like a whippet over to my office, which is at the back of the house next to the conservatory. He brought me up to speed about the change of plan and I had to hot-foot it out of here toot sweet to get to Oxford in time."

The sergeant looked at her for a moment, but said nothing. He turned and addressed the stationmaster.

"Mister McGurk, have you seen either of these people before?"

McGurk stood up. Charles shivered slightly as he remembered the man's strong hand on his shoulder and the sight of him crashing to the ground after Polly had knocked him out. The stationmaster walked across the room, hobbling slightly. Oh Lord, thought Charles, did she do him some kind of permanent injury?

"I've never seen the young lady before," he said. "And this man ... " he paused. "... is not the person who alighted from the London train."

The sergeant breathed through his nose, a snort either of relief or annoyance, Charles couldn't tell.

"Well that seems to wrap things up," said the Duke. "I'm sorry we can't help you more with your enquiries, sergeant. Pickles, do show these gentlemen out."

"This way, please," said Pickles, applying a firm hand to the back of Constable Prodgers, which propelled him forward faster than he would have wished. Charles was impressed by the strength shown by the tiny butler.

"Well, I'm glad that's all over," said the Duke, and he shuffled slowly over to a drinks cabinet. The Labrador looked up from his position on the floor and registered that the Duke had re-located. With great difficulty, he pulled himself up onto his four paws and slowly headed back to his original position near the fireplace.

The Duke took some glasses down from a shelf in the drinks cabinet. "Mister Washbrook, can I get you something to drink? Whisky and soda, perhaps?" he asked.

"That would be absolutely fine, Your Grace," replied Charles.

"Oh please, let's forget about this 'Your Grace' nonsense. Do call me Tarquin."

37

"Thank you, Tarquin. And you must call me Charles."

Charles yelped as Polly kicked him firmly in the calf.

"Call you what?" asked the Duke.

"Walter," said Charles, gritting his teeth to avoid howling with pain.

"Oh, right! I thought you said Charles."

"Charles is actually his real first name," said Polly. "It's what his parents call him."

"Parents?" repeated the Duke. "Are your parents still alive, Walter?"

"Alive? Um ... oh yes!" said Charles. "Not only alive but also kicking."

"My goodness, they must be quite old."

"Yes, well into their nineties, both of them. But both fit as an orchestra full of fiddles."

"Fit as an orchestra full of fiddles," repeated the Duke, "what a lovely expression. Do sit down, both of you, you must be exhausted."

Charles sat on a rock-hard chaise longue facing the coffee table. Polly took off her leather jacket and threw it over the back of the chaise. There was a clink as something fell out of the pocket. The Labrador looked up and waddled over to see if it was something to eat. It was a completely inedible metal whistle. He looked up at Polly, a hint of suspicion in his eyes, then plodded back to his favourite spot, lay down with his head on his paws and sighed loudly.

"Sherry for you, Polly?"

"Oh, rather," said Polly, getting down on her knees to retrieve the whistle, which she stuffed into one of her boots. When she sat down again, she tapped Charles on the knee and motioned with her eyes towards the wall over the fireplace. He didn't understand what she wanted him to do, so she jerked her head more rapidly. Eventually, he looked in the direction she was indicating.

Hanging over the fireplace was a portrait. Charles didn't recognise the subject, but the painting was most definitely in the style of Van Gogh. This must be the portrait of Robert Louis Stevenson, the one he had to copy.

The Duke poured drinks for them, put them on the coffee table and went back and poured a large whisky for himself. He then planted himself in his armchair, crossing one voluminous thigh over the other. He smiled contentedly and was just about to say something when the door opened and Pickles re-appeared. "Your Grace, there's a phone call for you," he said.

"Not now, Pickles, I want to spend some time getting to know Walter."

"It's your wife calling long-distance from Worthing."

"My ex-wife, Pickles, please refer to her in the past tense, as I do. Tell her whatever it is, I can't afford it."

Pickles walked over and whispered something in the Duke's ear. His eyes widened and his jaw dropped. "Oh Lord," he said. "How *does* she manage to get into such pickles?" He glanced up at the butler. "No offence intended, Pickles."

"None taken, Your Grace."

"Walter, this may take a little time. I completely understand if you would prefer to retire and get some shut-eye, so I'll say goodnight now. We'll reconvene in the morning. Snowball! Heel!" The Labrador looked up, saw the Duke walking away, and worked up an impressive speed to reach the door at the same time as his master.

With the Duke and the dog out of the drawing room, Charles breathed out quietly, relieved that the first hurdles of this ordeal seemed to have been negotiated without too much trouble. Pickles walked lightly across the room towards them, paused, and then began to speak. "Mr Washbrook, I'm very pleased that you made it safely to Great Park. Are you hungry?"

"Yes, I *am* a bit peckish, now you come to mention it," said Charles.

"I thought you might be," said the butler. "Unfortunately, the kitchen staff are given Monday afternoon off, a rather unusual arrangement, I admit, but it's the way things are at Great Park. Would it suffice if I arrange for some cold pheasant sandwiches to be served in your room? I can also send a bottle of claret to wash them down. How does that sound?"

The mention of food made Charles's stomach rumble. Pheasant sandwiches, what a nice idea, and washing them down with claret sounded very good indeed. Pickles went out of the room for a moment, called for someone, and gave them instructions. "That's all arranged," he said. "And your case has been taken to your room. I hope after a good night's sleep, you'll feel ready to start work."

"Absolutely," said Charles.

"I trust that Polly has apprised you of the Duke's requirements?"

"Oh yes indeed," replied Charles, relaxing into his role as a world-renowned portrait painter. "One portrait of said Duke, just as fast I can rustle it up."

"Quite," said Pickles. "And you're happy with the type of portrait the Duke requires?"

"Um... yes, of course."

"Have you done a portrait of this kind before?"

"Yes. Probably. Er ... a portrait of what kind exactly?"

"*Au naturelle.*"

40

"I'm sorry?" said Charles.

"*Au naturelle,*" repeated Pickles. "The Duke wishes you to do a portrait of him in the nude."

Charles's whisky and soda stopped halfway to his lips.

"Is everything all right?" asked Pickles. When Charles didn't answer, the butler shouted the same question, loudly and closer to his ear. Charles jumped nervously and the drink spilled down his oversized coat.

"Would you like to take your coat off?" asked Pickles. "You must be quite hot in it. It's ... very large."

"Don't worry, he wears it all the time," said Polly. "It gives him inspiration."

Pickles turned to Polly. "You seem to know quite a lot about Mister Washbrook's personal habits," he said.

"He's a friend of the family," replied Polly.

"Yes, I remember you telling me that. He does however seem to be a little surprised to hear about the kind of portrait the Duke requires. Are you sure you passed the message on to him?"

"Oh absolutely, loud and also clear, guide's honour," replied Polly. "I expect he forgot. He *is* tremendously old, after all." Polly and Pickles continued to talk about Charles as if he wasn't there.

There was a knock at the door. Pickles went to open it and a young man with a mop of curly blond hair put his head round the door.

"Everything's ready, Mister Pickles," said the young man.

"Thank you, Flockton. Mister Washbrook, the sandwich and claret are in your room. Would you care to retire?"

"Um... yes, I suppose so."

Flockton waved his arm, indicating that Charles should join him. "This way, Mister Washbrook," he said.

41

Charles got up slowly from his chair and huffed his way towards the door.

"Don't you need this?" asked Pickles, holding out Charles's walking stick, which was leaning against the coffee table.

"Oh yes, sorry," said Charles. "Mind like a sieve sometimes." He took the stick, thanked Pickles and followed Flockton out of the room.

The young man said he was delighted to meet a famous artist and chatted non-stop as they walked up the stairs. He was eighteen and had recently been appointed under-butler at Great Park. They walked up three flights of stairs and along a dark corridor, and then Flockton opened the door at the end.

"Welcome to the Corner Suite, sir," he said. The room was immense. In the middle was a table covered in a white tablecloth. There was a platter with a silver lid, an open bottle of red wine and two glasses.

"This is the best guest room in the house, sir," said Flockton. "Windows on two sides, and a marvellous view of the estate. Just be careful of that thing against the wall," he added, pointing at a tall structure made of grey metal piping.

"The radiator? What about it?" asked Charles.

"It's very old," said Flockton. "Just don't lean against it, it'll burn the skin off your arse." He wished Charles a good night's sleep and left, promising to bring a bowl of hot water at seven o'clock sharp.

Charles locked the door, took off his dark glasses and the grey wig and threw them on the bed. He poured himself a large glass of claret, drank it in one go and filled the glass again, then took the lid off the platter and picked up one of the sandwiches. When he bit into it, he felt a searing pain in his back teeth and spat out a small metal ball, which pinged on the plate and bounced onto the floor. He took another tentative bite of the sandwich and swallowed it. Chewing carefully, he managed to eat the whole thing without encountering any more bits of metal or causing further damage to his molars.

Wine in hand, he stood in the middle of the room and contemplated the immediate future. The Duke, a man so fat that he was almost as wide as he was tall, wanted to be painted in the nude, a prospect that made Charles feel quite nauseous. He was wondering what possible ways there were to improve the situation, jumping out of his third-floor window being the most attractive of them, when there was a knock at the door. He grabbed the wig, put it on quickly and went to stand at the door.

"Who's there?" he shouted, accidentally reverting to the original falsetto voice.

"Charles, it's me," said Polly. "Quick, let me in."

He unlocked the door and Polly slipped into the room, expertly turning the key in the lock behind her. She looked at him and burst out laughing. "Just as well I wasn't one of the servants," she said. "You've got the wig on backwards."

He pulled off the wig and threw it onto the bed. "I find little to be amused about in the current situation," he said.

"Oh Charlie boy," she said, pouring herself a glass of claret. "Come on, it isn't that bad! Tell me, what would you be doing if you weren't here? You'd be mooching around London with no money and no immediate prospects of earning any. At least here, you're going to have three good meals a day and a roof over your head, for who knows how long. And ..." she added, giving him one of her dazzling smiles, "you have me for company any time you want." Polly was good at emphasising the bright side of things, but Charles still had issues he wanted to raise.

"This bally beard," he complained. "It won't come off."

"I know," she said. "And we don't want it to come off, either."

"How am I supposed to wash my face?"

"I have some stuff that will un-glue it. Every couple of days, I'll take it off for you, you can have a good wash and I'll give you a new beard," said Polly. "It'll be fun, just you and me in the bathroom with a pot of glue."

"Marvellous," said Charles. "Bloody marvellous."

Polly's smile disappeared and her face clouded over. "I do wish you would show a little more enthusiasm for all this," she said.

"Enthusiasm? For something that could land me in prison?"

Polly laughed. "Prison? Don't be an ass. It's much more likely that we will finish up very rich indeed." Suddenly, she was all smiles again. She sat down on the bed and took off her riding boots.

"Let's lie down for a sec," she said. Charles was unsure if he had heard her correctly, but when she leapt onto the bed, he went round to the other side. Polly lay back, wriggled around to get comfortable, and sighed loudly. Charles sat down, took off his shoes and lay down next to her.

Charles had no idea what Polly wanted, but he was sure it wasn't any kind of physical advance, so he just lay still and kept his arms to his sides. She put her hands behind her head on the pillow, taking deep breaths. Out of the corner of his eye, Charles saw her breasts rise and fall under her white blouse. He did his best to suppress a moan of frustration.

44

"There's still so much to think about," said Polly. "You don't have an evening suit, do you?"

"An evening suit? No, of course not. And the jacket of the only suit I possess is torn to ribbons."

"Don't worry about that," she said. "I'll get someone to repair it. But you're going to need an evening suit for dinner. You're about the same height as Gilbert, and he's put on a bit of weight recently, so I'm sure there's an old one that he doesn't wear any more. I'll get Pickles to have a look in his wardrobe."

Charles remembered that Pickles had got them out of a hole with the police by saying they had received a telegram from him. "What was that all about?" he asked.

"Oh, Pickles doesn't like the police snooping around," she replied. "They've been here a couple of times since I arrived about some paltry thing or other. Strictly *entre nous*, I think Pickles has a past. He used to hang out with a fairly lively crowd in London back in the twenties. That's where he met Tarquin."

Polly leaned up and rested her chin on one hand, and looked at Charles. "Tell me something," she said. "How are you going to copy the portrait? We can't just take it down and bring it here, can we?"

"Oh, that won't be a problem," said Charles. "I can paint it from memory."

"Really? Do you have one of those, what are they called, photogenic memories?"

"Photographic."

"That's it. Do you have one?"

"I think so."

"Amazing! How does it work?"

"Well, I just look at something, it fixes in my memory, and I kind of go into a trance when I'm painting. Sometimes I can't remember anything about the process, and then I look at the canvas and it's ... well, it's a perfect replica of the painting I memorised."

"That's incredible. Does it happen when you paint people? I mean, in the flesh?"

"Sometimes, yes. I kind of stare at them for a minute or so, then I just paint like a mad person." This was the first time that Charles had ever talked about the unusual system he employed, and he was enjoying getting the information off his chest. He had always felt there was something odd about the method and, by association, his own mental state. He was very pleased when Polly reacted as if it was an amazing gift.

"I say, what enormous, good luck!" she said. "So, this means, you could just dash off the Van Gogh now?"

"Well, I could have a stab at it," replied Charles. "But I didn't really have a proper look at it. To be perfectly frank, my mind was on other things, what with the police being here and everything."

"Right. But if you get another chance to have a decent gander at it, you'll be able to go away and paint it without having to look at it again?"

"I suppose so."

"Oh my goodness, Charles, I love you to pieces." She turned on her side, put her arms round his neck and kissed him on the cheek.

Charles felt his heart pumping madly. Polly put her head on his chest, breathed deeply, and then spoke. "Chas, I just want you to know that I'm really glad we have each other and I really don't know what I'd do without you."

"Thank you."

More silence. Eventually Charles decided it was time to tell Polly how he really felt about her. "The fact is, Pol," he said, "you're the most interesting person, no, not interesting ... *fascinating* ...yes, the most fascinating person I've ever met, and if we weren't related, which of course we aren't really, not blood or anything, I mean, if we weren't brother and sister like this, I would really, I ...."

Polly's even breathing indicated that she was asleep on his chest. Charles sighed and pulled a blanket up to cover them both. Then he lay motionless until he too drifted off to sleep. The two of them lay there until the morning light began to show through the heavy curtains.

Chapter 4
Are there Goodgames in Worcestershire?

Charles first met Polly in July 1936. He had just turned twenty-two and she was nineteen, and they met on the day that his father Horace married her mother Leonora at Chelsea Register Office in West London. It was Horace's first time at Chelsea Register Office, but it was a place that his new wife Leonora was very familiar with. She had married her first husband Ronnie Capstan there, and she had also been in attendance in 1928 when her American friend Wallis Warfield Spencer married her second husband Ernest Simpson. Leonora told friends that she gave that partnership five years at the most.

After the ceremony, the small wedding party strolled a few hundred yards down Kings Road to have a sumptuous lunch at the Pheasantry Restaurant, where Charles was delighted to find himself seated next to Polly, the most beautiful girl he had ever seen. As she excitedly told her new stepbrother about her life, he discovered she was also the most energetic, the most amusing and the most alarming person he had ever encountered.

By the age of twenty, Polly had attended and been expelled from four private schools. She had also abandoned studying at a finishing school in Switzerland after one of the teachers criticised her for not doing any work. It was clear that she was unsuited to any kind of formal education, and she also enjoyed spending time with undesirable people. To try to keep her out of trouble, her parents sent her off to Paris with an invitation to stay with the family of the Duke of Aquitaine. Polly alarmed the women and charmed the men, and soon got engaged to the Duke's second son Fulgence, whilst at the same time discovering the delights of Paris with the help of a group of Brazilian dancers and musicians, usually arriving home in the small hours when the family was asleep. When Fulgence discovered what she was up to, he ordered her to stop seeing her new friends. Polly broke off the engagement and went back to London, taking the heirloom diamond engagement ring with her, where she sold it, living off the proceeds for the next few months.

Charles spent the entire afternoon listening to Polly and occasionally glancing at his new stepmother Leonora, a tall, imposing woman, who spent the afternoon drinking champagne as if it was going out of fashion. Charles wondered how on earth she had managed to finish up married to his father.

The Goodgame/Capstan marriage was indeed an unlikely one. Horace was a widower, a tubby man of medium height with wispy blond hair that was turning grey. He had been living a quiet life on the coast in Norfolk, spending his time painting watercolours, but after the disappearance of his first wife Martha, he had moved to the Belmont Hotel in Lyme Regis, which is where he met his second one.

Leonora was taller than him and had long bottle-black hair. She wrote novels whose heroines were usually involved in scandals and reverses, which they came through, tormented and scarred, but defiant. In one of them, *The Tangled Truth*, the heroine Thelma Dane left her husband Bertram and ran away with a lover after faking her own death by drowning. By coincidence, Horace's first wife Martha was one of Leonora's biggest fans and *The Tangled Truth* was by her bedside on the day she disappeared.

Leonora's first husband was Ronnie Capstan, an entrepreneur whose specialised in selling shares in Latin American gold and silver mines. The problem with the shares was that the mines had usually run out of whatever precious metals they had contained several decades earlier.

In December 1935, Ronnie told Leonora that he wished to divorce her and marry his mistress. He told her would move out of the house they shared in Bloomsbury, and she could continue to live there, but a week later, she received a letter from a solicitor telling her that the owner of the house would like to move in at the earliest convenience. It transpired that six months earlier, Ronnie had sold the property to a minor member of the royal family, with occupation guaranteed in six months' time.

A month later, Ronnie was arrested and charged with dishonestly handling stolen property, namely a Rolls Royce Phantom, a Bentley Speed Six and several other luxury cars that had disappeared from the streets of Mayfair and Belgravia. Even if he had been invited to Leonora's wedding a few months later, he would have been unable to attend, as he was now detained at His Majesty's Pleasure in Wormwood Scrubs.

Ronnie was in prison and his bank account, which contained her royalties, was frozen, so Leonora went ahead with the divorce, which *The Times* society page described as 'sudden and surprising'. The newspaper also noted that the Capstans were 'very close friends' with the new King Edward but knew better than to print the juicy part of the story, the fact that Leonora Capstan was one of the former Prince of Wales's many lovers. She had only slept with Edward twice and was so unimpressed that she never bothered to answer the dozens of messages he subsequently sent her. She introduced him to her friend Wallis Simpson and was relieved when the American took him off her hands.

Forced to leave her Bloomsbury home, Leonora went to live with her best friend Diana Bagshot, the widow of Viscount Grimbledon, who had an apartment in Saint John's Wood and a house on the Dorset coast. One afternoon, the two women were having tea at the Belmont Hotel in Lyme Regis when Leonora noticed a man with a huge hat sitting outside on the terrace. He was painting a picture of the promenade, the beach and the sea beyond.

The man was Horace Goodgame.

She walked out onto the terrace to have a closer look at him and tried to engage him in conversation. "Isn't it just divine?" she said.

Horace didn't reply.

"Isn't it just *divine?"* Leonora repeated, rather louder this time.

"I'm sorry? Were you talking to me?" asked Horace, who was unused to being addressed by women he didn't know.

"Yes. The view, it's divine, isn't it?"

"Oh yes," observed Horace. "That's why I'm painting it." This simple statement of fact caused the woman to gurgle with laughter, which puzzled him.

"I'm Leonora Capstan," she said. "How do you do?"

"Horace Goodgame," replied Horace. "Pleased to meet you."

"Goodgame?" repeated Leonora. "Are you one of the Worcestershire Goodgames?"

"Are there Goodgames in Worcestershire?" asked Horace. "Well, blow me down with a feather." Again, he was surprised that this innocuous remark caused Leonora to dissolve into peals of laughter. She walked across the terrace and looked at his painting, which was actually one of his better ones. "That's absolutely marvellous," she said. "Is this a hobby or are you a real artist?"

Horace found the distinction rather interesting. "Oh, it isn't a hobby," he said. "It's what I do."

"Really? Have you sold many paintings?"

He considered the question for a moment. As often happened when he was thinking, he wrinkled his nose, looking like a rabbit newly emerged from a warren. Leonora was quite taken with the sweet look on his face when he did this.

Horace had sold about a dozen paintings in his life, mainly of his neighbour's houses in Norfolk. They usually paid him with a basket of farm produce or the butchered carcass of a pig. "Well, yes, I suppose I have," he said, sounding immensely modest, as he always did.

"How marvellous. Is your ... um ... wife here with you?"

"I'm afraid I'm widowed."

"I'm so sorry," said Leonora. "Would you care to join us for tea?"

Because Horace was staying at the Belmont, Leonora presumed that he was well off. Whether his wealth was derived from painting or something else, she cared not a jot. He was a fairly attractive widower, and she was, not to put too fine a point on it, as poor as a whole family of church mice.

After their first tea together on that spring afternoon, Leonora made sure that she spent a lot of time with

53

Horace, taking bracing walks along the promenade and to the end of the Cobb, the harbour wall, and having dinner at the hotel. She found him reasonably amusing company, and liked his honesty and transparency, characteristics wholly lacking in her ex-husband Ronnie. She was delighted to find that he lived off the dividends of a trust fund, and his only son Charles was old enough to look after himself and wasn't a drain on family finances. Leonora also learned that Horace had an immensely rich brother whose lived at a very fancy address in South Kensington. She decided that he was a very good catch, but she became a little frustrated that he never talked about the possibility of marriage, even when they had been stepping out together for two months.

She decided to take matters into her own hands.

One evening in May, she arranged a candlelit dinner at the Belmont, booking a table near the window overlooking the sea. Once dessert had been eaten and Horace was sniffing a glass of brandy, she went on the attack.

"Horace, wouldn't you like to make an honest woman of me?"

Horace took his nose out of the brandy glass and looked at her. "Make a what?"

"An honest woman."

"Sorry, I don't follow."

"A girl has to think of her reputation."

"Which girl?"

"Me, Horace. We've been seeing each other for more than two months now."

"Have we?"

"Yes, people are beginning to talk."

"Are they? What about?"

"You and me, Horace. Neither of us is getting any younger, and if we're going to do it, we should do it sooner rather than later."

"Do what?"

Leonora was running out of ideas. There was only one thing for it. She would have to seduce him.

When the meal ended, she suggested a walk along the promenade. Horace mumbled something about wanting to turn in, but she took his arm and propelled him out of the front door of the hotel.

It was a balmy night after a warm cloudless day, and the setting sun was disappearing to the west. She steered him down the steps to the beach, where there was a row of brightly-coloured huts. She tried the door of the first one and was delighted to find that it was open. Inside the darkening space, there was a wooden chaise longue covered by a mattress. She checked there were no witnesses walking along the beach and pushed Horace inside.

"What are we doing?" asked Horace.

"We are going to cement the Goodgame Capstan alliance," she replied, pulling towels off a shelf and placing them carefully on the mattress.

"We're going to do what?"

She pushed him and he sat down with a bump. There were wheels at the back of the chaise, and it lurched towards the door. Leonora took off her silk wrap, her shoes and her stockings. Finally, she took off her red dress, revealing her black lace undergarments.

Horace had never seen a woman in her underwear before. "Are you feeling all right?" he asked.

"I'm feeling perfectly fine," she replied. She squatted in front of him, took off his jacket and began unbuttoning his shirt. With one skilful practised move, Leonora pulled his trousers and underwear down below his knees. She was relieved to see that he was getting an erection and the venture had a chance of success. With the skill of someone who had had sex in the most unpromising places, she straddled him and connection was achieved.

With his trousers and underwear wrapped round his feet, and still wearing his shoes and socks, Charles managed to do what he had rarely done in his life and achieved congress with a woman, which he celebrated with a loud groan. Leonora tried to stand up, but her feet slipped backwards, and she landed heavily on him, causing the chaise to shoot forward and crash into the door. The door came off its hinges and fell outwards onto the beach. Horace then added momentum by pushing sharply with his heels. The chaise clattered over the fallen door, out of the hut and onto the beach, where it stopped dead, causing the two of them to cartwheel into the sand.

Horace stood up and tried to run back inside, but he tripped over his twisted trousers and fell flat on his face. Leonora spat out a mouthful of sand, stood up and walked past him. He got to his feet and hopped into the hut behind her.

The following day, they started planning the wedding.

Leonora made it clear that she was not prepared to live in Norfolk, or Lyme Regis for that matter. As soon as they had agreed on a date for the wedding, she took a train to London and rented an unfurnished seven-room apartment in Barkston Gardens, Earls Court and arranged for the furniture that had originally been in her Bloomsbury house to be moved there. When Horace visited the apartment for the first time, he thought it seemed very nice and he chose one of the rooms as a studio.

They honeymooned at the Hôtel du Palais in Biarritz and then moved into the Earls Court apartment. A month later, she went to stay with her friend Diana Bagshot in Dorset for a few days and by the time she returned to London, Horace had moved back to his Norfolk home at Hunstanton. Thereafter, the newly-weds spent very little time together in London, which suited them both perfectly.

Beyond his bright blue eyes and winning smile, plus a large collection of wide-brimmed hats and an accidentally comic way with words, there wasn't much to Horace Goodgame. He had never needed to worry about making a living because of the generous trust funds he and his brother Ernest were left when their Aunt Agatha passed away in 1910. Ernest had invested his share, first of all in automobile manufacturing, which earned him a tidy sum in dividends every year. Later, when tensions began to build in Europe, he bought shares in a clothing company which specialised in military uniforms, and the value of his investment improved dramatically.

As soon as he had money in the bank, Ernest did what he had always wanted to do and escaped from the stifling boredom of the family home at Fakenham in Norfolk. He bought himself a house at Pelham Crescent in South Kensington and thereafter spent a lot of time at the theatre and in various Soho clubs, wine bars and coffee houses, building up an eclectic circle of friends, acquaintances, and hangers-on.

Horace left his trust fund at Krumnagel's Bank in the Strand, and continued to do what he liked best, which was to paint watercolour landscapes near the family home, his simple lifestyle more than adequately funded by the cheque for thirty pounds that the bank sent him every month.

Horace regularly attended Sunday services at Saint Edmund's Church and would usually stay on afterwards to have tea and biscuits with the rest of the congregation. One Sunday morning in 1913, he met Martha Donkin, who had recently moved to Fakenham to live with her older sister, having left the rented cottage she shared with her mother on the coast in Hunstanton when her mother passed away. Horace found Martha easy to talk to and chatted with her after church every Sunday. A few weeks after their first meeting, she suggested getting married and Horace agreed, then wondered if he had heard her correctly. He had, so it was too late to change the plan, even if he had wanted to.

After they were married, she said she wanted to go back to live in Hunstanton, so Horace sold the family home in Fakenham and bought a house, number 24 Cliff Terrace, in the town where his new wife had been born. The house had a conservatory, which he used as a studio, and he diversified his output by sitting on the beach and painting watercolour seascapes.

His ability as a painter was modest but, as his brother Ernest always used to say, Horace had plenty to be modest about. However, for a short time, his style was favourably compared to that of another Horace, Horace Tuck, a Norfolk artist whose paintings were exhibited in galleries around the country.

On 28th July 1914, the day the Great War broke out, Martha gave birth to a boy, who they named Charles. She found the whole business of childbirth so distressing that she told Horace that it must never happen again, and took strenuous measures to avoid further intimacy of any kind with her husband. Neither parent paid much attention to the child, and they employed a big-boned village woman called Emily Roebuck as a nanny. Emily terrified Charles so much that he used to hide in the woodshed whenever it was time for a bath.

On a brisk September morning in 1935, Martha left the house, saying she was going for a swim. She placed her clothes in a neat pile on the beach and disappeared. Although her body was never found, the coroner in King's Lynn eventually issued a death certificate, which gave drowning as the cause. Almost the entire adult population of Hunstanton crowded into Saint Edmund's Church for the funeral, the women of the village sobbing their way silently through the service, the men stoically waiting until they could slip into the Wash and Tope Inn next door for a couple of pints of ale. After the service, Horace went home and continued working on his latest painting.

A woman called Edna Normington, who had been widowed a few months before, moved into Horace's house and did the cooking and cleaning. Life continued pretty much as it had before, the presumed death of Horace's wife making very little difference to his quotidian routine. His only immediate family members, son Charles and brother Ernest, spent the next day with him and then went back to London.

When Charles returned to Hunstanton at Christmas, he was alarmed to see that his father had put on a lot of weight and was deathly pale. "Papa, you need to get out more," he said.

"Get out where?"

"Get some air. Walk along the beach, or something."

"Too bloody cold for that," replied Horace.

Back in London, Charles told his uncle Ernest about his father's sickly condition. "He never gets out at all. He says he will when the weather gets better."

"Hell will freeze over before the weather gets better in Norfolk," replied Ernest, shuddering as he remembered the bleak years he spent there before he escaped. "He needs to get down on the south coast for a while. I have a chum who owns a hotel in Lyme Regis. He owes me a favour. We'll park your father down there. He can't get up to any mischief in Dorset."

Charles nodded in agreement, convinced that his father would find it hard to get up to anything approaching mischief if he spent a month in a Parisian brothel. Horace always did what his brother Ernest ordered him to do, so he relocated to the Belmont Hotel, a move that would eventually lead to him marrying a racy but penniless novelist.

Chapter 5
I'm the victim of fraud on a grand scale
Monday 15th February, Krumnagel's Bank, London -
windy and overcast

Six months after the wedding, Horace received a telegram from Krumnagel's Bank, where his trust fund was administered, asking him to visit them as soon as possible. He rang the bank and asked what it was about, and was told the matter could only be discussed in person. On a cold Monday morning in February, the same day that his son Charles was setting off for Stanford Saint Mary to paint the Duke's portrait, Horace took an early train from Hunstanton to King's Lynn, changed onto a train to Kings Cross, and then took a taxi to the main branch of Krumnagel's Bank in The Strand.

He arrived at one o'clock, lunchtime, the busiest time in the bank's day. Horace stood for a moment and looked up at the front of the austere neo-Gothic building, and then at the people milling in and out. At the entrance was a tall man wearing a long purple overcoat with yellow epaulettes and a cap with a jutting peak. This was Reg Plumpton, a former sergeant major in the London Regiment and now chief commissionaire at the bank. Horace had rarely seen such a colourful and impressive figure.

"I say, do you work here?" he asked.

Reg tried to ascertain if the tubby man in the big hat was joking. "Nah, mate," he said. "I'm waitin' for a number nine bus."

"Really?"

"Course I work here. How can I 'elp you?"

"I have an appointment."

Reg went inside and summoned another employee, dressed more soberly in a grey suit. Eventually, Horace was shown into the office of the assistant manager Rupert Burgess, a small stooped man with a shiny bald head and wide luxuriant sideburns that almost met under his chin.

Burgess was not the bearer of good tidings. "Good morning, Mister Goodman," he began.

"Goodgame," Horace corrected him.

Burgess looked at the papers in front of him. "Ah yes, apologies. Well, we haven't met before, but I was appointed assistant manager of the bank a few weeks ago and I assumed responsibility for your trust fund, bequeathed to you by..." Burgess put on his glasses and tried to decipher a spidery signature at the bottom of a document on the desk. "... Angola Meatchase?"

"Agatha Merchant," said Horace. "My aunt Agatha, my father's sister."

"I see. Well, I'm afraid I have some rather bad news for you, Mister Goodman ...er ... Goodgame. The fund is ... well, it's not in very good shape. In fact, it's practically empty."

Horace stared at him for a moment. "What exactly do you mean by 'practically empty'?" he asked.

"Practically empty," Burgess repeated, searching for another way of stating the obvious. "There's hardly any money in it. In fact, if money continues to be withdrawn at the current rate, it will soon be *completely* empty." He opened a large ledger on his desk until he reached a page with Horace's name at the top and looked at the hand-written entries. "In the past eighteen months, we have made a series of cash payments to Martha Goodgame, amounts ranging from ten to ... goodness, as much as fifty pounds."

"To Martha Goodgame? That's not possible."

"Would she be your wife?"

"Well yes, she was my first wife," said Horace, "but she drowned."

"She ... I'm sorry?"

"She drowned. In Hunstanton. She went for a swim and never came back."

"She never came back ..."

"Yes. There was a funeral and everything. I can show you the death certificate if you don't believe me."

"Well obviously, I'm very sorry to hear about that," said the assistant manager. "But I have to ask you when this most unfortunate event took place."

"September, the year before last."

"I see." Burgess peered at the documents in front of him. "Well, either Mrs Goodgame been siphoning money from beyond the grave or..."

"Or what?"

"Or you are, to put it bluntly, the victim of fraud on a grand scale."

The assistant manager explained that someone impersonating Horace's late wife had made withdrawals almost every week for the past eighteen months. The trust fund was now, as Burgess repeated for the umpteenth time, practically empty.

When Horace asked why the bank had allowed the impostor to withdraw money, Burgess produced a typewritten letter informing the bank that in future Mrs Goodgame would be making withdrawals in person at the Strand branch. The letter was signed 'Horace Goodgame'.

Horace stared at the letter. It was dated 1st September 1935, a week before Martha disappeared. "I didn't write this," he said.

"Do you have any idea who did?"

"Of course not. Although it does look like my signature."

On receipt of the letter, the bank had written asking him to call the bank to confirm the arrangement.

"According to the notes, you then called the bank and did as the bank had requested," said Burgess. "You confirmed the arrangement."

"But I did no such thing," said Horace.

"I see ..." said Burgess, wondering what to do next. The records indicated that withdrawals had started about ten days later and the trust fund, which had been worth more than seven thousand pounds, had reduced substantially. His new wife Leonora had also used Horace's cheque book, which caused even more strain on the fund.

In addition, because the bank clerk who was responsible for sending the dividend cheques to Horace wasn't checking the state of the account, the monthly payments of thirty pounds had remained the same. The appointment of Mister Burgess as the first competent assistant manager for a long time meant that this and other examples of poor procedure had been uncovered. "I must ask you not to make any further withdrawals from the fund," he said. "And I'm afraid the monthly cheques will cease forthwith."

Horace sat silently for a moment. When he got up, he shook hands with the assistant manager, thanked him and made his way out of the office and onto the street. Reg the commissionaire saluted as he passed.

Horace saw a taxi approaching and flagged it down. As it pulled up in front of him, he remembered that as of now, the only assets he had were the coins in his pocket. He wondered if taking a taxi was actually a good idea.

"Where to, guv'nor?" asked the driver, cheerfully.

"How much will it cost to go to Earl's Court?" asked Horace.

"About two bob," replied the driver. "Cheap at twice the price."

Charles put his hand in his pocket and pulled out all the coins he possessed. He had eleven shillings and ninepence. This might have to last him for the rest of his life.

"It's all right," said Horace. "I'll walk."

The smile disappeared from the driver's face. "Fair enough," he said. "Think before you stop a cab next time, all right? We're busy people."

"Yes, of course. Um ... can you tell me which way is Earl's Court?"

"Just walk in a straight line," said the driver, pointing east towards Aldwych, and drove away. Horace set off the way the driver had indicated, walking in the opposite direction from his intended destination. Four hours later, red-faced and perspiring, he arrived at Barkston Gardens. The journey on foot should have taken him no more than an hour and a half, but his route took him east as far as St Paul's Cathedral before he decided to ask for further directions. Some fifty minutes later, he passed Krumnagel's on the Strand again, and eventually found his way home via Piccadilly, Knightsbridge and South Kensington, passing within less than a hundred yards of his brother Ernest's house.

Leonora was sitting at her desk in the drawing room with a glass of white wine in her hand. "Horace!" she said. "What a surprise!" Then she saw the rivulets of sweat pouring down his red face. "Good God, what on earth has happened to you?"

"I just walked from the Strand," he explained.

"What on earth for?"

"Um.... it's a bit complicated."

"Well, never mind that now. I need your advice."

After half a year of marriage and only a few weeks of actual co-habitation, Horace was very familiar with Leonora's use of language. The words 'I need your advice' usually meant that she was going to tell him something she had decided, and which would probably cost him money.

"As you know, all my novels are set in London," she began.

"Are they?"

"Yes, and I've decided it's time for a change of scene, so I've set my latest story in Venice. I think my readers will appreciate it."

She had offered the manuscript of her latest novel to a publishing company called Blandings and Worcester and she had been assigned an editor called Arabella Simpkins, a young woman who had studied Classics at St Hilda's Oxford. The first set of notes that Arabella sent to Leonora were not promising. She said that something needed to be done to spice up the Leonora Capstan formula, which was in danger of becoming tired and predictable. For a start, why were all the novels set in London? Leonora replied that London had served her well enough for her first five novels, but Arabella insisted that it was time for a change, and a new location was essential, somewhere colourful and exotic. She suggested Venice, Istanbul or Casablanca. Whilst this author/editor relationship was not one made in heaven, Leonora admitted to herself that Arabella's suggestion of Venice was an awfully good one.

Horace offered no opinion about how Leonora's readers would respond to the change of setting. Leonora found the silence a bit awkward.

"So, what do you think?" she asked.

"Marvellous," he said, turning over the eleven and ninepence in his pocket.

"Good," she said. "I'm so glad you agree."

"Agree?" he repeated. "Agree to what?"

"To me spending a month in Venice to do some research."

"Splendid idea. How are you planning to pay for it?"

"I'm sorry?" said Leonora.

He told her what he had learnt in the morning. Leonora listened, her mouth falling open by degrees as the story unfolded. "Oh God, it's *The Tangled Truth*," she said, referring to the plot of one of her previous novels.

"Er ... quite," said Horace, although he didn't see how 'the tangled truth' was in any way apt to describe the situation. "All very confusing."

"So, we have no money?"

"That's more or less the long and the short of it," he said. "I'm the victim of fraud on a grand scale." Repeating the assistant manager's words gave him some comfort, albeit temporarily.

Leonora stared at the destitute man that she had foolishly agreed to marry. After a moment's thought, she said: "Well, there's only one thing for it. You will have to ask that rich brother of yours to help us out."

Horace had already thought of this idea but rejected it, mainly on the grounds that he was frightened of Ernest and imagined the older more confident man would lambast him for his stupidity, and not for the first time.

"Well, I don't know ..."

"Horace, it's the only solution. I want you to go over there now and sort it out." Leonora picked up her glass of wine and the bottle and walked out of the room. Back in her bedroom, she sighed with despair as she thought about the terrible choices of men she always made. For the first time, she regretted putting that floozie Wallis Simpson in touch with her former lover, Bertie, or King Edward the Eighth as he was otherwise known. Was it too late to snaffle him back?

*****

At Krumnagel's Bank in the Strand, Burgess returned the box containing the Goodgame ledger and correspondence to its appropriate place in a filing cabinet, and then opened the door to the outer office where his secretary Rita O'Riley was sitting.

"Miss O'Riley, could you come into my office for a moment, please?"

Burgess dictated a memo for her to type out and pin on the notice board, to be read by all counter staff. It told them to be on the lookout for a woman calling herself Martha Goodgame. On no account was anyone to pay any money to this woman, who was impersonating the deceased wife of one of the bank's clients. If the woman came to the bank again, a citizen's arrest should be made, and she was to be kept prisoner at the bank, pending the arrival of the police. There were handcuffs in Mister Burgess's office if she needed to be restrained.

Rita went back into her office, put some paper in her typewriter, and typed out the memo. She then walked through into the busy banking hall, where seven tellers were seated at the counter, all but one of whom were dealing with customers. Behind them were another half dozen employees sitting at desks, with piles of papers and cheques in front of them, copying information into large ledgers. They all stopped what they were doing and looked at Rita as she pinned the memo on the noticeboard. Bernard Smithers, the only teller who was not actually dealing with a customer, walked up to see what it was about.

"So, what have you got for us today, Rita?" he asked.

"A warning," she replied, with a beaming smile.

"Oh I say, a warning," he repeated. "Have we done something wrong?"

"Maybe you have, maybe you haven't," she said. "You'd better take a look." She pinched him on the cheek and turned to go back to her office.

Smithers blushed to the roots of his hair and turned to see if any of his colleagues had seen what happened. They had. Most of them were glaring at him. He smiled and turned back to read the memo and the smile froze on his face.

"Oh Jesus!" he said. He turned and ran to the door that led to the public area of the bank, opened it and ran across the hall, past Reg the commissionaire at the front door and out into the street. He looked left and right and then he saw two women who were walking briskly towards Trafalgar Square.

"Hey you two!" he yelled. "Stop!"

When the women saw him, they ran across the road, an action which caused several motor vehicles to brake sharply, resulting in a collision between an omnibus and a van belonging to the Fotheringay's Sausages Company. Smithers thought about giving chase but, not having received permission to leave the premises during office hours, he decided against it.

"Somefin up?" asked Reg, as Smithers raced past him and back into the bank. He knocked frantically on the door separating the public and office areas and yelled to be let back in. Then he ran to Mr Burgess's office, took a deep breath and knocked on the door.

Smithers told Burgess that he had just paid twenty pounds to two women, one of whom identified herself as Martha Goodgame, and had only read the memo to staff warning them about the fraud after they had left the premises. He had immediately run out into the street and saw the women walking away down the Strand. Burgess asked Smithers why he failed to pursue them, and the counter assistant quoted verbatim the bank regulation that stated: *No employee shall leave the premises without the express permission of the manager (or his representative) between the start of work at nine o'clock and the designated end of work, be it six o'clock Monday to Thursday, five o'clock Friday or one o'clock on Saturday.*

The assistant manager sighed with annoyance when he heard this. He had no knowledge of this archaic regulation and resolved to add some kind of codicil which allowed employees to chase people down the street if they were suspected of fraudulent behaviour. How the bank had managed to survive into the mid-twentieth century with such old-fashioned rules was a mystery.

Burgess sat in silence wondering what to do next. He was never good at making decisions and the situation regarding the Agatha Merchant trust fund needed urgent attention. The beneficiary, Horace Goodgame, had accepted that he would no longer receive any income from the fund, but there was every chance that when he had time to reflect on the situation, he would sue the bank for the negligent behaviour that had caused his inheritance to disappear. The assistant manager had no idea whether such a claim had any chance of success, but he was sure of one thing. When the gang of ancient Krumnagels who ran the company from their Bavarian mountain retreat at Schloss Elmau looked beyond the current manager Godfrey Krumnagel and further down the pecking order to finger the person responsible, they would probably decide that the fault lay at the feet of one R. Burgess Esquire.

As was usual on a Monday (and many other days of the week if truth be told), Godfrey wasn't actually at work, so Burgess picked up the phone and called his boss's home number in Surrey, but there was no answer. He called Rita back into his office and dictated a telegram to her. It read: IMPORTANT NEWS STOP BANK CUSTOMER SUBJECT TO GRAND FRAUD STOP PLEASE ATTEND CRISIS MEETING SOONEST. Rita left the premises and headed for the Post Office in Aldwych, where she waited in line for half an hour before she was able to send the message. When she returned, she told Burgess that the telegram would be delivered to Godfrey Krumnagel's house 'within the hour'. The assistant manager sat by the phone, and when there was no call from his boss, he decided there was nothing to be done but wait until the next day before trying to contact him again.

Burgess was the kind of person who always found something to worry about. He went home to Tunbridge Wells and spent the evening sitting in an armchair, drinking tea and silently staring at a print of The Stag at Bay on the wall.

Chapter 6
Why on earth would I blackmail you?
Monday evening, Earls Court and South Kensington -
cold, turning frosty

Horace sat in his studio for about an hour, summoning up the courage to visit his brother Ernest, and finally set off in the direction of Pelham Crescent, a fifteen-minute walk from Barkston Gardens. It had been a cold day and there was a touch of frost on the ground. It was only the third time that Horace had visited Ernest's house, so he checked the number on the gate before walking up the grey and white mosaic path, which was lined on either side with a row of large pots, containing all manner of exotic plants. Not a grain of soil was out of place. Ernest liked things to be just so.

There were lights on in the house, but no one came to the door when Horace knocked. He thought about going home, but feared Leonora's angry reaction, so he walked round the side and through a metal gate, seeing the long and beautifully maintained back garden for the first time.

He heard laughter and looked down the garden to see where it was coming from. There were two wooden buildings, one of them a white chalet partly hidden by trees at the far end of the lawn. The sound was coming from that direction. Horace walked down the garden and looked through the window of the chalet. The interior was dimly lit and he couldn't see anything, but the people inside were clearly having a lot of fun. When Horace stepped onto the porch, the board beneath his foot creaked and the laughter stopped. He knocked loudly on the door. There was no reply, so he opened it and walked in.

The only light was provided by three candles on a white wicker table. The chalet was very warm, the air was thick with sweet-smelling smoke, and there were several wine bottles and glasses on the table and a large ashtray containing the remains of thin hand-rolled cigarettes. On a sofa, amongst brightly coloured cushions, were three naked men, one of whom was Ernest. The trio had frozen in a most unusual tableau, and they were all staring at the new arrival. One of the men broke the silence.

"Ernesto! I didn't realise you'd invited another friend."

"I didn't," said Ernest. "This is my blasted brother."

Ernest's two companions immediately sprang up and hopped around the chalet gathering up their clothes, Ernest stared at his brother, his eyes blazing with anger. "Horace, would you mind going back to the house and waiting for me there?"

"Of course, Ernest. As you wish."

Horace left the chalet, closing the door behind him. He walked down the garden and through the French windows into the conservatory. He thought about sitting there to wait for his brother, but it was a freezing cold night, so he continued through into the house, and finally parked himself on a sofa in the front sitting room.

He tried to recreate the sight he had just seen but was convinced his mind must have been playing tricks on him. Candlelight, smoky atmosphere, the smell of perfume - and three naked men in a position that only a trio of circus contortionists could have been comfortable with. He wondered if he had dreamt the last part.

He looked around at the room. He was no expert about furniture, but he was pretty sure the stuff in Ernest's

74

house was expensive. What was it his brother had made a fortune out of? Clothing? Ernest had clearly spent a lot of money making himself comfortable. Maybe he had a few pounds to spare to help his brother out of a hole. Or maybe he would tell him never to darken his door again.

A door slammed at the back of the house, and Horace braced himself for the appearance of his brother. Ernest stormed into the room, now fully clothed, wearing a pink shirt with ruffles on the sleeves and the collar, and purple leather trousers. On his feet, he wore a pair of camel-coloured canvas shoes that for some reason reminded Horace of adventure stories he had read as a child.

No one meeting the two brothers would ever imagine they were related. Ernest was taller, broader and definitely more muscular and had the classic features of a talking pictures matinée idol - a lean face with high cheekbones and a narrow nose. His moustache was a thin line and his hair was greased back, although at this particular moment, it wasn't as neat and groomed as it usually looked. His activities in the chalet had caused bits to stick out at the side, giving him a less threatening look. The hair, eyebrows and moustache were dyed black, otherwise his colouring would have been more similar to Horace's, but Ernest had none of his brother's excess fat.

The older brother stood over his nervous sibling. Horace stood up and offered his hand to be shaken, but Ernest was not in a hand-shaking mood. "What the hell do you think you're doing, coming here without warning?" he asked. Before Horace could answer, Ernest continued his angry rant. "And don't think for a minute you're going to benefit from this," he said. "I'm not going to let you blackmail me. I know people who could make your life hell if you----"

"Blackmail you?" said Horace. "What are you talking about? Why on earth would I blackmail you? You're my brother, for goodness sake. Flesh and blood and whatnot."

This evidence of filial affection stopped Ernest in his tracks. He took a deep breath and began to speak in a quieter voice. "Sit down, Horace."

Horace sat back on the sofa.

"Do you promise you will say not a word about what you have seen tonight?"

"Oh absolutely. Scout's honour."

Ernest walked over to a bureau, opened the glass door and took out a decanter of dark liquid. Without asking Horace if he wanted a drink, he poured two full glasses and handed one of them to his brother, who sniffed it cautiously. Ernest emptied his in one go, and breathed out noisily.

"More brandy?" he asked.

"I haven't drunk this one yet," said Horace, apologetically.

Ernest went back to the bureau, poured himself another glass and came back and sat down opposite his brother. "What are you doing here?" he asked.

As clearly as he could, Horace explained what he had discovered when he went to the bank.

The situation seemed clear to Ernest. "You know what this means, don't you?" he said.

"No. What does it mean?"

"Martha is still alive."

"What? How can she be? She died. There was a funeral. You know that, you were there."

"Yes, I was. But if you remember, Martha wasn't."

"I'm sorry?"

"Horace, her body was never found. The fact of the matter is, she could still be alive. She could have staged her own death."

"Why would she do that?"

"Oh, come on, Horace. I didn't know Martha very well but, well ... yours wasn't a love affair that caught fire, was it?"

"I'm sorry?"

"I'm being as clear as I can. Neither of you were very passionate, were you?"

"Oh no, absolutely not!" said Horace, as if he'd been accused of witchcraft or devil worship.

"Maybe she was involved with someone else," suggested Ernest. "Did she ever spend any time away from home without explanation?"

"No. Well, I mean, she used to visit an aunt in Suffolk."

"And did you ever talk to her while she was there?"

"How would I do that?"

"On the telephone?"

"Oh, her aunt didn't have a telephone."

"I see." Ernest thought for a moment. "This aunt, what's her name?"

"Gertrude."

"Was she at the funeral?"

"What?" Horace thought for a moment. "No, she wasn't."

"Was she at the wedding?"

"I don't remember."

"Do you ever remember meeting Aunt Gertrude?"

"No. I never met anyone from Martha's family apart from her sister. All the others were long gone."

"All long gone, eh? Apart from Aunt Gertrude."

"Yes." Horace sighed. "Do you think Aunt Gertrude was an invention?"

"I think it's a definite possibility, but that's not really important right now. You have a financial problem, which I'm happy to help you with in the short term. But in the longer term, you're going to have to sort things out for yourself. Which means you're going to have to cash in your assets."

"I don't have any assets," said Horace. "That's why I came to ask you for help."

"Of course, you have assets," replied Ernest. "The house in Hunstanton."

"What about it?"

"You can sell it."

Horace almost jumped off the sofa at this suggestion. "Sell the house? But where would I live?"

"You rent a place in Earl's Court, don't you?"

"Yes. But what are you suggesting? That I live in London? With Leonora?"

Ernest shook his head and smiled. "I gather that's what *married* people do," he said.

They moved from the sitting room into Ernest's office, a compact room which was lined with bookshelves and dominated by a large partner desk. Ernest went over to a bookshelf and pulled out a book, *Stamboul Train* by Graham Greene. When he opened it, the middle was hollowed out and contained a key. He took it out, unlocked the top drawer of the desk and took out a cheque-book.

"I'm going to write you a cheque for fifty pounds," he said.

"That's very kind," said Horace. "I promise I won't ask you for anything again."

"You most certainly won't," replied Ernest. "You won't get a penny piece more out of me. This is merely to tide you over until you sell the house. You're not in a position to live in two places at once. Sell it as fast as you can."

"What about Mrs Normington?" asked Horace.

"Who's Mrs Normington?"

"She's the woman who does for me."

"Does she live in the house?"

"Yes."

"Throw her out."

"But..."

"Horace, these are hard times. Take no prisoners."

"Yes, Ernest."

Horace thanked his brother, put the cheque in his pocket and walked towards the door, but Ernest called him back.

"You'd better tell Leonora the other news as well," he said.

"What other news?"

"That your marriage to her is probably bigamous."

"Oh lord," said Horace. Receiving the cheque from Ernest had lifted a large weight from his shoulders. Being told that he was a bigamist replaced it with an even larger one.

Ernest showed Horace out of the front door, and this time they did shake hands. The older brother then returned to his office, put the cheque book back in the drawer, locked it and replaced the key inside *Stamboul Train*. He was about to walk out to the chalet to clear away the evidence of the evening's activities when the telephone on his desk rang.

He picked it up. "Hello?" he said. "Yes, it is. Walter, is that you?"

The caller was indeed the artist Walter Washbrook, but he had clearly had a lot to drink, and he started to babble when he heard Ernest's voice.

"Walter, slow down, I can't understand a word you're saying," said Ernest.

"I have to come and see you," said Washbrook. "I'm in the soup. It's a matter of life and death."

"Walter, you're always in the soup about something, and it's always a matter of life and death."

"Ernest, this is the real thing. I've landed myself in some very deep manure."

It had already been a rather stressful evening, and Ernest wasn't in the mood to deal with another of Walter's problems. "Walter darling, I'm tired and I'm going to bed," he said. "Come over and see me tomorrow evening, I'm sure we can sort it all out then."

Chapter 7
Laboramus et insudamus
Monday evening, Earls Court and St John's Wood -
very frosty

When Leonora heard Horace leave the apartment, she picked up the telephone in the hall and called her friend Diana, who invited her to dinner. On the way to St John's Wood, Leonora reflected on her friend's life. Not yet forty years old, Diana Bagshot was the widow of Viscount Grimbledon, who had died aged sixty, having fathered no children and with no other immediate family, leaving his wife properties and shares worth a fortune. After a suitable period of mourning, she was now a very merry widow indeed. In the spring and summer, she had more invitations to dinners and parties than she could handle, and to help her through the long winter nights, she had a stable of young men in London and Dorset. Somehow, she managed to keep all her adventures a secret, there was never a whiff of scandal about her, and she was welcome in the finest houses in England.

Some women had all the luck.

Over dinner, Leonora described the dire situation she was in.

"Good Lord, Leo," said Diana. "You do have the most abominable luck with men. Pity you didn't stick it out with Teddy. You could have been living the life of Riley now that he's gone and abdicated."

"I did think about trying to steal him back, but he *is* a bit of a nightmare. He does like to go off with the most awfully disreputable women."

"Yes. Like you and me," said Diana.

After dinner, they sat in front of the large marble fireplace in the drawing room, drinking sherry. Leonora noticed a painting that was above the mantelpiece. "I haven't seen this before," she said. "Have you just bought it?"

"No," replied Diana. "I've had it for a while. I had it over my bed. I decided I wanted something a little more stimulating there, so I swapped it for the nude that used to be here."

"Oh yes, I remember that. A lovely image." She stood up and looked at the painting more closely. "Is this one of Horace's?" she asked.

"Your Horace? No, no, of course not. But it *is* something I bought from Horace's son. I forget his name."

"Charles?" said Leonora. "I didn't realise you knew my stepson."

"Polly introduced us at your wedding," said Diana. "We talked a bit about art, and he got the impression that I was a collector. He brought some paintings to show me, and I bought this one."

"I see."

"It's by a different Horace. Horace Tuck."

"Never heard of him. Is he fashionable?"

"Apparently, yes. Tucks are changing hands for more than a hundred pounds at the moment, so I'm thinking of selling it. In fact, I've got someone from Sotheby's coming to value it. He's coming tomorrow morning, in fact."

"I see."

"How is Polly, by the way?"

"No idea," said Leonora. "That child is a law unto herself. I'm really quite annoyed with her, actually. When she got expelled from Bedales, I packed her off to

Paris with an introduction to the Duke of Aquitaine. And his second son proposed to her."

"Goodness. And what happened?"

"They got engaged, he gave her a ring, and then she broke off the engagement. And apparently, she didn't give the ring back, which is terribly bad form in France."

Diana had always had a soft spot for Polly Capstan, and hearing this only increased her admiration of Leonora's daughter. "So, what's she up to now?"

"I don't know. I haven't seen her since she went to France, and I haven't a clue where she is or what she's doing." She continued to stare at the painting. In the bottom right-hand corner, there was a sweeping H, very similar to the one her husband put on his paintings.

"Are you sure this isn't one of Horace's? I mean my Horace?"

"I hope it isn't," said Diana. "With the greatest respect, I wouldn't be able to sell a Horace Goodgame for a hundred pounds."

"Neither would I," said Leonora, with a sigh.

Beneath the painting, leaning against a carriage clock, was a gold-embossed card, an invitation to a weekend shooting party. Leonora picked it up and read it.

"Who's the Duke of Burfaughtonleigh?" asked Leonora, slurring her words a little.

"Apparently, it's pronounced Burley," said Diana.

"Who is he?"

"I don't know him personally, but he was a friend of my husband's," said Diana. "Ever since Eustace died, he's been pestering me to join one of his weekend parties at his pile in Gloucestershire."

"What's he like?" asked Leonora.

"I've never met him," said Diana. "I get invitations like that all the time. I never accept them."

"But you're always going to parties."

"Only in London, and one or two in Bath. As far as the country house scene is concerned, I'm a complete unknown. And I'm happy for it to stay that way."

"So, you aren't going?"

"No. I have ... other plans for the weekend," said Diana.

Leonora looked at the invitation again. "This Burfaughtonleigh chap, or Burley or whatever, is he a bachelor?"

"Bachelor or divorced, I imagine. He must be if he sends out invitations to weekend parties and doesn't put a wife's name on them. You can find out in Debrett's."

Outside in the hall, the telephone rang.

"Do excuse me," said Diana. She uncurled herself on the sofa and left the room. Leonora heard her friend pick up the telephone. "Hello?" she said. "Oh, it's you. Look I'm busy...." and then she fell silent for a while. When she started speaking again, she spoke so quietly that Leonora couldn't hear what she was saying, but she was clearly annoyed. Eventually Diana slammed the phone down and shouted a word that Leonora had never heard her use before.

Diana came back into the room and marched past Leonora as if she wasn't there, picked up her handbag from the coffee table and walked over to the desk in the bay window. She sat down with her back to her friend and started opening and closing drawers, rustling papers around as she did. She took something out of one of the drawers and put it in the handbag.

"Is everything all right?" asked Leonora.

Diana turned round quickly. "Oh, Leonora," she said. "I have a small problem. Do you think you could do me a favour?"

"If I can, absolutely."

"The thing is, I have to go out for a while."

"Now? But it's nearly eleven o'clock."

"... and I may not be back tonight," she continued, ignoring Leonora's time check. "I need someone to be here tomorrow morning when the chap from Sotheby's arrives to value the paintings. Could you possibly stay the night?"

"Well, yes of course," said Leonora.

The telephone rang again in the hall and Diana hurried out of the room. She left the door of the drawing room open and this time she spoke in a loud voice, so Leonora heard everything, clear as a bell.

"Hello? Oh God, listen! I told you I will get there as fast as I can. What? Well, give him an aspirin or something. And don't let him leave the building .... I don't know, for goodness sake, use your imagination!" Again, the phone crashed back onto its cradle.

"Bloody imbeciles, the pair of them." She picked up the telephone again and dialled a number. "Operator, can you get me Juniper 4741? Yes, Executive Limousines." There was a pause. "Executive Limousines? This is Lady Grimbledon at 14 Chetwynde Mansions. I know it's very late but I need to get into Central London and I was wondering if you could send a car. Yes, as soon as possible. How long? Oh, marvellous, thank you."

Diana went into another room, cursing and shouting. Leonora had never heard her friend like this before. What had happened to put her in such a bad mood? Two people were involved and one of them seemed to be suffering in some way. Who? Where? And why did she have to go out at eleven o'clock at night?

Diana came back into the sitting room, carrying a small overnight bag. "So, can you do that for me?" she asked. "Spend the night here and let the chap from Sotheby's in?"

"Yes, of course. I told you I'm happy to oblige."

"If you need anything, Johnson the porter's number is next to the telephone in the hall. Strictly speaking, we're only supposed to call him between eight in the morning and ten at night, but I think he sleeps next to the phone, so you can call him more or less any time."

"I'm sure I'll be fine. I *have* stayed here before, remember."

"If you do call Johnson, don't tell him I'm not here. Tell him I'm asleep."

"I understand."

Diana seemed to have recovered her composure and smiled at Leonora. "I do value you as a friend, Leo." Leonora was about to express the same feelings, but Diana cut her off. "However, if I ever hear that news of tonight's events went beyond these four walls, our friendship will end."

"Diana, you know you can trust me."

"There are keys to the apartment on a hook next to the front door."

There was a buzzing sound in the hall, indicating that her car had arrived. Diana picked up her handbag and overnight bag, pecked Leonora on the cheek and left the room. The door of the apartment slammed behind her and Leonora heard the sound of her heels clacking down the marble staircase. Leonora went to the bay window and saw Diana get into the back of a large black car, which turned and headed towards Central London.

Leonora poured herself another glass of sherry, picked up the Duke of Burfaughtonleigh's invitation and sat in front of the fireplace. The shooting party was taking place at the end of the week, guests were to arrive on

Friday evening or Saturday morning, and there would be an afternoon of shooting on Saturday followed by a formal meal in the evening. On the back of the invitation were instructions how to get to Great Park. Guests who wished to come by train would be picked up at Stanford Saint Mary station by one of the Duke's staff and should indicate which train they would be arriving on. RSVPs by Wednesday 17th at the latest.

Leonora decided that she would pretend to be Lady Grimbledon and accept the invitation. Diana had said that she was a 'complete unknown' on the country house circuit, so why not? She had been on a couple of shooting weekends before, so she knew the form. Women weren't expected to know how to shoot, they simply went out with the men and applauded when they managed to blast the brains out of some stupid pheasant or partridge.

What could possibly go wrong? In the unlikely event of someone knowing that she wasn't Diana, she would simply say that she was standing in for her friend, who had been unavoidably detained in London.

She opened the wide drawer in the middle of the desk and was delighted to find writing paper with Diana's name and address across the top. It even had the Grimbledon coat of arms on it, a knight on horseback and dragon rampant, and the family motto - LABORAMUS ET INSUDAMUS - We Toil and We Sweat.

We toil and we sweat, indeed. Leonora had known the Honourable Eustace Grimbledon before his demise, an overweight simpleton who had never done a day's proper toil in his life. The only time he ever produced anything resembling sweat was when he walked up the stairs to his bedroom at Grimbledon Hall, usually after dinner and copious amounts of brandy, a journey that he failed to complete on the last day of his life, tripping on the top step and tumbling down the rounded stone staircase, breaking his neck *en route*.

Leonora took a piece of paper out of the drawer and began to write an RSVP. With no access to a car or chauffeur, she would have to go by train. How was she supposed to find out train times? She looked at the clock. It was twenty to midnight. She would have to call Johnson the porter. She walked into the hall, picked up the phone and dialled his number.

The phone rang three times before it was picked up, and a drowsy voice said, "Hello? Porter speaking."

"I'm so sorry," said Leonora. "Is that Mister Johnson?"

"Yes, your ladyship," replied Johnson. He clearly had a system which told him which apartment the call was coming from.

"Um... actually this isn't Lady Grimbledon. I'm a house guest." Remembering that Diana did not want Johnson to know she was out, Leonora added: "Lady Grimbledon is asleep now, but I'm still awake. I'm ... I'm working on one of my novels."

There was a pause. "I'm sorry, madam, I don't quite understand."

"My name is Leonora Goodgame. You may know me as Leonora Capstan."

"I may know you as what?"

"Leonora Capstan. I'm a novelist."

"I'm a bit confused, madam."

"Right. Well, the thing is, I need a railway timetable. Do you have one?"

"A railway timetable?"

"Yes."

"Which company?"

"I'm sorry?"

"I do have timetables here, madam, one for each company. Which company do you want? LMS, GWR, LNER or Southern?"

"Oh goodness."

"Which destination do you want information about?"

"Stanford Saint Mary."

"And where would that be, madam?"

"Gloucestershire."

'You'll want GWR, Great Western. Do you want me to check it for you, or should we bring it up?"

"Oh, do please bring it up."

"Now, or should we wait until the morning?"

"Could you possibly bring it up immediately?"

"Certainly, madam."

A few minutes later, there was a knock at the door. When Leonora opened it, she expected to see an old man, half-asleep and wearing a dressing gown. To her surprise and delight, a tall, muscular young man was standing there. He was wearing narrow black trousers and a white shirt that was unbuttoned half-way to his waist. He was barefoot and had clearly just woken up.

"Well, Johnson," she said, putting on her most dazzling smile. "Very pleased to meet you."

"I'm actually Johnson's nephew," said the young man, stifling a yawn. "Uncle Jasper asked me to bring this up." He held out a well-thumbed railway timetable.

"How lovely. Would you care for a drink?"

*****

While Leonora was getting into bed in St John's Wood, her ex-husband Ronnie Capstan was also turning in, a few miles away in West London. Ronnie's circumstances were more spartan than hers, but he was also smiling contentedly as he climbed up the ladder to the top bunk in his prison cell at Wormwood Scrubs.

His good humour was the result of news that he had received a couple of hours before, that he would be released the next morning after serving less than a year of a three-year prison sentence for dishonestly handling stolen goods.

Acquaintances of Ronnie Capstan had been shocked by the severity of the sentence that had been handed down by Mr Justice Brodkin and also surprised that someone on a charge of theft had been tried at the Old Bailey. What the newspapers had failed to report was that Brodkin's Rolls Royce Phantom was among the stolen goods. When he discovered that the perpetrator had been apprehended, the judge made sure he tried the case and sent Ronnie down for three years, a huge sentence considering it was a first offence.

As he lay on his upper bunk, listening to his cellmate Freddie 'Fingers' Fogarty talking in his sleep below, Ronnie was turning over his options on release. First of all, where was he going to live? *Faut de mieux*, it seemed his only option was to fetch up at his sister Cornelia's house in Hampstead, where she lived in some style with her husband Sir Arthur Wickham-Thynne. Ronnie thought his sister was a brainless snob, and he could barely stand to spend any time with her, but released prisoners can't be choosers so, if he wanted her to put him up, he would have to put up with her.

Secondly, what was he going to do for money? He had a strongbox at Krumnagel's Bank in the Strand, which contained about two hundred pounds in cash, plus a number of items that he might be able to sell, two Rolex watches, a silver cigarette case and a diamond necklace that he bought for his mistress, the woman he had planned to marry. Fortunately, he had never given it to her, and when he was sent down, she broke off the engagement and with almost indecent haste got engaged to someone else. To Humphrey Fotheringay, in fact, the heir to the Fotheringay's Sausages empire, who had once been engaged to Polly Capstan.

The contents of the strongbox would keep Ronnie going for a few months, but he had to think of something in the long term. This wasn't quite so straightforward. As Fingers Fogarty burbled on below him, probably dreaming about his next court appearance, Ronnie made a mental list of the people who owed him favours and also the ones about whom he had a little dirt he could dish. In particular, he thought about the three or four people who appeared in both lists.

One name stood out amongst the others in this last group - Tarquin Woolnough, the fourteenth Duke of Burfaughtonleigh.

Chapter 8
He's the biggest bastard I know
Tuesday morning, Great Park - turning colder, threat of snow

Charles and Polly were asleep, stepsister sprawled across stepbrother. There was a knock at the door. They both woke up with a start.

"Gilbert?" said Polly. She looked up and stared at her brother, puzzled. "Oh, Charles! What's happening?"

"I think it's the boy with my hot water," said Charles, stung more than he would like to admit by hearing Polly say the name of the Duke's son.

"Hold on a sec," she said. She jumped off the bed, walked as lightly as she could across the creaking floorboards and climbed into the wardrobe. Charles got up, kicked Polly's riding boots under the bed, put on his wig and dark glasses and unlocked the door to allow Flockton into the room. After he left, Polly stepped elegantly out of the wardrobe, smiling like a naughty schoolgirl. "First time I've had to do that for a while," she said. When she saw that Charles wasn't amused, she added "Only joking!", and kissed him on the lips. She put on her boots, kissed him again and walked quickly to the door, looking both ways before she disappeared.

The hot water steamed invitingly in the bath. Charles added some cold, then stepped in and sat down. He stared at the wall in front of him, trying to remember when he had felt as unhappy and confused as he was now, and an image of bath time at his boarding school came into his mind.

When he was seven, he'd been packed off to a school called Brambletye at East Grinstead in Sussex, which was more than a hundred miles from his home in Hunstanton, as the crow flew. As the train trundled, it was a lot further, a complicated and time-consuming journey that involved taking three trains and also finding your way across London, which neither of his parents enjoyed doing. Horace and Martha never visited Charles while he was there, and when he went home to Norfolk at the end of term, he spent most of his time alone, wandering along the beach collecting shells.

One day, during the summer just after his tenth birthday, when his parents were taking an afternoon nap in their separate rooms, he went into Horace's studio, put an empty canvas on an easel and started to copy one of his father's paintings. His first attempt was terrible, so he painted the canvas white and started again the next day. He really enjoyed this new pastime and took advantage of the time when the studio was empty.

His ability to copy improved and by the end of the summer, he was reproducing his father's very average work in perfect detail. Painting became an addiction, and he looked forward to the times he had to spend at home. As the years passed, his talent developed in a most unusual way. As soon as he put brush to canvas, he would go into a trance, not even aware of the process as the image flashed across the canvas. He was able to make a mental picture of the painting he wanted to copy and then complete it from memory. When he had done all his father's paintings, Charles started copying from the many books in the house that featured the works of famous artists. By the age of sixteen, he had skills that a serious art forger would be proud of. Two years later, after presenting a portfolio which consisted mainly of improved versions of his father's paintings, Charles was offered a place at the Royal College of Art. He moved to London, where his uncle Ernest reluctantly agreed to give him a roof over his head. The roof was on a shed in the back garden of the house in Pelham Crescent.

After art school, Charles got a job at the Arte Moderne Gallery in Bond Street, which was owned by Ronnie Capstan's brother-in-law, Sir Arthur Wickham-Thynne, but what he really wanted to do was make a living as a portrait painter. His uncle Ernest gave him his first opportunity when he found out that one of his South Kensington neighbours was 'looking for an artist to do a likeness'. The neighbour was a dynamic woman in her eighties named Veronica Stoodley. Miss Stoodley was barely five feet tall, with long straggly white hair and a stone-coloured face. She dressed in brightly coloured clothes and wore long false eyelashes and large amounts of black eye-liner, which made her face look as if two crows had crashed into a cliff. She clearly didn't give a hoot what anyone thought about her.

Charles was captivated by her when they met and was very much looking forward to painting her extraordinary textured face. It was only when he arrived at her house to begin work that he discovered she actually wanted a portrait of her dog. The mutt in question was a Bichon Frise, a small white animal that barked aggressively at him when he arrived. Its pedigree name was Fishwick Braccorian Wellington Saint Leger. Miss Stoodley called him Fish.

Charles explained to her that to do a portrait, it was necessary for the person (or animal) being portrayed to sit still for lengthy periods of time.

"That won't be a problem," she said. When it was time to start, she sat next to Fish and any time he so much as turned his head from one side to the other, she shouted 'FISH!!!' in her incredibly deep voice, and he froze. So did Charles.

Spending time with Miss Stoodley turned out to be the most fun he had had for a long time, and when he finished painting the dog, he insisted on doing a portrait of the owner too, free of charge. At first, she told him not to be a nincompoop, one of her favourite words, but she was clearly flattered, and they spent another enjoyable few hours together, but he refused to take money from her for the sketch he had done. Subsequently, she spread the word about him, and work flowed in. One after another, her ancient friends invited him to paint their dogs, cats, parrots, and other inhabitants of their expensive homes in West London. He gave up working at the gallery, and for two years he was in constant demand. He made enough money to rent a studio on the riverside near Hammersmith Bridge, big enough for him to live and work in.

None of Miss Stoodley's friends and acquaintances were anywhere near as interesting as she was, and one or two of the dogs he had to paint were quite hostile, one of them biting his leg quite savagely. He was already thinking it was time to stop doing pet portraits when a commission arrived from a retired army brigadier called Arnold Wigley, a man who was used to giving orders and being obeyed. Wigley wanted Charles to paint his pet boa constrictor, but when the snake coiled itself round Charles's leg and he lost all feeling in his foot, he thought it was time to stop. He informed the brigadier of his decision and Wigley did what he always did when things went against him and threatened to have Charles horse-whipped.

A few days later, Charles bumped into Miss Stoodley in the street. She was interested to know what had happened between him and the brigadier, and Charles explained that he felt threatened by the boa constrictor and hadn't meant to upset one of her friends, especially as she had been so helpful with his career.

"Don't say another word about it," she said, "Wigley is a bully and, frankly, he's the biggest bastard I know."

They were standing at the gate of her house, and she invited Charles in for a cup of tea. When they went into the drawing room, Fish the Bichon Frise was dozing in front of the fire and perked up when he saw the only young person he had spent any time with in the last two years.

"Funny," said Veronica. "He's been quite morose since you stopped painted him. I think he quite likes you."

More than the boa constrictor, that's for sure, thought Charles.

"How would you feel about looking after him?" she asked.

Charles was surprised by this request. "Look after him? I ... um ... I don't think I'm allowed to keep pets in my studio."

"I don't mean to look after him for good, you nincompoop!" she said. "I have to go out for a while. He barks the place down if I'm not here for more than five minutes and my bone-idle maid refuses to go anywhere near him. He bit her once."

"Oh goodness! Was it bad?"

"No! Just a scratch! It only needed five stitches and a tetanus injection, I can't think what she was complaining about."

Charles looked at the dog with a mixture of fear and respect.

"Can I leave him with you for half an hour?" she asked.

"Um..."

"Good. If you get hungry, pull that cord," she said. "Gisèle might agree to rustle up a ham sandwich for you."

Veronica picked up her large purple and pink handbag, smacked the dog on the nose quite violently, and headed out of the house. Fish growled, but Charles tentatively stroked him for a while, and the dog sat down by the fire and went to sleep, his tail wagging slowly from time to time.

Veronica had said she would be out for half an hour, but it was more than three hours and well into the evening before she returned. Charles had pulled the cord two or three times, but there was no sign of the bone idle maid, and every time he made a move towards the door to try to find some food for himself, Fish started barking and ran around in a demented way.

When Veronica came in, she put a purple Harrods bag on the table in front of Charles. "Did you pull the cord?" she asked.

"Yes."

"Did the maid come?"

"No."

"Right, no surprise really," she said. "I remembered as soon as I'd left that it's her day off, so I got you this."

Charles took a package out of the Harrods bag. In it was a huge slice of pork pie.

"I'll get you a plate and some mustard," she said, and disappeared into the kitchen. "Do you want a glass of beer to wash it down?"

"Yes, please."

So it was that Charles became a frequent visitor to Pelham Crescent and spent a lot of time looking after the dog. He even met Gisèle, the maid, a quiet Frenchwoman who didn't look much younger than Miss Stoodley. She eventually agreed to make him a ham sandwich, but just the once.

However, he received no more commissions to do portraits, either of people or beasts, possibly because Brigadier Wigley had informed all and sundry that Charles was not a reliable individual. He was running out of money and beginning to think it was time to look for alternative employment, maybe even go back to work at the art gallery.

Then Polly summoned him to Great Park. And now here he was, sitting in a bath of cooling water, with the prospect of painting the overweight Duke of Burfaughtonleigh's naked body.

Chapter 9
Should I take off the dressing gown?
Tuesday morning, Great Park - turning colder, threat of
snow

Charles got out of the bath, dried himself off and put on
a charcoal grey mechanic's overall, the garment he
always wore when he was working. Guessing that his
working space might be a bit cold, he also put on a shirt,
an old pullover and a pair of thick long johns. He picked
up his dark glasses and went out in search of breakfast,
and was halfway down the corridor when he realised he
wasn't wearing the wig. He went back for that, checked
that he had put it on the right way round, and set off
again, before returning a second time to collect his
walking stick. There were so many things to think about
when you were playing the part of an old man.

He clacked his stick down the stairs and when he
reached the ground floor, he stopped, wondering which
way to go. Flockton appeared and led him to the dining
room, a long dark empty room with a table that could
seat about twenty people. The under-butler asked
Charles if he would like a cooked breakfast, and he said
yes.

While he waited for his food to arrive, he picked up a
copy of *The Times* that was dated the previous Friday.
Flicking through the pages, Charles discovered that
Foreign Secretary Lord Halifax was on his way to
negotiate with German Chancellor Adolf Hitler. After
the announcement in parliament, which according to *The
Times* was met with almost universal approval, Winston
Churchill made a speech warning of the dangers of

appeasement, saying he knew for a fact that the Germans were developing missiles that could rain destruction on London. The article said that Churchill had been shouted down by members of his own party. On another page, Charles read that MPs had also voted to fund the building of air raid shelters in London and other towns and cities.

Staying at Great Park suddenly seemed like a pretty good idea.

Later, while Charles was munching on his fried eggs, bacon, sausages and mushrooms, Polly came in, poured herself a cup of coffee, drank it quickly and told Charles it was time for him to have a look at the place where he was going to work. He was reluctantly pulled away from his unfinished breakfast and marched down a long dark corridor and out of the back door of the house. Across the courtyard was an extension that was newer than the neo-gothic original, a right-angled addition that ended in a bright, airy conservatory, where his oils and portfolio of canvases and a sturdy easel were already in place. A Victorian chaise longue with green leather upholstery stood in the middle of the room. Charles presumed that this was where the Duke wished to be painted.

"Is this all right?" asked Polly.

"It's perfect," replied Charles. Light was coming in from skylights, which was exactly how he liked it. He smiled and thought that, if he could just deal with the sight of the naked Duke, this wasn't going to be too much of an ordeal.

"I'm so glad," said Polly. "My office is right next door. If you need anything, you know where to find me." She came over to him and put her arms round his neck. "I do love you, you know," she said, and kissed him on the lips.

Before he could say anything, she hurried out and along the path to her office. Charles breathed out, feeling more relaxed than he had done since his arrival. He adjusted the wig, so that it wasn't in his eyes, and then opened the wooden box which contained his brushes and oils and also a small box of charcoal pencils. He took out two of the wider ones and rested them on the ledge of the easel.

He was about to choose a brush when there was a knock at the door. "Come in," said Charles, bracing himself for the Duke's theatrical entrance.

The door opened and a short, thin man walked in. He had a mountain of black curly hair and was wearing a pink silk dressing gown and pink slippers with pompoms.

It was Pickles. He was wearing the Duke's wig.

He sat down on the green leather chaise longue, adjusted the dressing gown and coughed nervously. For a few moments, he and Charles looked at each other in silence. Eventually, the butler spoke.

"Good morning, Mister Washbrook," he said.

"Good morning, Pickles," replied Charles. "Nice day for it."

"I imagine you would like some kind of explanation."

"Not at all, everything's fine!" said Charles, rather too loudly. He began to laugh, with just a touch of hysteria in his voice.

"The situation is like this ..."

"No, let me guess!" said Charles. "The Duke wants me to paint your body in the nude, and then when I've finished that, he will replace you on the chaise longue and I will paint his face."

Pickles coughed again. Less nervously this time.

"Am I close to the truth?" asked Charles.

"Yes, Mister Washbrook. That's more or less the plan. Thank you being able to work it out for yourself."

Charles thought back to the days before he had come to Great Park, when his only problems were dogs who wanted a lump of his thigh and boa constrictors who fancied him for lunch. "So ... just let me get something straight," he said. "You told me the Duke wanted the portrait *au naturelle*."

"That is correct."

"In other words, a portrait in the nude."

"Yes."

"So ... the dressing gown, how does it -- I mean, is it part of the portrait?"

Pickles explained what the Duke wanted. The pink dressing gown should be nestling (the Duke's exact word) around his waist.

"And the slippers?"

"Also part of the portrait."

Charles nodded his head, thinking to himself that the Duke of Burfaughtonleigh had the worst aesthetic taste of any client he had ever painted. "Well, in for a penny, in for a pound," he said.

"Thank you so much, Mr Washbrook."

"Pickles, do please call me Walter."

"I'm not sure the Duke would approve of my being on first name terms with one of his guests," said Pickles. "But here in the privacy of the studio, I'd be honoured to do that. Thank you, Walter."

"Let's get started," said Charles.

"Should I take off the dressing gown now?" asked the butler.

"Just let it drop round your ... um ... waist," replied Charles.

"Should I remain silent?"

"Oh no!" said Charles. "Banter away. Conversation is good at this stage."

"That's good to know."

"And don't feel offended if I sort of stare at you for a while. It's the way I work."

"I see," said Pickles.

As he had promised, Charles looked intently at Pickles on the green chaise longue for about a minute, then picked up a piece of charcoal and began to work. He now had a powerful image in his mind of what he wanted to do, so he barely needed to look at Pickles as he began to make sweeping motions across the canvas. He was so bound up in what he was doing that he didn't hear when Pickles asked a question.

Pickles addressed him a second time. "Walter?"

"Oh, I'm sorry, I was miles away."

"My apologies then. If you would prefer me to remain silent ... "

"No, no, I just get a bit involved with what I'm doing."

"You certainly do," said Pickles, with a note of admiration in his voice. "And may I say, you are so supple. You move like a much younger man."

Charles swore quietly under his breath. He had completely forgotten that he was supposed to be in his sixties. "I expect they huff and groan a lot," Polly had said. He instinctively put his hand to his back, in the way he imagined old people did when they were in pain, and groaned noisily.

"You're right," he said, "I should slow down a bit."

"I think I understand what's happening to you," said Pickles.

"You do?" said Charles.

"Yes. I have a small confession to make."

'You have?"

"I actually trained to be a ballet dancer."

"You did? How interesting. I must say I did think you moved like a dancer."

"Oh Walter, that's extremely kind of you. Actually, I was never remotely good enough to make a living at ballet, but for a time, I worked in cabaret shows in London. And I was thinking about Doctor Theatre."

"Doctor Theatre? Who's he?"

Pickles laughed. "It isn't a who. It's an expression used by thespians and other performers to describe what happens if they're required to work when they're ill or suffering from an injury."

"Ah! I see."

"The show must go on, as they say. Usually, they find that the mere fact of walking on stage in front of an audience makes whatever ailment it is disappear."

"Extraordinary."

"When I saw you moving back and forth so gracefully, like a much younger man, that was my first thought. Doctor Theatre has taken over Walter's body."

"Funny you should say that," said Charles. "I think I just put my back out. I'm not getting any younger." Charles's back was indeed hurting and had been since he got up. Probably because of the position he had to sleep in with Polly draped across his chest, not a fact he felt he could share with Pickles. He sat down on a metal chair. Even through his long johns and overalls, the seat was quite cold.

"If you're feeling tired, we can stop now," said Pickles.

"Absolutely not, just feeling a bit of trouble here," replied Charles, pointing at his right hip. "The old hip gives me a bit of gip," he said, with a chuckle, rather pleased with his accidental poetry. "Let's carry on."

106

Charles was finding the experience far less troublesome than he had expected. Pickles was a perfectly wonderful person to pass the time of day with, and the fact that he was half naked and wearing a huge wig and pom-pomed slippers seemed to matter not one jot.

Later in the morning, Pickles asked if they could take a break. "The Duke has some guests coming to lunch all the way from London," he said. "A theatre impresario by the name of Bernard Delgado and I believe he's bringing a friend."

"Right, well yes, we can stop right now. Not a problem."

"I also have one or two other urgent matters to deal with," said Pickles. "I don't know if Polly told you, but there will be a shooting party at Great Park this weekend."

"No, she didn't."

"Do you shoot?"

"Do I shoot?" repeated Charles.

"Yes."

"Shoot what?"

'Pheasants, partridges. Game birds."

"Good Lord, no. How barbaric."

"Did you enjoy the sandwich that was in your room last night?" asked Pickles.

"The sandwich? Oh yes, it was very tasty."

"Well, that was a pheasant shot by the Duke himself during our last shooting weekend."

"Ah," said Charles. That would explain the small metal ball in the middle of it that nearly broke one of his back teeth.

"But I do agree with you. As you say, barbaric," said Pickles. "There will be no obligation to actually shoot, or indeed to spend time outside during the event. And there will be a banquet on Saturday evening, which should be amusing. And of course, you're more than welcome to avail yourself of the facilities in the house, as you are at any time. There are various works of art around the house that you may wish to see."

"Yes, indeed," said Charles. He decided to find out more about the painting he was supposed to copy. "I did notice that rather wonderful painting over the fireplace last night. It looked like a Van Gogh."

Pickles hesitated for a moment. "Yes, it almost certainly *is* a Van Gogh."

"*Almost* certainly?"

"It's a portrait of the author Robert Louis Stevenson, and it was acquired some fifty years ago by Aloysius Woolnough, the twelfth Duke of Burfaughtonleigh, the present incumbent's grandfather, the man who actually built Great Park."

Charles did a calculation in his mind. Fifty years ago, the late 1880s, the time that Van Gogh was actually painting. Anyone acquiring one of his paintings in those days must have got it straight from the studio.

"Aloysius Woolnough was a great traveller and art collector," Pickles continued. "And the story goes that he actually met Van Gogh in the south of France and purchased the painting from the artist himself."

Straight from the studio, indeed.

Pickles told Charles what he knew about the portrait. Apparently, the artist had met Robert Louis Stevenson in Arles sometime in the 1870s, when the writer was returning to London after a visit to the French Riviera, a place he had visited in the hope of improving his health. The Scot and the Dutchman got on immediately and Van Gogh persuaded his new friend to sit for a portrait, which

108

was unfinished by the time Stevenson had to leave. Unfortunately, when the writer returned to Arles a few weeks later to complete the sitting, he found that the artist had succumbed to one of his many bouts of mental illness. The two men argued and Stevenson walked out, never to return.

"We don't know the exact circumstances," said Pickles, "but because the painting wasn't in the possession of the artist's family and has never been exhibited in an art gallery, there appears to be no record of it in any of the official files relating to the work of Van Gogh. However, over the years, various experts have examined it and they all believe there are features that indicate quite clearly that it's the genuine article."

Charles listened to this explanation with great interest. So it may or may not have been painted by Van Gogh. One possibility was that he started it and it was finished by one of his acolytes, a fairly common occurrence and one that caused lots of disputes in the art world. But Charles was absolutely certain of one thing. If there was any doubt at all about the provenance of the painting, it would be very difficult to sell it, even on the black market. He had to tell Polly about this as soon as possible.

In the meantime, he could relax and enjoy life at Great Park. If he could just remember to behave like an old person all the time, huffing and groaning a bit more and generally feeling his age, he saw no reason why he shouldn't look forward to everything country life had to offer, even the barbaric prospect of the Duke's trigger-happy guests blowing game birds to kingdom come at the weekend.

Pickles left to organise lunch for the Duke and his guests and Charles stayed on in the conservatory, making small changes to the portrait. He heard someone running across the courtyard and was delighted to see that it was Polly. She opened the door of the conservatory, looked to see if she was being followed, and closed the door behind her.

"What ho, dearest stepsister!" he said, cheerfully.

Polly was, however, out of breath and looking anxious.

"Everything all right, Pol?"

"No. Charles, you're going to have to leave."

"I'm -- what?"

"You're going to have to make yourself scarce - immediately."

"Why?"

"There's a chap here from London, a theatrical type called Bernard Delgado."

"I know. Pickles told me."

"Please listen, will you? When he discovered that Walter Washbrook was here, he said he wanted to meet him."

"Well, I can deal with that," said Charles.

"No you can't," replied Polly. "Apparently, Delgado and Washbrook were at school together."

"Oh lord!"

"Yes. So leave now. If you go out this door, you can leg it to the stable. It's over to the left. Then you can take the Alfa Romeo and drive somewhere. Anywhere, just go!"

"I can't drive."

"Oh for God's sake, Charles, you really are useless!"

There was a noise of laughter coming from the courtyard. "They're coming," she said. "Quick! Get out there and ... I don't know, hide in the trees!"

Chapter 10
Did you say your name was Goodgame?

Tuesday morning, St John's Wood - cloudy with outbreaks of thunder

Leonora woke up when she heard the phone ringing. She leapt out of bed and managed to get to it before the caller rang off. When she picked it up, she heard a mechanical noise, a coin being pushed into the slot of a public call box. Leonora had never received a call from one of those before.

It was Diana. She was calling from Brewer Street in Soho, although she didn't say where she was, wanting to keep her mysterious late-night assignation a secret. She wanted to remind Leonora that the man from Sotheby's was due at Chetwynde Mansions to check the Horace Tuck painting. Leonora reassured her that she was ready to meet the art expert, put the phone down and went into the sitting room. She picked up the letter she had written on Diana's headed notepaper the night before, accepting the invitation from the Duke of Burfaughtonleigh to attend the shooting party at Great Park at the weekend. She read it again, took a deep breath and signed it *Diana, Viscountess Grimbledon*. What had been a mad, bad and dangerous idea the night before now seemed even madder, worse and more dangerous, but she was determined to go ahead with it. She would attend the shoot, dazzle the Duke and make him fall in love with her. And then take it from there, wherever it might lead.

She was about to put her RSVP into an envelope when it occurred to her that she didn't want the Great Park people to reply to the Saint John's Wood address or call her on Diana's number. She crossed out the address and telephone number on the letterhead, wrote her own number in Earl's Court and added a hand-written note, asking them to contact her only on this number. If they were suspicious, so be it. If they called her, it would be all systems go. When the envelope was sealed, she telephoned the porter and asked him to send his nephew up to take the letter to be posted.

She couldn't remember the young man's name, but she had spent an enjoyable half hour with him the night before, and for a moment thought about asking him to stay for a little longer, but it was more sensible to make sure the letter was posted, and anyway she had to get ready to meet the Sotheby's man. She wanted a bath, so went into the guest bathroom and turned on the enormous copper taps. Diana's apartment block had been built in the early nineteenth century, but it had been fully modernised and had features that put her modest apartment in Barkston Gardens to shame. You could, for example, get hot water all day long. She just hoped she would have time for a soak before the Sotheby's man arrived.

As it turned out, she wouldn't. With the bath only half full, the buzzer sounded, indicating that someone was at the street door. Diana's apartment even had a system where you could speak to the person who was trying to get in, another amenity lacking in Earl's Court. She turned off the taps, went to the front door of the apartment and picked up the handset.

"Hallo?" she said.

"Lady Grimbledon?" said a voice.

"This is Lady Grimbledon's apartment, yes."

112

"Good morning, Lady Grimbledon. I'm from Sotheby's. I've come to look at one of your paintings."

Oh well, she thought, he'll just have to take me as he finds me. At least she was wearing some of Diana's expensive nightclothes, a dark blue cashmere bathrobe and beneath that a black silk nightdress. "Yes, yes, do come up," she said, pressing the button next to the handset. She heard a noise and the street door opened and then there were footsteps on the marble staircase. When she opened the door, she was delighted to see another good-looking young man. He had a similar muscular build to the one who had left earlier and was even taller. He seemed equally impressed to see her.

"Good morning, your ladyship," the man said.

Leonora thought about pretending to be Diana but decided that this might be one impersonation too many. "I'm not actually Lady Grimbledon," she said.

"Oh, I beg your pardon."

"No, no, don't worry. My name is Leonora Goodgame. You may know me as Leonora Capstan. I'm a novelist."

"I'm sorry?" said the man.

"Leonora Goodgame. Was Capstan, now Goodgame. Pleased to meet you."

The man smiled and nodded, clearly as unaware of her literary activities as the porter had been. He introduced himself as Lawrence Kimberley-Waugh, which excited Leonora even more. She found a combination of youth, muscularity and a double-barrelled name very attractive. Kimberley-Waugh said that he was delighted to have the opportunity to evaluate a Horace Tuck painting because he had written an essay about the Norfolk artist as part of his Art History studies at Cambridge. In fact, he had never been near Cambridge in his life, but this was the preamble he always used in situations like this.

Leonora very much liked the look of the young man so, in order to keep him in the apartment a little longer, she offered him a cup of coffee. As she walked back and forth across the kitchen, she was aware that he was watching her with interest. They drank the coffee and flirted with each other before the Sotheby's man looked at his wristwatch and said that perhaps he ought to start work. Rather reluctantly, she took him into the drawing room and showed him the painting over the fireplace.

"Thank you," he said, giving her a dazzling smile, which she found very exciting indeed. When he looked at the painting, however, his smile faded. He leaned forward and looked at the flamboyant 'H' in the bottom right-hand corner of the canvas. He shook his head, then looked even more closely at the main image, a colourful but rather flat pastoral scene.

"Well, this is certainly quite a decent copy of Tuck's style, but it isn't genuine," he said. This was what Leonora had feared. The previous evening, when she saw the landscape for the first time, she was sure that it had been painted by her husband Horace. Why on earth had her stepson Charles pretended it was by this other Horace when he sold it to Diana?

"Would you happen to know who it was painted by?" she asked.

"Well, it's funny you should ask that," said Kimberley-Waugh. "I had a similar experience with a Tuck a month or so ago, and I discovered that the real artist was ...." He paused and looked at her. "Did you say your name was Goodgame?" he asked.

Leonora nodded.

"Are you by any chance related to an artist called Horace Goodgame?"

Leonora walked towards him. She loosened the tie on the bathrobe as she approached him. It fell open to reveal the black silk nightdress.

"Is there anything I can do," she asked, "that would persuade you not to tell Lady Grimbledon what you know?"

Chapter 11
Oh, I say! Dark goings-on at the bank!
Tuesday, The Strand, London - cold with a threat of rain

Siegfried-Wilhelm and Rolf-Theodor Krumnagel opened their bank in London in 1776 and their great-great-great-recurring grandson Gottfried was the current executive manager of the main branch in The Strand. Gottfried, who preferred to be known as Godfrey, was an enthusiastic and energetic individual, the only problem being that his enthusiasm and energy were rarely directed towards banking. Rupert Burgess, who had been assistant manager at the bank for less than a month, was a natural worrier, and agonized over whether to approach his boss about the Agatha Merchant trust fund, but he felt that the fraudulent activity relating to it was serious enough to alert the chief executive. Unfortunately, Godfrey had failed to answer the phone or respond to the telegram he sent.

The next morning, Burgess wrote a second telegram, wording it to convey the importance of the situation. MATTER LIFE AND DEATH STOP CRISIS REGARDING CRIMINAL EMPTYING OF MERCHANT TRUST FUND STOP INSIST ON MEETING AT BANK SOONEST. He decided MATTER LIFE AND DEATH was too dramatic and crossed the words out. He re-started the message with the words VERY SERIOUS STOP PLEASE READ AND REPLY NOW STOP.

At midday, Rita went back to the Post Office and stood in line. She was lost in thought and impatiently pacing back and forth, when she suddenly felt something under her wedge heel and heard a high-pitched yelp behind her. When she turned, she saw a tall, good-looking man with wavy blond hair and piercing blue eyes. His face was contorted in pain.

"Awfully sorry," he said. "But you just stepped on my foot."

"Oh goodness!" said Rita. "Are you all right?"

"Just a few broken toes, I think," said the man. "Don't worry," he added. "I think I'll live."

"I can only apologise again," said Rita. "I suppose we all get a bit impatient when we need to send a telegram, don't we?"

"We do indeed," said the man.

Now that a connection had been made, the two engaged in conversation as the queue for the telegram desk shuffled forward. Rita was pleased that the man wanted to talk to her but decided that the telegram was secret bank business and she shouldn't divulge the details. Instead, she let the man talk about himself. She was very impressed when he told her that he worked for Sotheby's, the company that sold and auctioned works of art. He said he'd been on an assignment in Saint John's Wood that very morning and had discovered that a painting thought to be by a famous artist was actually a fake. He made the whole escapade sound like the plot of a crime novel, exactly the kind of thing that Rita enjoyed reading, and she was entranced by the story. She was even more excited to learn that he was sending a telegram to a grand house in the country, telling them that he would be arriving the next day to attend a shooting party. When they reached the front of the queue, they stood next to each other at the counter, where they were handed forms by the two women who were operating the telegraph machines. When they finished

118

writing their messages, the Sotheby's man picked up Rita's and read it out loud.

"Very serious stop please read and reply now stop," he said. "Oh, I say! Dark goings-on at the bank! I really want to know more about this!"

"Name and address of recipient please," said one of the women, impatiently. There was some confusion when they handed over their forms. The words were hurriedly typed in and money changed hands.

When Rita and the man were out in the street, he begged her to explain what her message was all about. Rita said she had to go back to work but agreed to meet him later at Lyon's Corner House on the Strand, a few hundred yards from the bank.

It was nearly two o'clock when she got back to the bank, and Burgess was pacing up and down in his office. She confirmed that the woman at the Post Office had said the telegram would be delivered within the hour.

Burgess sat down at his desk and put his head in his hands. "It's pointless, really," he said. "I've rung him three times and no one answered the telephone. He's hardly likely to be sitting in the garden on a cold day like this so he's obviously not home. There's no way of getting hold of him at the moment."

In fact, Godfrey Krumnagel *was* at home. He had spent Sunday and Monday in bed, because he had a severe cold and fever, picked up on Saturday when he had foolishly accepted an invitation to play golf at Effingham on a freezing cold day. His wife Clarissa was unsympathetic about his condition and had gone shopping in Knightsbridge. Before leaving, she told their new Belgian maid Jozintje that if her sick husband asked for food, she should heat up some of the chicken soup she had left in the fridge. Jozintje's soup preparation

119

wasn't successful. Godfrey had just one mouthful of the gloopy brown concoction before deciding he'd rather go hungry. He took three sleeping pills and was dead to the world for the next two days.

Jozintje felt alarmed at being left in charge of the house and was too afraid to pick up the phone when it rang on Monday. When the telegram boy turned up, the maid put the brown envelope he gave her on a table in the hall.

It was Burgess's third phone call on Tuesday morning that woke Godfrey up, but he was too slow to get to the phone before it stopped ringing. He wandered into the kitchen, told Jozintje that he was feeling better, and asked her to make him a pot of coffee and a fry-up. The maid's grasp of English was poor, and the only parts of his instruction that she understood were 'coffee' and 'up', so while he sat in the conservatory smoking a cigarette and reading *Punch* magazine, she made a pot of coffee and took it up to his bedroom.

After reading for about half an hour, he walked into the kitchen, where the maid was sitting at the table reading a volume of the Oxford English Dictionary.

"Where's my coffee and fry-up?" he asked.

Jozintje pointed to the ceiling. "Upstairs. In bedroom," she said nervously.

Godfrey raised an eyebrow and headed towards the stairs to see what she had put in his room. He was about to walk up the stairs when there was a knock at the front door. Godfrey opened it and accepted a telegram from a young messenger, who then turned and walked back along the curved gravel path towards the gate where his bicycle was parked.

Godfrey ripped open the brown envelope and looked at the message, which read: HOW ARE YOU COMMA

YOU OLD RASCAL STOP WILL BE ARRIVING WEDNESDAY PM STOP HAVE INCREDIBLE STORY TO TELL STOP HAVE BRANDY READY STOP LET'S START DRINKING NOT STOP STOP LKW.

It made no sense at all. He called out to the boy, who walked back up the drive to the front door.

"Sorry, old son, not for me." He gave the telegram and the torn envelope back to the boy, with a sixpence tip to make up for his wasted journey. He then walked upstairs to his bedroom, where he found a pot of coffee on the bedside table. He sighed, picked it up and went back downstairs. At the bottom of the stairs, he saw the first telegram next to the phone on a table in the hall. After reading this one, he picked up the phone and called the bank.

When he heard Burgess's assessment of the situation, Godfrey agreed that there might be a problem, but didn't see the need for an emergency meeting. "I'm still getting over a cold," he said. "I'll be in the office first thing tomorrow morning."

Burgess put the phone down, relieved that he had at least been able to make contact with the manager, but the strain of working for Krumnagel's Bank was beginning to get to him. He sat down at his desk and, for the first time ever during office hours, he opened his copy of *The Times* and turned to the Situations Vacant page.

Rita knocked on his office door and walked in when invited. "It's five o'clock, Mister Burgess," she said. "May I leave now?"

"Yes, of course."

"See you tomorrow, sir."

"Yes, indeed. Have a nice evening."

Rita was hoping to do just that. She had applied some eyeliner and refreshed her bright red lipstick. She left the office, walked through the bank foyer and left the building. The Strand was dimly lit by gas lamps as she made her way in the direction of Trafalgar Square and Lyons Corner House. She stood just inside the door and was disappointed that she couldn't see the man from the post office anywhere. Then she jumped in surprise as someone pinched her waist. She turned and saw the Sotheby's man standing behind her, smiling his most dazzling smile.

"Sorry," he said. "Did I startle you?"

"Yes, you did a bit."

"Well, we all like to be startled sometimes, don't we?" he said.

"Um ... no, not really," said Rita.

"Let's sit over there by the window," he said, "so we can watch the world go by."

When they reached the table by the window, Rita pointed to the RESERVED sign on it, but the man told her not to worry. A waitress came over to the table, shaking her head and waving her finger at the two of them. She was about fifty, very overweight, had matted brown hair and was wearing the regulation Lyons uniform, black dress, white pinafore and a white cap with a black band. She looked extremely sour-faced and unhappy.

"You can't sit here," she said. "The table's reserved."

"Well, we're here now," said the man. "Whoever reserved it will just have to sit somewhere else, won't they?" The waitress was about to say something, but he took a shilling out of his pocket and put it in her hand. Instead of telling them to move, she picked up the reserved sign and put it on the table next to theirs. She

122

then started cleaning the new table, which was covered in cake crumbs.

"So..." said the man. "Tell me about these exciting events at the bank."

Rita was still a little concerned about divulging details of her work, but she couldn't resist talking about the woman who was masquerading as the wife of one of the bank's customers, and who only two days before had been exposed as a fraud.

"One of my colleagues actually ran down the street after her, but she got away!" said Rita. "Now we're going to call the police!"

The waitress at the next table wiped cake crumbs slowly back and forth and listened to Rita. Then she walked over to a wooden booth near the door, where another large woman was sitting behind a metal cash register. The waitress leaned into the booth to whisper something to the cashier.

"That tart in the window with that fancy-looking man ...." she began.

"What about her?" asked the cashier.

"She works at Krumnagel's Bank."

"And?"

"She says they're going to call the police."

"Well, we can't go back anyway, not after that bloke chased after us," said the cashier. "Just behave normally. We'll work out what to do tonight."

The waitress walked back to the table where Rita and the man were sitting and took out a pencil and a notepad, which was attached to the strap of her apron by a piece of string. She was about to take their order when someone behind her spoke.

"Martha?" It was another waitress, a thin woman with a pale complexion. She was wearing the same black and

123

white outfit. On the larger woman, the uniform was stretched to its limits to contain her, on the smaller woman, it hung loosely off her thin body.

Martha turned round quickly. "What is it?" she hissed.

"You moved the sign away from the table by the window. It was reserved for this gentleman."

She indicated a man behind her with a sweep of her bony arm. It was Rupert Burgess. When he saw Rita and the tall blond man sitting at the table, he shook his head and put up both hands, as if apologising for being there. He was the last person to make a fuss in a situation like this. "It's all right," he said. "I'll forget about it for today."

Rita stood up quickly. "No, no, Mister Burgess. If this is your table, please, we can move somewhere else."

"It's all right, Rita, I'm fine," he said. He mumbled something to the two waitresses and left.

Martha returned to Rita's table. "Are you ready to order?" she asked.

The man ignored her. "Who was that man?" he asked Rita.

"That's Mister Burgess my boss," she replied. "He's the assistant manager at the bank. He's the one who found out about the woman who's been taking money fraudulently. She's been pretending to be someone who's actually dead."

"That's very exciting," he replied, smiling at her and taking one of her hands.

"The dead woman had a really unusual name," said Rita, taking her hand away.

"What was it?"

"Martha Goodgame."

The waitress dropped her pencil on the table, turned and hurried out of the tea shop and into the street. Rita and the man stopped talking and watched her as she left.

124

"How odd," said the man.

"Yes," agreed Rita. "I wonder why she ran away like that."

"Yes, that's odd, too," he replied. "But I was thinking of something else. The woman I saw in Saint John's Wood this morning was also called Goodgame."

He leaned across the table and took Rita's hand. "By the way," he said, gazing into her eyes. "I didn't introduce myself. My name is Lawrence Kimberley-Waugh."

Chapter 12
There are Swedes visiting the house?
Tuesday, Great Park - grey, turning cold

When Polly told him to disappear, Charles put on his hat and dark glasses, picked up his walking stick and ran to the door on the other side of the studio. Outside, he found himself in a part of the garden he had never seen before. He turned to speak to Polly, but she had closed the door.

"What am I supposed to do now?" he asked, through the window.

He couldn't hear what she replied, but she pointed to the left, and then to the right. Lip-reading her words, he made out 'stable' when she pointed to the left, and something that looked like 'Arse Scottish' when she indicated to the right.

"Arse Scottish?" he repeated, feeling helpless.

She opened the door briefly, said "Garth's cottage!" and slammed it shut. Behind her, three men entered the studio through the door opposite. Polly turned away and nonchalantly walked towards the new arrivals, holding out both arms in welcome. Charles turned away to get out of sight, standing with his back to the wall, wondering what to do next.

To his left was a tall wooden outbuilding, which he presumed was the stable she was referring to. It had large double doors, one of which was open. He ran there and stopped at the door to catch his breath. Even though there were four skylights in the roof, it was gloomy, and it took him a while to see what was inside.

On the right, there were four of the original horse stalls, all empty. Equine pursuits clearly didn't feature in the Duke of Burfaughtonleigh's life. The stalls on the other side had been removed, and four vehicles were parked in a line. Furthest away was an old red tractor, then there was a shooting brake with wooden slats across the bodywork and next to that two black Humber Pullmans, one of which appeared to be older than the other. The last and nearest vehicle was the Alfa Romeo that Polly had driven to Stanford Saint Mary station to pick him up. Flockton the under-butler was polishing its bonnet and he looked up when Charles appeared at the door. Charles saw him and began to hobble, leaning heavily on the stick and huffing and groaning.

"Everything all right, Mister Washbrook?" asked Flockton.

"What? Oh, yes... I was just, er ... getting a bit of fresh air."

"Excellent idea, sir."

"I was just wondering... do you know Garth?"

"Garth Prodgers? The gardener?"

Prodgers. Charles tried to remember where he had heard that name before. "The gardener, yes. He lives in a cottage somewhere, doesn't he?"

"Yes, sir. Willow Cottage," replied Flockton. He walked up to where Charles was standing at the door of the stable and pointed beyond the house. "It's down the drive towards the main gate. There's a track off to the right and the cottage is at the end of it."

"I see," said Charles. Why had Polly suggested that he go there? There was no way he could set off down the drive without being visible from the main house. He knew he had to stay out of sight of the Duke's lunch guests, but what was he supposed to say when he came back? That he had been taken by an urge for a walk in the grounds and walked all the way to Willow Cottage?

A man who was supposed to have trouble walking three or four paces? This impersonation thing was one of Polly's craziest ideas, and now it was all unravelling.

"Are you all right, Mister Washbrook? Is there anything I can do?" Flockton put his hand on Charles's shoulder. Charles stared at him and shook his head frantically from side to side.

"Do you want me to go and tell the Duke you aren't feeling very well?"

"No!" said Charles, so loudly that the boy jumped a few inches off the ground. "Sorry. No, that won't be necessary," he added more quietly. "I just need to sit down for a moment." He walked to the Alfa Romeo and sat on the bonnet.

"If there's anything you need, just ask," said the under-butler, and went back to polishing the cream mudguard. Charles sat in silence, pondering what to do next.

At the opposite end of the stable was another entrance, also with double doors. Suddenly, there was a loud creaking noise as someone pulled a wooden bolt, and one of the doors swung open. Garth the gardener walked into the stable.

"Ah, well, here you are, Mister Washbrook," said Flockton. "Speak of the devil. Garth! Come over here!" Garth stood still for a moment, staring at the two men and then walked slowly towards them.

"Garth, this is Mister Washbrook," said Flockton. "He's a painter. Not like a painter and decorator," he added for clarification. "He paints pictures of people."

Charles stood up to as Garth approached them. Remembering the gardener's crushing handshake when they first met, he was greatly relieved that the giant didn't offer his hand. No doubt this would have been rather presumptuous behaviour between a member of the household staff and an esteemed visitor. Instead, he said something that might have been 'Pleased to meet you' or even 'Want to punch you', the exact meaning being lost behind his moustache and beard. He bowed slightly and touched the hair at the top of his forehead. Charles wondered if this was what people meant when they talked about tugging forelocks. Being unsure what kind of response this merited, Charles raised his hat.

"Mister Washbrook, what was it you wanted to see Garth about?" asked Flockton.

"It's all right," said Garth, his high-pitched voice surprising Charles once again. "Polly has informed me that Mister Washbrook would like a ride in the tractor."

"Oh, is that right, Mister Washbrook?" asked Flockton. "What an interesting thing to do."

Charles stared at Flockton and then at Garth. A ride in the tractor? Why on earth would Polly suggest he wanted to do that? But, as often happened with him, the penny took a moment to drop and once it had, the idea of taking a spin on the tractor seemed like the best idea in the world. Later, he could explain his absence by saying that he had gone outside for a breath of fresh air, he had seen Garth driving the tractor and asked if he could have a ride. "Jolly right!" he said, with relief in his voice. "It's something I've wanted to do all my life."

Garth turned and walked towards to the tractor, which was parked with its engine facing the wall. Charles followed him and stood behind the large ageing vehicle, not sure what to do next. The gardener climbed into the driver's seat, pulled out the choke and turned the ignition key. There was a spurt of oil from the exhaust, which splattered all over Charles's overalls, then Garth pumped the accelerator and a cloud of black smoke gushed out. A little too late, the gardener turned round to warn

Charles, but his words were lost in the chugging of the engine.

"Probably best to move out of the way until the smoke clears," said Flockton.

Charles coughed violently, nodded and moved to one side. There was a loud clanking sound as Garth engaged reverse gear, and the ancient vehicle turned out of its parking space. Flockton ran in front of the tractor and opened the second of the double doors.

Garth indicated the space on the seat next to him, and Charles leaned his walking stick on the side of the vehicle and leapt up, impressing Flockton with his agility. The under-butler passed him his stick, wished him well and went back to polishing the Alfa Romeo. The gardener drove the tractor out of the stable and turned right.

It was cold and Charles's working overalls were not designed for a trip of any distance in an open vehicle. He was also concerned that when they got to the end of the stable wall, they would be in full view of the studio that he had recently vacated and which could now contain the Duke's lunch guests, one of whom had known Walter Washbrook since schooldays. Fortunately, Charles was sitting to Garth's left, and was therefore almost invisible to anyone in the house.

The tractor chugged slowly to the end of the wall and into the open. Charles took off his dark glasses and glanced in front of Garth to look at the house. He could see into the studio clearly, and he was relieved that there was no one there. Garth looked straight ahead and drove towards the main drive that led to the entrance gate to Great Park. Charles shivered and folded his arms round himself to try to keep warm.

"There's a blanket behind you," said Garth. He spoke so quietly that Charles didn't hear him the first time, so the gardener turned to him and said more loudly: "Behind you. A blanket." Charles looked and saw a brown blanket in the space behind the seat. He picked it up and wrapped it round his shoulders. It was full of dust which made him sneeze, but at least he didn't feel as if he was going to freeze to death.

"Thank you," he said. Garth nodded and grunted a response. About a hundred yards from the main gate, they turned down the track towards Willow Cottage, and Garth parked the machine in the same muddy patch where Charles had fallen down when he first arrived. He clambered off the tractor and this time placed his feet carefully on the wet surface.

Garth opened the door of the cottage and indicated that Charles should go in. Inside, a log fire was burning, and the cottage was warm. He collapsed on the sofa, leaned back and blew out a noisy sigh of relief. "Thank you, Garth. You saved my bacon," he said. "And what a stroke of luck that you turned up when you did."

"I came to the stable because Polly told me to," said Garth. Polly had run out to see him in the greenhouse, explained that Charles had to make himself scarce for a while, and told Garth to take him to Willow Cottage. Charles reflected yet again on his stepsister's resourcefulness and quick thinking.

"I have to get back to the greenhouse," said Garth. "Because of the swedes."

"I'm sorry?" said Charles.

"Swedes," repeated Garth.

"There are Swedes visiting the house?"

132

Garth looked at him to see if he was making a joke. "Swedes. Like turnips. We grow them in the greenhouse. Cook wants some to make a stew for lunch on Saturday."

"OK, well, have fun," said Charles. "Er ... what should I do now?"

"I think Polly will look after everything," said Garth. "She usually does."

"Right ho. So ... I suppose I'll just stay here and see what happens."

"There are a lot of books to read," said Garth.

"Yes, I saw them when I was here yesterday," said Charles. "You seem to have quite a collection."

"They belonged to the late Duke, the Duke's father," said Garth. "He had a very large library, especially history books. This Duke isn't interested in anything like that, so he asked me to take them somewhere and burn them." He paused for a moment, then continued. "I don't think you should do that with books. So I brought them all here." Garth looked away, as if he was embarrassed to have said so much. "There are more upstairs as well."

These were more words than Charles had heard the gardener say since he met him. "You did the right thing, Garth," he said. "The Duke is an imbecile if he thinks books should be burned."

Garth turned and pointed to a small room to the side of the fireplace. "If you want food, there are a few things through there in the larder," he said. "Mainly swedes at the moment." And for the first time, the two men laughed out loud together. "And there are more logs outside the back door if you run out," Garth added.

There was a metal box next to the fireplace with three of four logs in it. "I think I should be all right with the ones that are there," said Charles. "I'm not planning to stay that long."

133

"Well, you never know. It's getting colder. I'm thinking there'll be snow tonight."

Charles thought how remarkable it was that he and Garth were having a proper conversation. He was rather excited that the gardener now trusted him enough to be so expansive, and he didn't feel afraid of him anymore.

After Garth left, Charles put another log on the fire and looked at the clock over the fireplace. If it was right, it was nearly two o'clock. It was an hour since he had left the studio in a hurry, and now he was stuck at Willow Cottage, a long walk from the main house. Unless Polly came to collect him, he would have to make his own way back to the house. If someone saw him walking back, it could lead to more awkward questions about his absence. Unsure what to do next, a common situation for him, he picked up a book and started reading.

About half an hour later, there was a knock at the door. Charles stood in front of the fire and tried to remain quiet. The door opened and Polly walked in. "Oh, lovely and roasty-toasty in here," she said. "The lunch guests have all cleared off. Are you ready to come back to the house?"

"Before we go anywhere, we have to talk," said Charles, showing more assertiveness than he had ever done before with his stepsister. "So please sit down."

Polly sat on the sofa, crossed her legs and looked at him. "I'm sitting down," she said, indicating her position with a theatrical wave of her hands. "What do you want to talk about?"

"The Robert Louis Stevenson portrait."

"What about it?"

"I've been talking to Pickles, and I don't think it was painted by Van Gogh."

134

"You're wrong," said Polly. "All sorts of people have been here and said it was."

"That isn't what Pickles told me," said Charles. "And with respect, he's been here longer than you and knows more about the story. It may well have been started by Van Gogh, then given to someone else to finish. All great artists are surrounded by acolytes, and Van Gogh was no exception. If I knew exactly what year it was painted, I could probably tell you who it was," he added, rather proud of the research he had done into the Dutch artist's work. "The point is, the complete portrait was almost certainly not painted by Van Gogh, so I can't imagine anyone, even in the criminal fraternity, will want to touch it with a bargepole."

Polly was silent for a moment before replying. "I still want you to paint it," she said.

"But Pol ---"

"Charles, listen to me." She stood up and took his chin in one hand and squeezed it. He didn't like it when she did that, and not only because it hurt. The icy look in her eyes always frightened him. "I know someone in London who is prepared to take the painting off our hands, so you have to paint a copy. And I suggest you start it tonight."

She let go of his chin. He rubbed it until the blood started to circulate again in his lower jaw. "Now let's get back to the house," she said. "Don't forget to tell Tarquin that you need a bit of fresh air from time to time, which is why you went out for a walk. Then you saw Garth---"

"Give me a bit of credit," said Charles. "I've already worked that bit out. I went outside for some fresh air, saw Garth in the tractor and asked if he would take me for a spin round the grounds."

"Well done."

"I'm not *completely* useless."

135

"Of course, you aren't!" said Polly, giving him another of her sunburst smiles. The way she was able to change her moods so quickly always made him uneasy. She put her arms round his neck and squeezed him. "You know, you're my favourite person in the entire world."

They went out of the cottage and walked towards the Alfa Romeo, which was parked right in the middle of the muddy patch. Charles tip-toed to the car and still slid twice before he made it safely into the passenger seat. Polly just walked up and got in, as if the mud made no difference to her ability to stay upright. She drove back to the house, turned off the main drive and took the car to the stable, parking next to two black limousines. "Just one more thing," she said, as she switched off the engine.

"What's that?"

"This Delgado chap who was here for lunch, I told you that he's known Walter Washbrook since they were at school, didn't I? Well, just listening to some stories he was saying and putting two and two together, I think Delgado is a pederast."

"A what?"

"A homosexual."

"Good Lord."

"Indeed. And the thing is, reading between the lines, he gave the impression that Walter Washbrook is, too."

"Oh bugger..."

"Quite," said Polly.

Chapter 13
Is he one of us?
Tuesday, South Kensington - cold, chance of snow

Walter Washbrook (the real one) bore little resemblance to Charles Goodgame's impersonation of him. He was a tall man who had been slim when he was young but filled out substantially as he progressed through middle age, thanks to a life of eating well and exercising rarely. He had grey hair, but not like the matted wig that Charles wore. Walter's hair was long and thick and was brushed back from his forehead. He kept it tamed in a ponytail, one of the very few men in London who wore his hair this way. He didn't have a beard, but his sideburns were long and bushy and his chin was square and fleshy. He didn't wear spectacles, and he didn't need a walking stick. Aged sixty-something, he was a handsome man, but his piercing blue eyes, narrow nose and wide mouth were set in a blotchy red face, witness to his overindulgence in food and drink and his lack of physical activity, such as walking or regular sex, although he would have liked more of the latter, if it was available.

He was in constant demand as a portrait painter and lived a comfortable life alone in a cottage in Godfrey Street, off the Kings Road in Chelsea. The magazine article that Polly Capstan had read described him as *a mature bachelor who has never married.*' His sexual preferences were common knowledge and of no particular importance in the world that he frequented, and his secret was safe with the people he socialised with.

However, it wasn't the same with the wealthy but unimaginative people whose portraits he painted. He was constantly aware of the prejudice and animosity among his clientele shown to anyone with an alternative lifestyle, so he kept his private life out of conversations with them.

Walter had met Ernest Goodgame in 1924 after the premiere of Noël Coward's play *The Vortex* at the Everyman Theatre in Hampstead. After the show, Walter and Ernest ended up at adjoining tables in a Hampstead pub called The Flask, and the occupants of both tables mingled and shared their views of the play. Some of their friends were shocked by it, but both Walter and Ernest thought it enjoyable and refreshing.

An art gallery owner and entrepreneur called Arthur Wickham-Thynne, who would be later knighted for services to the arts, had been at that first performance and was also in The Flask afterwards. Sitting at a different table, he listened to the conversation between Ernest, Walter and their friends and decided to finance the play's transfer to the West End, one of his many theatrical successes. He also made a small fortune when *The Vortex* played to packed houses for two years on Broadway.

Over the next decade or so, Walter and Ernest socialised a lot. The artist attended numerous dinner parties at the house in Pelham Crescent, and he was there one evening when Charles glanced into the dining room on his way to the bathroom. The young man with sandy hair caught the eye of the portrait painter, who was sitting next to the host. "Who was that chap who just walked past the door?" he whispered to Ernest.

"My nephew Charles," replied Ernest. "He lives in the garden."

"Does he now?" said Walter. "Is he one of us?"

"No, he's boringly normal."

"Pity."

Now, a few months later, something had happened that could ruin his reputation. At a party on Saturday evening, a woman had threatened to expose him as a homosexual. The woman was Cornelia Wickham-Thynne, the wife of Sir Arthur Wickham-Thynne and the sister of Ronnie Capstan.

When their livelihoods and reputations were in danger because of some unfortunate event, many men turned to Ernest Goodgame for help, and Walter was no exception. "I have to come and see you," he said, when he telephoned on Monday evening. "I'm in the soup. It's a matter of life and death."

Ernest hadn't been in the mood to deal with any more drama for one evening, so he told the artist to come over the next day. When Walter arrived, Ernest took him into the sitting room. An almost full glass of brandy was sitting on the coffee table. Walter picked up the glass and sniffed it.

"Is this yours?" he asked.

"No," said Ernest. "I poured it out for my brother yesterday."

"Can I drink it?"

"Well, let me get you a fresh one. Anyway, I thought you preferred rum."

"I don't give a tuppenny fuck what I drink tonight," said Walter, emptying the glass in one go. "I just want to get very very drunk and then perhaps kill myself."

Ernest sat next to Walter and put his arm round his shoulders. He knew better than to tell Walter to stop being stupid or to calm down. Walter was prone to fly into rages if people told him to do that. To his credit, he always apologised immediately after losing his temper.

"You'd better tell me what happened," said Ernest.

A week before, Walter had started a portrait of a woman called Emma Fitzroy, who was the wife of Sir Burlington Fitzroy, the Member of Parliament for Gloucestershire South. The Fitzroys had a very fancy house in Cheyne Walk on the Chelsea Embankment, where Walter spent three very enjoyable days with Lady Fitzroy before he took the portrait back to his studio in Godfrey Street for the finishing touches. His hostess was witty and fun to be with and, best of all, she had a stock of his favourite Cuban rum, a large amount of which was consumed while he was working. They drank so much during the three days they spent together, it was a wonder that he was able to paint anything approaching a likeness of her, and also that she managed not to fall off her chair while she was posing.

When Emma invited him to a buffet lunch "with just a few dozen of our closest friends" on Sunday, Walter was delighted to accept, thinking he might pick up some business from amongst her other guests. She told him he could bring a friend, so he invited an actor called Clarence Dalton.

"I arranged to meet Clarence at the Pig's Ear in Old Church Street before the party, and we had quite a bit to drink," said Walter. "We were three sheets to the wind by the time we got to Cheyne Walk."

The new arrivals were not impressed with the people who were already at the party. Walter recognised a couple of cabinet ministers from their newspaper photographs and there were two journalists that he vaguely knew. The ministers were talking in loud voices and boring the pants of anyone who listened.

"It was dull, dull, dull," said Walter. "The only women at the party were the wives of these big cheeses, and they were all bored out of their skulls and getting rat-arsed as fast as they could. Really, Clarence and I almost turned straight round and walked out."

Ernest was listening as patiently as he could. "So, what actually happened?" he asked.

"For Christ's sake, I'm trying to TELL you what happened, if you will just LISTEN!!"

"Sorry," said Ernest.

"Sorry," said Walter.

"No matter. Do carry on."

"Anyway, as I say, Clarence and I were about to heave off ... Jesus, I wish we had. But at that moment some new people arrived and there were a couple of younger people who looked a bit more interesting. And then Arthur Wickham-Thynne walked in. Do you know him?"

"I think so. It's Sir Arthur, isn't it? He's an art dealer or something, isn't he?"

"Yes, he owns two galleries, one in Jermyn Street and the other in Bond Street."

"Oh yes, I remember now. My nephew Charles worked in the one in Bond Street."

Walter wasn't listening to any of Ernest's replies. "He's exhibited my stuff at his place in Jermyn Street a couple of times. Nice fellow. But his wife, her name is Cornelia .... my God, what a bitch!" He stopped talking and put his head in his hands. "Is there any rum left?"

Ernest went over to the cabinet and looked at the line of bottles. "I'm afraid I don't have any Cuban left, Walter. I only have Jamaican."

"I don't care if it's fucking Chinese rum. I'm going to get totally blotto and then throw myself in the river."

Ernest poured a generous measure into a glass and put it on the coffee table in front of the artist. Walter picked it up, emptied it in one go and slapped it back on the table, where it made a cracking sound, which made Ernest wince. It was an expensive glass.

Walter continued his story. "So, in swans Wickham-Thynne and his God-awful wife, and we start chatting. She's such an old witch, she said she'd been to the exhibition of my portraits, and she left after five minutes because they all looked the same. Bloody philistine. Anyway, I'm talking to her husband, who's a decent cove, and all the time she's standing there, huffing and puffing and looking around to see if there's someone more important that they could be talking to."

"Walter, I can see that the party must have been a fairly tedious experience for you," said Ernest, "but so far I haven't heard anything that would suggest that you need to chuck yourself into the Thames."

"All RIGHT!" yelled the artist. "The important bit is coming UP! Just give me a chance to EXPLAIN, will you?

"Sorry, Walter."

"Sorry, Ernest."

"No matter. Do go on."

"So, the Wickham-Thynnes wandered off to talk to someone more important than me and I looked around to see what Clarence was up to. He was talking to one of the young fellows who were wandering around with trays of drinks and stuff. Very pretty boy."

Alarm bells started ringing for Ernest when he heard the words 'very pretty boy'. He knew Clarence Dalton, and could imagine what he might do when he had too much to drink and saw a young man he found attractive. Walter had felt equally concerned when he saw the two

142

of them disappear out through a French window, so he walked across the room and followed them out onto a terrace overlooking the garden. It was quite cold and getting dark, but the garden was lit by a series of gas lanterns. Clarence and the waiter had walked as far as a clump of bushes at the far end. The bushes weren't very high, and the tops of their heads were visible, so Walter decided it would be prudent to have a word with them.

By the time he reached them, the two men were kissing. Walter walked towards them and pulled them apart. "Look here!" he said. "This is neither the time nor the place!"

Clarence put his arm round the artist's shoulders. "Walter, darling, don't be such a bore. Come and join us." He pulled the three of them into a clinch, but the young man shouted something in a foreign language, wrenched himself out of the embrace and ran through the bushes away from the house. Walter thought it was because he wasn't interested in a threesome with an old man, but then someone behind him spoke.

"Just as I thought!" It was a woman's voice. Walter and Clarence turned round to see who was speaking. It was Cornelia Wickham-Thynne, who had followed Walter out of the house. "I knew all along that you were a filthy pervert, Washbrook!" she said.

At first, Walter was simply annoyed with her. How could she possibly have made such an asinine judgement about him after the short time they had spent in each other's company? But this feeling was swiftly replaced with a sense of shock. By the time his power of speech had returned, she had marched off back into the house.

Clarence became alarmed as well. Although he had never seen the woman with staring eyes before and had no idea who she was, he knew full well it wouldn't take her long to identify him. He had introduced himself to Emma Fitzroy when he arrived, explaining that he was Walter's guest. They decided to leave by the same route as the waiter, who had found a way through the foliage and into an alley that ran behind the house.

"And then what did you do?" asked Ernest.

"We legged it back to the Pig's Ear and ordered double brandies," said Walter. "Gave us a bit of Dutch courage. We talked about what she might do and decided if the worst came to the worst, say if the police got involved, we could brazen it out, it was our word against hers and all that. Things didn't seem so bad for a while."

That positive feeling soon drained away. Walter made his way back to Godfrey Street and sat in his studio, staring at the nearly completed portrait of Emma Fitzroy. Now that he was alone, the situation became more desperate the more he thought about it. He looked at Emma's face in the portrait and imagined her listening to Cornelia Wickham-Thynne as she poured out her poisonous news about the two guests in the garden.

"So just to be clear, this all happened three days ago?" asked Ernest.

"Right."

"And have you heard anything since then?"

"What do you mean? From Wickham-Thynne's wife?"

"From anyone. It's Tuesday already. The reptiles have been back at work for two days."

"Reptiles?"

"Journalists. She could have called some newspaper and told them what she saw. If she had, they would have sent someone round to knock on your door by now."

"No, nothing like that," said Walter.

"Give me a moment to think."

144

Walter had chosen the right person to come to. Over the years, Ernest had helped a succession of men whose livelihoods had been put in danger by some indiscretion, hazardous because of where it happened or who had witnessed it. His method of dealing with situations like this was always the same, as he explained to Walter now.

"You know my feelings about bijou problems like this, don't you?" he said.

"Do I?" replied Walter.

"Fight fire with fire," said Ernest.

"Come again?"

"We need to find some naughty little secret about Lady Wickham-Thynne, or even better about Sir Arthur, and we tell them what we know."

"Marvellous," said Walter. "And how are we supposed to do that? For all we know, she may have spread the word to all sorts of people by now."

"She may indeed," replied Ernest. "But as I say, fight fire with fire. We just need to find something salacious about the Wickham-Thynnes. Everyone has a dirty little secret and I'm sure Sir Arthur is no exception."

Ernest left Walter in the sitting room with the bottle of Jamaican rum and went into his office. He sat at the desk and flicked through a slim black leather book, making a list of people he wanted to call, then he picked up the phone and dialled the first number on the list. It was Clarence Dalton.

"Hello, Clarence? It's Ernest Goodgame. Yes, I know it's late, but I need to talk to you. I'm with Walter now, and I just wanted to find out more about what happened on Saturday." Ernest listened and made notes. There was no time for small talk, so he thanked Clarence, ended the conversation and dialled the second person on his list, the theatre impresario Bernard Delgado.

Half an hour later, he walked back into the sitting room, where Walter had fallen asleep on the sofa. He woke the artist up and told him what he had found out.

"I have discovered a few things that might be useful," he said. Ernest now knew that Cornelia Wickham-Thynne's had a brother called Ronald who was in Wormwood Scrubs, having been convicted of dishonestly handling luxury cars.

"As it happens, I know who this man is," said Ernest. "My brother Horace is married to his ex-wife."

"Really?" said Walter. He was drunk and half asleep, and his anxiety meant that he wasn't really connecting with anything that Ernest was telling him.

"I talked to Bernard Delgado," said Ernest. "You know Bernard, don't you?"

"Yes of course. We were at Saint Benedict's together."

"Really? I didn't know that. Anyway, Bernard gave me a wonderful piece of information about Arthur Wickham-Thynne, the witch's husband."

"What is it?"

"Before I tell you, do you remember where you and I first met?"

"What? No."

"We'd been to see a Noël Coward play and we were at a pub called The Flask in Hampstead," said Ernest. "Is the picture becoming any clearer now?"

"Oh well, yes of course I know The Flask," said Walter, whose knowledge of places where you could get a drink was encyclopaedic, "but what has it got to do with the price of eggs?"

"Walter, we're trying to find some dirt on Wickham-Thynne or that poisonous wife of his. I can't find anything about the wife, except that her brother is a cad of the highest order, but Bernard Delgado told me that

Sir Arthur is having an affair with one of the barmaids at The Flask, which is near where he lives, apparently."

Walter sat up and shook his head to clear it a bit. "That sounds quite useful," he said.

"Yes. So the first thing I need to do is get Wickham-Thynne's telephone number. It isn't listed in the directory."

"Oh, I have that," said Walter. He took a scrap of paper from his pocket. "He gave it to me when I exhibited there. I rooted it out this morning and I was wondering if I should call him. He's a decent bloke, I don't want to annoy him, I just don't want his blasted wife to spill the beans about what happened at the party."

Ernest sat down next to his friend and put his arm round his shoulder again. "Walter," he said, "this is no time to talk about decent blokes and not wanting to annoy people. We have to use the information to frighten the wits out of Wickham-Thynne and destroy his reputation. Or at least threaten to do so."

"Oh dear," said Walter. "I don't want to do that."

"Walter! Concentrate! It's your reputation and your livelihood that's at stake here! Or his. And the fact of the matter is, if we reveal that he's an adulterer, he won't be in a lot of trouble. Except with his wife, of course, but that's not our problem. On the other hand, if this information about you comes out, you could go to prison. Now, do you understand why we have to do this?"

"Yes, I suppose so. So, who told you about Wickham-Thynne?"

"I told you. Bernard Delgado."

"Good old Bernard."

"By the way," said Ernest. "Bernard was a bit surprised to hear that you were in London."

"What?"

"Bernard said that he was surprised you were in London."

"Why? This is where I live."

"Quite. But he said he went for lunch to some stately home in Gloucestershire today, and he'd only just got back when I called him. He was under the impression that you were there."

"Where?"

"At this stately home where he had lunch."

"What on earth would I be doing there?"

"They told him that you were painting a portrait of the chap who owns the place, the Duke of something, and Bernard wanted to say hello to you but you disappeared."

"Painting a portrait of a Duke?" repeated Walter. "What are you talking about?"

"I'm just telling you what Bernard told me."

"Where was this again?"

"Oh Walter, I do wish you'd listen. Bernard had lunch with a Duke somewhere in Gloucestershire, and they told him that you were there doing a portrait. You weren't in Gloucestershire today, were you?"

Walter's face went even redder than normal. "Of COURSE, I wasn't!" he shouted." I was sitting ALONE in my studio, WORRYING myself SICK!"

Ernest finally lost patience. "Oh for God's sake, Walter, shut UP!" he said. "If you start shouting like a spoilt child again, you can leave and never come back."

"Sorry, Ernest."

"Apology accepted."

"But tell me again what Bernard said."

Ernest sighed with annoyance. "He said that he had lunch at some stately home in Gloucestershire and he was told that you were there painting the portrait of the Duke who owns the place."

"Well, I wasn't."

"Yes, I know. I suppose Bernard got the wrong end of the stick. He often does."

Chapter 14
The nose. Keep it clean

Tuesday, Wormwood Scrubs, London - cold and windy

There were only three inmates at Wormwood Scrubs that Ronnie Capstan chose to communicate with and on the last morning of his incarceration, he sat with all three at a long breakfast table in the noisy canteen. On his left was Billy Whitlock, a small wiry man with curly black hair and staring eyes. When Ronnie arrived at the Scrubs, he very quickly decided it would be prudent to befriend this mad-eyed creature, even though he was unlikely to see the outside of prison any time soon.

Whitlock, who was known as Billy the Badger, was in prison for the seventh or eighth time, having been convicted of a variety of offences, usually the result of a disagreement with his enemies in the criminal fraternity. His way of dealing with an underworld dispute was to fight it out with his opponents or set fire to their workplaces, so his convictions ranged from grievous bodily harm to arson. The police were also pretty sure he had murdered a former colleague named Tommy Spraggs after Spraggs had reneged on a gentleman's agreement regarding sharing the spoils of a bank robbery. The victim's body was never found, but the word on the street was that it was under the foundation stone next to the main entrance of the re-built Hackney Town Hall in Mare Street. The contractors on that project were O'Halloran and Whitlock, the Whitlock being Billy's uncle Ted.

The Badger's nickname derived from his deathly white complexion and the black rings round his eyes.

Ronnie thought that he looked more like a panda than a badger but doubted whether any of his fellow inmates had ever seen a photo of the exotic black and white Chinese bear, and thought it best not to argue about the finer details of animal characteristics with people whose first instinct in a discussion was to punch your lights out.

Whitlock was the kind of person it was best not to argue with at all. Despite being quite small, he was by some distance the scariest inmate of the Scrubs and was known to lose his temper if anyone disagreed with him about anything. The discussion could be about the best team in the First Division, which pub in South London served the best pint of bitter, or even a more professional argument about which was the most difficult type of safe to crack - a simple divergence of opinion could send the Badger into a frenzy, which regularly required him to be subdued by four or five prison officers.

Ronnie had noted that Whitlock's moods were usually connected to whether or not he had enough tobacco to get him through the week. By arranging for extra tobacco rations to be smuggled in for him, Ronnie secured the Badger's undying friendship and the lifer had been Ronnie's minder throughout his time inside.

Seated to Ronnie's right was his second breakfast companion, Tony 'Cracker' Perkins, probably the number one safebreaker in the south of England, who still bore scars on his cheek caused by Billy the Badger's fingernails after they had discussed safe-cracking, difficulty thereof. When Perkins insisted that a German-built Burg-Wächter had given him most problems, the Badger bowed to his superior experience in the matter, but not before their argument had ended with him throwing his opponent to the ground and leaving him with scratches on his face that could have been delivered by a wild animal. The two men shook hands after the fight, declared no harm done, before both were marched off to solitary confinement.

Sitting opposite them was the third of his trio of regular dining companions, Alberto 'The Sicilian' Cagliari. Cagliari had been head waiter at one of Soho's most famous Italian restaurants, Casa Camorra in Greek Street. He also worked as a freelance enforcer, collecting protection money from non-Italian businesses in the centre of London and handing out punishments as and when required.

The Sicilian had been arrested after smashing the windows of a Chinese restaurant in Glasshouse Street near Piccadilly Circus, a necessary course of action because the owners had repeatedly ignored requests for payment of money owed. Unfortunately, he chose to carry out the punishment on a night when forty police officers were celebrating the retirement of the chief superintendent from nearby Vine Street Station. As he made his escape, he was alarmed to see that he was being chased down Shaftesbury Avenue by more than a dozen of the dinner guests, all of whom were over six feet tall, muscular and, as it turned out, faster runners than he was.

After they returned their bowls and mugs to the service hatch in the wall of the canteen, Ronnie and his three companions shook hands and he turned to head back to his cell in Block A. On his way out, he was confronted by a prison guard, an overweight and sweaty man called Broughton. Ronnie disliked all the guards at Wormwood Scrubs but he loathed Broughton the most.

Ronnie moved to one side to pass the guard, but Broughton stepped across to block his path. Ronnie sighed and put his hand on the man's chest to push him out of the way but the guard stood his ground.

"Get out of my way, Broughton."

"Mister Broughton to you, Capstan."

"Broughton, in case it hasn't registered in that cement-filled head of yours, I'm being released today. I can call you whatever I like." He pushed the guard to one side and walked past him and along the corridor.

"Capstan! Come back! You have to go to the governor's office!"

Of course. Prisoners who were about to be released had to have an audience with the governor, who would wish them well and give them a lecture about the dangers of re-offending. Ronnie sighed, then turned and followed Broughton, who headed towards the administration area. Their route took them down grim corridors and through three doors that had to be unlocked then locked again behind them. Eventually, they reached a section where the walls were covered in dark wood panelling and there was a red carpet on the floor. At the end of the corridor was a door with two wooden plaques on it. On the top one, in faded gold lettering, were the words *Prison Governor* and the one underneath had the current incumbent's name: *Ernest Murgatroyd*. Broughton knocked quietly on the door. There was no sound on the other side.

"You'll have to knock louder than that," said Ronnie. "The old fart's as deaf as a post."

"Sod off, Capstan," said Broughton. Without looking, he rapped his knuckles sharply in the direction of the door again. Unfortunately, the door was now open, and a thin man with a bald head was standing there. Broughton's attempt to apply a meaty knock on the door instead smacked the man firmly on the nose. There was a cracking sound, and the governor of Wormwood

154

Scrubs fell backwards and landed on the floor with a crash.

Later, after Nurse Harrison had stuffed Murgatroyd's nose with cotton wool, the final interview began. The governor was famous for trying to ingratiate himself with any prisoner he thought was upper-class. "I have to say, Mister Capstan, it has been a great honour to have you spend time here with us in such humble surroundings," he began. He pronounced 'honour' with an aspirate 'h' and 'here' and 'humble' without one. "However ..." he added, again without an 'h', pausing to adjust the blood-soaked cotton wool that was about to fall out of his left nostril. "However," he repeated, "you have served your sentence, and it is time for you to take your rightful place back in the community."

"Thank you, Murgatroyd," said Ronnie. "I say, can I use your telephone?" Ronnie needed to call his sister Cornelia so that he could arrange to be picked up. Without waiting for a reply, he picked up the dark green telephone on the governor's desk. There was no signal. "How does it work, old boy?"

Murgatroyd's eyebrows raised slightly at the lack of certain words in Ronnie's request - words like 'Mister' and 'please' - but he chose not to take issue. "Dial nine, and you will be connected to the operator, Mister Capstan."

The operator put him through to his sister. Cornelia agreed to send her chauffeur Turnbull to pick him up. "You won't be able to miss him," she said. "My new Rolls is powder blue."

"Thanks," said Ronnie. "Any chance of a spot of lunch when I get there? The food in this place is worse than the reheated vomit they gave us at Winchester."

"I'll get Anatole to throw something together," said Cornelia. "And Arthur has a lovely case of Bordeaux I think you'll be amused by."

An hour later, Ronnie was standing outside the tall front gate of the prison, his brown suitcase at his feet. He was wearing the clothes he had worn on the day of his trial, a dark blue jacket with an Old Wykhamists badge on the breast pocket, white shirt, spotted cravat, red waistcoat, tan trousers and expensive brown brogues. He could have been heading for lunch at a gentlemen's club, although there were very few clubs in London which would have welcomed him through their doors anymore.

The tall metal gate creaked open, and two other men stepped out. One of them walked off down the approach road without saying a word. The other was a tall slim man with greying hair, who was wearing a dark blue double-breasted suit. He had only arrived at the Scrubs two weeks before, and he and Ronnie had never spoken.

"You're Ronnie Capstan, aren't you?" said the man. He had what the governor would have described as a 'very heducated voice'. "My name is Alexander Malleson."

Ronnie ignored him and looked in the opposite direction. At that moment, a large car turned into the approach to the prison and made its way up towards the gate. Good, thought Ronnie, here's the Roller, I can get away from this boring fool. However, the car wasn't a powder blue Rolls Royce, it was a black Bentley. When the driver pulled up and got out of the car, he said "Good morning, sir" to Malleson and opened the back door.

"Just a moment," said Malleson. "I just want to say something to my friend." The driver nodded and got back into the car.

Friend? Cheeky bastard, thought Ronnie.

"I imagine you were a bit surprised when Brodkin sent you down for three years," said Malleson. Ronnie looked at him in astonishment. How did he know the name of the judge who had presided over his case? "You were very unlucky. Your case should have come before a district judge, and you might have got away with a fine and a suspended sentence. Did you ever wonder why you were tried at the Old Bailey?"

"You said you had some advice," said Ronnie.

"That's right. And here it is. Keep your nose clean."

Ronnie laughed. "Is that it?"

"Yes, that's it."

"I will try ever so hard to remember."

"You'd better. Because if you don't, the second time you come up before the bench and get convicted .... well .... they don't mind people like us behaving badly once. Twice, that's a different matter. You will go down for a very long time. I should know, it happened to me."

"You were only here for two weeks."

"That's because I was transferred from Parkhurst prior to release."

Amongst the many things that Ronnie had learned during his time inside was the status of the other houses of correction in the country. Parkhurst Prison on the Isle of Wight housed the country's most violent and dangerous criminals. You had to very bad, or very unlucky, to end up there. Malleson saw the look of surprise in Ronnie's eyes.

"Believe me, you will not enjoy the experience the second time around."

Ronnie said nothing.

"Do you need a lift anywhere?" asked Malleson.

"No."

"Good. Well, best of luck." Malleson turned and got into the back seat of the Bentley, then wound down the window. "Remember," he said. "The nose. Keep it clean." Ronnie stared at the car as it drove down the approach and turned right, heading west towards Chiswick.

The fact that Malleson knew the circumstances of his trial alarmed him. He had been dismayed to discover that his case would be heard at the Old Bailey, and now he was annoyed with himself for not asking the man how he knew so much. Yes, why *was* he tried at the Old Bailey? And why *did* he get such a long sentence?

Another car turned into the approach road. This time it was his sister's Rolls Royce which glided silently towards the gate house. The chauffeur, whose name was Turnbull, got out of the car, picked up Ronnie's suitcase and deposited it in the boot. He then opened the rear passenger door and stood silently waiting for Ronnie to get in. With one last look at the prison, Ronnie eased himself into the car. He wanted to relax and enjoy the ride to Hampstead, but Malleson's words had disturbed him. Ignoring him had been a mistake. In the next few months, Ronnie was going to need all the help he could get.

The car drove down the approach road and turned left, gliding smoothly towards his sister's house in north London.

Cornelia Wickham-Thynne was the youngest of the three Capstan children and had realised at quite an early age that her only assets were her looks. She had picked up all the life skills she needed at finishing school in Switzerland. The young women she met there taught her all she needed to know, which could be summed up in three rules - marry someone rich, don't have children, and keep the house if there's a divorce. She and her two best friends at the school tried to follow the rules to the letter, but one had already broken the second by having a child. The other had adhered to all three and was now in possession of a grand house in the Cotswolds after marrying and divorcing Humphrey Fotheringay, the heir to the Fotheringay's Sausages empire. Getting a divorce wasn't easy, but she had managed it on the grounds of 'non-consummation of the marriage'. After putting up with Fotheringay's clumsy and unsuccessful attempts at love-making for a few months, she decided she'd rather have the house than the husband and the rest just required a good lawyer.

Cornelia had ensnared Arthur Wickham-Thynne after meeting him at the Fotheringay wedding some fifteen years before. Arthur was a quiet, hard-working young man who was already making a name for himself in the newspaper business, but what impressed Cornelia most was the fact that he was the great-grandson of Queen Victoria's sister Princess Feodora of Leiningen and therefore in the outer circle of the royal family. Indeed, in the event of an anarchist bomb going off at a Buckingham Palace Garden party and selectively killing about four dozen of the people there, Arthur and Cornelia would be within sight of the throne. From the time she discovered she was *that* close to being Queen of England, she had a recurrent nightmare in which the Archbishop of Canterbury was placing a crown on her head, and it fell off and smashed to pieces. She would wake up with a start, images of crown jewels bouncing down the tiled floor of Westminster Abbey racing before her eyes.

They lived on the corner of Well Walk and Gainsborough Gardens, walking distance from

Hampstead High Street. Cornelia didn't like the area, mainly because of the people who lived there. Their neighbours included a novelist, a theatre director and a retired racing driver. Worst of all, the old man who lived next door drew political cartoons for a national newspaper. Quite apart from the fact that he walked up and down his back garden wearing shorts in the middle of winter, he also left the curtains to his front room open even when the lights were on and could be seen from the street late at night drawing pictures at his desk in the window, sometimes wearing only a grey dressing gown.

This was the kind of person they had to share the street with. There was literally no one who was even a junior member of the aristocracy.

Her ambition was to get away from these vulgar bohemians and move to a different part of Hampstead, where they could be amongst a better class of people. She had identified the house she wanted to move to, a mansion in half an acre of land on The Bishops Avenue north of Hampstead Heath. The estate agent who showed her round said the man next door was a cousin of King Zog of Albania and across the road was a family of Russian émigrés who were probably related to the Romanovs. Royalty! Proper aristocrats!

Arthur liked living in Well Walk expressly because of the people who lived there. He owned two art galleries, including the one that Charles Goodgame had worked in, and had interests in a weekly magazine and three newspapers, one of which featured the work of the cartoonist next door. When Arthur was at The Flask pub, he was usually with the cartoonist, the novelist, the theatre director and especially the retired racing driver. And if he wasn't with them at their favourite table by the window, he was otherwise engaged with one of the barmaids, a chirpy young woman from Lancashire called Betty Burton.

By four o'clock on the day of his release, Ronnie Capstan was sitting in the conservatory facing the back garden in Well Walk, nursing a large brandy and recovering from the four-course meal that Anatole had prepared. Having given the Belgian instructions for a less substantial three-course dinner to be served at eight o'clock, Cornelia poured herself a large gin and tonic and joined her brother.

"I see Leonora got married while you were otherwise engaged," she said, settling herself into her favourite armchair. "To some oik from Norfolk that no one has ever heard of, apparently. Really, the woman has no taste at all."

"Eth, can we not talk about Leonora?" said Ronnie. Cornelia had been christened Ethel Gladys Capstan, and in her teens had decided that she needed a more up-market name, changing it to Cornelia when she was at her Swiss finishing school.

"Suit yourself," said Cornelia, taking a hefty swig of her drink. "So, what are your plans?"

"Oh, this and that. Various irons in various fires."

"Do you fancy a bit of common or garden blackmail?"

"Please don't make jokes," he said. "I've only just got out of clink." There was a pause. "Who do you suggest I blackmail?"

"A chap called Walter Washbrook. Have you heard of him?"

"No. Who is he?"

"He's a painter and a homosexual."

"Is he?" he said. "Well, I imagine there are a few of those around."

"But it's disgusting!" said Cornelia. She told Ronnie how she had caught Washbrook and two other men doing unspeakable things to each other in a garden in Cheyne Walk just three days before.

"If you're so upset about it," he said, "why not get one of Arthur's newspaper chaps to expose him?"

"I probably will. I just thought I'd wait and see if my darling brother wanted to take advantage of it."

Ronnie said nothing, thinking what a drunken snob his sister was, and not for the first time regretting that he hadn't been born into a family of people as talented as himself.

"What are you doing this weekend?" asked Cornelia.

"Eth, I have just been released after a hellish time in prison," he replied. "For the next week or so, I have no more ambitious plans than to eat Anatole's food every night and get blotto on Arthur's wines and spirits."

"Well, of course you're welcome to do that," she said. "The thing is, we've been invited to a shooting party in Gloucestershire and Arthur informed me last night that he can't come. I thought you might like to take his place."

Ronnie looked at her in alarm. "Don't worry," she added. "I don't mean that you have to impersonate Arthur, just come with me. And I did ask for two rooms. I always insist that Arthur sleeps in a separate room, wherever we are. He snores like a pneumatic drill. So, what do you think?"

"I think I'll pass on that one," said Ronnie. "Country house weekends can be awfully tedious."

"Well, I'll show you the invitation," she said. "That might change your mind." She went out of the room, and when she came back, she was carrying a large card with gold lettering on it.

162

"The shooting party is at Great Park," she said. "Remember where that is?"

The name was familiar, but Ronnie couldn't place it.

"Country residence of the Duke of Burfaughtonleigh," she said.

"It's pronounced Burley," said Ronnie.

Chapter 15
What exactly does morvliss mean?
Wednesday, London - grey skies turning to blue

The sun shone on Leonora through the kitchen window of her Earls Court apartment as she drank her morning coffee and practised the story she was going to tell Horace about the weekend. Having responded to an invitation to the shooting party at Great Park as Viscountess Grimbledon, she now needed to prise out of her husband enough money to pay for her train ticket to Stanford Saint Mary and other expenses that might accrue. She hadn't seen her husband since Monday and at this time of the morning, if he was in Earls Court, he would probably be asleep on a mattress in the corner of his studio, but there was no sound from his room.

She was about to go to see if he was there when the telephone rang. It was on a table in the hall just outside the kitchen, so Leonora took her coffee with her when she went to answer it.

"Hello, Fremantle 3803?"

"May I speak to the Viscountess Grimbledon, please?" The caller was Pickles, the Great Park butler. Leonora had been prepared for the call and didn't panic. She began by pretending to be her own domestic servant. "I'll see if milady has done wiv 'er ablutions," she said in a high-pitched squeak, adopting an accent that she thought sounded like a working-class person. She turned away from the phone and called down the hall: "Lady Grimbledon? Is you available a'all to take a call on the telephone?" She then put the phone and her coffee down, tip-toed down the hall and stamped her feet as she returned. She picked up the phone again and said: "Thank you, Mavis. Hello, this is Lady Grimbledon speaking."

"Good morning, milady," said Pickles. "My name is Montmorency Pickles, and I'm head butler at Great Park, home of the Duke of Burfaughtonleigh. We received your RSVP this morning. May I first of all convey the Duke's delight that you have accepted the invitation?"

"You're most welcome," said Leonora. "I'm looking forward to it."

"As are we, Lady Grimbledon," said Pickles. "And am I right in thinking that you will be making the trip by train?"

"Correct."

"Excellent news. We will of course send someone to collect you from Stanford Saint Mary station," said the butler. "Can I just confirm that you plan to be on the London train, which arrives at ten to three?"

"Ten to three. That is correct."

"Good. Well, we're very much look forward to meeting you on Friday."

"Morvliss," she said. She was absolutely certain that upper class people pronounced 'marvellous' as a two-syllable word with an 'or' sound in the first syllable, followed by 'liss'. "I will see you anon." She put the phone down, picked up her coffee and sipped it.

"What exactly does morvliss mean?" Leonora jumped a few inches and spilt coffee down her dressing gown when she heard Horace's voice. He had come out of his studio during the conversation and was standing behind her.

"Good God, Horace, you startled the wits out of me. I've spilt coffee all down myself. I do wish you wouldn't do that."

166

"Do what?"

"Creep up on me."

"Sorry, I just walked out of my room the way I always walk out of rooms. I wasn't aware that I was creeping up on anyone."

"Well, try to be more careful in future."

"Is your friend Diana here?"

"No," said Leonora. "Why do you ask?"

"I heard you call out 'Viscountess Grimbledon'. And you asked her to come to the phone. And you did it all in a funny voice. You sounded like a parrot. What was that all about?"

This wasn't going according to plan at all. Leonora had rehearsed what she proposed to tell Horace about the weekend, and he was asking stupid questions. "I have no idea what you're referring to," she said. "But we need to talk."

"Do we?" asked Horace.

"Yes, we do." Leonora indicated the sitting room. "Would you mind coming in here for a moment?"

"Certainly."

They walked into the room and Leonora ordered him to sit on the sofa, which was extremely soft and festooned with colourful cushions. Horace sat down as requested, and half disappeared under a riot of scarlet, orange and bottle green. Leonora remained standing in order to keep the upper hand in the conversation.

"Did you see your brother?" she asked.

"I certainly did," replied Horace.

"And did he give you some money?"

"Yes. He gave me a cheque for fifty pounds."

"Marvellous."

"Yes, indeed. Morvliss," said Horace, chuckling.

Leonora was getting a little impatient with him. He didn't usually behave in such a light-hearted way. "Where is it?" she asked.

"Where's what?"

"The cheque for fifty pounds."

"At Krumnagel's Bank. I deposited it yesterday. And I walked all the way there and all the way back to save money," he added proudly.

Leonora was not at all pleased to hear that the cheque was now in the bank. She was hoping they could take it to a branch of Ernest's bank to cash it. The people at Krumnagel's would no doubt be reluctant to let the Goodgames take any more money out in the foreseeable future.

"Well, that's a confounded nuisance," she said.

"Why? It means we have enough money to see us through the next few weeks."

"Yes, but I'm afraid I need some cash now," said Leonora.

"What for?"

"I've been invited to speak at a literary event in the west country," she announced.

"Really?" replied Horace. "What about?"

"My novels," she said. "I'm the guest speaker at the West of England Literary Festival in Gloucestershire. It runs from Friday evening until Sunday."

"Well, that sounds nice," said Horace. "Can I come?"

"No," said Leonora, just a little too sharply. "I'm afraid not."

"I see. What do you need money for?"

"The train fare and one or two other items."

"Aren't the organisers paying your fare?"

"No. I mean yes. They will reimburse me on presentation of receipts."

"Well, the bank let me withdraw five pounds yesterday."

"Oh, how wonderful. If you can give it to me, that would be perfect."

"All right." Horace put his hand in the inside pocket of his jacket and produced an old leather wallet. He took out five one-pound notes, paused and then put two of them back. He handed the other three to Leonora. "I hope you don't mind if I keep two pounds," he said, "I'm going to Norfolk today to sell the house."

"What? You're going to sell the Hunstanton house?"

"That's correct."

"Where on earth are you going to live?"

"Well, as I pay the rent on this place, I thought I might as well live here with you. I gather it's what married people do."

"Yes, indeed. Well, Horace, that would be ... "

"Morvliss?" he offered.

She glared at him. "I'm sure you have all sorts of things to do, and I must get on," she said.

"Right ho," said Horace. With difficulty, he pulled himself up by grabbing the arm on the left of the sofa with both hands, rolling to one side and springing up. It was like trying to get off a large half-inflated balloon. He then walked towards the door, stopped and turned back to face her. "Just one other thing," he said.

"Yes?"

"Well..." he said and paused for a moment. "It turns out I might be a bigamist."

*****

Meanwhile in Hampstead, Cornelia Wickham-Thynne was sitting in the conservatory, making a list of things to do before Friday's trip to Gloucestershire. First and foremost, she wanted to ask Arthur for the name of a journalist she could talk to in order to spread some dirt about Walter Washbrook.

The more she thought about this, the more she liked the idea of sharing her shocking news about the old bugger. Washbrook was quite famous, so exposing him as a pederast would probably make the front page of one of the tabloids, the *Daily Mail* or perhaps the *Sunday Pictorial*, newspapers that none of her acquaintances would admit to reading, but which they all did. The thought of telling them that it was she who had tipped off the press made her dizzy with excitement.

She poured herself a cup of coffee and, as she occasionally did if the sky was grey, or indeed if it was winter blue as it was today, she added a small glass of brandy to give it a little extra flavour. She drank half the cup in one mouthful and was enjoying the effect when she heard the telephone ring in the hall. She hurried out of the conservatory to answer it, but Arthur emerged from his study at the same time and got to the phone first.

"Hello?" he said.

"Is it for me?" asked Cornelia, hopefully.

Arthur shushed her, waving his hand irritably behind his back.

"Is it for *me*?" she repeated.

He turned and whispered aggressively: "Will you give me a moment to find *out*?" He turned his back on her and made some noises of assent to the caller, then turned and shook his head, so Cornelia returned to the conservatory.

Usually when Arthur was on the phone, he was barking instructions to his stockbroker or some underling at one of his galleries. His assertive speaking style only softened if he was talking to someone, he considered an equal, such as the owner of one of the newspapers he had shares in, or that dreadful racing driver who lived up the road.

This phone call wasn't like any of those. Arthur was barely saying anything, and when he did, it was in a very quiet voice. The only words she heard him say were "Yes", which he said about ten times, each time more quietly than the last, and "I understand" which he said three times, the last one slightly louder, preceded by "I've already told you". Finally, he said: "That won't be necessary" and put the phone down. A slammed door indicated that he was back in his study.

Cornelia wanted to know who the caller was, and she was also keen to talk about Walter Washbrook, so she walked through the hall and into Arthur's study. Her husband was sitting at his desk, his head in his hands. He looked up sharply when she walked in.

"I want to talk to that nice young man you introduced me to at one of your newspaper things," she said.

"Which young man was that?" he asked. His voice was quieter than usual. He seemed to have something on his mind and wasn't in the mood to talk.

"The one who writes all the scandal stuff for *The Pictorial* or *The Mail,* I can't remember which. He wrote the piece about that vicar from Luton who visited a brothel."

"Why do you want to talk to him?"

"You know why. I want to expose Walter Washbrook as the dirty pervert that he is."

Arthur stared at her for a moment, a look of horror on his face. "You will do no such thing," he said.

Cornelia looked at him in surprise. "Why on earth not? These people are evil, they're destroying the moral fabric of the country. They *have* to be exposed."

171

Arthur stood up and walked slowly round to the side of his desk where she was standing. "If you even mention Walter Washbrook again, I will ... " he paused.

"What?" Cornelia really wanted to do this and wasn't going to take no for an answer. "You will what?"

"I will divorce you."

Before Cornelia could reply, the door opened and Ronnie appeared, wearing one of Arthur's dressing gowns and a pair of his slippers. His mussed-up hair suggested that he had only recently got up.

"Good morning, both," he said. "Arthur, old bean, I had a rummage around in your wardrobe and borrowed this dressing gown, I hope you don't mind. And I found these slippers under your bed."

Arthur was about to reply when the phone rang again. Cornelia turned to leave the study to answer it, but Arthur brushed past the two of them, went out into the hall and grabbed the phone before she could reach it.

"What do you want?" he asked, in a brusque voice. Cornelia was about to admonish him for being so rude, and then remembered he had just threatened to divorce her, so she held her tongue. "Wait a moment." He turned and handed her the phone. "It's for you." He walked back into his study, ushered Ronnie out into the hall, then closed the door and turned the key in the lock.

Cornelia put the phone to her ear. "Lady Wickham-Thynne?" she said. It was Pickles, making another call to check with the Great Park weekend guests.

"Yes, everything's fine," she said and put the phone down.

Everything clearly was not fine. She stared at the mirror in front of her. Suddenly, she looked much older.

Ronnie yawned loudly. "Any chance of some coffee, Eth?" he asked.

*****

In Saint John's Wood, Diana Bagshot had important issues of her own to deal with. One of her guilty secrets was the fact that she paid the rent of two Italian waiters who lived in a flat over a bookshop in Berwick Street in Soho in return for a little fun and games when she was feeling bored. Unfortunately, both men were in a spot of bother. One of them was the man who had allowed Clarence Dalton to kiss him at the Fitzroy party in Cheyne Walk on Saturday night. The other was suffering from a drug overdose and was the reason for her sudden departure from Saint John's Wood on Monday night.

Diana had become a widow when she was thirty-seven. According to the obituary in *The Times,* the world had been 'truly shocked and saddened' by the unexpected demise of her husband Eustace, the eleventh Viscount Grimbledon, whose ancestors had fought alongside Wellington at Waterloo and Nelson at Trafalgar. He himself had served in the Great War, bravely holding down a desk job, where he oversaw the transfer of hundreds of thousands of young men from cities, towns and villages all over England to the trenches of Northern France and Belgium, from where most were unable to return.

Inheriting the Grimbledon title came with an unusual requirement for Eustace, namely that the new Viscount had to be married. At the age of forty-five, he had never been remotely interested in cohabiting with anyone, male or female, and he had always hoped it would be possible to ignore this ancient family edict and simply move into Grimbledon Towers and carry on eating, drinking and writing the occasional book. However, his mother Gertrude, now the Dowager Viscountess Grimbledon, refused to allow Eustace to continue his bachelor life, and threatened to choose a bride for him if he was incapable of finding one for himself.

In fact, he managed to find one remarkably quickly. At the first weekend house party he attended after his father's funeral, he met twenty-two-year-old Diana Eastwood, a very beautiful young woman who had hoped to train to be a doctor, but that idea had been quashed by her mother Constance, who had impressed on her the importance of marrying well.

"For goodness sake, don't do what I did," Constance warned, as Diana progressed through her teens, coming top of the class in maths and science.

What was it that her mother had done that was so wrong? She was the daughter of a lord and had fallen in love with the gardener. Ignoring the pleas of her family, Constance ran away to Scotland and married him at Gretna Green, after which her father disinherited her and never spoke to her again.

The wedding of Eustace and Diana took place in a very different setting to the spartan parish church at Gretna Green. They tied the knot in the Norman church at Grimbledon Magna, a hamlet of some two dozen cottages, a church and a pub, about a mile from the family home. Afterwards, the wedding party made their way back to Grimbledon Towers, where a whole pig was roasted. The otherwise dull event was enlivened when the Dowager Gertrude swallowed a huge piece of fatty pork and choked to death. She was at the top table next to her son and, when she suddenly sat bolt upright and slumped forward onto the table, he thought she was having a nap. A few minutes later, he nudged her to let her know that the speeches were about to begin, and when she didn't respond, he decided to let her sleep through them. It was only when one of her oldest friends tried to congratulate her that they realised that she wasn't just sleeping.

"Well, that's a bit of bad luck," Eustace said to his best man, James Walsingham-Booth. "If she could have only popped her clogs a few weeks ago, I wouldn't have had to go through with this rigmarole." Walsingham-Booth, a younger man with more intense sexual desires, nodded in agreement, and made a mental note to try to seduce the new bride at the earliest opportunity.

So it was that Diana married young and in haste, and definitely repented at leisure. Her hopes of at least having children to alleviate the stultifying boredom of Grimbledon Towers were dashed when it became clear that Eustace preferred large amounts of food and drink to sex. On the rare occasions that he attempted the latter, he usually dozed off, his member having gone limp and his large frame pinning Diana down, until she punched him in the kidneys to wake him up.

Eustace met his fate one night after a dinner of the usual several courses washed down by a lot of wine, with two or three generous glasses of brandy to finish off. On his way to bed, he tripped on the top step of the circular stone staircase and tumbled down, breaking his neck as he crashed to the floor. There was no one to inherit the title, so Diana abandoned the cold grey corridors of the Towers and bought a house on the coast outside Lyme Regis and a London apartment in Saint John's Wood. Life became a colourful adventure, and without a hint of scandal.

Until now.

She had met Luca and Vincenzo when they were working at Casa Camorra, where they were waiters. One night, Diana was the last diner to leave after a meal with friends, and the boys were also on their way home. She asked them to wait with her until a taxi came, during which time she discovered that they lived in a small room over a butcher's shop in Kilburn, half a mile from where she lived at Chetwynde Mansions. She invited them to share the taxi, and somehow they stayed with her as far as Saint John's Wood. And one thing led to another.

She arranged for them to move into a flat in Soho, walking distance from where they worked, and where she could visit them without fear of being recognised by the bohemians and beggars who frequented that part of the city.

But now they were causing her trouble. Luca had a heroin habit and had overdosed two nights ago. He ran out into the street and started shouting at passers-by, one of whom alerted a police officer. Vincenzo managed to get him back upstairs into the flat before the police arrived, and then called Diana in a panic. It was clear that he was having trouble looking after Luca by himself, so Diana decided to go to Soho to sort thing out.

There was only one person she could think of who could help, someone she could trust to keep quiet about her situation. His name was Alexander Malleson, a former Harley Street doctor who had just been released from prison for selling addictive substances to his rich patients. He was one of the very few people Diana could confide in. On Wednesday morning, she called his number in Chiswick and told him about Luca's addiction problem.

"There are clinics that deal with problems like this springing up all over the place," he said. "Some people I know run a place near Cheltenham. It's pretty pricey, though."

"The cost won't be a problem," said Diana. "What's much more important is - can I trust the people there to be discreet?"

"Leave it with me," he said. "I'll get in touch with them."

An hour later, Alexander called her back. "They can accommodate him on Friday," he said.

Two days later, Alexander drove Diana to Brewer Street, where they picked up Luca. They then headed west out of London and came to a halt outside The Hollies, a large house between Cheltenham and Prestbury. They had actually driven past Great Park on the way.

By chance, another new patient arrived at the same time. Her name was Emma, and she was the wife of the Member of Parliament for Gloucestershire South, Sir Burlington Fitzroy.

Chapter 16
Shape up! The boss is here!

Wednesday, Krumnagel's Bank, The Strand - cold and overcast

When Reg Plumpton pulled up the lock bar and opened the huge metal door of Krumnagel's Bank on Wednesday morning, he was astonished to see the manager, Godfrey Krumnagel, standing on the doorstep waiting to come in.

Godfrey had stepped out of his Bentley a few moments before and told his chauffeur Bert Branch to come back in two hours to drive him to Effingham, where he had a game of golf booked at midday. Bert was delighted, the arrangement giving him the chance to spend some time at the Lyons Corner House only a few hundred yards away. He parked on Duncannon Street by the side of Saint Martin-in-the-Fields Church and five minutes later, he was sitting in the window of Lyons, reading the racing pages of *The Daily Herald* and smoking a cigarette. Bert liked that particular Corner House because Emily the cashier and Martha, one of the waitresses, were his neighbours in Peckham. He planned to drink a mug of tea and eat a couple of fancies and hoped that Emily might just forget to give him a bill. He was disappointed when he walked in to see that someone else was sitting behind the big silver till in the wooden booth near the door.

Inside the bank, unaware that Godfrey was on their doorstep, seven tellers sat idly at their windows and the clerks at desks behind them chatted. When Reg saw Godfrey, he turned and yelled a warning to the rest of the staff. "Oi, you lot! Shape up! The boss is here!"

Seeing the manager walk through the door like an ordinary customer, and at such an early hour, threw the place into a state of frenzy. The seven tellers signalled frantically to the two real customers who followed Godfrey in from the street, imploring them to come to their window. The six clerks stationed at desks behind the tellers ran back and forth to get ledgers off shelves, colliding with each other as they did so. Reg stamped one foot after the other on the marble floor, saluted the manager and marched to his position on the front doorstep, shouting "Left! Right! Left! Right!" as he progressed out of the building.

When the two customers had chosen a teller to go to, things calmed down in the foyer. There was another burst of activity when Godfrey asked for someone to open the door that linked the public and private areas of the bank. The clerks all ran to the notice board and grappled with each other before one of them managed to get the key off its hook and let the manager in.

Godfrey thanked them, walked down the corridor and opened the door to his secretary Avril Long's office. Avril was astonished to see him there so early. He smiled at her, went through into his own office and opened a cupboard behind the desk. He took out a blue and white striped mug and instructed her to get him some tea and two bacon rolls from the Strand Cuppa Café, which was a few doors down the street. He preferred the tea they made at the Cuppa Café to the concoction that was on offer in the bank itself, and he was addicted to the bacon rolls made by the owner's wife Freda. He asked Avril to make sure Freda smothered the rolls in brown sauce, then walked out into the corridor and knocked on the door of his assistant's suite of offices.

Burgess never knocked on the door, so Rita thought it was Avril coming to say hello. She shouted, "Come in, darling!" and was then mortified to see Godfrey's head appear round the door.

"Burgess here?" he asked.

"Oh, I'm so sorry, Mister Krumnagel!" she said. Even without this rare sight of the manager, Rita was already in a state of panic, anxious to apologise to Burgess for having denied him the table he had reserved at Lyons the night before.

"Sorry? What for?" asked Godfrey.

"Calling you 'darling'!"

Godfrey laughed. "No problem. So ... is he here?"

"No, sir, he hasn't turned up yet. Not like Mister Burgess at all."

"Tell him I'm in my office when he gets here," said Godfrey. He smiled at Rita and disappeared. Rita was reminded what a cheerful man Godfrey was and how nice it would be if he chose to spend a little more time on the premises.

It was indeed strange for Rupert Burgess to be late for work. His train from East Sussex had been delayed, a dead goat on the line outside Tunbridge Wells being given as the reason by the train inspector, who marched up and down shouting 'Not my fault! Dead goat!" and ignoring the angry retorts from the passengers.

By the time Avril got back from the café with Godfrey's rolls and tea, his assistant manager was arriving at Charing Cross Station, nearly two hours behind schedule. Burgess alighted from the train and hurried across the concourse, as briskly as a fifty-four-year-old man who never took any exercise was able to do. It was the first time since he had been appointed assistant manager that he wasn't at his desk when the doors opened.

When he got out of the station, he walked across the road and passed the window of the Lyons Corner House. A man sitting at the very table he had reserved the night before raised a hand holding an untipped Woodbine cigarette and waved it in Burgess's general direction. Burgess vaguely recognised the man but didn't feel confident enough to wave back, so he raised his hat. It was a few seconds before he realised it was Branch, Godfrey Krumnagel's chauffeur. What on earth was he doing there at this time in the morning?

Burgess thought about what had happened the previous evening. Having a cup of tea and a slice of apple crumble at Lyons Corner House was one of his few pleasures in life and Tuesday evening was the only time he allowed himself this simple extravagance. He had a regular booking at 5.15pm at the table by the window, and he would try to answer at least five clues in *The Times* crossword before he finished the crumble. The previous evening, he had been dismayed to see that not only was the table occupied, but the intruders were his secretary Rita O'Riley and a young man with wavy blond hair and a smug face. He hadn't wanted to make a fuss and left the premises rather than sit somewhere else and embarrass Rita. But now he was feeling a little put out and resolved to ask her at the earliest opportunity what had happened.

When he arrived at the front door of the bank, Reg Plumpton saluted him and asked him how he was. Burgess liked Reg a lot and often stopped to talk to him but because he was late, he mumbled a reply and walked past him.

"Mister Krumnagel's here, sir," said Reg.

Burgess walked back to where Reg was standing. "What did you say?"

"Mister Krumnagel's here, sir. He was actually standing right here at the door when I opened up!" Reg made it sound as if a creature from outer space had fetched up at the bank and asked to open an account. Burgess cursed his luck. The one time his train was delayed was the only day his boss arrived at the bank before him. No doubt his late arrival would be relayed to the Krumnagels who controlled the bank from their mountain retreat at Schloss Emlau in Bavaria.

"I'd better go and talk to him," he said.

The arrival of the assistant manager caused a smaller, less seismic disturbance. When he asked to be let into the office area, only two of the tellers and one of the clerks ran to the notice board to get the key off the hook.

Burgess went quickly into his office, put his raincoat and hat on the stand, warned Rita that he wanted to talk to her shortly and went to see his boss. Godfrey was sitting at his desk and was halfway through the second bacon roll when his assistant manager knocked on the door of his office. Burgess apologised profusely for being late, and Krumnagel waved the roll airily to indicate that it didn't matter. Burgess thanked him and discreetly wiped brown sauce off the sleeve of his suit.

After the usual enquiries about wives and children - Burgess had one of the former and three of the latter, Godfrey had one of the former and none of the latter - they got down to business. The assistant manager explained about the fraudulent withdrawals from the Agatha Merchant trust fund and his interview with its beneficiary, Horace Goodgame. Godfrey asked what Goodgame's reaction had been when he was told his monthly cheques would be stopped, and Burgess

183

answered that he seemed to take the news very calmly. He had simply acknowledged the problem and left the bank.

"I imagine it was the shock that silenced him," said Godfrey. "But I think you're absolutely right that we need a strategy in place in case he decides to take action against us. Let me have a look at the file."

Burgess was delighted that the manager was taking a serious interest in the case, and relieved to hear Godfrey's calm and thoughtful response. He would have been the perfect boss if he could just bring himself to turn up for work a little more often. Burgess went back to his own office and told Rita to take the box containing the correspondence and ledger relating to the Merchant trust fund into the manager's office, and then he wanted to talk to her.

When she came back, Rita sat opposite Burgess and began to cry.

"Oh please ... " said Burgess, who had a pathological fear of witnessing any expression of emotion.

Rita took out a handkerchief and blew her nose noisily. "Mr Burgess," she said. "I'm so terribly sorry about what happened last night! What that horrible man did was unforgiveable!" She had discovered that spending time with Kimberley-Waugh was not a pleasant experience. His flirting became more intense, and he kept asking her to go back to his flat in Upper Montagu Street. When she said no for the seventh or eighth time, he paid the bill, and they went out into the street. He then hailed a taxi and pushed her into it, jumped in afterwards and instructed the driver to head towards Marylebone. Rita screamed at the top of her voice and the taxi screeched to a halt. She got out, then turned and slapped Kimberley-Waugh hard on the face.

She chose not to tell Burgess about that, but there was something that she had learned at the tea shop that she felt she ought to pass on to him. The problem was, she didn't want to tell him that she had been discussing bank business with Kimberley-Waugh, so she re-ordered the conversation.

"Mr Burgess, there's something I need to tell you," she said.

"Go on," said Burgess.

"Well," she started, then paused to get her thoughts in order. "That man I was with," she continued. "I met him yesterday when I was sending the telegram to Mister Krumnagel. And I foolishly agreed to have tea with him, and then he stole your table."

"I know that. Unless there's something else ---"

"There *is* something else. He works for Sotheby's the art people. When we were having tea, he mentioned that he'd met a customer of theirs and her name was Goodgame."

Burgess looked up from examining his hands. "Are you sure?" he said.

"Absolutely," said Rita. "And there's more. When he mentioned the name 'Goodgame', the waitress who was taking our order suddenly ran off."

"She did what?"

"She ran off. She dropped her pencil on the table and just ran out into the street. It caused an awful turmoil in the tea shop."

"I can imagine," said Burgess, "but what has this got to do with anything?"

"The point is," said Rita, pausing as she came to the most important part of the narrative, "another waitress came over to serve us. As she was serving us, the ... the man I was with ... said Goodgame was an unusual name.

185

The new waitress said that the woman who had run away used to be called Goodgame!"

"What?"

"She calls herself something different now. And her name is Martha!"

"Good Lord." Burgess stood up suddenly. "I know which one Martha is. And I also know that she lives with Emily Roebuck, the cashier."

Even though he had always found the cashier to be a rather frightening figure, they were on first-name terms. A large sturdy woman of about fifty, Emily Roebuck had taken a shine to Burgess when he accidentally left two florins - *four shillings* - as a tip when he paid his bill. In fact, it had been a mistake. He had meant to pick up the coins from the little silver tray that Emily presented him with and replace them with a one-shilling piece that was in his pocket. Unfortunately, it took him so long to locate the shilling that Emily picked up the tray and poured the two florins into a jar on the shelf next to her. Burgess looked in horror as he lost the money but felt too embarrassed to ask for it back. As a result, his reputation as a big tipper was established, and thereafter he always felt he had to tip over the odds.

"Mister Burgess?" Rita's words brought him back from his thoughts about his lost florins.

"Right. Thank you, Rita." Burgess was still uncertain what to do next but he felt sure Godfrey would have an answer. He took his hat and coat from the hat stand and knocked on Godfrey's door, went in and explained the situation. Godfrey had sent Avril out for a third bacon roll from the Strand Cuppa Café, and he was in the middle of eating it, so Burgess kept his distance to avoid getting sprayed with brown sauce again.

"We must go straight down there," said Godfrey. He stood up sharply, roll in hand, and brown sauce looped in the air and landed right in the middle of Burgess's bald patch. Godfrey wasn't aware of what had happened, and so Burgess put his hat on to avoid the embarrassment if he saw it.

The two men marched out of the office, and their sudden presence in the working area of the bank caused another bout of activity, as if two foxes had invaded a chicken coop. Everyone settled down when they disappeared into the street and walked off down the Strand towards Lyons Corner House.

Despite his fondness for fry-ups and bacon rolls, Godfrey was quite fit, thanks to the amount of time he spent on the golf course. The non-golf-playing Burgess struggled to keep up with his boss as he strode down the street. When they walked through the door of the tea shop, they were met by the thin waitress who had tried to seat Burgess at his table the evening before.

"Good morning, Mister Burgess, very nice to see you," she said. The sour expression on her skeletal face showed that she was merely spouting words Lyons employees were instructed to say when regular customers turned up. "I'm afraid your usual table is occupied at the moment." Burgess looked towards the window, where Bert Branch the chauffeur was circling the names of the horses, he planned to put a wager on in the afternoon.

"Actually, we haven't come for tea," said Godfrey. "Are either Mrs Goodgame or Mrs Roebuck here?"

"There's no one by the name of Goodgame working here," said the waitress. "And it's Miss Roebuck, not Mrs."

Godfrey sighed. "Fine, Miss Roebuck. Is she here?"

"No."

"Do you know where she is?"

"No."

Godfrey knew it was time to take his questions to a higher level.

"I want to see the manager," he said.

"Manageress," the thin waitress corrected him.

Godfrey had had enough. "Just tell me who's in charge here!" he said in a voice so loud that every conversation in the tea shop stopped. In the silence, Bert looked up from his research into the racing, saw his boss, put his pencil back in his pocket and started reading the front page of the newspaper.

"There's no need to raise your voice," said a woman who was sitting behind the till in the wooden booth. "I'm the manageress. How can I help?"

Godfrey introduced himself and said that he needed to speak to two of her employees in connection with bank business. The manageress listened and nodded her head, but when Godfrey asked her for the address of the two women, she refused to give it. He thought about going out into the street and enlisting the help of a police constable, but before he could do that, he heard his name being called. Bert the chauffeur had stood up and was indicating that the two men should come over to his table.

Godfrey walked over to talk to him. "What is it, Bert?" he asked.

"Mister Krumnagel, sir," said Bert, "is you looking for Emily Roebuck?"

"Yes. But these people are not being very helpful."

"Right. Well, listen..." Bert lowered his voice. "I know where she lives. She's my neighbour down in Peckham.

188

And the woman she lives with also works here. Her name is Martha Donkin."

"Excellent news, Bert," said Godfrey. "Take us there immediately."

"Yes, sir. Oh, and Mister Burgess?"

Burgess was holding his hat in his hand, having taken it off as he always did when he entered Lyons. "Yes?" he asked.

"You've got brown sauce on your head, sir."

Chapter 17
Why are men so sodding *difficult*?
Wednesday, Great Park - snow in the evening

After the drama of escaping from the Duke's guests on Tuesday, Charles spent most of Wednesday painting a half-naked Pickles. In the middle of the afternoon, the butler said, "Walter, I'm going to have to ask you the most immense favour."

"Fire away," said Charles.

"In this morning's post, we've had confirmation that a Viscountess will be attending the shooting party. I have to say that this news has put the whole household into something of a tizz. She's been invited to several events, but this is the first time she's accepted."

"Good-oh. So, what's the favour you're asking?"

"Well ..." said Pickles. "Tradition has it that when anyone with a higher peerage ranking than the Duke himself stays in the house, that person is invited to use the best room we have to offer, which is the Corner Suite on the third floor." He paused to see if Charles understood the implication of this.

"Oh! You mean the room I'm in?"

"Exactly."

"Well, no problem at all. I'll move my stuff out as and when."

"That won't be necessary, Walter. The under-butler who took you to your room will see to that. And you won't have to move until Friday."

"Right ho."

"I'm sure we will all find the lady an interesting person to meet," said Pickles.

"I'm sure we will," replied Charles. "What's her name?"

"Lady Diana Bagshot. She's the widow of the late Viscount Grimbledon."

Charles made a groaning noise.

"Are you all right?" asked Pickles.

"Just got a stabbing pain," said Charles, pointing to his left hip.

Pickles looked puzzled. "Yesterday it was your right hip that was causing you pain," he said.

"Moved across," said Charles, with a touch of desperation in his voice. "Bally pain won't sit still." He sat down on the metal chair with a bump. Diana Bagshot, the woman he had mis-sold a painting to, was coming to Great Park at the weekend. He thought for a moment, then decided it wouldn't be a problem. His disguise as Walter Washbrook seemed to be working, so she wouldn't recognise him. When all was said and done, despite the fact he had to pretend to be an old man with a bad hip, he could breathe a sigh of relief. So he did.

His cheerful mood changed almost immediately when Polly came into the conservatory to tell them that Gilbert Woolnough had arrived. Gilbert, the Marquis of Stanford, the Duke of Burfaughtonleigh's only child, the man that Polly never stopped talking about and whose name she had uttered when she woke up after spending the night in Charles's bed.

Pickles apologised and said he would have to make sure the new arrival had everything he needed.

"It's OK, Monty," said Charles. "Let's call it a day, shall we?"

The butler thanked him, put on his pink silk dressing gown and hurried out of the conservatory towards the main house. It had turned cold as evening approached and snow was beginning to fall. Polly picked up a copy of *Vogue*, lay down on the chaise longue and started reading. "You'll like Gilbert," she said.

"Do you think so?" replied Charles. "I rather doubt it."

"Why? He really is a lot of fun. He makes me laugh more than anyone I know."

"Does he now?"

"Mmm..." said Polly. She looked at the tiny gold wristwatch she was wearing, which was a present from Rupert Fotheringay, heir to the Fotheringay's Sausages empire, the first man she got engaged to. The face of the watch was so small she had to hold it right in front of her eyes to see what time it was. "It'll be dinner in half an hour," she said. "You can meet him then."

"I'm not feeling very hungry."

Her smile disappeared and Charles knew he was in trouble. She marched over to him, took his chin in her hand and squeezed it until it hurt. "Look, if this is you being jealous, then you can stop it right this minute," she said. "Get it into that fat head of yours that Gilbert is just a friend, nothing more!"

Before she could say anything else, Pickles appeared at the door, dressed in his normal dark suit, white shirt and tie. He stopped when he saw them standing face to face. "I'm not interrupting something, am I?" he asked.

"No, not at all!" they said, almost simultaneously.

"How's Gilbert?" asked Polly.

"Young Mister Woolnough seems to be very well," replied Pickles. "He's having an aperitif in the blue drawing room and wants to know if you would care to join him."

"We'd love to," said Polly.

Pickles looked at the two of them for a moment and then went out and closed the door behind him. Charles started to speak, but Polly cut him off. "Charles..." she sounded more conciliatory this time. "... you don't believe me, but you're the only man in the world I trust."

"I just wanted to say----" he started.

"Listen to me! Every man I meet, and I mean *every* man, without exception, thinks that I'm a brainless fool."

"I'm sure that isn't true," said Charles.

"It *is* true," replied Polly. "And they also think I have the morals of a Parisian Street girl. So, they all want to do the thing with me and throw me on the scrapheap."

"Do what thing?"

"You know what I'm talking about!"

He did know what she was talking out. "Including Gilbert?" he ventured.

"Stop going on about bloody *Gilbert!* Yes, he was the same as all the others to begin with, but when I made it clear I wasn't interested, he started treating me like a friend. And he did me a very good turn by persuading his father to take me on as his secretary. And in spite of your *lack* of belief in my abilities, Charles, he knows that I'm doing a good job and so does Tarquin. But I wouldn't trust either of them as far as I could throw them."

"Which wouldn't be far with the Duke," said Charles, trying to lighten the atmosphere and failing miserably. He wasn't good with serious conversations, particularly with Polly. He looked on in alarm as she slapped both of her cheeks in frustration.

"Why are men so sodding *difficult*?" she shouted. "Why won't any of you just treat me like a normal *person*? I deserve *better!*" She sat down on the metal stool and put her head in her hands. He was worried that she was going to start crying and had no idea what he would do if she did, so he patted her shoulder.

194

She pushed his hand away. "Don't do that!" she shouted. "I'm not a bloody dog!"

"I just wanted to say," he said, "... that I plan to start work on the Van Gogh tonight."

Polly looked up at him and the dazzling smile returned. She stood up and put her arms round him and kissed him. "Let's go and have an aperitif with Gilbert," she said.

"If you insist."

In the blue drawing room, an overweight man was standing in front of the fireplace, a glass of dark liquid in one hand and a cigarette in the other. There was another taller man standing at the window.

"Hey! Gilbey!" shouted Polly.

"Hey, Polly-wol!"

Charles was delighted that it was the fat man who spoke. The heir to the Burfaughtonleigh estate was the complete opposite of the type who normally flocked around Polly. He was taller than his father, the same height as Charles in fact, but while he wasn't as fat as the Duke, Gilbert was certainly obese, with a drinker's midriff and a neck so wide that it seemed to be part of his shoulders. And although he wasn't yet egg-bald like his father, that was his destiny. His hair was thick on the sides, and swathes of luxuriant side hair were combed from the left across the top of his head, where hair was, so to speak, thin on the ground.

He was very clearly his father's son, but there was something he appeared to have inherited from his mother. His nose was a bulbous red thing, like something a clown would wear, and its size was emphasised by the droopy moustache he sported under it. He looked like Groucho Marx, who Charles had seen in *A Night At The Opera* a few weeks before.

Gilbert ambled over, blew smoke out of the side of his mouth, and kissed Polly sloppily. "Damn good to see you."

"Good to see you too, poppet," said Polly. "Let me introduce you to the incredibly famous and talented portrait painter, Walter Washbrook."

"Pleased to meet you, Washbrook," said Gilbert. Charles knew that aristocrats never used the word 'Mister' when they addressed men for the first time. He decided to do the same with Gilbert.

"Pleased to meet you too, Woolnough," he replied. Gilbert glared at him, stung by this insult to his seniority, but didn't say anything.

"Pol, I want you to meet a friend of mine." Gilbert turned to look at the man who was standing at the window, opening and closing the lock mechanism. "Lawrence, you bastard! The filly I was telling you about *est arrivée!*"

The man turned and walked towards them. He was tall and broad-shouldered, his blond hair was swept back and his smile was gleaming. Charles hated him instantly.

"Pol, this is Lawrence Kimberley-Waugh, a cad of the highest order. Keep your hand on your ha'penny when LKW is around."

"You're too kind, Gilbert," said Kimberley-Waugh, fixing Polly with a dazzling smile. Polly almost melted in the warmth of the look. Charles felt physically sick. "Delighted to meet you, Polly."

"Thank you," said Polly.

"Lawrence works for Sotheby's in London," said Gilbert.

"Really?" said Polly. "In that case, I'm sure you'd like to meet Walter too!"

196

Kimberley-Waugh looked at Charles, who felt a pang of anxiety that this man who worked in the art business might know the real Walter Washbrook. Instead, the young man produced another smile. "Awfully nice to meet you at long last, Mister Washbrook. I am of course familiar with your work."

"Good-oh!" said Charles.

Before he could say more, Kimberley-Waugh turned to Polly again. "So, you're the famous Polly," he said. "I've heard a lot about you."

"Well, I hope it's all good," said Polly. "Gilbert, Walter and I have been hard at work all day and we're jolly thirsty."

Gilbert walked over to the drinks cabinet and prepared aperitifs for them, and when the gong sounded, Polly and Charles went off to their rooms to change for dinner. Charles put on the evening suit that Polly had found for him, and he hoped that Gilbert wouldn't notice that it was one of his old ones.

By the time he got down to the dining room, the rest of the guests were all seated. The Duke was, as usual, at the head of the table, with Snowball the snuffling Labrador under his chair. Next to him was a pasty-faced man wearing spectacles with heavy black frames. This was Lionel Pudsey, the Duke's accountant, a man with a permanent scowl on his face, the reason for which became clear as each course of the meal was served. As he miserably informed the servers as they approached with each new dish, Pudsey had a stomach ulcer, and there was virtually nothing he could eat. He spent the entire meal gloomily nibbling lettuce leaves and drinking water. No one noticed when he left the table after the main course.

Gilbert and Lawrence also left when the dessert dishes had been cleared away. The Duke invited Charles and

Polly to join him in the drawing room for a brandy and Charles was about to excuse himself, but Polly squeezed his thigh under the table, which shocked him into silence.

"We'd love to," she said.

"I'll see you there," said Tarquin, and waddled out of the dining room with Snowball.

"What did you squeeze me like that for?" asked Charles, when the Duke was out of sight. "I nearly squeaked like a parrot! I want to start work on the Van Gogh as soon as I can."

"Yes, but this way, you'll get another chance to look at it."

"Actually, I'm fine already!" Charles had a perfect mental image of the painting, down to the last brush stroke, so he didn't need to see it again. Even so, he and Polly joined Tarquin in the drawing room and spent the next hour listening to more anecdotes about the old days. The Duke was a good raconteur, and his stories involving members of the royal family and government ministers were made more tantalising by the removal of the names of the people involved.

"I can't possibly tell you which of the three was there when I woke up, darlings, but I *can* tell you that he went on to hold one of the great offices of state." Tarquin paused and chuckled at the memory. "And to think, if we'd left him outside, naked on SUCH a cold night, he may never have survived to serve as a member of His Majesty's government *at all*!"

Tarquin finally dozed off and began to snore gently as the last logs on the fire crumbled to ash.

It was time for Charles to get started on the portrait. He was going to paint the copy in his bedroom, so he had to do it without an easel, but he reckoned he could probably place the canvas on the wall between the metal radiator and the door frame of the bathroom. He told Polly he needed some materials from the conservatory, so they tip-toed out of the room and made their way down the hall and across the garden.

There was no moon to light their way, and snow was falling quite heavily. Charles put a framed canvas under his arm, two brushes and some charcoal in his pocket and picked up the box of oils, and they made his way back across the garden to the main house. They walked down the hall and then up the dark wooden staircase to the first floor, where a single lightbulb in the ceiling provided a small amount of light.

"This is where we part company," said Polly. "Best of luck, young Master Goodgame. Let's hope we all come out of this alive!"

"Yes, colonel!" he said, clicking his heels and saluting, which caused the canvas under his arm to fall to the floor with a crash. He bent down to pick it up. "God bless King and country," he added.

"I love you," said Polly, putting her arms round his neck. Charles couldn't return the hug because of the canvas and the wooden box he was holding, so he stood there and tried not to get over-excited.

"I heard a crash," said a voice in the darkness. "Is everything all right?"

Polly sprang away from Charles as Pickles emerged from the shadows, wearing a dark bathrobe and slippers. He looked at the two of them, made a grimace in Polly's direction, and then smiled as he addressed Charles. "Do you need anything, Mister Washbrook?" he asked.

"No, everything's fine," said Charles. He wanted to lean on his walking stick at this point, as he always did when he was talking to anyone at Great Park apart from

199

Polly, but he wasn't holding it. He tried to remember where he could have left it.

"I'm just taking this stuff to my room to do a bit of re-organizing," he said. "The oils need ... sorting out," he added.

"At this time of night?" asked Pickles. "Can't it wait until the morning?"

"It's just something I like to do late at night," said Charles.

"These artists are queer fellows," said Polly.

"Indeed." Pickles walked past them down the corridor to his intended destination, the first floor bathroom. When the door closed behind him, Charles swore quite loudly. "This is all going horribly wrong!" he said.

Polly put her fingers to her lips. "Everything's fine," she whispered. "Just carry on as normal." She disappeared off along the dark corridor, and Charles went upstairs to his room on the third floor. As he had hoped, he was able to wedge the canvas between the radiator and the bathroom door. Once it was there, he took out a piece of charcoal and sketched the shape of Stevenson's head.

Then his mind went blank.

His vibrant mental image of the painting simply disappeared. He stepped back from the canvas and shook his head. His extraordinary ability to remember paintings down to the tiniest detail had vanished. What on earth had gone wrong? Was it because he was tired? Or because of the alcohol? He had certainly drunk more in the three days he had been at Great Park than he would normally consume in a month. He sat on the bed and breathed in and out a few times. Then he stood up and looked at the canvas again. The charcoal outline of

Stevenson's head looked more or less the right shape, but he couldn't recall the painting itself in enough detail.

He needed to see the real thing again. No, more than that, he had to have the portrait with him while he worked. He thought about taking his canvas and paints down to the blue drawing room, but he wouldn't be able to see the portrait in the dark, and he couldn't turn on the lights for fear of attracting attention. It would be just his luck if someone heading for a midnight piss came into the drawing room to see why the lights were still on.

He would have to bring the portrait back to his room, work on it during the night and take it back before the house woke up.

He walked down the stairs and paused where he could see the bathroom that Pickles had disappeared into. There seemed to be no light coming from under the door, so he continued down into the main hall. In the darkness, he could just make out the door of the drawing room, almost directly opposite the foot of the stairs, so he tip-toed across the creaking floorboards, but tripped on something and fell flat on his face. The something was Snowball the Labrador, who was lying on his favourite part of the carpet and wasn't pleased about being woken up. The overweight dog thought about getting up and having it out with whoever it was who had fallen over him, but the effort was just a little too much, so he lifted his head, barked twice and then lay back down again.

Charles stood still against the wall, waiting for the dog to go back to sleep. There was a loud rattling noise as someone tried to open the door of the drawing room from the inside. Charles darted across the hall and hid behind the staircase.

The Duke emerged. "Snowball!" he said in a slurred voice. "Where the dickens are you?"

Charles watched between the stair rods as Tarquin stumbled forward and bumped into the dog, who growled again. When Snowball saw that it was the Duke, he sighed loudly and put his head back on his paws.

"I don't know why you prefer sleeping down here in the hall when there's plenty of room at the foot of my bed," said the Duke. He hiccoughed and belched loudly, and then made his way slowly up the stairs.

Charles waited until he heard a door slam upstairs, then walked slowly across the hall and grasped the handle of the door to the drawing room. Opening it made a noise that seemed to echo through the house, so he closed it more slowly.

Through the window on the other side of the room, he could see the snow falling and the embers of the log fire provided a little light. He walked over to the fireplace and tried to take the picture off the wall, but he couldn't reach it because the mantelpiece was too wide. He needed to get higher up, so he looked around for something he could stand on. There was a wooden chair by the window, next to the long drapes that had not been pulled shut. He walked to the window and stopped to look at the view.

Outside was another courtyard. There were small bushes along the edges, all of which had snow on their branches and there was a fountain in the middle. It was a magical sight and Charles paused to enjoy it.

There was a crash in the hall outside. Someone else had collided with the sleeping Snowball and landed on the floor. This was one interruption too many for the Labrador. Charles heard the dog growl, a noise which got louder and turned into a full-blown spell of barking. The victim was making a shushing noise to quieten him. There was a moment of silence, but the dog started barking again and someone said: "For Christ's sake, Snowball, put a sock in it!" The voice of whoever it was seemed to calm the dog down. He whimpered for a while, and then everything went quiet again.

The door to the drawing room opened and two people walked in. Charles moved swiftly behind the long curtain.

One of the people said: "Where's the light?" and the other said: "Don't turn the bloody light on, we don't want the servants snooping around."

The first voice belonged to Lawrence Kimberley-Waugh and the second was Gilbert Woolnough's.

"Where's the painting?" asked Kimberley-Waugh.

"Don't you remember? It's over there, above the fireplace."

"I remember, but I can't see a bloody thing in here."

Charles looked round the edge of the curtain as the two men made their way slowly across the room to the fireplace.

"I can't reach it," said Kimberley-Waugh. "Help me move this table." The two men moved the heavy coffee table closer to the fireplace, and Kimberley-Waugh stood on it and took the painting off the wall. He took a small torch out of his pocket and checked the back of the frame. "OK," he said. "I can get this out quite easily, so I can just take the painting without the frame. That will be a great help."

Behind the curtain, Charles gasped quite loudly. They were planning to steal the Van Gogh! Kimberley-Waugh got onto the coffee table again and put the painting back over the fireplace. When he stepped down off the table, he turned his ankle on something which was lying on the floor and shouted in pain.

"Keep your voice down!" hissed Gilbert.

"What the blazes is this?" said Kimberley-Waugh, picking up a stick.

"A walking stick," said Gilbert. "I expect it belongs to that chap who's here painting papa's portrait."

"Oh right, Washbrook. He's an odd cove, that's for sure," said Kimberley-Waugh. "I must say he isn't at all what I expected him to be like."

"Do you know him?"

"I know who he is. He's quite famous. He painted a lot of portraits of the royal family back in the twenties. But I would have expected someone a bit more ... I don't know, a bit more substantial."

"Well, never mind that, let's concentrate on the matter in hand," said Gilbert. "To make this look like an outside job, you're going to have to break in."

Charles ducked quickly out of sight as Kimberley-Waugh turned towards the window. "It's all right, I've done my homework," he said. "I checked the lock on that window earlier. It would be the easiest thing in the world to open it with a knife from the outside. Then of course, I can leave it open when I leave."

The two men walked over to the window. They were inches away from Charles. "Just one thing," said Gilbert. "It's snowing."

"Well spotted, Mister Holmes," said Kimberley-Waugh. "Not a lot gets past you, clearly."

"Listen, you fathead," said Gilbert. "If you plan to steal the painting by breaking in through this window, then there will have to be two sets of footprints, one coming to the window and one going away again."

"Oh right..."

"Not only that, but the burglar will have to show tracks all the way to the driveway."

"I hadn't really thought about that," said the art expert.

204

"So, not the ace criminal mind after all, are you?" Gilbert tapped on the window and breathed a long sigh of annoyance. "This snow is a blasted nuisance. It would help if it melted by the weekend, but fat chance of that happening."

"You still think we should wait until Saturday night before we take it?"

"Absolutely. We should think of getting it out of here about one o'clock."

"One o'clock. Right. And what do I do? Drive to London with it?"

"Of course not, you idiot! You have to be at breakfast, otherwise you'll be chief suspect! Don't you ever listen to anything? I'll tell you one more time."

He outlined the plan, speaking slowly and emphatically. Once he had the portrait, Kimberley-Waugh was to get a bicycle from the stable and ride it down the driveway to the gatehouse, the small stone building near the main road.

"Do I leave it in the gatehouse?" asked Kimberley-Waugh.

"No, there's a kind of woodshed off to the left behind it. Leave the painting there, then ride back to the stable, put the bicycle away and come back in through the back door, which I will leave open, but remember to bolt it shut once you're in. When the dust settles, we can pick up the painting and take it back to London in the Alfa."

Kimberley-Waugh looked at the falling snow. "You expect me to ride a bicycle in this weather?" he said.

"Yes," said Gilbert. "Just remember how much loot you're going to make out of this caper. Getting your balls frozen for a few minutes is going to be well worth it. By the way, what do you think about this painting? My father isn't absolutely sure that it's genuine."

"Sorry, I can't help you there, squire. Not my area of expertise. It looks like a Van Gogh to me, but all I can do is what I promised. Hand it over to some people in London. If they aren't sure about it, they'll probably smuggle it to New York. Some Yank with more dollars than brain cells will want it."

"I'm very pleased to hear it. It won't be the first time I've pulled the wool over a gullible American to make a packet."

"Oh yes, I remember," said Kimberley-Waugh. "That jewellery you said belonged to Queen Victoria. Didn't you sell it to the American ambassador?"

"It wasn't the ambassador, but it *was* someone from the embassy."

"Brilliant."

"Yes. It's amazing what you can get away with when you're the son of a Duke," said Gilbert. "Just make sure you keep that information to yourself. That stuff belongs to my mother, and I imagine she thinks it's still here in the house. Not sure what I'm going to do if she ever comes back to find it."

"And now the Van Gogh," said Kimberley-Waugh. "Stripping the family assets one by one."

"Yes. I'm a bit annoyed with you, I was hoping you could confirm that it was genuine," said Gilbert. "What *is* your area of expertise anyway?"

"British watercolourists."

"God, how boring."

"Someone has to do it. And they always send for me when there are paintings to be evaluated. That's what I was doing yesterday when I bumped into that Goodgame woman."

Charles nearly jumped out from behind the curtain when he heard his name. At first, he couldn't imagine

206

who Kimberley-Waugh was referring to, but it soon became clear. Horribly crystal clear.

"Actually, I didn't tell you what happened," said the expert.

"Yes you did!" said Gilbert. "You had her, I know that. You don't have to rub it in that you get more sexual intercourse than I do."

"But I didn't tell you *why* she offered herself like that. It was all because this painting was supposed to be by a chap named Horace Tuck, who's quite famous."

"I've never heard of him."

"Well, I can't help it if you're a bloody philistine. The fact is, the painting wasn't by Tuck, it was by a nonentity called Horace Goodgame. And this woman was his wife."

Charles almost fainted.

"She had a painting by her husband on the wall," said Gilbert. "What's so strange about that?"

"No, that's the point. It wasn't on *her* wall, it was on the wall of a friend of hers, a woman called Diana Bagshot, who's Viscountess something. Someone had sold her this worthless painting and told her it was a Horace Tuck. The Goodgame woman let me have her to stop me telling anyone."

It was all Charles could do to stop himself fainting and falling at the feet of the two men.

"*Are* you going to tell anyone?" asked Gilbert.

"Well, I have to. Lady Whatever asked Sotheby's to authenticate the painting, so she'll be expecting some kind of letter."

"I see."

"But I did quite enjoy dipping the wick with that woman. She was pretty lively for a woman of her age. "

"And what was her name again?" asked Gilbert.

"Leonora Goodgame. Or Capstan."

"Or what?"

"Capstan, I think. She's a novelist."

"Jesus Christ. Capstan is Polly's name."

"What?"

"Polly, the girl who works here. Her name is Capstan, and I seem to remember her saying her mother writes novels."

"Well, I'll be damned," said Kimberley-Waugh, and laughed out loud.

Gilbert's voice changed and his manner became less friendly. "If you've been shafting Polly's mother, you're going to keep very quiet about it. Polly is very, very special to me and if she finds out what you did, she'll be devastated. If you so much as mention any of this while you're here, I will skewer your balls and roast them on the fire."

"OK, calm down, will you?"

"Never mind calm down. Just make sure you keep absolute schtum about this. Not only here, but when you get back to London. Remember I know things about you that you wouldn't want people to find out."

"Are you threatening me, Woolnough?"

"Yes, I am. And you know better than to try and threaten me back. I can play very dirty if the mood takes me. And while we're on the subject, keep your hands off Polly."

"What do you mean?"

"You know perfectly well what I mean. I was watching the way you were giving her the glad eye tonight. She may give the impression that she's easy to get into bed, but I can tell you she's absolutely not interested in anything like that."

Kimberley-Waugh laughed again. "Is that what she told you?" he said.

"You bastard!" said Gilbert. From behind the curtain, Charles heard some kind of scuffle between the two men.

"All right! Leave me alone!" said the art expert. "Woolnough, you're so damned violent when you're angry! Just knock it off, will you?"

"I will remind you one more time," said Gilbert. "I could ruin your career with one phone call."

"All right, all right!"

"Or I may just call the chap who runs that gallery, what's his name? That Wickham-Thynne character, and shine some light on the great unsolved mystery of ----"

"All RIGHT, damn you! Don't rub it in. I make ONE little mistake in my entire working life and you want to crucify me for it!"

"I bet if I dig deeper, I'll find there are more *little mistakes* that you haven't told me about. Anyway, don't ever give me any reason to go down that route. Leave Polly alone."

"Don't worry," said Kimberley-Waugh. "No filly is worth losing your job over."

"Good," said Gilbert. "Now, we'd better make ourselves scarce before the servants start rattling around. They get up about four to start the fires and whatnot."

After the two men had left the room, Charles came out from behind the curtain and sat down on one of the armchairs in front of the fireplace. He was in shock. He had to tell Polly what was going on. Painting the Van Gogh was going to have to wait. He picked up his stick, walked carefully across the dark room, opened the door, tip-toed past Snowball and went upstairs to bed.

Chapter 18
I hope I won't have to use my shotgun

Wednesday, Peckham, South London - high winds, thunderstorm brewing

People walking down Asylum Road Peckham stared in astonishment as a brand new Bentley, the 3.5 litre Thrupp and Maberly Sport version, glided past them and parked outside Emsworth Dwellings, a tenement block on the corner of the Old Kent Road. Sightings of Bentleys were rare as hen's teeth in Peckham, even though a local resident was actually employed to drive one. Godfrey Krumnagel's chauffeur Bert Branch lived at number 43 on the third floor of the block, but he had never parked the boss's car in his own street before, because that would have been just asking for trouble.

Godfrey had discovered that the two women he believed to be responsible for the fraudulent withdrawal of money from the Angela Merchant trust fund were Bert's neighbours, living two doors away at number 45 Emsworth Dwellings, and he had come down to Peckham to confront them.

Aged thirty-six, Godfrey was too young to have taken part in the Great War, but there was no doubt that his tactical and organisational skills would have been very useful to the armed forces. Before they set off for Peckham, he called New Scotland Yard and told them he planned to make a citizen's arrest of two people he believed to be responsible for the embezzlement of several thousand pounds from his bank. He was immediately put through to a man who identified himself as Inspector Sparrow.

Sparrow wasn't impressed by Godfrey's plans. "A citizen's arrest is neither advisable nor necessary," he said, in the patronising voice he used when dealing with members of the public who he thought were either uneducated or crackpots. "If you give us details of the people involved, we will interview them and decide if they should face charges of any kind."

"*Au contraire,* Inspector Skylark --- "

"Sparrow," said Sparrow, annoyed by Godfrey's mistake, which was deliberate.

"I beg your pardon, Mister Sparrow."

"INSPECTOR Sparrow!" This was exactly what Godfrey wanted to do. He knew from experience that the only way you could get the full attention of law enforcement officers was by ruffling their feathers. "My dear inspector," he said, "a citizen's arrest is both advisable AND necessary. In fact, it is essential. And for everyone's sake, I hope I won't have to use my shotgun."

"SHOTGUN?" Sparrow didn't want to be the last police officer this lunatic spoke to before he shot someone. "Where exactly are these people?" he asked. Godfrey handed the phone to Bert, who gave the address and directions how to get there.

Assistant manager Rupert Burgess was alarmed at his boss's plan to perform a citizen's arrest and tried to persuade him to leave the matter in the hands of the police, but Godfrey was determined to see it through to its possibly bitter end. On the drive from the Strand, Burgess sat silently in the back of the Bentley, his hands grasped tightly together, imagining all sorts of violent outcomes to this misguided adventure.

When Bert brought the Bentley to a halt outside the building where he lived, Godfrey surveyed the surroundings and decided that the car should not be left unattended in a street that looked as poor, neglected and frankly dangerous as this one. He instructed Burgess to stay with the car while he and Bert went upstairs to find the two women. Burgess had never been anywhere like Asylum Road in his life and was quite nervous about being left alone in such a run-down street.

"It's all right, sir, I'll look after the car," said Bert, picking up on Burgess's anxiety. "To be perfectly honest, I'd rather not be there when you meet the ladies."

"Fair enough," said Godfrey. "Where do they live?"

Bert pointed up to the top floor of the soot-blackened building. On every level, there was an outside walkway and, even on a cold February day like this one, there were lines of washing hanging out. "Number 45, sir, on the third floor," said the chauffeur.

"Thank you," said Godfrey. "I'm a bit surprised the police aren't here already. When they get here, show them where to go, will you?"

"Right you are, sir," said Bert. It wasn't unknown for the police to pay a visit to Asylum Road. The reason they hadn't arrived that morning was that Sparrow had been unable to get through to the police station in Peckham High Street and, fearing that a shooting might be about to take place, he ordered a car to take him there from New Scotland Yard. In addition to the driver, he was accompanied by another officer and there was a battering ram in the boot of the car. The three of them were at that moment passing through the centre of Camberwell.

Godfrey opened the boot of the Bentley and took out a pair of handcuffs. "It's a pity the bank only has one of these," he said, "I suppose we will have to handcuff the women to each other. What do you think, Burgess?"

"Whatever you say, sir."

"What I suggest is this," said Godfrey, handing the handcuffs to his assistant. "You handcuff the women to each other while I'll cover you with the shotgun." Godfrey produced the gun from the boot, put it to his shoulder and pointed it at Burgess. Burgess squealed, dropped the handcuffs, and put his hands in the air.

"Oh, do stop behaving like a child, Burgess," said Godfrey. "The blasted thing isn't even loaded." He snapped the gun open, looked into the two barrels, and saw that each one contained a cartridge. "Actually, it *is* loaded. Sorry. Just as well I didn't pull the trigger."

The assistant manager was already a bag of nerves and the sound of the gun snapping shut made him jump. He was regretting handing over responsibility for the car to Bert, but there was no going back. Any evidence of his indecisiveness or lack of courage would surely get back to the Krumnagel family in their Bavarian Mountain retreat at Schloss Elmau. Burgess had to bite the bullet, hopefully not literally, and accompany his boss up the stairs to who knew what fate.

Godfrey decided Burgess couldn't be trusted to look after the handcuffs, so he picked them up and put them in his jacket pocket.

"Follow me," he said.

There was a concrete staircase up to third floor of the building. A thunderstorm was forecast, and a strong wind was beginning to blow. The bedsheets and clothing hanging on the walkways were billowing around and flapping loudly.

The two women who lived at number 45 were Horace Goodgame's first wife Martha, who now called herself by her maiden name Donkin, and Emily Roebuck, the nanny who had been employed to look after Horace and Martha's son Charles when he was growing up in

Hunstanton. As Horace's brother Ernest had correctly guessed, Martha had faked her own death by drowning, and the two women had moved to London, where they worked at Lyon's Corner House in The Strand. Every time they withdrew money from Krumnagel's Bank, they were prepared for the fact that someone might raise doubts about them. If that happened, their plan was to run out of the building and disappear down a side street to mingle with the crowds of traders and customers in Covent Garden. Which is exactly what they did when bank teller Bernard Smithers shouted at them on Monday. The two women knew it was inadvisable to stay in the same place for too long, so they moved from one rented flat to another every few months. It was unfortunate for them that the one they were living in now was just two doors away from the one where the bank manager's chauffeur lived.

Godfrey ran up the concrete steps two at a time, which meant he had to wait at the top before his unfit assistant manager caught up with him, holding his chest and gasping for air. With bedsheets hanging on washing lines waving noisily around them, Godfrey outlined his plan of action. "We knock on the door and tell them we're from the council, and we've come to check something," he said. He paused for a moment. "What would we need to check?"

Burgess had never been anywhere near housing like this and hadn't a clue what they would find. "I don't know," he said. "Do they have running water?"

Godfrey snorted with annoyance, wishing he'd asked Bert for more details about the flats before climbing the stairs. He walked to the wall and looked down into the street. Bert was leaning against the Bentley, smoking a cigarette and reading the racing pages of *The Daily*

Mirror. He nearly jumped out of his skin when his boss yelled his name from the third floor. He turned round and looked up. The wind was swirling around now, and it was starting to rain. It was hard for the two of them to hear each other.

"What kind of facilities do these flats have?" shouted Godfrey.

"SORRY?"

"WHAT KIND OF FACILITIES DO THESE FLATS HAVE?"

Bert had never heard the word 'facilities' before, but thought he heard the word 'bats'. He presumed Godfrey was talking about the two women. "WHAT ABOUT THEM?" he shouted back.

Further along the walkway, a woman was standing at the door of number 45. She saw a man with a shotgun shouting down to the street. She looked over the balcony and saw Bert standing next to the Bentley and quickly went back into the flat, where a woman was washing dishes in the kitchen.

"It's time to go," she said.

The other woman was Emily Roebuck, who had devised the scheme to steal Horace's money, many years ago when her friend Martha Donkin first told her about the man she had met at church and who seemed interested in her. At first Martha had been reluctant to agree to the scheme, but after twenty years of uneventful marriage, she had agreed to fake her own death and begin the complex process of emptying the Agatha Merchant Trust Fund. The two women had moved to London to be able to visit the bank regularly, but they had agreed that the moment it became too dangerous to pursue their fraudulent activity, they would leave the city and head back to East Anglia, where they would find a country cottage to turn into a bed and breakfast.

Now was clearly that time.

They walked into the bedroom, put on their coats and picked up the suitcases and handbags they had packed after the previous night's alarm at Lyons Corner House. Emily Roebuck looked carefully out of the door. The man with the gun was still engaged in an unsuccessful conversation with the man down below in the street, their neighbour Bert Branch.

"Let's go," she said. They turned left and quickly headed to the staircase at the other end of the walkway. When they reached the bottom, they took the back exit from the tenement, walked through a passage to the Old Kent Road and stood at a bus stop. When a 137 bus eventually pulled up, they got on and went off in the direction of Waterloo Station.

The wind-affected conversation between Godfrey and Bert wasn't progressing well so the manager decided to give it up. "Come on, Burgess," he said. "I suppose we can say we've come to check for rising damp." Godfrey looked around to see where his assistant was. "Burgess! Where are you?"

With a great effort, Burgess disentangled himself from one of the sheets, which was not only damp but also smelt horribly of petroleum carbolic soap. He felt as if he was emerging from a flooded garage. Godfrey shook his head, annoyed that his incompetent assistant was his only support on this important mission. He was also wondering why the police hadn't arrived and was feeling less confident about their ability to arrest the two women. "Come on, Krumnagel," he said to himself. "We can do this!"

He grabbed Burgess by the arm to release him from his damp prison. They zig-zagged through the washing and arrived at the door of number 45. Godfrey was about to knock on the door when it occurred to him that damp probably couldn't rise to the third floor of a building, so he changed the reason for the visit to a check for dry rot. Taking a deep breath, he pressed the buzzer. After a few seconds, he rapped firmly on the door.

The door creaked open. Martha had failed to close it properly. Godfrey pushed the door open a little more and stepped into the hallway. There was a room immediately to his left, which he could see was empty. "Is anybody here?" he asked, loud enough to be heard by anyone in the other rooms. "We're from the council. We've come to check for rising damp." Too late, he remembered he had changed the reason for the visit. "And also dry rot," he added.

No reply. There was a wall down the right side of the hall and a door at the end. There were two more rooms beyond the one he could see into. "Let's search the place," Godfrey whispered to Burgess, who was standing behind him, trembling like a leaf. "You look in the rooms on the left, I'll look down there."

With the shotgun under his arm, Godfrey set off towards the kitchen at the end of the hall. Burgess delayed his part of the search by carefully closing the door of the flat behind him and then walking slowly to the second door on the left.

He was about to peer into the room when there was a loud banging on the front door. Burgess thought about going back to open it, but decided to ask Godfrey first. As he walked down the hall, someone shouted: "Police! Open up!" Burgess poked his head into the kitchen, where Godfrey was looking at some papers he had found on the table. The shotgun was in the crook of his elbow.

"Mr Krumnagel, sir?" asked Burgess, not wanting to do anything that might interrupt his boss's search.

"What is it, Burgess?"

"I think the police are at the door. Should I let them in?"

"OF COURSE, you should let them in!"

"Right, sir. Doing it now." Burgess hurried back to the front door. The insistent banging on the door had stopped, and he wondered if the police had decided to go away.

He soon found out.

As he reached the door, he heard someone shout: "COMING IN!" He opened the door and two policemen carrying a battering ram ran past him, their momentum taking them all the way down the hall. Godfrey appeared at the door of the kitchen and the battering ram hit him full in the stomach. As he fell to the ground, the gun went off. There was a scream of pain, followed by a torrent of bad language. Another gunshot rang out and the front policeman tumbled over sideways, pulling the second one down with him.

An older police officer came into the flat. It was Inspector Sparrow. He swore loudly when he saw the three men writhing around and the battering ram rolling from side to side next to them. He turned to the bald man cowering behind the door. "Are you Krumnagel?" he asked.

"No, no," said Burgess. "That's Mister Krumnagel there." He pointed a shaking finger at the three men, who were trying to disentangle themselves from each other.

"He's the one with the shotgun," he added helpfully.

Chapter 19
Now you're really talking nonsense!
Thursday, Great Park - persistent snow showers

Charles woke up at seven o'clock when Flockton knocked on his door. He dragged himself out of bed and mumbled words of gratitude to the young man for bringing another bowl of piping hot water. He poured the water into the bath, added some cold from the single tap, and sat in the shallow and lukewarm mixture. He had arranged to meet the Duke at ten o'clock and was planning to add his host's face to Pickles's small muscular body that was already on the canvas.

When he got out of the bath, he put on his grey overalls, wig and dark glasses and shuffled down to breakfast. He was hoping to talk to Polly in the dining room, but when he got there, she wasn't alone. She was sitting at the end of the long dining table, deep in conversation with Lawrence Kimberley-Waugh. They were smoking cigarettes and drinking coffee, and she was laughing at something he had said. Charles felt the same pain in his gut that he had suffered when Polly had first met the Sotheby's man the previous day.

Polly looked up and smiled when she saw him. "Ch - *Walter* darling! Come and join us. Larry has been telling me some awfully funny things about goings-on in the art world. I'm sure you have a few stories of your own to add."

"I'm in a bit of a hurry, actually," said Charles. "I have to meet the Duke in the conservatory."

"What? Tarquin said he was meeting you at ten," said Polly. She squinted at her watch, holding the tiny face close to her eyes, so she could see what time it was. "You've got plenty of time. And you need to eat something to build up your strength." She whispered something to Kimberley-Waugh which made him laugh out loud.

Charles mumbled something about checking his brushes and turned to leave the dining room. He wondered if Polly would be quite so attracted to Kimberley-Waugh if she knew that he had slept with her mother. When he reached the door of the dining room, he looked back, just in time to see the Sotheby's man put his hand on Polly's hand. Polly didn't take hers away.

"Polly!" He hadn't meant to speak so loudly. Polly turned to look at him with a frown on her face.

"Yes?"

"I need to talk to you," he said. "If you can drag yourself away, perhaps you can meet me in the conservatory." He walked down the hall and out into the snow-covered garden between the main house and his workplace.

Hardly two minutes passed before Polly walked into the conservatory, a thunderous look on her face. Charles knew she was going to yell at him, so he raised a hand to stop her. "Before you set off at me," he said, "I think you should know why Lawrence Kimberley-Waugh is here."

"What do you mean?" said Polly. "He's here for the shoot."

"He's also here to steal the Van Gogh."

"What rubbish. Don't be silly."

"I am not being silly. And if you will break the habit of a lifetime and listen to me for once, you will find out why."

Polly sat down on the green chaise longue and Charles told her about his nocturnal adventure in the drawing room. When he finished, she looked up at him. "What on earth were you doing down there in the middle of the night?" she asked.

Charles explained that his power of recall, his photographic memory or whatever it was, had deserted him. Hopefully it was just a temporary thing, but as he couldn't remember the portrait in the same detail as before, he was beginning to think that the affliction might be permanent.

"I seem to have gone blind as far as that's concerned," he said. "Anyway, I took a bally big risk in order to do what you want me to do." He had hoped Polly might at least show a modicum of gratitude. Instead, she stared straight ahead and said nothing.

"There's something else as well," he began. He wasn't sure how much to tell Polly about the incident at Diana Bagshot's apartment in London. "I'm not sure how or why this happened," he said, "but Kimberley-Waugh met your mother."

"What?" said Polly. "Now you're really talking nonsense!"

"Polly, listen to me. He really did."

"How do you know?"

"Because they talked about it last night."

Polly looked at him as if he had gone completely mad. "Charles, I really think you're making all this stuff up just to put me off Larry." Hearing her use the short form of his name was enough to set off the pain in his gut again, but he was more upset that she chose not to believe him.

"I'm sorry if that's how you feel," he said. "The fact of the matter is people are going to find out about that painting of my father's. My reputation will be shot to pieces and I will probably never get any work again as a portrait painter. I'm going to finish the Duke's portrait today or tomorrow, then I'm going to get the train back to London and ... just disappear from view."

Polly stood up and walked towards him. He had decided that this was the end, and he wasn't going to let her sweet-talk him into changing his mind, but before she could say anything, there was a knock on the door. They both turned to see the Duke leaning theatrically on the door frame, wearing a long overcoat, a large black hat and wellington boots.

"Room for a little one inside?" he said, adopting what he thought was a Cockney accent. "I'm a bit early. I hope that isn't a problem."

Charles and Polly said 'No' at the same time, and Polly walked towards the door. "I was just leaving," she said.

"Oh Polly, hold on a minute," said the Duke. "I've left a few notes about the weekend on your desk. There are still one or two things to sort out."

"Don't worry, I'll get it all done."

"The main thing is the sleeping arrangements," said the Duke. "I think we were completely wrong to ask Walter to vacate his room to accommodate Lady Grimbledon."

"Really?" replied Polly.

"Yes," continued the Duke. "I think that Walter should stay where he is, and the Viscountess can have the Forest Suite."

"The one next to yours?" said Polly. "Are you sure? No one has used the Forest Suite since---"

"I'm aware of that, but perhaps Beryl can make herself useful and get it ready."

"Right," said Polly. She breathed out and shook her shoulders, as if to rid herself of one mood and adopt another, transforming into the efficient secretary.

Tarquin walked over to the chaise longue and sat down. "I must say you're doing a magnificent job with this portrait," he said. "Do you think it'll be finished by the weekend?"

"Oh, absolutely," replied Charles.

"That's marvellous. There are some wonderful people coming to the shoot. Apart from Lady Grimbledon, there's a chap called Arthur Wickham-Thynne, he's a theatre impresario and he also owns an art gallery in London."

Charles felt faint and sat down on the metal chair next to the easel. Sir Arthur Wickham-Thynne, his former employer at the Arte Moderne Gallery in Bond Street, a thoroughly decent person, very honest and straightforward for such a wealthy man, and someone who had wished Charles the best when he decided to pursue a career as a portrait painter. In different circumstances, Charles would have hoped to go back to work at the gallery, but if Wickham-Thynne found out about the fake Horace Tuck, that was unlikely to happen.

"Are you feeling all right, Walter?" asked Tarquin.

"Yes, just a little bit dizzy," said Charles. "I think I might have drunk a little bit too much last night, what with the aperitif, the wine and your excellent brandy."

"Yes, it *is* rather good, isn't it?" Tarquin took off his hat and overcoat to reveal that, like Pickles before him, he was wearing a red silk dressing gown. He was still wearing Wellington boots. "What do you think?" he said, laughing his deep laugh. "Should I keep the boots on?"

"I'm afraid I've already done the feet," said Charles. "But I can add the boots if you like."

"No, of course not! I know you've done all points north up to the throat," said Tarquin. He rummaged in the pocket of the overcoat and took out a pair of red slippers, which were adorned with pompoms like the ones that Pickles had worn. "I just want to add a touch of *réalité* to the proceedings by wearing the same things that dear old Pickles was wearing."

With some difficulty, Tarquin leaned over his bulky stomach, pulled off the boots and threw them to one side, and then struggled to get his hands close enough to his feet to actually put the slippers on. Then he leaned back and breathed in and out. When he had recovered his breath, he said, "Walter, before we start, there's something I have to tell you."

Charles stood still, his brush in his left hand.

The Duke cleared his throat nervously. "I have some bad news," he said.

"Bad news?"

"Well, I have a small problem to solve. As usual, it's about money."

Charles relaxed a little. At least the bad news wasn't that Tarquin had rumbled his disguise. The Duke lay back on the chaise longue, crossing his pom-pom slippered feet in front of him, and began to speak in a slow, measured way that Charles hadn't heard before. The message was simple: he was in serious financial difficulties and the good ship Great Park was sinking. He had made a list of possible ways to put things right, and the shooting party was the best idea he could come up with. He hoped that he could persuade one or more of his guests to invest in the property, effectively becoming co-owners. "And this is my second good idea," he continued, waving an arm in the direction of Charles's easel.

Charles was puzzled and looked round the room. "What do you mean?"

"Having my portrait painted by Walter Washbrook."

"Really?" said Charles, feeling a little alarmed. "You think the portrait will help?"

"Of course. It will add gravitas to the place. I mean, I checked around before I asked Polly to contact you, Walter. You're clearly the number one portrait painter in the country."

"Well, I don't know about that."

"Really, you're top dog! I can't wait to tell the world that I've been done by Walter Washbrook!" Tarquin laughed out loud, and Charles stared at the canvas. He had never considered the possibility that his fake Washbrook would be seen by God knows how many of Tarquin's friends and neighbours.

"There are lots of paintings around the place with more gravitas than a Washbrook," he said, trying to play down the advantage.

"Actually, there aren't," said Tarquin.

"Of course, there are. The Van Gogh, for instance."

"The Van Gogh, yes. You're right, if I could sell that, it would solve all my problems."

"So why don't you?"

Tarquin lowered his voice and looked towards the door of the conservatory to make sure that no one was eavesdropping on the conversation. "The fact is, Walter, we can't be certain it's genuine."

Charles continued to apply brush strokes to the canvas, trying to pretend that what he was hearing wasn't that important. "Really? I thought someone from Sotheby's came and vouchsafed it."

"Not exactly. What he actually said was that it was probably *started* by Van Gogh and finished by someone else. But the fact that there's no record of the painting in the list of his works is a problem. He said I could probably find a buyer in America. They have less rigorous checks there! I may just do that in the end. Anyway, the point is, you *will* get paid for your wonderful portrait. It's just that I may have to pay you in kind."

"Um..."

"Don't worry, Walter darling, I don't mean I'm going to paint a portrait of you. I owe you thirty pounds. What I propose is that in lieu of payment, I give you something from the house that's worth twice as much as that. I had all the gold and silver plate valued recently ......"

He paused for a moment and suddenly looked very sad.

"knowing that I will have to sell some of it ... or even all of it.... Anyway, I've identified one or two pieces that you could have. There's a marvellous gold chalice, it's Egyptian, hundreds of years old. I think my grandfather basically stole it from some museum in Alexandria back in the eighties. It's probably worth a hundred pounds. You might want to keep it, or if not, you'll have no trouble finding a dealer who will be more than happy to take it off your hands."

Charles continued to apply touches of paint to the portrait, thinking about the absurdity of leaving Great Park with a gold chalice in his suitcase and the Van Gogh painting in his portfolio.

"Not a plan you like the sound of?" asked Tarquin.

Charles shook his head. "No, I mean yes, of course, I understand the situation."

"The chalice is actually rather beautiful, it would look lovely on .... do you have a mantelpiece at home?" asked Tarquin.

"I think so," replied Charles.

"You think so?"

"Yes, a mantelpiece. I have two, I think." Charles felt at his most vulnerable when he was asked to give any precise details about Walter.

"You have a place in Chelsea, haven't you?" asked Tarquin.

Charles had absolutely no idea where Walter Washbrook lived. "Oh yes, indeed, lovely little place."

"I know Chelsea quite well," said Tarquin. "Where exactly do you live?"

Charles's mind went blank. Even though he spent quite a lot of time in Chelsea, he couldn't think of the name of a single street in the area. The only address he could call to mind was where his uncle Ernest lived, so that was the name he said.

"Pelham Crescent? Oh, I say!" said Tarquin, mightily impressed. "But that's South Kensington rather than Chelsea, surely. And those houses! Hardly 'a little place', Walter!"

"I used to have a little place in ... Flood Street," said Charles, finally dredging a Chelsea Street name from the recesses of his mind. "I only recently moved."

"Pelham Crescent, well, well, well ...." Tarquin looked into the distance, a smile spreading across his face. "I do love that part of London. I remember going to a party in Pelham Crescent once... it was all a bit wild and woolly down there in those days. I'm trying to remember the name of the chap who threw the party. Goodfellow, Goodhugh, something like that."

"Goodgame," said Charles. Behind his dark glasses, he closed his eyes, astonished that he had said the name out loud.

"That's right!" exclaimed Tarquin. "Ernest Goodgame! Do you know him?"

"I know *of* him," said Charles. "I believe he lives somewhere nearby."

Tarquin's tone became more serious. "I'd be a bit careful about getting to know Ernest Goodgame too well," he said. "I don't know what he gets up to these days, but back in the twenties, he had a bit of a reputation."

"I'll make sure I steer well clear of him then." Charles wished for all the world that Tarquin would change the subject, or maybe stop talking altogether and let him get on with finishing the portrait. Instead, the conversation became even more stressful as Tarquin finally mentioned Bernard Delgado, the man he thought was their mutual friend. He asked about their time at school together, questions that Charles batted away with bland answers, even suggesting that he and Delgado weren't really that friendly with each other.

"Bernard did say something that puzzled me a bit," said Tarquin. "He said how much he liked your pony-tail. I told him you didn't have one, but he insisted that you had."

Like a perfect googly that catches the batsman in a sensitive part of his anatomy. the remark made Charles's knees buckle, but he remained silent, continuing to paint.

"Did you use to have one?"

"Have what?"

"A pony-tail. Bernard said you kept your hair tied back. Awfully bohemian, I must say. Why did you decide to get rid of it?"

"Why did I decide to get rid of the pony-tail?"

"Yes."

"It was .... getting in my way when I was working."

"What? How would a pony-tail get in the way of you painting something?"

Charles didn't answer, hoping that Tarquin would think he was a bit deaf.

"I mean, unless the wind blew it in your face, or something, I can't see how----"

"Oh, for heaven's SAKE!" Charles jumped up and down twice, let out a howl of anguish, and threw his paintbrush to the floor, where it clacked as it bounced off the tiles.

Tarquin stopped speaking. There was a moment's silence and then he slowly finished his sentence. "... how that would affect your ability to paint. Walter, are you feeling all right?"

Charles decided enough was enough. It was too tiring, too stressful, too bloody impossible to stay in character as Walter Washbrook, and anyway all motivation to do so had vanished. He was doomed, ruined. Right now, he felt not the slightest inclination to continue with the whole charade.

"Tarquin," he said, "it's time to come clean."

"I'm sorry?"

Charles took off his dark glasses and put them down on the metal chair, then he pulled off the grey wig and threw it dramatically across the conservatory. It hit the tall lamp next to the chaise longue and fell into Tarquin's lap, where it lay, looking like luxuriant pubic hair. Tarquin looked at his groin area, then at Charles. "Can you please explain what's going on?" he asked.

Charles would have been happy to come clean about everything, but he knew he could land Polly in the soup. If she lost her job, she would never speak to him again. And it would be madness to say that they were planning to steal the painting, an admission that could lead to another visit from the boys in blue at Cheltenham Police Station. What he really wanted to do was think of an explanation for his behaviour that would avoid incriminating his stepsister but would also suggest there was something not entirely kosher about Lawrence Kimberley-Waugh.

"I'm not Walter Washbrook," he said.

"Who are you?" asked Tarquin.

"My name ----"

"Charles! What on earth are you doing here?" Polly was standing at the door. "And why are you wearing a false beard? And where's Walter?"

"This is Walter," said Tarquin. "Or rather this *was* Walter." He looked puzzled for a moment. "Who's Charles?"

Polly stared at Charles. "This is my stepbrother Charles Goodgame," she said.

"Goodgame? Any relation to ---?"

"Charles, have you been masquerading as Walter Washbrook all along? I simply don't believe it."

"Can someone please tell me what's going on?" asked Tarquin. He stood up to try to gain some authority, adjusting his pink silk dressing gown. The grey wig fell from his groin and landed on one of his pom-pom slippers.

As requested, Polly explained everything, and very convincing she was, too. When Tarquin said he wanted to be painted by Walter Washbrook, she declared, she contacted the only person she knew in the art world, her stepbrother Charles Goodgame. "The man you see before you now," she said, pointing at Charles as if he were a defendant in a courtroom. "He told me that he would contact Mister Washbrook and arrange for him to visit Great Park. And all the time," she continued, "he was planning this act of gross deceit." She stopped speaking, as if she were ending the opening statement for the prosecution at Charles's trial.

"Mister Goodgame, is this true?" asked Tarquin.

Charles looked at Polly. An unspoken message passed between them. This version of the story had the advantage of containing no hint of criminal intent, at least not involving the Van Gogh.

"Yes," said Charles. Polly's shoulders relaxed. "Actually, not quite," he added. "I talked to my old chum Walter and he said he was too busy and ... well, because he's a big fan of my work ..." Charles decided there was no reason to go down without a fight, "... he suggested that I might offer to do it. But as Polly had already told me that you didn't like that idea, Walter and I came up with this as ... as the next best solution."

There was a moment of silence as the three of them looked at each other. Then Tarquin burst out laughing. He shook with laughter, unable to control his merriment. He tried to talk, but the laughter made it almost impossible to get the words out. "Oh Walter, HA! HA! HA! or Charles, or whatever your HA! HA! HA! name is, that's the most HA! HA! HA! most amusing thing HA! HA! HA! I've ever heard in my...." Tarquin couldn't finish the sentence. Laughing made his bulky body shake under the pink dressing gown. He sat back down on the chaise longue. Polly and Charles waited for the laughter to subside, which it did briefly before a new wave washed over his body.

Then Polly started to laugh, which for Charles made her even more beautiful. For a moment, it was as if the cares of the world had been lifted from her shoulders.

Tarquin stopped for a moment and looked at Charles. "And that wig," he said. "It looked so ridiculous on you!" The two of them set off laughing again. Polly was shaking so much she could hardly stand, so she sat down next to the Duke. They leaned against each other and rocked up and down simultaneously.

"I'm glad you can both see the funny side of it," said Charles. "I realise that it was a bad decision to agree to Walter's idea."

Tarquin stopped laughing out loud, but continued to rock silently up and down, a large smile on his face. "This is more fun that I can remember having since I inherited Great Park," he said. "The fact is," he continued, "you've done an absolutely wonderful portrait of me."

"Thank you," said Charles.

"At least of my body." And he started laughing again.

"Tarquin, if you don't like it, I can change it," said Charles.

"Noooo! Not at all! I love it!" Tarquin wiped his eyes and took a deep breath. "I'm so sorry, I really needed that laugh. Things have been so difficult recently." He took Polly's hand. Charles remembered shaking hands with Tarquin on Monday evening, when he thought his hand was being eaten by a toothless lizard.

"Well, this is a pretty pass," said the Duke. "What are we going to do about it?"

"I haven't any idea," said Charles.

"Well, I do..." said Tarquin. He paused. "Why don't we just continue as if nothing had happened?"

There was a silence while everyone thought about this. Polly was the first to speak. "You mean ... Charles just puts his wig back on and continues to be Walter?"

"Yes," said Tarquin. "Or we can make a phone call to Cheltenham Police Station and ask that nice Sergeant Conway to pay us another visit. What do you think?"

Charles and Polly looked at each other.

"I'm putting two and two together here, Walter ... I mean Charles," said Tarquin. "Now that I can see the real colour of your hair, I'm guessing that you..." He looked from Charles to Polly. "... and you, Polly, were the two people responsible for the assault on the Stanford Saint Mary stationmaster."

Like defendants facing charges in court, Charles and Polly opted to remain silent.

"So, what would you like to do, Charles? It's your call."

Chapter 20
Ooh, Horace! There's news!
Thursday, Hunstanton, Norfolk - cold, persistent snow
showers

Thursday dawned and Horace woke up on the mattress in the corner of his studio in Barkston Gardens. He was as usual feeling weighed down by worry. If he was lying on his stomach, it felt as if there was a rock on his back and if he was lying on his back, there was an even bigger rock on his chest. He sat up, rubbed his eyes and tried to work out what was upsetting him today. Ah yes. He had to travel to Hunstanton and start the process of selling the house at 24 Cliff Terrace.

He packed a few clothes and a toothbrush in a small travel bag and walked out onto Earl's Court Road. After spending one and fourpence on breakfast at the Corrillo Café, he walked down to Old Brompton Road and took a number 30 bus to Saint Pancras Station, where he boarded a train to Kings Lynn. There he changed onto the local service to Hunstanton, a set of rusting rolling stock that had been grinding back and forth along the Norfolk coast since the turn of the century.

On this cold February day, the train had already trundled up from Downham Market, stopping at Watlington and Setchley. After Kings Lynn, it was scheduled to wheeze slowly through South Wootton, North Wootton, Ingoldisthorpe, Snettisham, Dersingham and Heacham before reaching its, and Horace's, destination of Hunstanton. It would also stop at Wolferton, but anyone wanting to get off there would need a very good reason to do so because it was the nearest station to Sandringham, and the recently crowned King George was in residence. Those charged with his safety didn't want random oiks wandering up to the estate to gawk over the wall or generally make the area untidy. To discourage such behaviour, there was always a police presence on the platform at Wolferton, and anyone who couldn't prove they actually lived in the village was pushed back onto the train and given Anglo-Saxon instructions to go elsewhere.

Horace sat by the left-hand window of the compartment and caught an occasional glimpse of the metallic grey sea as the train crawled between towns. It was much colder than in London, and large snowflakes were swirling past the window.

He had tried to telephone his housekeeper Mrs Normington to warn her about his visit, but he couldn't get through. As a result, when he got off the train at Hunstanton and walked the half mile to the house, she was still unaware of his imminent arrival, and he was wondering how to explain that he was planning to throw her out onto the street.

It was already dark when he emerged from the little station, snow was falling heavily, and gusts of wind whipped up mini-tornadoes. Holding the lapels of his coat over his throat for warmth and with his head bent into the wind, Horace walked briskly along Cliff Parade. He passed Saint Edmund's Church, where the town had mourned the passing of his first wife Martha, then the Wash and Tope public house, where many pints of beer had been drunk by the menfolk of the village after the funeral. A few hundred yards past the pub, he turned into Cliff Terrace. When he reached number 24, he stood for a moment in front of the simple building that had been his home for the past quarter century, but which must now be sold to.... to do what?

Why did he have to sell the house? No other reason than to finance the lifestyle of his spendthrift wife. That was why.

Marrying Leonora had been a monumental mistake, and from the moment she found out there was no money in the bank, she dropped all pretence of being interested in their relationship. However, as far as Horace was concerned, marriage brought responsibilities and one couldn't allow one's wife to be destitute. No, instead one had to throw one's utterly reliable housekeeper to the wolves.

He walked up the short path to the front door. The door wasn't locked, and he opened it without knocking and walked in. Mrs Normington was asleep in an armchair in front of a log fire, with a large cat curled up on her lap. As far as Horace was aware, the house didn't have a resident cat, but his housekeeper was the kind of person who would give shelter to any waif or stray, human or otherwise, that pressed his, her or its nose against her window.

There was a bucket of logs next to the fireplace, so Horace quietly picked one up and threw it onto the fire. It was just his luck that instead of nestling on the fire, it hit the one log that was still burning, which bounced off onto his foot and rolled onto the rug, causing him to let out a small yelp of alarm. The cat woke up and leapt off the housekeeper's lap, digging its claws into her knees as it did so. Mrs Normington let out a high-pitched screech and then screamed even louder when she saw the shadow of someone standing in front of her.

"Mrs Normington, don't worry, it's only me," said Horace.

The housekeeper blinked a few times, then stood up. "Mr Goodgame!" she said, in a voice that could have indicated pleasure, shock or despair, and she enveloped him in a warm embrace. She had never done this before, so he was rather taken aback, but he was also happy that she seemed to be pleased to see him. He disentangled himself from her when a smell alerted him to the fact that the rug was on fire.

"Oooh, Horace! There's news!" she said, as Horace jumped up and down to put out the flames.

Mrs Normington was not one to waste time on formalities and rarely used expressions like "How are you?" or "How was your journey?". Once they had prevented the house from burning down, she proceeded to tell him about the recent tragic event that had rocked the town to its foundations. And it was this: Albert Looney the postmaster had dropped down dead two days before. One minute he was weighing the parcel of books Mabel Pickersgill was sending to her sister in Great Yarmouth, the next he was slumped over the weighing machine, dead of a heart attack at 53!

Mrs Normington was unable to remain still as she related the shocking news. The story of Albert Looney's demise took her and Horace from the living room into the kitchen, where she switched on the light and put the kettle on the stove. By the time she finished the story, four teaspoons of tea had been placed in a large chipped white teapot, steaming water poured into it, and the two of them were sitting at the kitchen table waiting for the tea to brew.

Horace had spent most of the time making short noises of interjection, "Ooohs" and "Aahs" and the occasional "Well I never!", if Mrs Normington paused for breath.

"The thing that everyone's asking," she continued, opening and closing cupboards in a hunt for biscuits to go with the tea, "is who's going to take over as postmaster? Albert's been in the job since his father died, also of a heart attack, by the way. Albert never married, so there are no more Looneys to take on the responsibility." She paused to allow the significance of this to sink in. "The postmaster at Hunstanton has *always* been a Looney, Mister Goodgame, so what's going to happen now?"

"Search me," said Horace. The Post Office at Hunstanton was a place he had always taken for granted, as unchanging as the red cliffs that faced the sea near the centre of the town. He used to go there the third week of every month to cash his Krumnagel's Bank cheque for thirty pounds, and Albert Looney himself was always the one handing over the money.

The building which housed the Post Office was a fine piece of architecture, still with its original Victorian wooden porch intact. Back in 1934, Horace had asked Albert if he could paint a picture of the exterior. Albert answered with a grunt, which could have meant yes or no, but as it was accompanied by a downward movement of the head, Horace took it as a yes. The postmaster had come out into the street to look at the painting while Horace was working on it and asked if he could buy it. Horace was so unused to people wanting to pay money for his paintings that he told Albert that he could have it for nothing. The next time he went in to cash his cheque, the painting was hanging behind the counter. With the banknotes, Albert passed him five postage stamps, which he did thereafter every time Horace came in for his money.

A generous man, Albert Looney. He lived alone above the shop and kept chickens in the large garden at the back, where he had a dog tied up to discourage foxes. Horace had never seen the dog, but the monthly financial transaction was often accompanied by prolonged barking from the back of the building.

As if she was reading Horace's mind, Mrs Normington started talking about Albert's dog, which was now without an owner. "It's a lovely little thing called Goliath," she said. "I was a bit worried about him, so I brought him over here and tied him up in the back garden. I hope you don't mind."

The animal in question clearly sensed that he was being discussed and started barking ferociously at the back of the house. Horace picked up his mug of tea and walked over to look through the kitchen window. He could see the dog straining at its leash, trying to free itself from a hook that was attached to the wall. Even in the half-light and through the falling snow, it was clear that Mrs Normington was not being entirely accurate when she described the dog as a 'lovely little thing'. It was a long-haired black beast the size of a small horse, whose barking became even more frantic when it saw Horace looking out of the window.

"He's a sweetheart, really," said Mrs Normington. She came to join Horace at the window and as soon as it saw her, the dog stopped barking and started making a high-pitched mewling sound, at the same time banging its huge tail against an old dustbin next to the kitchen door. It sounded like the percussion section of a small orchestra. The housekeeper shook her head from side to side and made a noise that sounded like "awpawpawpaw!" The dog fell silent and sat down next to the dustbin. "Shall I let him in?" she asked.

"NOOOO!" said Horace, terrified of meeting the animal face to face. "Not just yet," he added, more calmly.

What a woman Mrs Normington was, he thought. As well as being a wonderful cook and housekeeper, she could turn the Hound of the Baskervilles into an obedient lapdog. Even so, he was going to have to tell her the bad news about the house, and there was no point in delaying.

He went back and sat at the kitchen table. "Mrs Normington," he began. "Do come and sit down. There's something we have to talk about."

The housekeeper was still making awpawpawpaw noises at the dog and didn't hear what Horace said.

"Mrs Normington!" he said. His louder voice surprised them both. The housekeeper looked at him with raised eyebrows, said a final awpawpaw to the dog, and walked across to the table. She sat down, picked up her mug of tea and drank it dry. She licked her lips and smiled. Horace took a deep breath and was about to speak, but she started first.

"I've always thought it would be nice to run the Post Office," she said. "There are always people coming in and out, and it's where you hear all the gossip."

"Mrs Normington..."

"Trouble is, I expect you have to be able to read and write, and I can't."

"Really? You can't read and write?"

"Well, I can read a bit. And I can sign my name and write numbers."

"I'm sorry, I never knew."

"Oh, there's nothing to be sorry about," she said. "No one in my family ever learned to read and write. Mister

Normington, God rest his soul, he wasn't much better, but we muddled through."

Horace had been home for half an hour, and he still hadn't raised the delicate subject of the sale of the house. He put his hands over his face, rubbed his forehead vigorously and began talking. "Mrs Normington, I'm going to have to ask you to sit down ..." he started.

"I *am* sitting down," she pointed out. He took his hands down from his face and saw that it was true.

"Thank you," he continued. "And I'm going to have to ask you to listen, not speak and not get up to do anything." The dog started barking again, and the housekeeper started to get out of her seat. "Please, I'll ask you again, don't get up, just sit still and listen. I have something very important to say."

"I'm all ears," she said, folding her arms and leaning back on her chair.

"Do you remember that I get a monthly cheque in the post?" he said. "From the bank where my trust fund is managed?"

"Yes of course," said Mrs Normington. "From that fancy bank in London. What's it called? Krumblies or something, isn't it?"

"Krumnagels," said Horace. "Well, the fact is ... there will be no more cheques."

The smile disappeared from Mrs Normington's face, and her cheeks reddened. "Oh, that isn't very nice of them," she said. She looked ready to have it out with whoever was responsible for this terrible turn of events, if necessary, get a train to London and bang some banking heads together.

Horace tried to explain. "No, they had no choice. There's no money left in the trust fund. Someone's been making fraudulent withdrawals."

"Who has?" asked Mrs Normington. "I'd like to have a word with the person who's been doing that!"

Horace wasn't sure how to continue. Mrs Normington was the same age as his first wife, and they had known each other since they were children, but whenever Martha's name came up in conversation, the housekeeper always went icily quiet. She kept her thoughts to herself and never once said anything, out of respect for the dead. But Horace could tell there was no love lost between the two women. "It would appear that the person who was withdrawing the money was someone pretending to be ... my late wife Martha."

For the first time in her adult life, Mrs Normington was rendered completely speechless. Outside, the dog stopped barking, as if it realised the importance of the moment. The housekeeper got up and walked silently to the kitchen sink and poured the remainder of her tea down the plughole. She rinsed the cup and put it on the counter next to the sink, then walked to the kitchen door. Horace jumped out of his seat when she opened it, alarmed that the massive dog might run in and leap on him, but she quickly closed the door behind her.

It was snowing heavily, and his housekeeper wasn't wearing a coat. Horace waited for a while, then went to the window and tapped on it. Mrs Normington came and opened the door briefly and told him she needed a few moments to herself. He flinched when the door opened, expecting the dog to appear and bite a portion off his leg, but he nodded and went back and sat down at the table.

A few minutes later, she reappeared at the back door. When Goliath realised he was being abandoned, he started barking, but this time just a look from the housekeeper was enough to quieten him down. She sat down opposite Horace and began to speak.

"She's still alive, isn't she?" she said. Horace admitted that this was a possibility. "I never liked that woman," she said. "Of course, you didn't know her before her mother died, and she moved to live with her sister, but she was always a wrong 'un."

Horace looked at her in astonishment. "A wrong 'un?" he repeated. "What on earth do you mean?"

Mrs Normington looked at him for a moment before saying anything else. "Martha Donkin was trouble from the moment she was born," she said. "It was just as well she left Hunstanton when she did because there were people who would have liked to throw her out of town, including me."

"Why? What did she do?"

"How long have you got?" said the housekeeper. Now that she had the opportunity, she allowed herself to give vent to the deep anger she felt about a woman who, amongst other things, had tried to steal her Norman from her when they were courting. Martha Donkin had even written letters to him when he was away working on a farm in Lincolnshire. It was only when the future Mrs Normington went to the Donkin house and told Martha's mother that she would tear her daughter limb from limb if she didn't stop trying it on that the attempts to prise him away ended.

"I never believed that she drowned," she went on. "And when I saw the smirk on Emily Roebuck's face at the funeral, I knew they were up to something."

Horace was completely mystified by the direction of the conversation. "Emily Roebuck? My son's nanny?" he asked. "What has she got to do with anything?"

"They were thick as thieves, those two, ever since they were little." Mrs Normington was convinced that Martha Donkin had been in cahoots with Emily Roebuck for

246

years, probably hatching out the plan that would eventually lead to her pretending to drown in order to drain Horace's trust fund.

Horace tried his best to defend his first wife's reputation, but without much conviction. "I'm sure they weren't planning it for years," he said. "Maybe it ... just occurred to them one day."

The more he thought about it, however, the more Mrs Normington's words made sense. He remembered the conversations he had with Martha all those years ago when they were drinking tea after church. How she suddenly brightened up when she discovered he had a monthly income from a trust fund. She even asked him what he had to do if he needed more money. Could he take more out of the bank than the monthly allowance? Oh yes, Horace answered. He sighed as he remembered telling her he could authorise other people to take money out just by writing a letter to the bank.

"I suppose you're right," he said. "Anyway, the point is, I have no money and I also have a wife who ..." He searched for the least derogatory way of saying what he wanted to say. "... I have a wife who likes the good things in life. And my only asset is ... this house."

They stared at each other across the table. Without needing to hear the words spoken, she knew that this meant the house had to be sold and she would find herself homeless again.

"Well, if you have to sell the house, you have to sell the house," she said.

She saw that he was on the verge of tears, so she stood up and walked round the table and pulled him gently out of his chair until they were standing face to face.

"Horace," she said.

"Yes .... Edna?" he said. He had never used her first name before.

"Horace, these things happen for a reason," she said. "The fact that you have come home today to tell me this ... on this day of all days .... it seems it was written in the stars. It's clear what you have to do."

Horace stared at her. He noticed what warm friendly eyes she had, and what a lovely comforting smile. "You mean ..." he started.

"Yes," she said.

".... I should divorce Leonora and marry you?" He couldn't believe that he had heard himself say that.

Mrs Normington pulled away slightly, looking puzzled.

"No," she said. "You should become the new Hunstanton postmaster."

Chapter 21
This is a hospital, not a night club!

Thursday, Charing Cross Hospital London - storm clouds gathering

Godfrey Krumnagel woke at five o'clock in the morning and looked at his bandaged foot, which was in a sling attached to a pulley above his hospital bed. His throat felt as dry as burnt toast, so he pulled the cord to summon a nurse. When she arrived, he asked her if there was any chance of a gin and tonic or failing that, a cup of strong tea with plenty of sugar.

This wasn't his first call for help, but this time a tall, well-built Irish nurse responded. "Mr Krumnagel! This is a hospital, not a nightclub!" she said, in an unnecessarily aggressive manner, Godfrey thought. "We don't serve alcohol. And you will get a cup of tea when the morning staff take over."

"What time will that be?" asked Godfrey.

"Eight o'clock," replied the nurse. "Three hours from now."

"I'm afraid I can't wait that long," he said. "If you show me where the kettle is, I'll make some tea myself." He tried to get out of bed but fell headfirst onto the floor, his foot remaining in the sling. His scream of pain as he hit the floor woke his roommate Constable Eric Percival, who had injuries to hand and ear suffered when Godfrey fired his shotgun the day before in Peckham.

Inspector Sparrow had given orders that the bank manager should have a day and night guard at the hospital. The officer currently assigned to the task was Constable Melvyn Duddle, the other half of the battering ram team from the previous day's raid on the flat in

Peckham. He hadn't slept since the incident and was not feeling well disposed to the man he had to keep an eye on. He stumbled into the room and the nurse asked him to help her get Godfrey back into bed. She put his foot back in the sling and asked: "Do you have any handcuffs?"

The constable was about to tell her that members of the public were not supposed to use restraining equipment of any kind when Godfrey interrupted. "You want handcuffs? I have some in my jacket. Over there in the cupboard."

The nurse couldn't believe her luck. She went to the cupboard and took the handcuffs out of his pocket.

"What do you want them for?" asked Duddle.

She ignored his question. "How do these things work?" she asked.

"Now, just listen to me. I don't think ---"

"Oh do shut up."

The rings on both sides of the handcuffs were open, so she closed one on the metal frame of the bed. Then she grabbed Godfrey by the wrist and was about to attach the other ring to him when Duddle intervened.

"Hold off, you can't do that!" he said and started grappling with her. In the ensuing struggle, he managed to get himself handcuffed to Godfrey's bed.

"Well, you've only got yourself to blame for that," said the nurse. She put a chair next to the bed so that he could sit down. "Just whack him with your free hand if he tries to pull the cord again." With that, she left the room.

Duddle shook his head in disbelief and looked at Godfrey. "Do you have the key to these cuffs?" he asked.

"I'm afraid I don't," replied Godfrey.

"Oh for Christ's sake! Where is it?"

"I believe it's in the safe at my bank. Which hospital is this?"

"Charing Cross."

"Ah well, in that case you're in luck. My bank is just round the corner in the Strand. If you wait until eight o'clock, you'll be able to nip over there and get the key when the caretaker chappie opens up."

"Nip over there and get the key?? And how do you propose I do that? Drag you in the bed behind me?"

Godfrey ignored this very reasonable objection to his plan and added: "And while you're out, could you pop into the Strand Cuppa Café and get me a cup of tea and a bacon roll?"

The previous day, when Godfrey was hit in the stomach by the battering ram, he accidentally pulled the trigger of his shotgun, firing a cartridge straight at his foot. The cartridge burst into pieces, one of which pierced the brown leather shoe he was wearing and blasted a hole in his middle toe. As he hit the floor, he pulled the trigger again, discharging the second cartridge. Luckily, it hit the battering ram rather than the men holding it, but from there, part of it ricocheted into the hand of Constable Percival, the man now lying next to him in the hospital, and another fragment of the cartridge tore off a portion of the officer's ear. The last thing Godfrey thought before he passed out was the remarkable amount of blood that gushes out when someone's ear is blown off.

With the three bodies rolling around on the floor and the injured police officer screaming and swearing, Inspector Sparrow turned to Burgess for help, but the assistant manager fainted, collapsing on the floor behind the front door of the flat. Sparrow ran out onto the walkway and called down to Bert Branch the chauffeur, who was still guarding the Bentley.

Bert looked up at the third floor of the tenement block. He had heard the shots and feared the worst - that his boss Godfrey Krumnagel was lying dead, and he was out of a job.

Rain was lashing down, and thunderclaps sounded overhead. Sparrow called down to Bert to ask him where the nearest telephone box was. Bert shouted back that there was one round the corner in the Old Kent Road.

"GO AND DIAL 999!" yelled Sparrow.

"GO AND DO WHAT?" Bert shouted back.

"DIAL 999!"

"999?"

"YES!"

"WHAT'S 999?"

Sparrow ran down the concrete steps of the stairwell and came face to face with Bert. "You don't know what 999 is?" he asked.

"No," replied Bert.

"It's the new emergency number that can be called free of charge from any public call box."

"Right," said Bert. "By the way, is Mr Krumnagel still alive?"

"I HAVE NO IDEA!" shouted Sparrow. He calmed down a little before continuing. "I don't know," he said, more quietly. "We need to get an ambulance and some medical people here as soon as possible. That's why you need to dial 999."

"I haven't got any pennies," said Bert.

Sparrow took a deep breath to prevent him from getting even more angry than he already was. "You weren't listening," he said. "I told you it's free of charge. You just pick up the phone, dial 999 and you will be

252

connected to an operator. SO BLOODY WELL DO WHAT I ASKED YOU TO DO!"

Bert ran around the corner into the Old Kent Road and went into a telephone box. He explained the situation, and an ambulance was despatched to Emsworth Dwellings.

When Inspector Sparrow went back up the stairwell and into flat number 45, Godfrey was lying motionless in the kitchen and Constable Percival was sitting with his back against the kitchen door. The side of his head was covered with blood, and he had a handkerchief wrapped round his hand. Constable Duddle was kneeling next to him, dipping a dishcloth into a pan of hot water and dabbing Percival's ear with it. No one was speaking.

"Is he badly injured?" Sparrow was speaking to Duddle but it was Percival who replied. "I can hear what you're saying, sir," he said.

"Which is a miracle," said Duddle. "Half your ear is missing."

Godfrey groaned and sat up. Inspector Sparrow leaned down to talk to him. "Are you Godfrey Krumnagel?" he asked.

"Yes," replied Godfrey. "Who are you?"

Inspector Sparrow gave his name.

"Ah, Skylark, good of you to show up," said Godfrey. "I'm afraid our birds have flown."

"Never mind 'our birds have flown'," said the inspector. "I'm arresting you for attempted murder."

Godfrey looked around to see if there were any victims of attempted murder nearby. "Don't be ridiculous," he said. "These chaps attacked me with that great big metal thing, so I have every intention of getting you all arrested for attempting to murder *me*. But I won't press charges if someone will do something about my foot. I appear to be bleeding to death."

At that moment, two white-coated men carrying a stretcher ran into the flat. They quickly assessed the situation, put Godfrey on the stretcher, and asked Duddle to help his colleague down the stairs. The ambulance set off to Charing Cross Hospital, the nearest place where there were staff who could deal with gunshot wounds. When they arrived, both men were taken into the operating theatre, where what remained of Percival's ear was sewn up and several bits of cartridge were removed from his hand. Godfrey had a similar operation on his foot and the top part of his middle toe was removed.

When Inspector Sparrow arrived at the hospital at eight o'clock on Thursday morning, he was surprised to find both police officers in the room with the bank manager. Percival was sitting in one bed and Duddle was hand-cuffed to the other. All three men were chatting and drinking tea and the atmosphere seemed quite convivial. Godfrey was in the middle of explaining to the two police officers the importance of opening a bank account.

Sparrow's arrival silenced the room. Both constables attempted to salute the inspector. Percival yowled with pain as his bandaged hand hit his forehead, and Duddle's salute was scuppered because of the handcuffs.

"What on earth is going on?" asked the inspector.

"The nurse cuffed me to the bed," Duddle explained.

"She did WHAT?" asked Sparrow. He looked at the handcuffs. "These are not regulation issue," he said. "Where did they come from?"

"They're mine," said Godfrey.

"Give me the key," said Sparrow. "Immediately."

"Ah, well, there's the problem," said Godfrey. "The key is currently at the bank, just round the corner from here, in fact. It's in my assistant manager's office. If you pop over there, you'll be able to get it. And if you don't mind, could you get me a bacon roll on the way back?"

Sparrow ignored this request. "Mr Krumnagel," he said. "The two women you were so keen for us to arrest ... we have them in custody."

Godfrey sat up sharply when he heard this, spilling his tea on the hospital blanket. "That's marvellous news," he said. "Are you sure it's them?"

"Absolutely positive."

Sparrow was rather proud of the part he had played in the arrest, which had been a combination of luck and quick thinking. As soon as the ambulance arrived at Emsworth Dwellings, Sparrow had run downstairs to seek out the caretaker of the tenement block, a thin old man who spent his days listening to the radio in a narrow little space in the basement area. The man named the two women in number 45 as Martha Donkin and Emily Roebuck. He told Sparrow that he had seen them leaving the building just a few minutes before. From where he sat, he was able to see the bus stop in the Old Kent Road, and he told the inspector that the two women had waited several minutes before catching a 172 bus in the direction of Waterloo Station. They were dressed almost identically, wearing grey coats and black hats, and they were each carrying a suitcase, one black, the other sky blue. Sparrow worked out that if they travelled all the way to the station, he could get there in his car before the bus arrived. He ran into Asylum Road, jumped into the police car and drove off in the direction of Waterloo, some three miles away.

On the way, he overtook three number 172 buses and just hoped that the women were on one of them. When he reached Waterloo Station, he jumped out of the car and blew his whistle. He was very relieved when two police officers came running out of the station towards him. Standing with his back to the bus stop, he explained the situation and didn't see that a number 172 had just stopped behind him. "... and the two women are both wearing grey coats and black hats, and they're carrying suitcases ---"

"Do you mean those two, sir?" said one of the police officers. Sparrow turned and found himself face to face with the two suspects.

The women behaved very differently when they saw the three officers. Martha Donkin put her suitcase on the ground and stood still, but Emily Roebuck ran out into the street, where she was nearly run over by a van belonging to the Fotheringay's Sausages company.

One of the officers ran after her and struggled with her in the middle of the road, which caused a large number of motorists to toot their horn. He eventually brought her back to the pavement, and when both women had been placed in the back of the police car, Sparrow opened the two suitcases. One was full of clothes, but the other contained banknotes. Sparrow ordered one of the officers help him take the two women to Scotland Yard, where they were placed in a cell while the money was counted. There was nearly five thousand pounds in the suitcase.

Godfrey was delighted to hear this. "Old Goodgame will be pleased," he said.

"Goodgame?" repeated Sparrow. "Who's Goodgame?"

For the first time, Godfrey was able to explain the full story of the fraud that the two women had been perpetrating. "Keep that money safe," he said. "I know who it belongs to, and I'm very much looking forward to telling him that we have it back."

*****

Roebuck and Donkin were kept in custody at New Scotland Yard for two days, during which time Sparrow tried without success to get them to confess to theft and fraud. Neither uttered a word during their interrogation. Even when they were offered tea, they merely nodded their heads to indicate that they would like some. Sparrow also made sure that they were given very little to eat, but even that failed to make them talk, with the result that after forty-eight hours, the police had to release them. On Friday morning, they were free to go. Well done, the Habeas Corpus Act of 1679!

When they were given the suitcase containing their clothes, they rather brazenly asked for the other one to be returned as well. Inspector Sparrow said that would not be possible until they could establish who the money belonged to. He told them they were welcome to return to the station to find out, any time they chose. The two women laughed and walked out of the station.

For the next hour, they sat in Gordon's Wine Bar in Villiers Street where, to the annoyance of the otherwise male clientele, they laughed loudly and drank glasses of gin followed by pints of cider. They then crossed Westminster Bridge and walked down Southwark Street to Waterloo Station, where they collected another suitcase from the Left Luggage Office. They then took a bus to King's Cross and caught a train to King's Lynn in

Norfolk. At the Duke's Head Hotel, they booked a twin room which overlooked the marketplace and opened their newly-acquired piece of luggage, which contained another thousand pounds of Horace's money. Then they went downstairs to the bar and started making plans to find a local widower to embezzle.

Chapter 22
Why should I invest in a dump like this?

Friday, Great Park - heavy snow falling all day

It was the weekend of the Great Park shooting party and the staff were doing their best to make the old place look as good as a crumbling late nineteenth-century neo-Gothic pile could, at least on the inside. The woodwork was gleaming, the silver was shining, and the carpets had all been taken out into the courtyard and beaten to within an inch of their lives. The guest rooms looked immaculate, with clean sheets on the beds and fluffy towels in all the bathrooms. There wasn't much the staff could do to improve the dilapidated look of the exterior, with its unwashed stonework, warped window frames and loose gutters. The windows on the ground floor were all sparkling, but the absence of a safe ladder meant that some of the upstairs windows weren't.

The shooting party had been organised to try to help the Burfaughtonleigh family continue the life of privilege and comfort that they had grown accustomed to for nearly four centuries, since 1544 in fact, when Henry the Eighth bestowed the original dukedom on Hubertus Woolnough. Hubertus was an unpleasant character, a domineering husband and father, and a landowner who treated his tenant farmers appallingly. Apparently, he was no oil painting either, described in the 1556 folio *Ye Peeres of Ye Realme* as 'in stature shorte, notte hansome of looke, and mightily grosse of gyrthe', but he had deep pockets, and the Dukedom was a reward for his financial assistance to the King in the war against France. Henry also gave Hubertus a sizeable chunk of Gloucestershire and the new Duke commissioned the building of Woolnough Hall near the village of Burfaughtonleigh.

The grand house was an architectural eyesore of the highest order, and it appeared to be haunted from the moment it was completed. Visitors unfortunate enough to spend the night there saw or heard the ghosts of a whole coven of cackling witches. Over the centuries, there were several mysterious deaths. Thankfully, Woolnough Hall burnt down in 1864 and the family moved away from the bewitched site to Great Park, which was built several miles away near Stanford Saint Mary. The new house was an improvement on the old residence insofar as it was described as 'dull, with hardly any redeeming features'.

At least Great Park was still standing but funds were needed, and they were needed soon, before the old place crumbled and fell to the ground.

Tarquin instructed Polly to invite every titled person within a fifty-mile radius and she got a positive response from the usual suspects. Lords Winchcome, Nailsmith and Longhope and their respective spouses, plus the Duke of Tewksbury and his close friend Marcus Fitzwilliam, all said they would attend. The Dowager Lady Wootton said she would come too, and would no doubt turn up with her muscular gamekeeper Dogwood. But these were not people Tarquin could lean on for funds. The upkeep of grand houses was a struggle for most of their owners, but it would have been too humiliating to admit to his neighbours that he was on the verge of bankruptcy, and already halfway through selling off the family silver.

Polly also sent out invitations to all the rich and influential people Tarquin knew, or had at least met, in the hope of persuading them to turn up and hopefully cough up some funds. At a pinch, there was room for about twenty guests at Great Park, so two dozen people were invited and offered accommodation for the weekend. Who could refuse an invitation like that?

As it turned out, almost everyone. Tarquin was bitterly disappointed by the response. Theatre impresario Bernard Delgado was unable to attend, although he did accept an invitation to lunch earlier in the week, when he tried to meet his old school friend Walter Washbrook. However, Delgado was not the slightest bit interested in providing funds for Great Park. As he put it quite bluntly when Tarquin raised the matter: "Why should I invest in a dump like this? It's falling to bits!"

Tarquin was more successful in persuading another entrepreneur to attend, someone who also included theatrical productions in his investments. He had only met Sir Arthur Wickham-Thynne once but was extremely impressed by his business acumen and the pots of money he clearly made from his portfolio, which also included newspapers and art galleries. Sir Arthur had a very pushy wife, whose name Tarquin couldn't remember, and he wasn't looking forward to meeting her again, but as long as he could spend some time trying to prise money out of her husband, he could put up with that.

The RSVP which had delighted him most was from Diana Bagshot, the widow of Viscount Grimbledon. Tarquin had been at Cambridge with her late husband Eustace, and they had rooms on the same staircase in college. The Duke had read about Eustace's sudden death in *The Times* two years before, and subsequently sent invitations to Diana for a number of events at Great Park, none of which she even acknowledged, let alone replied to in the affirmative. And this time, she had not only replied but accepted! This one piece of news outweighed the fact that just about everyone else turned him down, including Godfrey Krumnagel of Krumnagel's Bank, Humphrey Fotheringay, the heir to the Fotheringay's Sausages empire, and Sir Burlington Fitzroy, the local Member of Parliament for Gloucestershire South. Sir Burlington had initially accepted, but then sent a telegram saying that he would be unable to attend. His wife Emma had just been admitted to the Hollies, a drying-out clinic a few miles away near Cheltenham. He failed to mention that in the RSVP.

If you compared Tarquin's lifestyle to that of his ancestors, there was no doubt he was roughing it. At the end of the last century, there had been more than twenty servants at Great Park, with others brought in for banquets and other special events. Nowadays, there were only eleven staff, and if things didn't improve quickly, some of those people would also have to go.

On this Friday of Fridays, things didn't start well. The Duke woke up with a raging headache and fever, and told Pickles he would stay in bed until his guests arrived. Pickles could see his employer was in no fit state to meet and greet the guests, so he tried to find Gilbert, but the son and heir had already set off for Cheltenham, where he planned to glean information from Pudsey the accountant about the family finances.

Charles had finished the Duke's portrait and it was now on an easel in the blue drawing room. In the morning, he decided he needed a break and, even though it was a cold morning and snow was still falling, he persuaded the Duke's chauffeur Winstanley to drive him into Stanford Saint Mary. Winstanley dropped him off at the Dog and Ferret and agreed to pick him up at five o'clock. Charles, still in his Walter Washbrook disguise, parked himself in a warm corner with a pint of ale.

He spent the morning doing a charcoal sketch of the interior of the cramped Elizabethan inn. At lunchtime, he bought himself a steak and kidney pie and another pint, and when the landlord said he was closing for the afternoon, Charles asked how much it would cost for him to remain in the bar for the rest of the afternoon. The landlord looked at the drawing and told him that he could stay if he would leave the sketch as payment.

As Charles sat quietly in the corner of the pub and the snow continued to fall outside, the London guests who had accepted Tarquin's invitation were setting off for Gloucestershire. Cornelia Wickham-Thynne and her brother Ronnie Capstan were travelling in the powder blue Rolls Royce, and Ronnie's ex-wife Leonora, who was planning to spend the weekend pretending to be the Viscountess Grimbledon, was at Paddington Station, about to board the train to Stanford Saint Mary.

Chapter 23
Are his eyes a bit close together?
Friday, Hampstead - snow moving in from the west

Turnbull the chauffeur held open the back door of the Rolls Royce for Cornelia and closed it when she was in her seat. He then walked round to do the same for her brother, but Ronnie had already settled himself behind the driver's seat and closed his own door. A creature of habit, Turnbull was a little put out to have his duties curtailed in this way, but his poker face gave nothing away. When it came to his relationship with his employers, his policy was to scowl and bear it.

Preparations to leave 46 Well Walk had taken place in silence. Several items of luggage had been loaded into the capacious boot, including a suitcase full of Arthur's clothes that Ronnie had requisitioned to get through the weekend. He hadn't asked Arthur if he could borrow the clothes, but a man has to keep up appearances, even if it meant temporarily stealing his brother-in-law's best evening attire, plus a three-piece tweed suit, a deerstalker hat and wellington boots that he could wear on the hunt. It bothered him slightly that he was a few inches shorter than Arthur, and several inches wider round the midriff but, as with any problem he had encountered in his life, Ronnie presumed it would all sort itself out somehow.

With his passengers settled in the back, Turnbull slid into the driver's seat, placed his copy of Bacon's Reversible Map of the United Kingdom on the seat next to him and started the engine.

"Do you mind if we don't talk?" said Cornelia, as the car pulled away from the house.

"Fine by me," said Ronnie.

And so it was that they spent almost the entire road journey from Hampstead to Great Park in silence, Cornelia looking out of the left-hand window, Ronnie out of the right. As far as Turnbull was concerned, this was as near to perfection as his working life could get.

After the initial shock of Arthur's threat to divorce her, Cornelia was now overwhelmed by a desire for revenge. She had few practical skills, but she knew how to devise a terrible punishment when she had been wronged. She was, if not the original, then at least a perfect copy of the woman scorned that hell hath no fury to compare with. She would get her lawyer, Sebastian Kugelhorn of Kugelhorn, Kugelhorn, Gummy and Schütz of Temple Bar, London EC4, to find a way to eject Arthur from his own house, a home that his family had occupied for several generations. She would then sell it and move to where she wanted to be, the mansion in The Bishop's Avenue north of Hampstead Heath.

Ronnie was also deep in thought, looking at the hoi polloi going about their business on the streets of London and thinking about the dramatic information he had discovered completely by chance, that Arthur was having an affair with the barmaid at The Flask pub in Well Walk. On Wednesday morning, after spending his first night of freedom under the Wickham-Thynne roof and wearing nothing but a string vest and a pair of long johns, Ronnie had wandered into Arthur's bedroom to look for some clothes. The telephone next to the bed rang and the ringing continued for so long that it seemed as if no one downstairs was going to answer, so Ronnie did. Arthur picked up the telephone at the same time and was unaware that his brother-in-law was listening to his conversation with Ernest Goodgame. Ronnie tried not to give himself away by uttering an oath or gasping in astonishment as he learned about Arthur's little secret.

When Arthur slammed the phone down, Ronnie waited a second before gently replacing the receiver on the cradle. He was sure that what he had just learned would come in useful at some point, but for the time being, he thought it best to keep the information to himself. He rooted around in Arthur's wardrobe and identified the clothes he would need to borrow for the weekend, then put on a dressing gown he found behind the door and some slippers from under the bed. Downstairs, there seemed to be a bit of an atmosphere between Arthur and Cornelia, so he went into the kitchen and hacked several chunks off a loaf of bread and smeared them with butter and marmalade. When Cornelia came in, she poured herself a cup of coffee and sat down opposite him. She seemed to have been stunned into silence by her conversation with her husband. Did she know about the affair? Ronnie felt that it still wasn't the right time to find out, so he read the racing pages of the newspaper and chomped noisily on his bread and marmalade.

Cornelia sipped her coffee, then stood up and walked to the door. "I'm going out," she said. "You'll have to look after yourself today." She disappeared without waiting for a reply.

Ronnie looked at the clock. It was almost pub opening time, so he went back to his room and put on the same clothes he had been wearing when he left prison the day before. Downstairs, he looked at his reflection in the mirror in the hall, smoothed back his thinning hair and left the house in the direction of The Flask.

When he walked into the pub, he looked at the two barmaids and decided that the one with smiling eyes,

267

long wavy hair and bright red lipstick was the more likely object of Arthur's affections. Ronnie was about to introduce himself to her when he saw someone he recognised sitting at a table by the window. It took him a few moments to put a name to the face - it was the racing driver, Henry Dumont. They had both been at Winchester, although Dumont was three or four years older.

He walked over to the table, pointed to the old Wykehamist badge on the breast pocket of his jacket, and offered to buy Dumont a drink. Dumont was a bit surprised by the stranger's excessive familiarity, but accepted the offer of a drink, although he would have preferred it if the man had cleared off after bringing him a double whisky and soda. Instead, he had the nerve to plonk himself down at the table and start talking.

Ronnie asked the driver to confirm that the younger of the two barmaids was Betty Burton, and also indicated rather crudely that he knew that something was going on between her and his brother-in-law. Ronnie then went back to the bar and introduced himself to Betty.

Despite repeated evidence to the contrary, he continued to believe that he was attractive to women, and Betty's stony response to his opening line failed to change his mind about this. "Well, hello ...." he said. "Are you the famous Betty? I'm Ronnie Capstan, Arthur Wickham-Thynne's brother-in-law. Arthur's told me ALL about you." And he winked. Betty screwed up her face as if she was going to be sick. He ordered a pint of bitter and tried to engage her in conversation while she pulled it. Betty answered his questions as economically as she could.

Now, as the Rolls Royce cruised smoothly through the Berkshire countryside, Ronnie's thoughts returned to the

268

phone call he had overheard between his brother-in-law and a well-spoken but slightly scary sounding man. The man hadn't asked for money. Why not? Ronnie couldn't see the point of blackmail if there was no financial reward. Also, Walter Washbrook was mentioned, the artist that Cornelia claimed she had seen committing an act of gross indecency in a garden in Chelsea. Arthur was told that if any information about this event came to light, Lady Wickham-Thynne would be informed of his adultery. All very strange.

Ronnie turned his mind to the more immediate matter of the weekend at Great Park. He had agreed to accompany Cornelia to the shooting party for the sole reason that he wanted to shake some money out of Tarquin Woolnough, a man he had met in London more than twenty years before. At the time, the fun-loving future Duke of Burfaughtonleigh had got into a number of scrapes with the law and there were a couple of things Ronnie imagined Tarquin would prefer to be kept secret. A simple exchange of funds would ensure this would remain the case. At least for the time being.

For pretty much the whole of his adult life, Ronnie had made a living out of deception, swindling and the occasional spot of blackmail. In order to cover his tracks, he used more than one name in his business dealings and was known variously as Ronald Carlton, Rupert Carrington and, for a short time, Arbuthnot Twistleton, the name he was using when he met Tarquin.

One of Ronnie's first business partners was Carlos Petworth, a South American who specialised in selling shares in silver and gold mines that were no longer operational. Petworth was an attractive and confident young man, with an Argentinian father, from whom he inherited a volatile temperament, and an English mother, who bequeathed him blond hair and a winning smile. He spoke English with an accent and felt annoyed that most people seemed to think he was untrustworthy because of it. He never realised that their low opinion of him had nothing to do with his accent. Anyone who went into business with Petworth soon found that he really *was* untrustworthy. He found a useful ally in Ronnie, a man with a posh voice and the gift of the gab. They went into partnership offering worthless stock in mines that had long since stopped producing meaningful quantities of whatever precious metal they had originally contained, but which in some way appeared to be thriving. The Potosí mine in Bolivia was a good example, where the last silver had been mined about a hundred years before. However, there was also a mining town in the US state of Nevada that had been named after Potosí, so it was possible to show potential customers newspaper reports indicating that stacks of silver were still being mined in a place with that name.

Ronnie spent a lot of time in gentlemen's clubs in London, targeting country members who were temporarily in the capital. The combination of his public school accent and a business card with a fake Mayfair office address persuaded dozens of gullible old men to exchange a cheque for shares which were worth less than the embossed paper they were printed on. Ronnie eventually found himself *persona non grata* in the clubs where he made his best killings. In some cases, his own bouncing cheques meant that he was barred from entering and he chose to avoid visiting others so as not to meet angry clients face to face.

His working relationship with Petworth didn't end well. The Argentinian's temper was a constant problem - he would explode with rage at the slightest disagreement. One day at Ronnie's house in Bloomsbury, Petworth pulled out a pistol, pointed it at his partner and pulled the trigger. There was a click, and nothing happened. Ronnie burst out laughing. "You're a joke," he said. "Your gun doesn't even work!"

Petworth pulled the trigger again. This time, a bullet flew over Ronnie's shoulder, smashing a fake Ming vase. Ronnie punched Petworth in the face, before taking him by the scruff of the neck and throwing him out into the street. His wife Leonora was very shaken when she heard what had happened, and even more distraught when she discovered that Ronnie had told the Argentine never to darken his door again.

She was very fond of Carlos Petworth. But that, as they say, is another story...

Looking for new ways to make a dishonest shilling, Ronnie fell in with a different bunch of crooks, whose main business was stealing and selling top of the range limousines. The boss of the gang, a man from Shepherd's Bush named Stilgoe, had people who could produce fake ownership documents and car number plates and who could re-paint cars, but he needed someone who could talk to the posh types he wanted to sell the stolen limousines to, and Ronnie fit the bill. From there, it was just a short step to Ronnie's appearance in front of Judge Brodkin at the Old Bailey and thirteen months in Wormwood Scrubs.

Turnbull steered the Rolls Royce out of Oxfordshire and into Gloucestershire. The sky darkened and snowflakes began to swirl around. The road ahead was already covered in snow, so the chauffeur slowed down and drove carefully along the tracks made by earlier vehicles. As the car passed through Stanford Saint Mary, Turnbull noted where The Dog and Ferret was, the inn where Cornelia had booked a room for him, and then headed out along the Cheltenham Road in the direction of Great Park.

"We're almost there, ma'am."

"Thank God for that, I'm dying for a piss," said Ronnie. He looked across at his sister, but her head was arched back on her seat, her mouth was open, and she was snoring gently.

The wall of the Great Park estate came into view on the right and as they approached the gate house at the foot of the main drive, a black Humber Pullman appeared, stopped briefly and turned left in the direction of Stanford Saint Mary. When it drove past the Rolls, the driver shouted "Watcha, cock!" through his open window and waved cheerfully. Turnbull took an instant dislike to the smiling face of the Great Park chauffeur and thanked his lucky stars that, after depositing his passengers at the house, he would be returning to the sanctuary of the Dog and Ferret and wouldn't have to spend any time in the man's company.

He turned into the drive and headed up towards the main house.

Ronnie looked at the ugly dark building that they were approaching. "Well, well, Tarquin," he said quietly to himself. "All a bit different from that place of yours in Old Compton Street."

*****

After Winstanley set off to collect Viscountess Grimbledon from the railway station, Pickles went into the library, which was at the corner of the house with a view of the drive, to wait for the arrival of the Wickham-Thynnes. They hadn't given a time of arrival, so the

272

butler stationed himself where he would be able to see them when they finally showed up. It also gave him a chance to take a break from overseeing the preparations for the shoot. He parked himself in an armchair and picked up a collection of PG Wodehouse short stories called *Young Men in Spats.* Pickles settled back in his chair and opened the book at his favourite yarn, *Trouble Down At Tudsleigh.*

He hadn't even reached the end of the first paragraph when he saw the headlights of a car heading up the drive in the early evening gloom. He sighed, put the book down and hurried into the hall, calling for Flockton the under-butler to join him to greet the new arrivals. The two of them were waiting at the top of the steps when the car pulled up and Turnbull switched off the engine. The driver got out, nodded to Pickles and walked round the car to open the door for Cornelia. There was someone in the nearside back seat, so the butler walked down and opened that door.

"Sir Arthur," he said. "Welcome to Great Park."

Ronnie emerged from the car, ignored the butler, and walked up to the window to the right of the main entrance, which was the library that Pickles had just vacated. The window was quite high off the ground and Ronnie had to stand on tip-toe and hold onto the sill to be able to see inside.

Pickles's face gave no indication of his initial impression that this knight of the realm appeared to be an ill-mannered lout.

A thin woman with a skeletal face and hair dyed dark red appeared on the other side of the car. After reminding Turnbull which of the several suitcases were hers and which one was Ronnie's, she walked up to the butler, smiled and held out her hand. Pickles took it and bowed.

273

"Lady Cornelia," he said. "We are delighted that you and Sir Arthur are able to join us."

The smile disappeared and she pulled her hand away. "I'm afraid my husband has been detained in London on important business," she said. Pickles raised one eyebrow and turned his head in the direction of the man who was still looking through the window.

"This is my brother, Mister Ronald Capstan."

Capstan. Polly's name, too. An unusual name, but Pickles found it hard to believe that this pudgy man whose eyes were too close together could be related to the pretty young woman who was his colleague. He resolved to check with her as soon as he had guided them to their rooms.

Having arranged with the new arrivals to reconvene in the blue drawing room in half an hour and leaving Flockton to struggle upstairs with the first three of Cornelia's suitcases, Pickles hurried across the snow-covered courtyard and into Polly's office.

"I have news," he said. "Lady Wickham-Thynne has arrived."

"Oh good! What's she like?" asked Polly. "And her husband .... um, Sir Arthur, isn't it? What's *he* like?"

Pickles cleared his throat. "Sir Arthur did not accompany her."

"Really? She came alone?"

"No."

"Oh. Who did she come with?"

"A man she claims is her brother."

"I see." She waited to see if Pickles was going to elaborate. "That's interesting."

"Yes."

"Monty, are you keeping something back about our new guests? Are you worried, Lady Whatever has bought some gigolo with her?"

That possibility hadn't occurred to Pickles, but he quickly dismissed the idea. Even though she was caked in make-up and looked as if she hadn't eaten for a month, Lady Wickham-Thynne seemed a fairly stylish and sophisticated woman, whereas her companion looked like a petty criminal. But there was no accounting for tastes.

He was still hesitant about telling Polly the name of this unexpected guest. "The thing is ..." he said. "The brother ... his name is Ronald Capstan."

Polly squealed and leapt out of her chair. "Oh my God! Are you sure?"

"That was the name Lady Cornelia gave. I haven't yet exchanged words with the man himself. Do you ... do you know him?"

"Is he about this tall?"

"Yes?"

"And are his eyes a bit close together?"

"Yes."

"Good Lord, he's my father! What on earth is he doing with this Wickham-Thynne woman?"

"Well, as I told you, she says he's her brother. Does your father have a sister?"

"Yes, he does. I never met her, but I'm pretty sure her name was Ethel. She used to send me a ten-shilling note for Christmas when I was little. Yes, papa definitely used to say it was from Aunt Ethel."

Pickles was now very confused indeed.

"But papa's here," said Polly. "I really don't know what to think about that. I thought he was still in prison."

"*What?*"

"Yes. He went to prison, last year, I think. I haven't actually seen him since he walked out on us. Certainly not since mama married Charles's dad."

"Charles? Who's Charles?"

Polly looked at Pickles for a moment before replying. So far, the Duke was the only person who knew that the artist currently in residence at Great Park was her stepbrother and not Walter Washbrook. Polly had always felt very close to the butler and didn't like keeping secrets from him, and she presumed he was going to find out the truth sooner or later from the Duke.

"Sit down for a moment, Monty. There's something I need to tell you."

Pickles sat in the seat on the other side of her desk. Polly took a deep breath, then told him what happened the previous day when Charles abandoned his disguise. The butler raised an eyebrow, and both of them shot up when Polly revealed that Tarquin had persuaded Charles to continue in the role of Walter Washbrook for the duration of the shoot.

Pickles sat in silence for a moment, then said: "Please explain how this came to pass."

Polly repeated the story that Charles had invented for Tarquin. "He's a pal of this Washbrook character, and the old chap is too busy, so they came up with this plan. I thought it was quite amusing." She could tell by the look on the butler's face that he didn't agree. "Sorry."

"Well, we'll worry about that another time. There are more urgent matters in hand. Lady Grimbledon should be arriving soon, and the Wickham-Thynnes, or rather Lady Wickham-Thynne and this man she came with, will be fetching up in the drawing room soon expecting aperitifs. I *was* quite looking forward to showing them

276

the Duke's portrait. I wish I didn't know what you just told me."

Polly bowed her head in silent apology.

"I was also hoping that the artist could be there to talk about it himself, but now I'm not so sure that's a good idea. Where *is* Walter, or Charles, or whatever he's called?"

"Do you know what? I haven't the faintest idea," said Polly. "I haven't actually seen him at all today."

As far as Pickles was concerned, Charles's whereabouts were less important than the absence of the Duke himself, who was still in bed. "I'd better go and see if the Wickham-Thynnes are ready for a drink," he said. "I know I am!" He stood up to leave. "Would you care to join us?"

"I'll come a bit later, if that's all right with you," she said. "I just need to compose myself." She walked round her desk and did something she had never done before. She gave the butler a hug. Pickles was not a natural receiver of hugs, and for a moment he squirmed and wriggled, then sighed and put his head on Polly's shoulder. She felt the shiny dome of his bald head against her cheek for the very first time. It made her feel simultaneously moved and just a tiny bit queasy.

"Everything's going to be fine," she said.

Pickles disentangled himself, breathed in and out quickly, nodded and walked elegantly to the door of her office. "Please do come as soon as you can," he said. "I could do with the moral support."

Chapter 24
I may be a lush, but I'm not a snitch
Friday morning, Hampstead - cold with grey skies

Arthur Wickham-Thynne watched the Rolls Royce containing his wife and her brother set off to Great Park. When the car crossed Christchurch Hill and disappeared from view, he went downstairs to his office and stood in front of the portrait of his grandfather, the Victorian explorer Montgomery Wickham-Thynne. He didn't know that it had been painted some fifteen years before by a young artist called Walter Washbrook.

There were many business matters that Arthur should have been dealing with that morning, but all he could think about was the phone call he received two days before, when a man asked him to confirm that he was in an 'adulterous relationship' with Betty Burton. To begin with, Arthur remained silent, refusing to make any comment. The man also knew that Arthur's wife had scandalous information about Walter Washbrook, and he suggested that if she were to share it with anyone, she would immediately be told about her husband's affair. Arthur indicated that he understood, without committing himself to any course of action. As it happened, immediately after the phone call, he had an opportunity to do something about the man's main demand. Cornelia walked into his office and told him that she planned to spread some dirt about Washbrook and Arthur threatened to divorce her.

In the forty-eight hours since then, the atmosphere in the house had been chilly. Arthur spent most of Wednesday literally locked in his office, coming out only to grab some bread and cheese and a glass of wine and tip-toeing to his room late at night when the house fell silent. Early on Thursday morning, he drove to his office in Shaftesbury Avenue, where a series of meetings kept him busy until the evening. He dined at his club and didn't return to Well Walk until nearly midnight, where he was relieved to find the house in darkness. Since the confrontation on Wednesday, he had managed to avoid seeing either his wife or her brother, and he was happy to keep it that way.

On Friday morning, Arthur felt a huge sense of relief as the car moved away, mainly because he was glad to see the back of his brother-in-law. He had never liked Ronnie, suspecting from the moment he met him that he was a crook, an opinion that proved accurate when he was sent to prison. The fact that Ronnie spent his first few days of freedom helping himself to Arthur's food, wine and brandy did nothing to improve the host's opinion of his loathsome guest.

Now, alone in the house, he once again started thinking about the phone call he had received two days before. The caller's only demand was that Arthur must make sure Cornelia said nothing about this man Washbrook. All very confusing. First of all, how did he know about Betty? And why did he make a connection with the portrait painter? And could Arthur trust him not to increase his demands and maybe ask for money? Arthur wasn't in the habit of sharing information about his private life, although there was no doubt that his regular drinking companions at The Flask had put two and two together regarding his relationship with Betty. Would any of them have blabbed about it? He had also talked about her to a theatre impresario called Bernard Delgado, but they were both drunk at the time, and

280

Delgado was notorious for not paying attention to any conversation that wasn't about him.

There was something else on Arthur's mind. After the initial shock of his threat to divorce Cornelia, he had begun to think - why not? Their marriage was a sham. They slept in different rooms, she was usually drunk as a skunk by midday, and she was no longer the nubile beauty he had married more than twenty years before. Plus, she was the most appalling snob. From the very beginning, she had made it clear that under no circumstances would she agree to have children. At the time, Arthur was fine with this arrangement, but more recently, he had begun to regret the lack of a son or daughter to continue the Wickham-Thynne line.

He had previously thought divorce was something deeply shocking, but now he wasn't so sure. He remembered the drama when Ronnie announced he was planning to divorce his wife - the alarming, theatrical Leonora - although that was as nought compared to the shockwaves following his arrest, trial and subsequent conviction for handing stolen goods.

And then there was the astonishing affair of King Edward, or rather ex-King Edward. Since his abdication just three months before, the world, at least the one Arthur frequented, seemed to have modified its views about divorce and much more besides. The affair of Edward and Mrs Simpson had divided the world into three camps. The first group thought that he had committed an act of treason by giving up the crown to marry a twice-divorced woman, and an *American* at that! The second smaller group quietly congratulated Edward for following the counsel of his heart, while the third group, including the people who actually knew him, imagined that after the ex-king had tried living without royal patronage for a while, he would dump Mrs S and come running back, begging forgiveness and pleading for a chance to live the rest of his life in peace. Paid for by the public purse, of course.

Divorcing Cornelia would mean Arthur would have to re-house her somewhere, but he knew she hated living in the centre of Hampstead. She had designs on an architectural monstrosity in The Bishop's Avenue, but she could forget about that. He would find her an apartment in Saint John's Wood and give her an allowance, enough to stay sozzled and buy a new hat every month. She would probably be as happy as Larry.

Suddenly it seemed like the best idea in the world.

The main reason to consider this dramatic step was the lovely Betty Burton herself. She was vivacious, funny, cheeky and smart, as well as being drop-dead gorgeous. But the thing he liked about her most was that she listened to him, and told him exactly what she thought about the way he conducted his affairs, probably the only person he dealt with who was consistently honest. He was pretty certain that he was genuinely in love with someone for the first time in his life.

Arthur looked at the portrait of his grandfather, his hero, the man he had spent so much time with when he was a small boy, and the person whose advice he sought when he began making his way in business. Most of all, the one whose opinions he respected more than any other. "Well, grandpop," he said. "I've made a rather big decision. I do hope you would have approved." He went out into the hall, put on his overcoat and hat and headed off in the direction of The Flask, a five-minute walk away.

The pub opened at eleven o'clock on weekdays, and by the time Arthur got there, the usual suspects had already arrived and were downing alcohol to relieve the tedium of a February Friday morning. As was often the case, the first person through the door that day was Henry Dumont. By the time Arthur walked in, Betty was serving Henry his second whisky and soda. Glass in hand, Henry had returned to his favourite seat at a table by the window.

"Arthur, you old bastard!" he said, when he saw his drinking companion. "Get a drink and come and join me!"

Being able to chat to Henry was one of the reasons why Arthur enjoyed spending time at The Flask, but today was not a day he wished to do that. He told Henry he would join him presently. First, he wanted to talk to Betty.

She came to face him at the bar. "Good morning," she said, "what'll it be?" There was a certain *froideur* in her voice.

"Well, that really depends on you," he said. "You might be interested to know that I'll be home alone this weekend." There was a pause. "Are you?"

"Am I what?"

"Interested to know that."

"Not really," said Betty. "Can I get you something to drink?"

Arthur was puzzled and alarmed by her tone of voice. Even though they tried to keep their relationship secret, she was usually much warmer than this in her over-the-bar conversations with him. He ordered a pint of bitter and then followed her down the bar as she went to pull it for him.

"Is everything all right?" he asked.

"Everything's fine."

The liaison between Arthur and Betty had started on a rainy day in May the previous year. He and Henry were sitting at the table where the racing driver had just planted himself, and Betty was walking around collecting empty glasses. When she reached their table, she stood still for a moment and started staring into the distance.

Arthur had asked her if anything was the matter. "I've come over all funny!" she said, slumping forward onto the table in front of them and smashing the two glasses she was holding. Arthur pulled her up into a chair and saw that she had cut her hand quite badly.

He asked for some cotton wool, clean towels and a bowl of hot water. He cleaned the cut in her hand and wrapped it in a towel. The wound needed stitches, so Arthur walked her out of the pub through the rain to his car and drove her to New End Hospital.

Betty cried all the way there, apologising for being such a clumsy idiot, and told him he shouldn't be wasting his time looking after her. He kept reassuring her that it could have happened to anyone and told her that he'd fainted when he first worked as a nurse in the Great War. Hearing him refer to himself as a nurse cheered Betty up. "I thought you 'ad to be a girl to be a nurse," she said.

Arthur had volunteered for the Royal Army Medical Corps when the war started in 1914. He dealt with casualties on the front line and three years later, he was incapacitated by a mustard gas attack on the Western Front. He and dozens of others were invalided back to England, and he never recovered enough to be sent back. Many of his comrades who remained in France were killed at the Battle of the Somme, which started a few weeks later.

Not the kind of thing to tell a barmaid with a gash in her hand.

The nurse at New End took Betty away to get the wound cleaned and stitched up. Betty told Arthur not to waste his time waiting for her. "I'll be all right, I'll catch a bus home," she said. He ignored her, telling her that it was raining, and she would be in no fit state to catch a bus. When she came out, her hand was bandaged, and she looked exhausted and in pain.

"Why are you still here?" she asked.

"Because I didn't want to abandon you," he replied.

"But why are you doing this for me?"

"I'd do it for anyone," he lied.

"You're a lovely man, Mister Wickham-Thynne," she said.

"Miss Burton, I do wish you'd call me Arthur."

"All right! I do like being called Miss Burton, though. You can do that any time you like!"

"Wait here a moment," he said. He walked into the nurse's office and asked how much the treatment would cost, and quickly wrote a cheque for the amount before going back to where Betty was waiting. He asked her why she had been feeling unwell and she said that she hadn't eaten for two days.

"Whyever not?" he asked.

"Sometimes I don't have the time, sometimes I don't have the money."

Arthur took her to a restaurant called Cabillaud Fraîche in West End Lane and they both enjoyed a fried fish supper. Her bubbly energy returned as she ate her fish and chips, washed down with white wine. She chatted non-stop, telling him about growing up in Bolton, how the only options to someone like her were working in a factory or as a maid, and how her grandmother had encouraged her to escape. She bought a one-way train ticket to London and wasn't planning to go back north any time soon.

"If I go 'ome, me dad'll chain me to t'kitchen table," she said, and burst out laughing. Arthur hadn't enjoyed a meal in a restaurant so much since ... well, he couldn't remember ever having this much fun while eating or doing anything else. He drove her to the rooming house where she lived in Kentish Town, she invited him in, and that was how it all started.

Now, nine months later, Arthur was feeling panic-stricken. He was on the verge of making a life-changing decision, but the object of his affections was behaving like a freshly-filleted piece of haddock in the cold store at Cabillaud Fraîche.

"Betty, I have something really important to tell you," he said.

She looked at him, then nodded towards the snug, the small dark room to the left of the bar, which was empty. "I'll be there in a minute," she said. Arthur walked through and sat down, and eventually she came through the connecting door, staring at him with a cold look in her eyes. "What do you want to talk about?" she asked.

"I'm not stupid, Betty. There's something wrong. What is it?"

"You really don't know?"

"No, of course I don't. That's why I'm asking. What's the problem?"

"Your brother-in-law."

"What about him?"

Betty could sense that Arthur really didn't know why she was upset. She paused for a moment and began to tell him. "His name's Ronnie, right?"

"Yes."

"He came in here t'other day and asked me I was the famous Betty."

"He did what?"

"You 'eard. He said: 'Are you the famous Betty? I'm Arthur Wickham-Thynne's brother-in-law. He's told me all about you.' And then he gave me the most god-awful greasy smile and ... and then he ...uuughhh...."

"What? What did he do?"

"He winked at me. God, he's a slimy little bleeder."

As always, Arthur was both shocked and stimulated by Betty's use of language. He shook his head in disbelief, but then couldn't stop himself from laughing.

"It weren't funny," said Betty.

"No, no, it weren't... it wasn't," said Arthur.

"If you're going to make fun of the way I talk, you can bugger off right now," she said, getting up from the table. Arthur reached out to take her hand, the same one she had injured on the rainy day in May. He looked at the scar in the palm, remembering its importance.

"Betty, please sit down for a moment." She did as he asked. "I have never ever said a single word about you to anyone, and certainly not to that execrable brother-in-law of mine."

"What does that mean?"

"What does what mean?"

"That word you just used."

"Execrable?"

"Yes."

"It means ... oh goodness, it means not very nice."

"I don't need telling that. I noticed him when he first come in." Her face clouded over as she remembered what happened. "Definitely a rum 'un, I thought. He looked around and went straight over to where Henry were sat and introduced himself. You could see that

287

Henry hadn't the foggiest notion who he were. Next thing you know, he were at the bar, buying Henry a drink."

"Did he mention my name then?" asked Arthur. "The first time he spoke to you?"

Betty thought for a moment. "No, I think he were sat with Henry for a while. Then he came back for more drinks and gave me the eye. Slimy sod."

"Bloody Henry," said Arthur. He looked across to the main saloon where Henry was standing at the bar again, his face a shade more beetroot than it had been when he crossed the threshold an hour earlier.

"There's something else I want to talk about," said Arthur. She was sitting at the table with her hands clasped in front of her. He put both of his hands on hers and was relieved that she didn't take hers away. She even smiled, which kindled flames inside him.

"What is it?" she asked.

"Well," he started. "I've made a really big decision. I want to ----"

"Arthur, dear boy!" Henry had wandered into the snug. He slapped them both on the back and planted himself at the table with them.

"Oh, for God's sake, Henry! Do piss off!"

"I will do as you wish, dear boy, just as soon as I've imparted the message, I was sent to ... umm ... impart. Now, what was it?" He blinked and shook his head. "Oh yes.... Betty! Doreen says she's overrun and needs all hands on deck."

Betty gave Henry a withering look and stood up. "Fine," she said, and walked through the door to the area behind the bar.

"Sorry," said Henry. "Was I interrupting something? Can I get you another drink?"

"No."

"No to interrupting something, or no to another drink?"

"Both."

"Fair enough. If you'll excuse me, I've a throat that's on fire and I need a pint of something to douse the flames." Henry made a move to get up, but Arthur yanked him by the sleeve of his jacket back down onto his seat. Because the racing driver wasn't in complete control of his limbs, he sat down with a thump and slumped sideways onto the floor. Arthur bent down and prised his eyes open with his fingers. He could see that his companion wasn't badly hurt, so he went to the bar and asked Doreen for a jug of cold water, which he poured onto Henry's head.

"Warra blazes!" Henry shouted and sat up.

"Get up off the floor," said Arthur. "I want to talk to you." When Henry failed to move, Arthur yanked him back onto the chair. He then slapped the racing driver quite firmly on both cheeks.

"Christ almighty, will you be careful?" Henry rubbed his face and ran his fingers through his hair and then looked at them, puzzled. "I'm wet," he announced.

"Yes, and if you don't listen to me, I'm going to throw more cold water in your face," said Arthur.

"Please!" pleaded Henry. "Not water! I hate the stuff!"

Arthur was determined to find out more about Henry's conversation with Ronnie Capstan, even though he imagined that his drinking companion might not be in the best shape to recall something that had taken place two days before. He took the lapels of Henry's jacket and pulled him closer to his face.

"Listen, he said. "The other day, you talked to my brother-in-law, a chap called Ronnie Capstan."

"Did I?" replied Henry. "Where?"

"Here. He came in and bought you a drink."

"A lot of people buy me drinks," said Henry, smiling at the thought of how popular he was. "What does he look like?"

Arthur tried to be fair in his description of his brother-in-law, but failed. "He's an ugly, spivvy looking man who brushes his hair back over a bald patch and his eyes are too close together," he said. "He looks like a petty crook, which he is."

Henry thought for a moment. "Was he wearing an Old Wykehamist's blazer?"

"Well, he was at Winchester, so yes, probably."

"Right! I remember him!" said Henry. "Popped up out of nowhere the other day. Came over and said hello." He screwed up his eyes to dredge up some more memories. "He said we were at school together, but I couldn't remember him. Told me he'd seen me driving at Brooklands back in the day. Tried to sell me some shares in a silver mine somewhere in South America."

"That's Ronnie."

Henry's mind was clearing little by little. "Just a mo, didn't the blighter say he was Cornelia's brother?"

"Well, he is, so he probably did. Think back, Henry. Did you say anything to him about me and her?" He indicated towards the bar with his head.

"You and the fragrant Betty?"

"Yes."

"Good Lord no, Arthur, what do you think I am? I may be a lush, but I'm not a snitch. Your secret's safe with me."

"Thank you, Henry. I really appreciate that."

"You're welcome."

"The thing is, my brother-in-law, the man you met on Wednesday ... after he talked to you, he went up and addressed Betty by name."

"Well," said Henry. "Maybe that's because it *is* her name." Henry opened and closed his eyes two or three times. "I remember it all clearly now," he said. "This brother-in-law of yours, Laurie ..."

"Ronnie. Ronnie Capstan."

"Right. He bought me a drink, sat down opposite me, and the first thing he did was point at the girls behind the bar. And he said - which one of those popsies is Betty Burton?"

"He said what??"

"What I just said. Which one of those popsies is Betty Burton?"

"Did you tell him?"

"Yes. Gosh.... and I've just remembered what he said next."

"What did he say next?"

Henry paused. "I'm not sure you want to know."

Arthur took hold of Henry's lapels again. "OF COURSE, I want to know. WHAT DID HE SAY?"

"If you will let go of my jacket, I will tell you."

Arthur released the jacket. "What did he say?"

"He said .... so that's the one Arthur's shagging."

Chapter 25
Who was the geezer in the back seat?
Friday, Great Park, early evening - snow falling

Eric Winstanley the Great Park chauffeur was delighted to see the Wickham-Thynne Rolls Royce arrive at the gates of Great Park and was looking forward to sharing anecdotes with the driver when he got back to the house. Winstanley was a former London taxi driver, who had moved to Gloucestershire in pursuit of a woman he met in a pub in the East End. Whatever hopes he had of sharing a life with her had evaporated, but he found country life to his liking, and he ended up renting a room over the blacksmith's forge in Stanford Saint Mary and making a modest living doing odd jobs. When he heard that Great Park was looking for a new chauffeur, he turned up with his own set of tools and asked if he could have a look at all the motors in the stable. He started the engine of each one, listened, then looked under the bonnet and made adjustments. In every case, when he started the car again, the engine purred, sounding less sluggish. The butler gave him the job immediately and Winstanley moved into the cottage behind the stable.

Unfortunately, the Duke took an instant dislike to the new chauffeur, annoyed at the man's way of addressing him - "Watcha, Tarks! How's tricks?" or variations on that theme. Every attempt Tarquin made to get the man to address him as 'Your Grace' fell on deaf ears. When the Duke asked Pickles to dismiss him, the butler reminded him that Winstanley was the only one who knew how to maintain the Great Park vehicles, including the aging tractor.

So, this cheerful son of Whitechapel remained in position, and now he was on his way to pick up a titled lady at the railway station. He was fairly certain that he would recognise a member of the upper classes amongst the gnarled sons and daughters of Gloucestershire who arrived on the same train but, just to be on the safe side, he scrawled her name on a piece of cardboard. He wasn't completely sure of the spelling, but he reckoned VYCOUNTUS GRIMEBULLDIN was close enough.

But he didn't make it to the station until much later ...

The 3.50 from London Paddington had arrived on time and Leonora was standing alone on the deserted platform. The snow had been swept away but there were random patches of ice everywhere. The small number of passengers who alighted had already shown their tickets to the man at the barrier, stationmaster Arnold McGurk. He was about to go back to his office when he noticed the tall woman who was still standing on the platform. He walked down to speak to her.

"Can I help you, madam?"

Leonora was always pleased when a well-built man came into view, especially such a fit-looking specimen, and one wearing a uniform. An image of him naked to the waist and chopping wood came into her mind. She gave him one of her most flirtatious looks and a broad smile. "Hello, my good man," she said. "I'm Diana Bagshot, Viscountess Grimbledon."

"Blimey," said the stationmaster. "I mean blimey, your highness."

"Darling, you don't have to call me your highness," she said. "You ... " She realised that she didn't actually know the correct way to address a Viscountess and ended her sentence enigmatically. "... just have to stand to attention when you speak to me."

294

McGurk had seen service in the Great War and was well able to do that. He straightened his back, snapped his heels together and only just stopped himself from saluting. "Yes, ma'am!" he said, rather loudly.

Leonora smiled. "At ease, soldier," she said, touching him gently on the arm. "I've been invited to a shooting weekend at Great Park by the Duke of ..." She couldn't remember the short pronunciation of his name. " ... Bur something or other... Burfort?"

"Burfaughtonleigh," said McGurk, pronouncing all four syllables. It was the name of a village a few miles from Stanford Saint Mary, and it was only the Woolnough family who chose to pronounce it 'Burley'. The mystery of who had knocked him out on this very platform a few days before was still unsolved, but McGurk was convinced it was someone from Great Park, so he almost spat out the name. Leonora wondered if she was heading off to some haunted castle that the locals lived in fear of. Not for the first time, she asked herself if she was doing the right thing to visit this unknown place.

"I was expecting to be met by one of the Duke's people," she said. The coat she was wearing wasn't keeping the cold out and she was shivering. "I say, is there somewhere I can wait? I'm absolutely freezing."

"You can sit in my office," he said. He picked up her suitcase and turned to walk up the platform. "Please follow me, your ... gracefulness." As soon as Leonora started walking, she slipped and turned her ankle on the ice. She swore quite loudly, which surprised the stationmaster.

"May I?" He put his hand under her elbow and guided her gently along the platform and into his warm sanctuary.

The only light in the room was provided by a log fire. There was a table under the window with an unlit oil lamp on it, and along the walls there were shelves full of books. In front of the fire there was a large armchair which Leonora sank into with a sigh of relief. She felt relaxed because it was warm, but also because it seemed like a safe place to be.

It was getting dark, so McGurk took the top off the lamp. He opened a drawer and took out a box of matches.

"Don't light it," said Leonora. "The fire is enough." She breathed out, feeling less tense than she had done for a while. The prospect of spending the weekend pretending to be Viscountess Grimbledon worried her a lot, and she was happy to stay right where she was, just for the time being.

"Would you like some tea?" asked McGurk. "And should I call Great Park to tell them that you're here?"

"Tea would be wonderful. But don't call Great Park. I'm very happy to stay here for a short while."

"As you wish," said McGurk. "Do you take milk and sugar?"

"Just milk."

There was a small recess opposite where Leonora was sitting, and McGurk disappeared into it and put a kettle on a gas ring. Leonora closed her eyes and fell asleep. When she woke, he was standing over her, holding a cup of tea. She thanked him and took the cup, feeling the hairs on the back of his hand as she did.

"What's your name?" she asked.

"McGurk. Arnold McGurk."

"I'm so pleased I met you, Arnold. My name is Leonora."

He looked at her, puzzled. "Beg pardon, milady?" he asked. "Didn't you say your name was Diana?"

Leonora bit her lip, annoyed at her mistake. How was she going to get through the weekend without doing that again? "Yes, my real name is Diana. Leonora is my pen name." Now she was mixing her two identities. It was going to end in tears.

"Pen name?"

"I'm a novelist. I write under the name of Leonora Capstan."

Capstan. McGurk had heard that name before and racked his brains to remember when and where. A blonde woman, the secretary at Great Park, the one with the mad-looking artist who was wearing dark glasses and a ridiculously long overcoat. The police sergeant from Cheltenham had called the woman Miss Capstan.

"Are you by any chance ----?" He didn't finish the question. There was a knock at the door of his little sanctuary and his time with the lady he had rescued from the icy platform was about to end.

*****

The journey from Great Park to the Stanford Saint Mary station should have taken Winstanley no more than fifteen minutes in the Humber. The reason he was late was that, second after waving cheerily at the Rolls Royce, he ran into a sheep. They bred a rather stupid type of sheep at Great Park and this one had broken out of the field behind Garth's cottage where he and his dim relatives were being kept before they were slaughtered. Winstanley jerked the steering wheel to the right, and the car skidded on a patch of ice and crashed into the ditch on the other side of the road. Worried sick that he had damaged the car, the chauffeur jumped out and checked for dents. There weren't any, but when he tried to back

297

out of the ditch, the rear wheels span around on the bank of snow.

He was only wearing his regulation chauffeur's black suit, so he took a blanket out of the boot and put it round his head and shoulders to keep warm. The sheep was still standing in the middle of the road, so he kicked it firmly in the backside. It let out a high-pitched bleat and scooted off towards Stanford Saint Mary. Winstanley trudged back to the main gate and started walking up the driveway to the house, carrying the VYCOUNTUS GRIMEBULLDIN sign under his arm. He would have to walk the quarter mile back to the house and get into the other limousine.

Turnbull was heading back down the drive in the Rolls Royce. He was very much looking forward to sitting in the bar of the Dog and Ferret and drinking a pint of beer and very probably one or two more. Then he saw what looked like the ghost of a medieval monk running towards him, frantically waving some kind of message. Turnbull tried to swerve round him, but the caped man moved quickly to his left and was still in front of the car. The chauffeur applied the brakes, and the Rolls went into a spin. With the skill of a bullfighter, Winstanley moved a little to his left and the back of the car missed him by a whisker as it careered past. When it came to a halt, it was facing the way it had come, its long bonnet pointing towards the house.

Turnbull got out of the car and walked towards the man, who he now recognised as the chauffeur who had shouted "Watcha, cock!" earlier. The man was smiling and would probably have said "Watcha, cock!" again if Turnbull hadn't taken him by the lapels and shaken him.

"What the flippineck are you playing at?" he said.

"Hold off," said Winstanley, pulling the other man's hands away from his coat, puzzled and upset at this treatment by a fellow member of the professional drivers' fraternity. "I'm the Duke's chauffeur, and I just had a prang outside."

"That's nothing to do with me," replied Turnbull.

"No, it ain't," said Winstanley. "But I need your help. Some posh lady is waiting to be picked up at Stanford, and she's probably getting her knickers in a knot wondering why no one's come to meet her. Would you be so kind as to take me there? And bring us back?" He smiled his most ingratiating smile and showed Turnbull the sign. "Look. I've got a sign with her name on it," he added.

Turnbull wanted to tell him to stick his sign where the sun didn't shine, but he had no idea what kind of relationship Lady Wickham-Thynne had with the occupants of this godforsaken house and didn't want to get himself into any trouble. Without saying another word, he got back into the car and turned it round to face the gate. Winstanley got in the passenger's seat, and they drove towards and main gate and out onto the road.

There was a conversation of sorts between the two men on the way to the station, if the definition of conversation can be broadened to include a monologue where the speaker fills in the responses that he isn't getting from the person being spoken to. Winstanley was well practised in this kind of discourse, as most of his conversations with the Duke were like this.

"Nice motor, this Roller, eh? Yeah? Nice to drive? I bet it is. V12 engine, I expect? Can tell from the hum. Or rather the lack of hum. Ha, ha, ha! And I expect this is the twin ignition version, am I right?" Turnbull failed to respond to any of this, although he was impressed by the

299

other man's knowledge of the car's advanced engineering.

Turnbull drove with extreme caution on the icy road and the Rolls came to a halt outside the station where Polly had parked the Alfa Romeo a few days before. Winstanley ran through the barrier onto the deserted platform, where he skidded on the ice and almost fell onto the railway line. He looked up and down and began to panic when he saw the platform was empty. He even checked to see if the titled lady had come a cropper and fallen over the edge. He was relieved that there was no sign of anyone having done that but was still alarmed that the Duke's guest of honour was missing.

As he ran out of the deserted station, he noticed a light in the window of the room next to the ticket office, so he knocked on the door. At first there was no reply, so he knocked again, and a man's voice invited him in. He opened the door, peered into the gloom and saw a woman sitting in an armchair in front of a log fire.

"Lady Grime-bull-din?" he asked, hoping he was pronouncing the name correctly. He held up his cardboard sign for confirmation. She said she was indeed the lady he was looking for but seemed less than excited about seeing him. She pointed to her suitcase and told him to carry it to the car, saying she wanted to finish her tea and would be out shortly. Winstanley picked up the case and took it to the Rolls and a few minutes later, Leonora emerged from the office. From where they were standing, the two chauffeurs could clearly see that she kissed the stationmaster on the cheek. They looked at each other in surprise, and even Winstanley was reduced to silence.

When Leonora was comfortable in the back seat, Turnbull turned the car and drove away from the station.

Winstanley glanced at the clock in the middle of the dashboard and realised it was already time to pick up Walter Washbrook from the Dog and Ferret. He tapped Turnbull on the arm. "Listen, me old china," he said. "I'm going to have to ask you to do me another favour. We need to pick someone up from the Dog and Ferret, which is a pub in the village."

The chauffeur knew exactly where the Dog and Ferret was. He was looking forward to the pint of ale he was planning to sup there when he managed to get rid of his passengers. "I think we should get her ladyship to Great Park as soon as possible, wouldn't you say?" he replied.

"Oh, absolutely," said Winstanley. "But bear with me, squire, there's a geezer who's also staying at the house, an artist ... a chap who does paintings," he added, in case Turnbull didn't know what an artist was. "He needs collecting and transporting back to Great Park. Come on, the boozer's just down the road, it won't take a second."

Turnbull sat in silence, his gloved hands gripping the steering wheel tightly, so Winstanley turned to address Leonora. "Lady Grimblydon, would you mind if we made a quick stop at the pub before we go back to Great Park? To pick up a gentleman by the name of Washbrook?"

"It's all the same to me," said Leonora. "I'm happy for us to pick up the gentleman in question." She was also interested to see what this 'chap who does paintings' looked like.

Turnbull started the engine and drove away from the station. As they approached the Dog and Ferret, the door of the pub opened and Charles came out, wearing his hat and long overcoat. Despite it being gloomy outside, he was also wearing the dark glasses that were essential to his disguise.

"Ah, stroke of luck," said Winstanley. "That's the bloke right there. Pull over."

Turnbull breathed out noisily to indicate how he felt about being given orders by another chauffeur. As the car rolled to a halt, Winstanley opened his door and jumped out, almost slipping on the icy path outside the pub.

"Whoops, nearly came a cropper there," he said, cheerfully. "Good to see you again, Mister Washbrook."

Charles looked puzzled, because he hadn't seen a blue Rolls Royce parked in the stable, in fact he had never seen a car like this in his life. Winstanley understood his confusion and explained. "Ah, you're probably wondering why I didn't fetch up in the Humber," he said. "Fact is, I had a prang on my way here, so Mister Turnbull kindly agreed to bring me here."

"Oh I see," said Charles. "Jolly good."

"We also have another illuscious passenger," said Winstanley, hoping he was pronouncing the word 'illustrious' correctly. He opened the rear door. "Allow me to introduce the very graceful Viscountess Grimblydon."

From the moment he had discovered that Viscountess Grimbledon was going to attend the shoot, Charles had been preparing himself to meet her again. He took a deep breath and clambered into the rear of the car. It was difficult to see anything with his dark glasses on, so he held out his hand in the general direction of the other seat and said: "Awfully pleased to meet you, Lady Grimbledon."

The woman took his hand and said: "Pleased to meet you too, Mister Washbrook."

Turnbull turned on the light over the rear seats, and Charles turned and looked at his companion properly. He now saw that the woman who had been introduced as Viscountess Grimbledon was actually his stepmother Leonora Goodgame.

"Good Lord!" he said.

"I beg your pardon?"

"Um ... I said 'Good to have you on board'."

Leonora decided this shabby-looking man was a bit senile, and certainly not worthy of her attention. She turned away and looked out of her window at the flakes of snow that were still drifting down. Charles wondered how on earth it was possible to mix up Diana Bagshot and Leonora Goodgame. And why had his stepmother not corrected Winstanley when he got her name wrong? He was about to explain to Winstanley that there had been some mistake, but as the real Walter Washbrook presumably knew neither of these women, he kept quiet.

Turnbull started the engine, turned in the road and headed back in the direction of Great Park. The Rolls drove smoothly out of the village and Leonora listened to the quiet hum of the engine. The car was clearly brand new and probably extremely expensive, which she found very pleasing. If the Duke could afford cars like this, he must be very well off indeed.

"This is a very nice car," she said. "How long has the Duke had it?"

"Ah well, the thing is, your ladyship," said Winstanley, "this isn't the Duke's jam jar. I'm the Great Park chauffeur, and I had a bit of an accident on my way to meet you. Mr Turnbull here kindly agreed to bring me here in his motor."

"I see," said Leonora, disappointed that the car belonged to someone other than the Duke, who she still hoped would turn out to be an attractive widower. "So, who does this car belong to?"

"Well, Mr Turnbull works for some very posh people. Isn't that right, Mr T?"

Turnbull nodded.

"What's the name of your lady again?"

"Lady Wickham-Thynne."

"That's the one. She and her husband Sir Arthur ..." Winstanley pronounced it 'Arfer', "... they just arrived. You'll be meeting them just as soon as we get back to the house."

"Sir Arthur didn't make the journey to Great Park," said Turnbull.

"Didn't he?" replied Winstanley. "I definitely saw two passengers in the motor when you arrived. Who was the geezer in the back seat?"

"Lady Cornelia's brother. Mister Ronald Capstan."

"Good Lord!" said Leonora. And Charles. Simultaneously.

*****

After his conversation with Polly, Pickles left her office and scrunched across the snow back to the house. It was already dark, more snow was falling, and it was turning cold. Back inside, he walked along the hall just in time to see Lady Wickham-Thynne and her brother coming down the stairs. He put on his most welcoming smile and said, "I trust you are both happy with your accommodations?"

"Yes, perfectly acceptable," said Lady Wickham-Thynne. Her brother said nothing. He was examining a vase that was on the dresser at the bottom of the stairs. So far, Pickles had not heard Ronnie Capstan utter a single word. The butler was beginning to wonder if the man who might be Polly's father might also be mute.

"Please come into the drawing room," said the butler. "I can prepare a pre-dinner cocktail for you, and I'm delighted to tell you that you will be the first visitors to Great Park to view a new portrait of the Duke."

"Where *is* the old toad?" asked Ronnie.

"I beg your pardon, sir?"

"Woolnough. Where is he?"

"I'm afraid the Duke woke this morning with a slight fever and thought it prudent to remain in his suite until dinner. His personal physician attended him and administered a medication designed to stabilise his temperature." The second sentence was untrue, there being no personal physician, on or off the premises. Pickles himself prepared a hot honey and lemon drink, and gave the Duke several aspirin tablets to see him through the day. He had also left a decanter of brandy by his bed.

The butler opened the door to the blue drawing room. "Do please come in."

The three of them entered the room, which was looking splendid. The servants had done an excellent job, making it look spruce and tidy. The portrait of the Duke was on an easel in the middle of the room and Snowball the Labrador was lying in front of it. He looked up to see who had entered and wagged his fat tail across the carpet when he saw Pickles, but then growled at the shifty-looking man next to him. Snowball was as astute as Pickles when it came to identifying dodgy visitors.

The new arrivals stood at the door and looked around the room, taking in the furniture, fixtures and fittings. Cornelia noted with approval the classic style of Tarquin's favourite armchair and the chaise longue next to it, and she was impressed by the floor-length crimson drapes on either side of the windows. Ronnie immediately noticed painting over the fireplace. "Is that a Van Gogh?" he asked.

"It is indeed believed to be a Van Gogh, yes," replied Pickles. "It's a portrait of the writer Robert Louis Stevenson. It was acquired from the artist himself, in fact, some fifty years ago by Aloysius Woolnough, the twelfth Duke of Burfaughtonleigh, the present incumbent's grandfather, the man who actually built Great Park." These were the carefully-chosen words that Pickles always used when talking about the portrait. He was certainly happier talking about the Van Gogh (or not) than he would be about the Walter Washbrook (definitely not).

He asked what aperitifs they would like and went over to the drinks cabinet to prepare a gin and tonic for Cornelia and a whisky and soda for her brother. "Do have a look at the Duke's portrait," he said. "It's quite literally hot off the press. The artist has been in residence here for a week and completed it yesterday."

The guests approached the new canvas. Ronnie looked it up and down and burst out laughing. "Is this supposed to be a joke?" he asked.

Pickles felt a jolt of anxiety and took a deep breath before he turned round. "I beg your pardon, Mister Capstan?"

"This is, what do they call it, a caricature, isn't it?" said Ronnie. "I mean, Woolnough can't actually look like that these days. He was fat as a bus when I knew him back it the twenties, so I can't believe he's developed a torso like that. Someone's painted his head on the body of an athlete, haven't they?"

Whilst he was pleased that his own body was being indirectly praised, Pickles was also dismayed by this reaction. Not for the first time, he feared that the portrait might cause laughter rather than admiration. Cornelia had only met Tarquin once, at an exhibition at one of her husband's art galleries, and she didn't remember anything about him. She thought she should try to repair the damage created by her brother's oafish comments about the portrait. "It's awfully good," she said. "Who did it?"

In view of what Polly had just told him, Pickles was now reluctant to mention Walter Washbrook by name, so he decided to talk about the artist's reputation rather than say who he was. "He's a very highly regarded portrait painter, and has painted various members of the royal family," he said.

His attempt to avoid saying the artist's name didn't work.

"Yes, but what's his *name?*" asked Cornelia.

"Walter Washbrook."

Cornelia emitted what can only be described as a loud harrumphing sound. She looked at Pickles, and her already florid face turned a shade more purple. "Did you say Walter WASHBROOK?" Her voice reached a strangulated top C when she said the surname.

"Yes," said Pickles, anxious that his distinguished guest was on the verge of blowing a gasket. "Is there something wrong?"

"Something WRONG? Don't you know ANYTHING about that man? He should be LOCKED UP and the key THROWN AWAY!"

There was a moment's silence. Even Ronnie was aware that the atmosphere was getting a little chilly. "Come on, Eth, live and let live," he said.

"Never mind 'live and let live'!" she snorted. "You say the man has been living here for a week? I cannot believe that you have allowed a KNOWN PEDERAST to stay

307

under this roof! Does your employer have NO morals AT ALL?"

Shocking though this revelation about the artist was, Pickles was running out of patience with these new visitors. Indeed, he was on the point of losing his temper, one of many things they tell you not to do at butler school, and was about to tell Cornelia she had some nerve belly-aching about another guest at a country house party. He was saved from butler suicide by someone rapping on the door. He turned as the door opened and Flockton's head appeared.

"Mr Pickles, sir?" he said.

"What is it, Flockton?"

"Lady Grimbledon has arrived, sir. And the artist fellow came back with her, sir. Mister----"

"THANK YOU, FLOCKTON!" Pickles was aware that his reply was just a little too loud. "I'll be out presently." He turned to his other guests. "If you will excuse me, our guest of honour has arrived." With that carefully-worded insult, he turned on his heel and steered his muscular dancer's body towards the door.

Chapter 26
Mister Capstan seems to have fainted

Charles and Leonora spent the journey back to Great Park deep in thought. Leonora was wondering what to do when she came face to face with her ex-husband Ronnie Capstan. He was here with a woman called Lady Cornelia Wickham-Thynne and was claiming to be her brother. Leonora knew that this couldn't possibly be the case because Ronnie only had one sister and her name was Ethel. Leonora had met her just once, on the day that she and Ronnie married, and had taken an instant dislike to her pushy new sister-in-law, who got very drunk and spent the afternoon trying to latch on to any man who had money or a title. After the wedding, Leonora refused to socialise with her, so whenever Ronnie fetched up in Hampstead to gorge on Anatole's food, he arrived alone.

Leonora decided that she would tell her ex-husband that she knew about his little secret and then continue to play the part of Viscountess Grimbledon. She was certain the fact that Ronnie was not who he claimed to be would work to her advantage.

Charles was confused. At first, he thought the chauffeurs had made a mistake calling their passenger Viscountess Grimbledon, but Leonora hadn't corrected them, so now he was wondering why his stepmother was pretending to be one of her own friends. And what about Polly? Did she know that her mother was about to arrive at the house? And was she also expecting to see her father, who apparently was already there? Charles knew that his stepsister had a fairly low opinion of both her parents, so he was trying to picture what would happen when they all met up.

It was snowing heavily when the car pulled up at the foot of the steps to the house. Winstanley hopped out of the car, opened the door on his side to let Charles out, and Turnbull did the same on the other side. Winstanley then ran up the steps and rapped the metal doorknocker twice. After a few seconds, Flockton opened the door.

"Here, Flocko, listen up," said Winstanley. "Fetch Pickles sharpish, cos we have some very important guests out here who are freezing their arses off." Flockton looked down the steps and saw Walter Washbrook and a tall woman with long black hair looking back up at him. "Right you are," he said. "Please do come in out of the cold!" he shouted down to the new arrivals, then ran into the house to inform the butler.

After a moment's hesitation, Leonora walked quickly up the steps. Charles followed her more slowly, remembering the first time he had entered the house, when he had leaned on a walking stick and huffed and groaned like an old person. He was alarmed to realise that in the intervening few days, he had abandoned both the walking stick and the huffing and groaning.

Inside, the new arrivals peered down the hallway as Flockton knocked on a door and opened it. Pickles appeared, and then a thin woman with red hair walked out into the hall. She started shouting at the butler but when she saw that there were people watching her, she turned and stomped noisily up the stairs. Pickles adjusted his tie, looked towards the front door and went to deal with the new arrivals.

"Lady Grimbledon," he said, with a warm smile. "We are delighted to welcome you to Great Park."

"I'm very pleased to be here," she replied.

"And Mister Washbrook ...." Pickles paused and looked meaningfully at Charles. "It's good to know that you managed to get back."

"Yes, all in one piece, more or less," said Charles.

"Excuse me," said Leonora. "Who was that woman you were just talking to? And what was she so upset about?"

Pickles smiled again and waved an arm to indicate it was nothing serious. "Oh, that was Lady Wickham-Thynne," he said. "It was just a little misunderstanding. I think she may be a little tired after her journey."

"And the man who claims to be her brother?" said Leonora. "Is he here?"

Pickles tried to hide his surprise at the question. "The man who ... you mean Mister Capstan? Yes, he's here." Pickles indicated down the hall. "He's in the blue drawing room. Er ... Lady Grimbledon, I'm delighted to tell you that you will be accommodated in the Forest Suite on the first floor. If you would like to -----"

"I wish to speak to Mister Capstan first."

"I'm sorry?"

"I'd like to speak to Mister Capstan before I see my accommodation."

"Certainly," said Pickles. Things were not going as planned and he was finding it difficult to keep calm. He gave Flockton orders to take Leonora's luggage to her suite and then led the way down the hall to the drawing room. Leonora followed him and Charles huffed and groaned after them. Pickles went to open the door, but Leonora put her hand up in front of him.

"I wish to speak to Mister Capstan alone," she said. She entered the room and closed the door behind her. Pickles and Charles looked at each other for a moment, then both of them started to speak at the same time. Charles deferred to the butler and let him speak.

"First of all," said Pickles. "I know that you aren't Walter Washbrook. Your name is Charles Goodgame, you're Polly Capstan's stepbrother, and you're here under false pretences."

"Oh." Charles took off his dark glasses and put them in the pocket of his overcoat.

"I've a good mind to inform the police..."

"Right."

"... but I gather the Duke has decided that you should keep up this ridiculous charade for the weekend, so I will say no more about it."

"Right ho."

"I don't understand why this has happened and I feel extremely upset to have been kept in the dark about it."

"Sorry."

Pickles pointed at the door of the drawing room. "I also know that the man in there is Polly's father," he said.

"Yes, I worked that out, too," said Charles.

"What? You know Mister Capstan?"

"No, never met him," said Charles. "But I've heard all about him from Pol. He's a bit of a character, by all accounts."

"Indeed," said Pickles. "And I gather he's only recently been released from prison."

"Right, I remember she said he'd been banged up for something."

Pickles sighed and suddenly looked very tired. "I must say that all this has been rather too much for me to deal with."

"Well, there's something else you ought to know," said Charles.

"Is it important? I don't think I can cope with any more surprises."

"Well, I suppose it *is* rather important."

"What is it?"

"That woman who just went in there ..."

"Lady Grimbledon? What about her?"

"Well, that's the thing," said Charles, and paused for a moment. "She isn't Lady Grimbledon."

"WHAT? Are you sure?"

"Absolutely certain."

"Who is she?"

"Her name is Leonora Goodgame."

"Leonora Goodgame? How do you know?"

"Clue's in the name. She's my stepmother."

"Your stepmother? Oh come on, this is getting ridiculous!"

"I agree. But that's not all. If you already know about me and Pol and put two and two together, you should be able to work out something else about her."

"I'm sorry, Mister Goodgame, I'm not very good at riddles."

"If the woman in there is my step*mother* and Polly is my step*sister*, then it stands to reason ...."

Pickles looked at Charles, his eyes open very wide. "Oh, please don't tell me...."

"That woman is Polly's mother."

Pickles held his head in his hands. "I don't think I can take any more of this," he said.

"I'll go and get Pol," said Charles, and set off at speed down the hall in the direction of his stepsister's office.

At that moment, there was the sound of a man laughing from inside the room, followed by a woman shouting. Then there was a loud thud, a scream, and finally something that sounded very much like a body crashing to the floor.

*****

Ronnie was standing in front of the fire inspecting the signature at the bottom of the portrait of Robert Louis Stevenson when the door opened. He stepped away and walked towards the window, without looking to see who the new arrival was. Leonora closed the door behind her and walked towards him.

"Ronnie," she said quietly.

He turned round. "Good God, Leonora! What on earth are you doing here?"

"I could ask you the same thing."

"I'm here with my sister."

"Don't be ridiculous. You're pretending to be the brother of some woman called Wickham-Thynne."

"I'm not pretending. She really is my sister. She's married to a chap called Arthur Wickham-Thynne."

"But this woman's name is Cornelia. You only have one sister, and her name is Ethel."

"Right both times. She changed her name and nabbed a rich husband, which was always the plan. Arthur couldn't make it to this tiresome event, so I gallantly agreed to step into the breach and be Eth's plus one."

There was a pause.

"So, how come you're here, Leonora? I didn't see your name on the guest list." Ronnie hadn't seen a guest list of any kind, but he was enjoying having the upper hand in the conversation.

Leonora had hoped to persuade Ronnie to keep quiet about her real identity by offering to do the same for him, but her bargaining powers were now seriously reduced.

"I'm here representing my best friend, the Viscountess Grimbledon, who at the last minute was unable to attend," she said. "She asked me to take her place. Unfortunately, there has been some kind of misunderstanding and the people here think I'm actually the Viscountess herself. To avoid any embarrassment, I've decided not to disabuse them of this notion. So, while I'm here, I will let them call me Lady Grimbledon."

Ronnie laughed out loud. "That's the funniest thing I've heard in ages. You should quit writing those tedious novels and start writing comedies instead."

"You think my novels are tedious, do you?" said Leonora. "I don't remember you saying anything like that when they were making money. Money which went directly into your bank account."

"Oh come on, I gave you money whenever you needed it. If I hadn't looked after it for you, you'd have spent the lot, and then where would we have been?"

"In prison, perhaps? Oh I forgot, that's where you ended up anyway."

"Indeed I did, and now I'm out. I've served my time and I'm a free man."

Leonora paused for a moment. "I wonder if the people here know all about your recent incarceration" she said.

"Don't even think about telling anyone."

"Really? You don't think they would be interested?"

"I'm warning you, Leonora."

"I think they would be *most* interested," she said. "That and the fact that you make a living by cheating gullible old people out of their savings."

Ronnie walked towards her. "If you choose to say anything about that, I'll have your guts for garters." He raised his hands, as if he was planning to take her by the throat.

"DON'T YOU DARE TOUCH ME!" she shouted. She backed away from him, colliding with the easel containing the Duke's portrait. The painting fell to the floor with a crash. Ronnie walked towards her, and Leonora picked up the easel and swung it in the direction of his head like a cricket bat, scoring a direct hit on his temple. He collapsed on the floor, falling onto the portrait, and his hand punched a hole straight through the Duke's forehead.

Leonora looked down at his inert body. Either he was pretending to be unconscious just to annoy her or he really was unconscious. She knelt, pulled his heavy body up by the shoulders and turned his face towards her. He wasn't the best-looking of men and his looks were not improved with his mouth open, his tongue hanging out and his eyes disappearing into his head.

There was a knock on the door and Pickles entered. In front of him, he saw the people he now knew to be Polly's parents. The mother was on her knees, and she was slapping the face of what looked like the lifeless body of her ex-husband. Leonora stood up, letting Ronnie crash to the floor onto the Duke's portrait.

"Oh hello," said Leonora, calmly. "I don't suppose there's a doctor in the house, is there? Mister Capstan seems to have fainted."

"The only one in the house with any medical training," said Pickles, "is the Duke's secretary." He looked Leonora directly in her eyes. "I will go and summon her. I think you may know her."

"Really?" asked Leonora.

"Yes. Her name is Polly Capstan."

316

"Polly Capstan," said Leonora. She closed her eyes, reeled to one side and fell to the floor in a dead faint. At that moment, Polly raced into the room, where she saw her parents lying on the floor, one on top of the other, with the Duke's portrait beneath them.

*****

When the new guests had entered the house, Winstanley hurried round to his cottage. He needed to do something about the car in the ditch, but he was also feeling quite hungry, so he took a loaf from the bread bin and some cold ham from the larder, and made a large sandwich which he slowly munched at the kitchen table. Then he put on an overcoat, scarf and hat and trudged through the snow to look for Garth. He found him in the stable scraping mud off the tractor's huge back wheels with a hoof pick.

No horse had lived at Great Park since the days of Tarquin's father, but the riding paraphernalia remained - saddles, harnesses, stirrups, nosebags, feed buckets, grooming brushes, hoof picks - nothing had been disposed of. It was as if everyone was waiting for things to return to the old days after the reign of the fourteenth Duke. In the meantime, if there were alternative uses for the equipment, all well and good, and a hoof pick was the perfect tool to unclog the treads of tractor tyres.

Winstanley explained that the Humber needed to be pulled out of a ditch on the main road. Garth went over to one of the stalls and picked up a long coil of rope. They climbed onto the tractor and Garth pumped the accelerator and the tractor engine began to chug loudly. Winstanley looked behind to see how much smoke the exhaust was emitting and made a mental note to check the carburettor as soon as he could. The tractor reversed in a semi-circle, Garth clanked it into forward gear and they drove noisily out of the stable, where a flurry of snow hit them in the face. Winstanley held the brim of his hat over his eyes and neither man spoke as they made their way down the driveway towards the gatehouse, where Garth gently pressed the brake and stopped the tractor.

Winstanley indicated to the left. "The Humber's over there," he said. "Just past the telegraph pole."

Through the darkness and the snow, Garth could hardly see the pole, let alone the car that was apparently in a ditch just past it, but he revved the engine and the tractor moved forward.

"Hold up!" said Winstanley, grabbing Garth by the arm. "Something's coming!" He could see the headlights of a car which was approaching rapidly from the direction of Cheltenham. Garth took his foot off the accelerator and pressed hard on the brake. Unfortunately, the part of the driveway they were on was covered in ice, and there was nothing he could do to stop the tractor rolling forward and out into the road. The driver of the car sounded his horn but the tractor kept moving forward, there was a sound of shrieking brakes and the car zigzagged past them and into the ditch, coming to rest next to the Humber.

The two men jumped off the tractor and ran across the road and down into the ditch. Winstanley noted with some concern that the car was a very expensive Bentley Derby 3.5 litre saloon. He opened the door on the driver's side, leaned inside and switched on the light over the dashboard.

A man was slumped over the steering wheel and a woman in the passenger seat was leaning against the door. She turned to look at the driver, then at Winstanley. At that moment, Garth opened the passenger door, and she had to stop herself from falling out. When she turned and saw the gardener's giant face, his beard flecked with snow, she howled, pulled the door shut and grabbed the arm of the driver. Garth decided it would be better if he made himself scarce, so he clambered out of the ditch and went back to sit on the tractor.

"It's all right, missus," said Winstanley, "we're here to help. We both work at the big house across the road." The woman looked confused, and she held the driver's arm even more tightly.

"What happened?" she asked. "I was asleep. Where are we?" She leaned over and stroked the driver's head. "Alex, are you all right?"

The driver opened his eyes and raised his head. "I don't know," he replied. He looked at her and then at Winstanley. "Who are you?"

"The name's Winstanley, sir."

The man groaned quietly, closed his eyes and leaned his head against the door frame. "I just want to go to sleep," he said.

"Can you please tell us what happened?" asked the woman.

"I think your husband was barrelling along a bit," said Winstanley. "And he went into a spin on the ice."

"He isn't my husband," said the woman.

"Fair do's," said Winstanley. Rescuing the two cars would be more easily achieved in daylight, so he decided the most sensible thing would be to get the two people back to the house and explain the situation to Pickles. He would know how to sort things out.

The woman shook the driver's arm. "Alex, will you please wake up?" The man opened his eyes and began to feel his arms and shoulders with his hands.

"Can you hear me, sir?" asked Winstanley.

"Loud and clear."

"I'm very sorry that your car's ended up down here. We're very near the house where I work, it's called Great Park, and I think it would be a good idea if you and your ... your friend come up to the house while we work out what to do."

The man nodded and turned to the woman. "He thinks we should go up to the house."

"I heard him," she replied.

The two of them got out of the car and opened the back door to retrieve their coats. The woman also took her handbag off the back seat.

"Any luggage in the boot?" asked Winstanley.

"No," said the man. "This was just a day trip. We were heading back to London. We've been ---"

"Alexander, I don't think the man needs to know any more," said the woman.

"Of course. Sorry, Diana."

Winstanley was wondering how all four of them could get back up to the house when he saw another car coming down the road from the direction of Stanford Saint Mary. Fortunately, it was travelling more slowly and when the driver saw the tractor in his headlights, he pulled up and stopped. Winstanley ran across the road waving his arms, and the driver, a short old man wearing a long black overcoat and a bowler hat, got out. Winstanley thought he recognised him but couldn't immediately remember where from.

"Excuse me, squire," he said. "I wonder if I could ask you a favour."

320

The man looked at the chauffeur. "It's Winstanley, isn't it?"

"Yes, sir." The chauffeur recognised the man's voice. It was Doctor Soames, someone he had ferried from Stanford Saint Mary to Great Park more than once to minister to the Duke. "Ah! Hello, doc!" he said. "What a pleasant surprise. There's been a bit of a to-do here and we need to get a couple of people up to the house. Could you possibly help out?"

"Of course," said the doctor. "As it happens, I was heading up to the house. I would have been here sooner, but I just ran over a sheep and killed it, I'm afraid."

"Ah," said Winstanley, knowing he was an accessory to the death of the blameless creature.

"I gather there's been some kind of accident," said the doctor. "At the house."

"Has there? Well, there's a turn-up. You leave the house for ten minutes and all hell breaks loose." Winstanley ran back to the car, and the two occupants walked across the road. Doctor Soames asked them a couple of questions about what had happened, then opened the back door of his car to let them in.

"When we get to the house, I'll examine you both," said the doctor.

"Actually, I'm also a doctor," said the man.

"Oh really? That's marvellous. I might have an emergency to deal with, so any help would be gratefully received. Someone's been hurt, a blow to the head, apparently. We'd better get up to the house right away, so I can assess what needs to be done."

Winstanley checked with Garth that he could turn the tractor round and take it back to the house, then asked if he could travel with the others in the car. Doctor Soames started the engine, reversed a little, then turned up into the driveway.

"Excuse me," said the woman, as the car trundled towards the house.

"Oh sorry, ma'am, how can I help?" asked Winstanley.

"Did you say this is Great Park?"

"Yes, ma'am."

"The residence of the Duke of Burfaughtonleigh?"

"It is indeed. The Duke prefers to pronounce it 'Burley', but the way you said it is exactly what the locals call it. Burfaughtonleigh. It's a village a few miles from here."

The woman started to laugh.

"Yes, it's a funny old name, isn't it?" said Winstanley.

"That isn't why I'm laughing," said the woman. "Isn't the Duke having some kind of event this weekend?"

"Right again, ma'am. Well, supposed to be. All sorts of nobs are fetching up tomorrow for a shoot. Although if it don't stop snowing soon, the birds ain't gonna wanna fly, are they?"

"How did you know about the event?" asked the man.

"I was invited," said the woman.

"Really?"

"Yes. Actually, I was going to reply to tell them I couldn't come, but I mislaid the invitation."

"And now we're here anyway. How strange."

The doctor pulled up at the bottom of the steps that led to the front door of the house. "If you'll excuse me," he said. "I'd better get along to see what's going on."

"Off you go, doc," said Winstanley. "I'll look after the new guests."

The doctor ran up the steps and knocked on the door. After a few moments, Flockton opened it and let him in, indicating where he should go to deal with the emergency. The under-butler was about to close the door when Winstanley called him.

"Hey, Flocko!" he said. "Can you ask Pickles to come to the door?"

"What is it this time?" asked Flockton. "He's a bit tied up at the moment. There's been an incident. That's why they phoned for the doctor."

"I understand that," said Winstanley. "But we've got another emergency to deal with. Unexpected guests. Pickles'll be able to sort it out in two shakes of a whatsit."

"Good grief! More guests?" Flockton ran back down the hall.

Winstanley turned to Alexander and Diana. "Would you like to step inside the house?" he asked. "And careful you don't come a cropper on the steps. The snow's turning to ice, so hold on to the rail."

All three walked carefully up the steps and into the house and Pickles walked towards them, with his usual welcoming smile. Winstanley decided to make introductions and keep the tractor's part in the accident a secret for the time being. "Mister Pickles sir, by way of explanation. This gentleman and lady just had a prang right by the gatehouse. Their car needs retrieving. To be honest, it would be best done in the morning when we can see what we're doing."

Pickles looked at the two guests, who seemed well dressed and, more importantly, well off. "Well, it's quite late, and the weather is terrible. I think I should be able to arrange a room for you."

"Two rooms?" asked the man quietly.

"Two rooms? Ah, yes, why not? Absolutely no problem at all," he said. "Welcome to Great Park. May I have the pleasure of knowing your names?"

"Of course," said the man. "My name is Alexander Malleson. And this is my friend Diana Bagshot, the Viscountess Grimbledon."

There was a moment's silence.

"Did you say Viscountess Grimblydon?" asked Winstanley.

"Grimbledon, yes."

"Well, blow me down with a feather."

The door of the blue drawing room opened, and a man and two women walked out into the hallway. The man was Charles Goodgame, the women were his stepsister Polly and her mother Leonora.

Chapter 27
Why were you pretending to be her?

Pickles stared at the new guests, took a deep breath and began to speak. "Did you say ----?" He didn't complete the question.

"Leonora!" Diana spotted her friend in the group of people standing further down the hallway. She ran down the hall and embraced her. "How wonderful to see you here!" she said.

"Oh my God!" said Leonora. Considering the circumstances, she recovered her composure remarkably quickly. "Diana! Lovely to see you, too!"

"Are you here for the shoot?" asked Diana. "I didn't realise you'd been invited. Why didn't you tell me? We could have come up from London together."

"I didn't think you were planning to come."

"Actually, you're right, I wasn't. Alexander and I were driving past, and we ended up in a ditch." She turned and gestured for her companion to join them. "Alex! This is my friend Leonora." She turned back to her friend. "Leo, this is Alex. I've told him lots about you."

"Yes, indeed," said Alexander. "So pleased to meet you, Leonora." They shook hands, and when he was able to retrieve his hand from her firm grasp, he turned to introduce himself to the circle of people who were silently looking at the new arrivals. He approached the eccentric-looking older man with dark glasses first.

"Alexander Malleson," he said, extending his hand. Charles stared at the hand and then held out his own.

"Um ... Walter Washbrook," said Charles. He glanced at Pickles, who huffed but remained silent.

"Walter Washbrook, did you say?"

"Yes," said Charles.

"Are you the chap who paints portraits?"

"Um ... yes."

"What a small world! You painted my mother about twenty years ago. Matilda Malleson. Do you remember her?"

"No. Sorry."

"Oh, how stupid of me!" said Alexander. "You probably knew her as Lady Thornberry."

"Oh right!" said Charles, feigning recognition of the name. "Yes, good old Lady T! What a trooper!"

Alexander was surprised to hear his deadly dull mother described as a trooper but didn't comment. He held out his hand to the pretty young woman who seemed to be hiding behind Charles. "Alexander Malleson," he said again.

"Polly Capstan," said Polly, very quietly.

"Oh my goodness! Polly, you're here, too!" said Diana, walking over and clasping her in an embrace. "What a lovely surprise! Are you here for the shoot, too?"

"What? Oh, no. I work here. I'm the Duke's secretary."

"Oh! How interesting!" Diana remembered Polly as a lively, vivacious young woman but she was looking listless and preoccupied. She put her arm round her shoulders. "Polly, is everything all right?"

"Um, no, not really. My father's here...."

"Ronnie's here?" Diana looked at Leonora. "Have you two made it up?"

"Good Lord!" said Alexander. "Ronnie Capstan is here?"

Pickles and Winstanley watched the conversation with great interest. The people who had just arrived at the house seemed to know pretty much everyone who was already there. The butler started to speak. "If I may be so bold...."

Polly put her hand on his arm. "It's all right, Monty," she said. "I think we all need to sit down. Why don't we go into the drawing room?"

"That's an excellent idea," said the butler. He opened the door and motioned everyone to enter. Winstanley knew without having to ask that the invitation wasn't extended to him.

The drawing room was a welcoming sight, a log fire was burning and there were no bodies lying on the floor. The Duke's portrait was back on its easel in the middle of the room, albeit with a hole in the forehead. Leonora, Diana and Alexander sat on the couch near the fire and Charles sat opposite them on the chaise longue. Pickles asked them what they would like to drink, opened the glass doors of the cabinet, and started preparing apéritifs.

Polly decided it was time for some explanations. "Mother, there's no point in delaying this any longer," she said. She pointed at Diana. "Why were you pretending to be her?"

"Why was she what?" asked Diana.

"For some reason, when my mother arrived, she told everyone that she was Viscountess Grimbledon."

"Good heavens! Did you, Leonora?"

"Yes."

"Whatever for?"

"It's a bit complicated. I ----"

There was a loud rattling noise and someone outside the room started cursing. The door eventually opened and a short, fat man with a bald head entered. He was wearing a purple dressing gown and red slippers with pom-poms. It was the Duke, who had forgotten to put on his curly brown wig. He was not in the best of moods.

He had anaesthetised himself during the day by drinking from the decanter of brandy that Pickles had left for him, and then fallen asleep. He woke up with a painful combination of head cold and hangover, so he yanked the cord next to his bed to ring the bell in Pickles's alcove next to the kitchen. Unfortunately, the butler was otherwise engaged trying to revive Ronnie Capstan, and heard neither the bell nor Tarquin's angry yelling when no one came to attend to him.

The Duke's mood changed as soon as he saw that there were guests. "Aha!" he said, a smile spreading across his face. "Hello, everyone! Welcome to my humble abode!" He scratched his head and when he realised he wasn't wearing his wig, he briefly considered returning to his room to put it on, but decided to soldier on without it. He glanced at the portrait on the easel and did a double take when he saw the hole in the forehead. He closed his eyes and shook his head, but when he looked again, the hole was still there. He shuffled on, ready to be the world's best host.

Alexander Malleson stood up and held out his hand, which Tarquin took between his pudgy palms.

"How do you do?" said Alexander.

The Duke tried to place the new arrival's face. "Sir Arthur?" he said, a note of uncertainty in his voice.

"Er, no. Alexander Malleson."

"I'm not sure I've had the pleasure," said Tarquin.

"I drove Lady Grimbledon here."

"Oh, I see!" Tarquin looked at the two women sitting next to each other on the chaise longue. "The Duke of Burfaughtonleigh, *à votre service*," he said. "I won't come too close, so you don't catch this terrible cold." He had a hazy memory of Arthur Wickham-Thynne's wife but neither of the women looked like the image in his mind. "So," he continued, "which of you charming ladies is the Viscountess Grimbledon and ... um ... which is Lady Wickham-Thynne?"

Diana didn't recognise the second name but decided to take charge of the situation. "I'm Lady Grimbledon," she said. "And this is my good friend Leonora Capstan. Or Goodgame, if you prefer. Leonora has been staying at my apartment in London, so I hope you don't mind that I invited her along, too."

Pickles raised his eyes at this development but said nothing.

"No, of course not, *enchanté* to meet *toutes les deux*," said Tarquin. He turned and looked at Polly with a puzzled look on his face and mouthed the word 'Capstan?'. When he turned back to face his guests, he was all smiles.

"I trust Pickles and my excellent staff have made you all welcome," he said. He then flopped down into his favourite armchair and crossed his legs. After making sure his dressing gown was covering most of his fleshy thighs, he ordered a gin and tonic from Pickles.

Outside in the hall, the telephone rang. The butler excused himself and went to answer it. When he came back a few minutes later, the atmosphere was considerably improved, and laughter sounded round the room. Tarquin was telling stories about rich and famous people he had met when he was younger, taking care not to identify them. He paused for a moment and the butler coughed to engage his employer's attention.

"What's the news from the front, dear boy?" asked Tarquin.

"I've just taken a call from Bernard Maxted, Lord Winchcombe's butler," said Pickles. "His Lordship won't be able to attend the shoot tomorrow due to the inclement weather."

"Oh, *quelle dommage*," said Tarquin. "Still, that's one less mouth to feed. And quite a large one," he added, grinning at his guests.

"I'm afraid Maxted was also calling on behalf of Lord Nailsmith and Lord Longhope," Pickles continued. "They can't make it, either."

The smile disappeared from Tarquin's face.

"Nor can the Duke of Tewksbury or the Dowager Lady Wootton."

"Good Lord, that's just about the entire local crew we invited."

"I don't have much experience of shoots," said Alexander. "But I would imagine it would be rather difficult to have one in this weather."

"With the greatest respect, Your Grace, I think Mister Malleson is right," said Pickles. "If you're agreeable, I could make two telephone calls, one to the dog people and the other to the agent who's providing the beaters. I think, in all honesty, it would be best to abandon hope of holding the shoot. We will of course do what we can to entertain those of you who managed to get here despite the weather. And there will be the grand banquet tomorrow evening."

Tarquin sighed and nodded and made a flicking movement with his hand towards the door. Pickles made his way back to the telephone in the hall.

"Well, this is all wonderful," said Diana. "I wasn't expecting to spend the weekend in a lovely country house, but I'm awfully pleased to be here."

"Me too," said Leonora. She was feeling relaxed for the first time since she arrived at Great Park. She squeezed Diana's hand and whispered "Thank you" in her ear. Even though the Duke of Burfaughtonleigh was not the attractive widower she had hoped for, the idea of a country house weekend now seemed a pleasant prospect. And at some point, she wanted to go back and re-acquaint herself with the muscular stationmaster at Stanford Saint Mary.

There was a knock at the door. Tarquin yelled "Come!", and the door opened. Flockton took a moment to realise that the bald man in the dressing gown was his employer. "Ah! Sorry, Your Grace," he said. "If it isn't too much trouble, Doctor Soames wants to have a word."

"Doctor Soames?" said Tarquin. The head of the man himself appeared. "Soames! Good Lord, what are you doing here?"

It took the doctor a moment to realise the bald-headed man who was speaking to him was actually the Duke of Burfaughtonleigh. "I was summoned by Pickles," he said.

"Why? Is someone ill?"

It was now the turn of Pickles's head to appear, in the gap between the two other heads which were already looking into the room. "There was an incident earlier, Your Grace," said the latest head. "I felt it wise to call Doctor Soames and request that he come immediately."

"An incident? What sort of incident?"

Pickles looked at the doctor and asked him to explain.

"I've been attending to Mister Ronald Capstan," said Soames. "Mister Capstan suffered a concussion, here in this very room. He's regained consciousness, but he appears to have lost his memory. At any rate, he's forgotten why he's here."

"Ronald Capstan, you say?" said Tarquin. "Who is he? I don't recall inviting anyone called Capstan." He glanced at Polly, and then at Leonora. Both of them Capstans. Had they invited him?

"Well, that's as may be," said the doctor. "The fact is, Mister Capstan needs to be taken to an infirmary immediately. I recommend the Montpellier Clinic in Cheltenham." Soames always recommended the Montpellier Clinic in Cheltenham because he earned money from his consultancy work there. "Furthermore," he continued, "the patient should travel in something rather more comfortable than my Austin."

"I would have been happy to take him," said Alexander. "Unfortunately, as you know, my car is in the ditch outside."

"Yes, of course," said the doctor. "I was wondering if the chauffeur was available."

"I'll go and look for Winstanley," said Polly. She walked past the doctor and out of the room.

"I'm sorry, I'm just a little confused," said the Duke. "This Capstan chap. Who is he and what's he doing here?"

There was a moment's silence. There were various people in the room who could answer the question. Pickles decided to reveal just enough to satisfy the Duke's curiosity.

"Mister Capstan came with Lady Wickham-Thynne," said the butler.

"Did he? Why?"

"He's her brother."

"Oh, I see," said Tarquin. "And the Wickham-Thynnes. Where are they?"

"I'm afraid Sir Arthur was unable to attend."

Tarquin let out a noise which sounded like a cough. It was in fact a grunt of annoyance. Sir Arthur had been his best bet for some financial assistance. "And Lady Wickham-Thynne?"

The door opened and the woman that Tarquin was asking about appeared. Cornelia had only woken up a few minutes before, her short red hair was sticking out at angles, and the make-up on her left eye was smeared across her cheek. After her earlier rant about Walter Washbrook, she had gone upstairs to her room, thrown herself on the bed and fallen asleep. As was always the case when she woke up, whatever time of day it was, her throat was parched, and she needed alcohol. She stared at the assembled group of people, recognising no one except the butler.

"I say," she said. "Any chance of a gin and tonic?"

Tarquin stared at the woman. He vaguely recognised her, but he couldn't be sure, and there were so many unexpected guests in the house, he didn't want to make any more *faux pas.* He looked at Pickles for help.

"Of course, Lady Wickham-Thynne," said Pickles. "Do take a seat and I'll fix something for you immediately."

Now that Tarquin knew who the new arrival was, he rose unsteadily to his feet and walked towards her. She recoiled at the sight of someone so inappropriately dressed. Tarquin grasped her hand and shook it sweatily. "Lady Wickham-Thynne!" he said enthusiastically.

She pulled her hand away from his grip. "And you are ...?" she asked.

Tarquin attempted a gentle laugh, but because of his cold, it sounded more like a sneeze. "Your host," he said. "I'm the Duke of Burfaughtonleigh."

Cornelia looked him up and down, from his mottled bald head to his red slippers with the ridiculous pom-poms on them. "Don't you think you ought to get dressed?" she said, and walked past him in the direction of the drinks cabinet.

Tarquin felt like saying something about her gaunt appearance and smudged make-up, but realised she was right. Even though he was in his own home, he had no business consorting with his distinguished guests wearing nothing more than a dressing gown and slippers. He wasn't even wearing underwear, a fact that more than one of his guests had already noted.

"You know what?" he said. "Lady Wickham-Thynne is absolutely right. I've been enjoying chatting with you all so much, I'd completely forgotten that I came downstairs virtually *déshabillé*. I will repair to my rooms and put this right immediately."

With that he turned to leave the room. Unfortunately for him, at that very moment the door opened again and smacked him on the forehead, throwing him backwards onto the floor. He hit the carpet with a thud and the belt on his dressing gown burst open, revealing the full extent of his *deshabille*. There were gasps of horror, everyone stood up and the two doctors in the room ran towards him.

"I'm absolutely fine," said the Duke. He raised himself onto his elbows and eventually sat up. "If you can just help me up." He wrapped the dressing gown around his bulky middle with one hand and held out the other for assistance. Alexander pulled him up and, with a yelp of pain, the Duke regained his feet.

Everyone in the room then turned to look at the man who had entered. It was Ronnie Capstan. He had a white bandage round his head and was looking blankly round the room. Doctor Soames approached him. "Mister Capstan, I asked you to stay in your room while I organise some transportation for you," he said.

Ronnie ignored the doctor. "Eth, are you here?" he asked, squinting as he tried to focus on the various people in the room. His sister was at the drinks cabinet, where she was fixing herself a gin and tonic.

"I'm over here, Ronnie," she said, looking across at him. "Goodness! What on earth have you been up to? You look frightful. Get yourself a drink." She downed her G and T and felt restored enough to socialise. She walked towards the circle of people sitting round the fire, but stopped when she recognised Leonora.

Ronnie chose that moment to give her a warning. "I'd look out if I were you, Eth," he said. "Mad Leonora is here somewhere, pretending to be Lady Something-or-other, and she biffed me on the head with a lump of wood."

"What?" asked his sister.

"Leonora hit me with a lump of wood."

Cornelia looked at Leonora. "Is this true?" she asked. "Did you attack my brother?"

Diana rescued the situation. "I think Mister Capstan must have got the wrong end of the stick," she said. "Or indeed the wrong end of the lump of wood." There was a murmured laugh from Alexander. "I'm the Lady Something-or-other he's referring to, Viscountess Grimbledon in fact, and Leonora is here as my guest."

Cornelia glared at her brother, then smiled sweetly at the Viscountess. "I see," she said. "Well, no harm done, I suppose. For those of you who don't know me, I'm Lady Cornelia Wickham-Thynne, wife of Sir Arthur Wickham-Thynne, who's the great-grandson of Princess Feodora of Leiningen, the sister of Queen Victoria. As such, he's forty-seventh in line to the throne." Cornelia didn't usually introduce herself in such a grand manner but with Dukes and Viscountesses in the room, she felt the need to establish herself as a *bona fide* toff.

"Well, this is all very pleasant," said Tarquin. "I'm feeling much better now, so if you'll excuse me, I'll just pop upstairs and get into my glad rags, then the party can really begin." He indicated his favourite armchair to Ronnie. "Perhaps you would like to sit here, Mister Capstan?" The two men stared at each other in silence for a few seconds. The visitor looked familiar from somewhere. Ronnie coughed his distinctive smoker's cough, and Tarquin remembered where.

"Oh, Lord .... it's Arbuthnot Twistleton," he said quietly.

Chapter 28
I'm not staying in this madhouse a moment longer

Arbuthnot Twistleton was the name Ronnie Capstan was using when he first met Tarquin Woolnough in a Soho nightclub more than twenty years before, when Tarquin was very much down on his luck. Ronnie had introduced himself and tried to sell his new acquaintance some shares in a South African gold mine. Tarquin wasn't interested in the shares, but the two of them kept in touch and eventually got involved in several business deals. Like most of Ronnie's working relationships, it ended acrimoniously, but at least Tarquin didn't try to shoot him, as the Argentinian Carlos Petworth had done.

And now, here he was, turning up at Great Park like the proverbial bad penny. And operating under a different name as well. The Duke said something quietly to his concussed guest as he shuffled out of the drawing room. Ronnie ignored him and continued to stare at the other people in the room. Doctor Soames put his arm under Ronnie's elbow and led him towards the armchair. Cornelia walked over and sat on the arm of the chair. "Ronnie, what the dickens are you talking about, saying that Leonora hit you with a lump of wood?" she asked.

Ronnie turned to her and blinked twice. "She did hit me with a lump of wood."

"What lump of wood?"

Ronnie pointed at the easel. "That one."

"That isn't a lump of wood, it's an easel."

"I don't give a fuck what it's called. She walked in here and nearly killed me with it."

The doctor approached the two of them. "Lady Wickham-Thynne, allow me to introduce myself," he said. "I'm Doctor Soames. I was summoned from Stanford Saint Mary after your brother was involved in an altercation."

"It wasn't an altercation," said Ronnie. "My ex-wife biffed me on the head with a lump of wood."

"Yes indeed." Soames had not formed a positive opinion of his patient, who had been rude to him from the moment he regained consciousness, but professional detachment helped him to continue without losing his temper. "The thing is, Mister Capstan is probably concussed, and he also sustained quite a nasty cut to his temple which needs immediate medical attention."

"Nonsense," said Cornelia. "He isn't concussed. He always looks like that. He just needs a stiff drink." She gave Ronnie the large brandy she'd poured for him. "He's going nowhere. He's staying here for the shoot."

"I gather the shoot has been cancelled," said Soames.

"Has it?" Cornelia marched over to talk to Pickles. "What's all this about the shoot being cancelled?"

"I'm afraid the weather, as you can see, has turned inclement," said Pickles. He thought it best to give the impression that the decision was out of his hands. "As a result, the beaters and the people who were to provide us with dogs are unable to fulfil their obligations."

"What on earth are we going to do, stuck out here?" asked Cornelia. "Get drunk, I suppose. Give me another gin and tonic."

While Pickles prepared her drink, which used up the last of the gin and most of the remaining tonic, Cornelia looked around at the various people in the room, trying to decide if any of them were worth talking to. Ronnie was sitting with his glass of brandy, staring in front of

338

him. The Viscountess and her friend were very attractive, but Cornelia wasn't about to join a group that included the awful Leonora. Finally, sitting alone on the chaise longue, was the strange-looking grey-haired man wearing dark glasses and a long overcoat.

Pickles passed her a drink. "Thank you," she said.

"You're welcome," said Pickles, pleased to finally hear a civil response from her.

"Who's the odd cove in the overcoat?" she asked.

Pickles hesitated, remembering her outburst when she heard that Walter Washbrook was in the house. Alexander Malleson chose that moment to ask Charles a question.

"Mister Washbrook?" he said. Charles was miles away and didn't hear his alter ego's name being called out. Alexander repeated his name in a louder voice. Charles still didn't hear him, but Cornelia did. She walked over and stood in front of Alexander.

"Did you say Washbrook?" she asked.

"Yes," replied Alexander.

"Are you talking about Walter Washbrook?"

"Yes."

"Where is he?"

Alexander found the question rather puzzling. "I'm sorry," he said. "I'm not sure I follow."

Cornelia huffed with annoyance. "I presume you're referring to the odious portrait painter who I gather is on the premises somewhere." She looked quickly round the room. "He isn't here, so where is he?"

Alexander frowned. "Yes, he is," he said, pointing at Charles. "He's over there."

Cornelia turned and squinted at Charles. Her eyesight wasn't perfect, and she eschewed the wearing of spectacles for reasons of vanity. Even so, she could clearly see that the man on the chaise longue was half the size of the man she had accosted in the garden in Cheyne Walk just a week before.

"What are you talking about?" she said. "That isn't Walter Washbrook!" She spoke so loudly that Charles finally became aware that he was the subject under discussion. Cornelia marched over to him and then pointed back at Alexander. "That man thinks you're Walter Washbrook," she said. "I know for a fact that you aren't. Who are you?"

"I'm sorry?"

"Who ARE you?"

Charles stood up slowly. First he removed his dark glasses, which he put in the side pocket of his overcoat. He coughed and put one hand on the mantelpiece underneath the portrait of Robert Louis Stevenson.

"You're absolutely right, I'm not Walter Washbrook," he said. "I'm merely impersonating him." He removed his grey wig. There was a gasp from the people on the sofa. "Walter is SO in demand ..." he continued, enjoying his moment in the spotlight. "... and he has a posse of talented young artists who do the work for him, of whom I am one. I volunteered to take this commission." There was another gasp as Charles tossed the wig onto the fire, where it crackled noisily and was consumed by blue flames.

Cornelia wasn't impressed. "What absolute balderdash!" she said. "I have no idea who you are, but I'm not staying in this madhouse a moment longer." She looked at Pickles. "You!" she shouted.

"Yes, Lady Wickham-Thynne?" said the butler. "What can I do for you, you drunken old soak?" He didn't say the second part, he just wanted to.

"I want to leave. Immediately. Call my chauffeur and tell him to get back here and pick me up. He's at the Pig and Whistle, or whatever the place is called."

"Certainly. I will call the Dog and Ferret right away."

"Ronnie!"

Ronnie turned to look at his sister. "Yes, Eth?"

"Come upstairs and pack your bag. We're leaving."

Ronnie drained the last of his brandy, gasping as the spirit hit the back of this throat, then dropped the glass on the floor and followed his sister out of the room. Pickles went into the hall and picked up the telephone.

Doctor Soames had had enough. He no longer cared whether Ronald Capstan lived or died, and decided it was pointless to continue trying to drum up business for the Montpellier Clinic. Without saying a word, he left the room, took his hat from the stand in the hall and let himself out.

Everyone looked at Charles, who was still standing at the mantelpiece as the last of his wig was consumed by the fire. Diana was the first to speak. "I'm sure I recognise you from somewhere," she said. "Have we met before?"

"Yes, we have," he said. "I once sold you a painting."

"Of course!" said Diana. "You're Charles Goodgame, aren't you?"

"Yes."

"Leonora!" she said excitedly. "Your stepson is here!"

Leonora wasn't really concentrating on the conversation around her. She was tipsy and thinking how much she'd enjoyed biffing her ex-husband with the lump of wood and wishing she'd done it several years earlier.

"Leonora, did you hear me?"

"What? Sorry, I was miles away," said Leonora.

"Horace's son Charles. He's here."

Leonora had spent very little time with Charles and, if truth be told, had erased almost everything about Horace's family from her mind. She looked at Charles, with his stuck-on grey beard and red hair. He looked vaguely familiar.

"My stepson, did you say?"

"You clearly don't remember me," said Charles. "I seem to have that effect on people. I am indeed your stepson. I met you when you married my father, and then on one or two occasions subsequently."

"Oh right," said Leonora. "How are you?"

"Very well," said Charles. "And how's my father?"

"Your father?"

"Yes, my father. Horace."

"Well, I imagine he's fine. He's always so busy, we don't see a lot of each other these days."

The door opened and Tarquin appeared, dressed in a flattering green velvet smoking jacket, black trousers and frilly white shirt and cravat. His curly brown wig was back on his head. He had just passed Cornelia and Ronnie on the stairs and had ascertained that they were planning to leave. He didn't know whether to be disappointed or relieved by this information and decided to forget about it and try to enjoy the party.

"Here I am, boys and girls! *Je suis prêt! La fête peut commencer*!" he said, with a playful laugh. Then he saw Charles standing in front of the fire, without his wig and dark glasses. "Ah. Charles, I see you've decided to reveal your true identity."

Chapter 29
Tonight's the night

Friday evening, Cheltenham - roads icy and dangerous

It was nearly five o'clock, dark and cold, when Gilbert Woolnough and Lawrence Kimberley-Waugh left Lionel Pudsey's office and trudged down the street to where the Alfa Romeo was parked. With his gloved hand, Gilbert swept the snow off the driver's door and then unlocked it.

"I'm a bit hungry," said Kimberley-Waugh, as they got into the car. "Can we get something to eat before we head back to Great Park?"

Gilbert said nothing. He started the engine, switched on the wipers to clear the snow from the windscreen, then turned the car in the road and pointed it towards Stanford Saint Mary.

"Can we ---?"

"I heard you! I don't want to spend any more time in this manure heap," said Gilbert. "We can stop at the Plough in Prestbury."

They had arrived in Cheltenham about midday and lunched at the Queen's Hotel. Gilbert scoffed down everything that was put in front of him, but Kimberley-Waugh found the soup tasteless, the steak inedible and the wine undrinkable. Gilbert tried to pay for the meal with a cheque from an old chequebook that he found in a drawer in his father's office, but the waiter brought it back to him, saying that the cashier had rejected it. Apparently, Krumnagel's Bank had re-designed their cheques, and this one was no longer in use. It was Gilbert's bad luck that the manager of the hotel had been

343

talking to the cashier when the cheque was presented. He was also a Krumnagel's customer and knew that it was a dud.

Between them, Gilbert and Lawrence scraped together enough cash to pay for the meal, but the incident made Gilbert even more determined to force Pudsey the accountant to stump up the loot he needed to fund a visit to France. He wanted to sell the rest of his mother's antique jewellery, the gems he told people had belonged to Queen Victoria. Having run out of customers in London, he decided the best thing would be to tap up some of his aristocratic contacts in Paris. He wanted to go in style, of course, first on the Golden Arrow to Dover, then across the Channel to Calais on the new luxury ferry the Canterbury, and finally to Paris first class aboard the Flèche D'Or. Nothing but the best for the Marquis of Stanford.

He shouted and stomped around Pudsey's office like a spoilt child, but Pudsey was defiant, refusing to give Gilbert any information about the family finances and making it abundantly clear that under no circumstances could he dip into the family funds. Gilbert left the office empty-handed.

He was a foot-to-the-floor, force-the-peasants-to-jump-out-of-the-way kind of driver, but snow was falling heavily on the road out of Cheltenham, so he had to slow down. When they arrived in Prestbury, he pulled up outside the Plough Inn and the two plotters went inside, bought pints of ale and slabs of game pie, and took them to a table near the fire. After noisily swallowing his piece of pie in three giant bites and downing the best part of his drink, Gilbert belched loudly and finally indicated what was on his mind.

"Tonight's the night," he said.

"I'm sorry?"

"We're going to do it tonight."

"What? Steal the painting?"

"Yes."

"I thought you wanted to do it tomorrow night."

"I did," said Gilbert, emptying his pint and placing the glass back on the table with a smack that momentarily quietened conversation in the rest of the inn. "But I have a feeling something's up at the house."

"What do you mean?"

"I don't like the way that Washbrook chap stares at me, I can see him doing it even though he's wearing those ridiculous dark spectacles. I think he suspects something. Get me another pint, will you? And some more of that pie."

Kimberley-Waugh was only halfway through his drink, so he went to the bar and ordered one pint and one more piece of pie. The first slab had been enough to quell his hunger, but he knew that his companion's capacity for food was far greater than his and he would be less ratty if he wasn't feeling peckish.

Back at the table, Gilbert noisily devoured his second piece of pie while Kimberley-Waugh finished his pint in silence and stared at the fire. He wondered if it was too late to get out of this caper. His partner in crime was becoming more aggressive and unpredictable by the hour and the Sotheby's man was regretting ever having met him in the first place.

Lawrence Kimberley-Waugh's main weakness was that he wanted to be liked by people of power and influence, or at least by those who belonged to the upper ranks of society. When he met Gilbert Woolnough at a party in London, his first impression had been similar to most people's - what a vile, obnoxious, conceited

345

specimen of humanity this overweight oaf is. And he has a nose that could win prizes in a competition for misshapen vegetables. However, when he discovered his new companion's status, he changed his opinion. The man's a Marquis, for goodness sake, so he's *allowed* to be vile, obnoxious and conceited. And who *cares* if his nose looks like a squashed turnip?

Gilbert had been equally pleased to make the acquaintance of Kimberley-Waugh. Even though he could see that his new friend had a ridiculously high opinion of himself, stopping in front of any mirror he walked past, Gilbert thought that his connections in the art world would come in useful. The idea of stealing the Van Gogh had been on his mind for a while, so his ears pricked up when Kimberley-Waugh told him what he did for a living. When the conversation turned to famous forgeries, the art expert had, in a drunken moment, admitted his involvement in the sale of a Turner painting that turned out to be a fake.

Like Ronnie Capstan, Gilbert was an expert at sniffing out blackmail opportunities. Whenever Kimberley-Waugh indicated the slightest reluctance to continue with the Van Gogh plan, Gilbert reminded him that he could ruin him with just one telephone call, if he so desired.

In fact, Kimberley-Waugh's entire life was a series of lies and inventions. Even his name was false. He was born Arnold Sidebottom, the son of a milkman and a laundry-worker in Hackney. His parents had no money for him to study, so when he left school, he went to work in a haberdashery shop. The first woman he slept with was one of the shop's customers, and he spent a lot of time at her house when her husband was away. He was an art dealer who was often abroad, usually in Paris,

Rome or Madrid, places young Arnold could only dream of visiting. He borrowed the man's degree certificate and got a printer friend to make a copy of it, with a couple of minor adjustments - the name of the graduate, the level of the degree and the date of graduation. He was also delighted to find headed stationery from art galleries in Paris and Milan, which came in very useful to forge work references. He now had a new name, a first class degree in Art History from Cambridge and work references from the owners of galleries in France and Italy. His lover was also able to find him employment at a Chelsea gallery. Subsequently, he used forged credentials to get a job in a larger gallery, and after that, he successfully applied to work at Sotheby's.

Now, on this cold evening in a country pub in Gloucestershire, the liar formerly known as Arnold Sidebottom decided as a last resort to cast doubt on the authenticity of the painting he was supposed to steal. "I'm pretty sure it isn't a Van Gogh," he said.

"You told me you didn't know anything about Van Gogh," replied Gilbert.

"I know a little. It's the canvas...."

"What about it?"

"It doesn't look old enough."

"Now you're just talking nonsense. The chap from Christie's said the canvas was definitely painted in the last century. So, if it's a fake, it's a nineteenth century fake, and that's good enough for me."

"Christies..." said Kimberley-Waugh, holding up his hands as if to say, what do you expect from that lot of amateurs.

"Don't try that on. They're just as good as your lot. Anyway, some imbecile American collector will buy it, you said that yourself."

Gilbert finished his pint and pushed his empty glass away. "Right, we're off," he said. He stood up, put on his long leather coat and walked towards the door. Kimberley-Waugh slowly got up and followed him.

The road from Cheltenham to Oxford was blocked by snow and a diversion was in place, so it took them nearly two hours to get back to Great Park. As they approached the main entrance to the estate, Kimberley-Waugh noticed two strange formations of snow on the side of the road that looked like cars with their noses in the ditch. He presumed they were strange-shaped bushes.

It was after nine o'clock, dinner would be over, and the art expert wondered if Polly would still be around and whether there was a chance of some time alone with her. Gilbert had other ideas. He stopped the car as soon as they had passed the gatehouse.

"Get out," he said.

"What?"

"Get OUT!"

"Aren't we going to the house?"

"In a moment. First, I want to show you where to leave the painting."

Kimberley-Waugh followed Gilbert past the gatehouse and along a path which led to a wooden hut. The area was shaded by trees and there was hardly any snow on the ground. Gilbert lifted the bolt on the door of the hut and pulled it open. Inside there were some rusting farm tools and a small pile of logs, covered in green mould, which smelt horrible.

"This is where you leave the painting," said Gilbert. There were just a few pockets of snow on the path that had made their way through the thick branches of the evergreen trees. "Not much snow back here," he said. "You shouldn't leave any footprints."

They got back into the car and drove towards the house, turning off the main drive and heading towards the stables. Gilbert parked next to the shooting brake and the older limousine and wondered why the new Humber wasn't there, and where his father would have gone on a cold, snowy night like this.

"Come over here," he said, and led Kimberley-Waugh over to the stalls on the other side of the stable. He showed him the bicycle he could use, and pointed to a selection of Wellington boots.

"I suggest you try some of those on," said Gilbert.

"For goodness sake, I wouldn't be seen dead in Wellington boots."

"Please yourself," said Gilbert. "There's always the chance that the police will find the prints of your Bond Street brogues and be able to identify the thief from them."

Kimberley-Waugh went into the stall and tried on boots until he found some that were his size.

"So, you know what you have to do," said Gilbert.

"Yes," said Kimberley-Waugh, with no enthusiasm. "At one o'clock, I go out of the back door of the house, make my way round to the small courtyard, break into the drawing room through the window ..."

"And how will you do that?"

"Using the kitchen knife, you gave me. Then I steal the painting, come in here to get the bicycle, ride down to that smelly shed near the gatehouse, leave the painting there, ride the bicycle back and enter the house by the back door."

"And lock the door."

"And lock the door. Then I go to bed and come down to breakfast and express my astonishment and concern that the van Gogh has been stolen."

"OK, no need to be sarcastic."

"After breakfast, we say goodbye to everyone and drive back to London."

"No, no," said Gilbert. "We have to stay for the shoot. Although how they're going to organise that in weather like this is anyone's guess."

"Another day in purgatory then," said Kimberley-Waugh. Secretly, he was pleased to be staying longer, as he still reckoned his chances of getting Polly into bed were better than even.

The two men walked out of the stable. As they disappeared through the large wooden doors, a man emerged from behind the tractor. He waited until they were out of sight, then he walked out of the stable, knelt down and brushed the snow to one side, scooped up some gravel and made his way to the back of the house.

Chapter 30
Please try not to get blood on the towels

Friday night, Great Park blue drawing room - cold and dark

The clock in the hall struck one, the only sound in the otherwise silent house, but not everyone was asleep. The thief crept down the stairs and opened the door to the drawing room. He waited until his eyes adjusted to the dark, then moved forward carefully, stopping when his foot touched some kind of wooden strut. It was the leg of the easel which held the Duke's portrait, now featuring a hole in the great man's forehead. The easel wobbled but remained upright, the thief moved past it and then stopped when he bumped his shin against the low table in front of the fire.

He pushed the table forward until it reached the brass rail in front of the fireplace, directly under the portrait of Robert Louis Stephenson. He then stepped onto the table and reached up to take the portrait off the wall. When he was back on the floor, he sat down on the chaise longue and turned the painting to see how the canvas was fixed into the frame.

He heard a noise behind him and a giant figure came out from behind a curtain and moved towards him. The thief swore and tried to run out of the room, but a muscular arm grabbed his shoulder, pulled him backwards and encircled his throat. As the thief struggled to get free, the giant said, in a voice that was occasionally falsetto: "Just stay calm, and nothing bad will happen to you."

He relaxed his arm, and the thief tried to make a bolt for it, but he was stopped in his tracks as the bigger man chased after him and threw him to the ground. The giant sat with his knees on the other man's back, which made him yelp like a wounded animal.

"You weren't listening. If you move again ...."

Before he could complete the warning, he heard a tapping sound behind him. He continued to hold the thief down with his knee and turned to see where the noise was coming from. Someone was standing outside in the courtyard and seemed to be chipping at the window with a chisel. There was a crunching sound and the lock slid open. The shadowy figure outside pushed up the window and put one leg through into the room. The new arrival was a tall, slim man and he seemed to be holding a knife.

The giant stood up, keeping one foot on the thief's back, and turned to face the new arrival. He was wondering how he was going to deal with both intruders at the same time when there was a noise from the opposite side of the room. The door opened and two people entered.

"Turn on the light," said a woman's voice.

"Right ho," replied a man.

Light filled the room and Polly and Charles surveyed the scene. Halfway through the window, frozen in surprise and holding his knife like a murderer caught in the act, was Lawrence Kimberley-Waugh. In the middle of the room stood Garth the gardener, his foot on the back of a man who was lying on the floor. That man was Ronnie Capstan.

Polly and Charles turned when they heard footsteps coming quickly down the stairs. It was Pickles, wearing a blue silk dressing gown.

When Polly was later asked by the police to describe what happened next, she failed to mention the man who leapt out of the window and legged it across the courtyard. She did tell them that the man on the floor, who she named as her father Ronald Capstan, had made another effort to escape the clutches of Garth Prodgers the gardener. What she didn't say was that, as Ronnie ran towards the door, she punched him hard on the nose, knocking him to the floor again.

When that happened, Charles gazed at Polly, open-mouthed with astonishment and desire. Was there nothing this beautiful creature was incapable of doing?

"You just knocked your father out," he said.

"Something else I learned at martial arts class." She smiled and squeezed his arm.

A trickle of blood started to ooze out of Ronnie's nose. He groaned, made an effort to get up, but collapsed to the floor again. Garth yanked him to his feet and pulled his arm up behind his back, making him yelp with pain again. "If you try to escape, I'll break your arm," he said.

"All right! All right!" said Ronnie.

Garth pushed his prisoner towards the door. "What shall I do with him?" he asked.

"Well..." began Pickles.

"Put him in the first floor bathroom and lock the door," said Polly. "From the outside," she added, in case Garth thought she meant he should lock himself in with his prisoner.

"Good idea," said the butler.

"Right," said Garth.

Polly looked contemptuously at the oily spiv who was her father. "Papa, you can clean up while you're in there," she said.

"But please try not to get blood on the towels," added Pickles.

Ronnie's reply was so crude and unpleasant that it made all his listeners apart from Polly blush with embarrassment. Dear reader, we will not shock you by printing it here.

They watched Garth frogmarch Ronnie up the circular wooden staircase to the first floor. They heard a door open, the sound of a man crashing to the floor, and then the door closed again.

"I'm not sure what's been happening here," said Pickles, "but I presume Mister Capstan was apprehended whilst attempting to steal the Van Gogh. Am I right?"

"This is my understanding of the situation," said Polly.

"I'm confused," said Pickles.

"Me too," said Charles. "Didn't we also see ---?"

"Not now, Charles," said Polly. "What are you confused about, Monty?"

"Well," said the butler. "Lady Wickham-Thynne left earlier. I thought Mister Capstan had gone with her."

"Evidently not," said Charles.

"I'm also wondering what's the best thing to do," said Pickles.

"Nothing for the moment," said Polly. "But we'd better call the police in the morning."

"I suppose in the circumstances we have no alternative," said the butler.

"I agree it isn't ideal," said Polly. "But I also think my father needs to be taken into custody. And I hope they throw away the key this time."

There was a murmur of agreement. Garth appeared at the door, holding the bathroom key. He looked embarrassed. "What should I do with this?" he asked.

354

"Throw it away," said Polly. Charles laughed, then apologised when Pickles glared at him.

"Garth, first of all, well done for preventing the theft of our most prized asset," said the butler. "And now give me the key, I will look after it."

"What about the other man?" said the gardener.

"What other man?"

"The one at the window."

"There was a man at the window?"

"Don't worry about that now," said Polly. "I think we all need a bit of shut-eye."

"Yes, of course. Everyone should go to bed," said Pickles. "However, I think I'll place a chair outside the first-floor bathroom and sit there for the rest of the night."

"Goodness, do you think that's necessary?" asked Charles.

"Yes," replied the butler. "We don't want any more altercations if any of the other guests decide they want to take a piss."

Charles sniggered. No one else did. He wished he didn't have such a juvenile reaction whenever he heard words like 'piss' and 'fart'.

"Right, time to turn in," said Polly. "Off you go and get some sleep. I'll just clear up down here."

Charles and Pickles made their way up the stairs, and Garth started to walk towards the back door.

"Garth!" whispered Polly.

The gardener stopped and looked round. "Yes?" he said.

"I need to talk to you."

Chapter 31
Are you acquainted with my gardener?
Saturday morning, Great Park, a pale sunshine glowing

Just after nine o'clock in the morning, Sergeant Conway and Constable Prodgers arrived at Great Park and parked their Wolseley Wasp at the front door, as they had done earlier in the week when they were investigating the assault on the Stanford Saint Mary stationmaster. They had made the perilous journey from Cheltenham, including a diversion caused by snowdrifts at Duntismore Abbotts, because Pickles had called the station, alleging that one of the Duke of Burfaughtonleigh's house guests had been caught in the act of stealing a painting and was now locked in a bathroom.

The butler met them at the door. "Let me show you the way," he said. He walked down the corridor and started up the winding staircase.

"Where are we going?" asked the sergeant.

"To the bathroom," said Pickles. "The miscreant is incarcerated there."

"The misk - the what?"

"The thief ... is locked ... in the bathroom..." said the butler, slowly.

"Right, I know that," said the sergeant. "And what exactly do you expect us to do?"

"Arrest him and take him to prison."

"I'm sorry, Mister Pickles. I'm afraid we can't do that."

"Why on earth not?"

"Well, we can't just arrest someone without evidence."

"Evidence? How much evidence do you need? The man was caught red-handed! He was apprehended as he was taking the painting off the wall, and he was about to make his getaway with it! Arrest him immediately!"

"Things don't work like that, Mister Pickles. Certain conventions have to be followed." The sergeant explained that he needed to interview everyone in the house, starting with the downstairs servants. Pickles snorted with annoyance and expressed his doubts that anything was more important than removing the odious Ronald Capstan from the premises, but reluctantly agreed to round up the staff for inspection. A few minutes later, the entire crew of cooks, maids and under butlers, plus Winstanley the chauffeur, were assembled in the gloomy subterranean kitchen. To the puzzlement of his colleagues, Garth Prodgers the gardener was told to go upstairs and wait in the blue drawing room.

Some of the servants were concerned the police might be looking for the perpetrators of various local crimes and misdemeanours, so there was some sweating and chewing of fingernails. Fortunately, Sergeant Conway was only interested in the attempted theft of the painting. As soon as it was clear that none of the staff had seen or heard anything during the night, he allowed them to get on with their work. Winstanley had the most challenging task, to rescue the two cars that were still nose-first in the ditch near the main gate.

Sergeant Conway told Pickles that he would like to question the family members and guests who were currently resident in the house.

"Certainly. Everyone is waiting in the blue drawing room," said the butler.

Conway couldn't believe his luck. A fan of Agatha Christie's detective stories, the sergeant had always dreamed of addressing a group of witnesses and possibly suspects in the drawing room of a country house. With his back straight and his chest puffed out, he raced up the stairs from the kitchen, along the wood-panelled hall and into the drawing room. Constable Prodgers had never seen his superior officer move so fast, and ran after him.

The Duke was in his favourite armchair and his three remaining guests were on the sofa to the left of the fireplace. Polly and Charles were on the chaise longue on the other side. Garth the gardener had turned down the offer of a seat and was standing behind the chaise longue. The Duke stood up as the two police officers entered, and everyone else stopped talking and looked the uniformed men up and down.

Conway and Prodgers took notebooks from their top left hand pockets and pencils from their top right hand pockets. They flipped open the notebooks and licked their pencils.

"Could I possibly have the names of all those present?" asked Conway.

"Of course," said the Duke. "I'm the Duke of Burfaughtonleigh, as well you know. And this is Lady Diana Bagshot, the Viscountess Grimbledon." Both police officers bowed their heads slightly. "And these are her friends, the novelist Leonora Capstan and Doctor Alexander Malleson, a medical physician."

Conway wrote *The duke of B, some titled lady, a novelist and a doc* in his notebook.

The Duke then pointed to Polly and Charles who were sitting next to each other on the chaise longue. "You've already met my secretary Polly Capstan," he said, "and the gentleman is her brother Charles Goodgame." Charles recognised the two police officers. They were in this very room when he arrived at Great Park, while he

359

was still getting used to his Walter Washbrook disguise. Was he being paranoid to think they were looking at him suspiciously? Didn't police officers look at everyone suspiciously?

Sergeant Conway was indeed looking at Charles, thinking about the still unsolved case of the assault on the stationmaster and the theft of his whistle. "We have reason to believe that the perpetrator of the crime was the person who disembarked from the train, who was described by a witness as a young man with red hair," he had said. However, he was dealing with a different crime, so the earlier investigation would have to wait.

The Duke then indicated Garth. "And finally, this is the member of staff who apprehended Mister Capstan attempting to steal the portrait that you see over the fireplace. My gardener. His name is Garth ...er ...Garth ... um..." He couldn't immediately recall Garth's family name.

"Prodgers," said Constable Prodgers.

"Oh, thank you," said Tarquin. "Are you acquainted with my gardener?"

"Yes," said the constable. "He's my brother."

The siblings grunted at each other, Garth's grunt being more high-pitched than his brother's. Everyone in the room looked at the constable and then at the gardener. Both men were huge. Garth had a bushy beard and unkempt hair, whereas his law-enforcing brother had no beard and no visible hair of any kind under or around his helmet. The guests wondered if he was actually bald as a coot. As if he was reading their minds, Prodgers put his pencil behind his ear and removed his helmet, cleverly managing not to dislodge the pencil with the strap. The young officer had a short back and sides that appeared to be kept in place with an entire tub of Brylcreem. The two

360

brothers looked like before and after images of the Wild Man of Borneo - when he was first captured and then after he had been tamed and prepared for an appearance at the London Palladium.

"Is everyone currently residing in the house present?" asked Sergeant Conway.

"No," said Polly. "The Marquis of Stanford isn't here."

"The Marquis of ...?" asked the sergeant, his pencil poised over his notebook.

"Stanford," said the Duke. "My son Gilbert. He doesn't appear to be here at the moment. And also, a friend of his from London. Mister Waugh, I think his name is."

"Kimberley-Waugh," said Polly. "Lawrence Kimberley-Waugh. He works for Sotheby's the art people."

Hearing the name of the man she had recently slept with made Leonora squeak involuntarily. When everyone looked at her, she started coughing. "Sorry," she said. "I think I'm coming down with a cold."

"Where *is* your son, your Grace?" asked Conway.

"I've absolutely no idea," said the Duke. "He wasn't at breakfast and the under butler said his room was empty when he went to wake him up."

"And Mister Kimberley-Waugh? Is he on the premises?"

"Apparently not," said the Duke.

"Does anyone have any information about their whereabouts?"

"Yes. I do," said Polly. "The Marquis told me yesterday that he and Mister Kimberley-Waugh were planning to spend the night in Cheltenham." She looked at Pickles, who opened his mouth to speak, but thought better of it.

Sergeant Conway breathed out. There was silence for a few moments while he made some notes. Constable Prodgers also wanted to make notes, but he was hampered by the fact that he was holding his helmet in his hand. He looped the chinstrap of the helmet over his arm and took his pencil from behind his ear, then forgot what it was he wanted to write down. He stood to attention when Conway spoke.

"Mister Prodgers," said the sergeant.

"Yes, sir?" said Garth, the squeak in his voice more noticeable because he was feeling nervous.

"Mister Pickles tells me that you apprehended the thief when he was attempting to steal the portrait. Is this correct?"

"Yes, sir."

"And the incident took place here in this room?"

"Yes, sir."

"At what time did this occur?"

"One o'clock this morning, sir."

"One o'clock in the morning," repeated the sergeant. He wrote *1am* in his notebook. Constable Prodgers wrote *one o'clock in the morning* in his.

"Mister Prodgers, I'm a little confused," said Conway. "Am I right in thinking that you were already here when the attempted theft took place?"

"Yes, sir."

"Why were you here?"

Garth looked quickly at Polly, who nodded at him.

"Miss Capstan asked me to be here, sir."

"Miss Capstan?"

"Yes, sir."

"Why?"

"She believed that someone was going to steal the painting."

362

"Why did Miss Capstan think that?"

"Why don't you ask me?" said Polly. "I'm perfectly capable of answering for myself."

"I beg your pardon, miss," said Conway. "You're absolutely right. I should have directed that question to your good self. So ... how did you know that someone was planning to steal the painting?"

Everyone turned to look at Polly. She took a deep breath and stood up. She was about to tell a story that she had devised that morning. "The thief, Mister Ronald Capstan, is my father," she said. "He came here for the shooting weekend with his sister, Lady Cornelia Wickham-Thynne, who had to return to London unexpectedly yesterday evening. We all thought that Mister Capstan had departed at the same time. However, at about ten o'clock last night, I was in the hallway on the first floor, and I heard my father's voice. I walked part of the way down the stairs and saw him on the telephone." She pointed to the door. "The one that's in the hall."

Sergeant Conway made notes of what he had just heard, reading the words aloud as he wrote them. "Mister .... Capstan ... was ... making ... a ... telephone call." Constable Prodgers wrote more or less the same words in his notebook. He had no idea how to spell Capstan, so he just wrote *Mister K.*

Polly said that she heard her father telling someone, presumably an accomplice, that he planned to wait until one o'clock in the morning when everyone was asleep, then steal the portrait and make his escape in one of the cars he had seen in the stable.

There were gasps of surprise from the people in the room when they heard this, including the ones who knew that none of it was true. Garth the gardener was the only person who managed to avoid making any kind of sound.

"So how did Mister Prodgers get involved?" asked Sergeant Conway.

"Well," said Polly. "I needed some help and I decided Garth, Mister Prodgers, would be the perfect person to ask. I hid until Mister Capstan was back in his room, then I went out of the house, with the intention of walking down to Willow Cottage."

"Willow Cottage?" repeated the sergeant.

Constable Prodgers leaned over and spoke quietly in his superior officer's ear. "It's where my brother lives," he said.

"Where is it?"

"Down near the main gate."

"I see. So, Miss Capstan, you walked through the snow ... *through the snow* ...." Conway's emphatic repetition gave the impression he was finding the story hard to believe. "... down to Willow Cottage, which is some distance away as I understand it, to get help from Mister Prodgers?"

"No."

"No? I thought you said ---"

"That was my plan, but fortunately, at the very moment that I walked out of the back door of the house, Garth was making his way back to his cottage. So, I bumped into him. Stroke of luck, actually."

"Mr Prodgers just happened to be walking past?"

"Yes."

"Bit of a coincidence, wasn't it?" said the sergeant.

"Not really," replied Polly. "He'd been working in the stable."

"In the stable? Doing what?"

"I think he was fixing the tractor."

364

"In the middle of the night?"

"It wasn't the middle of the night, it was about ten o'clock."

"It's still quite late to be fixing a tractor," said the sergeant.

"I have a very loyal and hard-working group of servants," said the Duke. He waddled over and patted Garth on the lower back, which was as high as he could reach.

"I see," said the sergeant. He instinctively felt that there was something fishy about Polly's story, particularly the bit about bumping into the gardener, but he couldn't see any alternative to accepting it without accusing at least one person in the room of lying.

Polly had avoided mentioning the appearance of Kimberley-Waugh because she wanted to make sure that Gilbert owed her a favour at some point in the future. Earlier, when Flockton the under butler had told her that the two men were not in their rooms, she presumed correctly that they had left Great Park during the night. Flockton had been quite annoyed when he found that neither of the men were in their rooms, after he had boiled water and carried it in a heavy metal bowl, first to Gilbert's room and then to Kimberley-Waugh's. "Wasted a lot of hot water, I did," he grumbled to Polly.

So, what really happened?

At about nine o'clock the previous evening, Polly was reading a book in her room when she heard a noise at her window. It was a sound she was familiar with. Garth had thrown some gravel to attract her attention. The gardener was an accomplice in her plan to steal the Van Gogh, but there was more to their relationship than that. Polly found Garth easy to talk to, and they regularly spent time together. When she needed advice, she would go down to Willow Cottage and sit with him in front of the log fire, and she also invited him to spend time in her room after he finished his gardening duties. It became the custom for him to throw gravel against her window on the first floor at the back of the house when he was free to talk. The nocturnal meetings became quite frequent, but they never did anything other than talk.

After hearing Gilbert and Kimberley-Waugh discuss the details of the theft in the stable, Garth gathered some gravel from under the snow, walked to the back of the house and threw the stones against her window. A few minutes later, they were sitting on Polly's bed, and he was explaining what he understood their plan to be.

"One o'clock in the morning, you say," she said.

"That's what they said."

"Garth, I'm going to ask you to do me a favour ..."

"I think I know what you want me to do," said the big man.

"You're such a poppet," she said, leaning up and kissing one of the less hairy parts of his face.

"I'll be waiting for him when he arrives," said Garth.

"And I'll make sure Charles and I come down and witness it."

And so Garth was waiting, but it was a different thief who arrived.

After listening to Garth's and Polly's testimonies, Sergeant Conway was silent for a moment as he read through the notes he'd made.

"Mister Pickles?" he said.

"Yes?"

"The alleged thief. Is he still in the bathroom?"

"Of course he is," said Pickles.

"I suppose we'd better go and take a look at him."

"Finally!" said the butler. "Please follow me." He led the way out of the drawing room and up the stairs, followed by the two police officers, Polly and Charles. As her daughter and stepson disappeared out of the door, Leonora leapt up and followed them.

"Where are you going?" asked Diana.

"I want to see the look on Ronnie's face when they arrest him," said Leonora, and rushed out of the room to catch up with the others.

The posse who followed Pickles up the stairs were now standing outside the bathroom on the first floor. Conway knocked on the door. He was about to speak, then realised he had forgotten the name of the alleged thief.

"What's the gentleman's name?" he asked.

"Capstan," said Pickles, Polly, Charles and Leonora.

"Mister Capstan!" said the sergeant.

There was no reply. The sergeant repeated the name, a little louder. There was still no reply.

Conway decided to continue speaking. "In a moment, I'm going to open this door and charge you with the attempted theft of a work of art. You have the right to remain silent, but it may harm your defence if you do not mention when questioned something that you later rely on ----"

"I say, can you get on with it?" asked Polly. "You can do all the formal stuff when you've got him banged up in a cell."

Conway was a little put out to be denied his dramatic soliloquy. "Very well," he said, and tried to open the door.

"It's locked," he said.

"Yes," said Pickles. "Otherwise he would have escaped, wouldn't he? Let me unlock it."

"Be very careful," said Conway. "The man may be dangerous."

"Oh, I have no intention of actually going *in*," said the butler. "I will unlock the door and let you officers of the law take over."

He turned the key in the lock and stepped back. Conway stepped forward, took a deep breath, and said: "Mister Caplan! I ---"

"CAPSTAN!" shouted Pickles, Polly, Charles and Leonora.

"Sorry. Mister Capstan! I'm coming in. Please don't make things difficult for us by resisting arrest." With that, he pushed open the door and he and Constable Prodgers ran into the bathroom.

It was empty.

Conway opened a cupboard to see if the alleged thief had managed to hide himself there, and even looked under the bath. Constable Prodgers tapped him on the shoulder and pointed at the window, which was open. The two police officers rushed over and looked out. There was a drainpipe that led to the ground, and down below they saw a man with a white bandage round his head opening the door of their Wolseley Wasp police car.

"Stop, thief!" shouted Conway.

Ronnie Capstan looked up at them, laughed and gave them a two-finger V sign. He turned to get into the car but at that moment, Garth ran down the steps from the front entrance of the house, pulled Ronnie away from the car and threw him onto the ground. He then got the would-be car thief to his feet and, for the second time in less than twelve hours, pulled his arm up his back and said "Just stay calm, and nothing bad will happen to you."

From the window above, there was the sound of applause. Garth and Ronnie looked up and saw Polly and Leonora at the window, smiling and clapping.

*****

Ronnie was bundled into the back of the Wolseley Wasp and handcuffed to a metal ring that was fitted there to restrain unwilling passengers. Sergeant Conway felt relieved. The suspect had tried to steal their car, so there was a real crime they could charge him with, or at least something more than 'possible involvement in the theft of a painting'. The sergeant had no idea what the actual sentence for attempting to steal a police vehicle might be, but it was sufficient to lock the culprit up until Monday, when he would appear before the local magistrate.

The snow had stopped falling, the sky was clear, and the sun was shining weakly in a pale blue sky. Everyone showered praise on Garth the gardener, who received more handshakes and backs slaps than he had previously had in his entire life. He retreated in blushing embarrassment to find useful things to do in the stable.

The Duke, Pickles, Polly, Charles and the three remaining guests watched as the police car set off down the drive. Then the tractor appeared from the side of the house, chugging and belching out smoke. Garth and Winstanley were finally on their way to rescue the cars that were still in the ditch near the main gate.

As the tractor disappeared from view, Tarquin waddled up the steps to the house, paused to catch his breath, then turned to his guests and suggested they should take an early lunch, an idea which met with universal approval, although not from Pickles, who would have to organise it. He hurried up the steps, into the house and down to the kitchen, where he told the staff to produce a three-course meal an hour earlier than they had planned, then he raced to the drawing room to provide pre-prandial refreshment, apologising that there was no longer any gin in the drinks cabinet.

The butler appeared calm, dealing with everyone's liquid requirements, but he was concerned about Polly's fictitious account of what had happened during the night. He also wanted to know what had really taken place in the drawing room before he arrived on the scene. Quite apart from anything else, who was the mysterious man who appeared at the window?

Polly and Charles were standing in silence by that very window.

"Thanks for everything you've done," said Polly. "You've been an angel."

"Mmm..." said Charles.

"What are you going to do? You can stay at Great Park for a while, if you like." She gave him one of her dazzling smiles. "You could paint me. I'd like that very much."

"I think I'd better go back to London." Charles had already decided that spending more time with Polly was a bad idea.

The smile disappeared from her face. "Please yourself."

"The thing is, I can't go back to my studio," he said. "I'm behind with the rent and the landlady will throw me out if I don't cough up. So ... my best bet is to go back to Uncle Ernest's place in South Kensington and sleep in the shed. I need to call him. Can I use the phone?"

"Feel free. It's in the hall."

"I don't know how it works. Will you help me?"

"Sure."

They walked out of the drawing room and Polly picked up the phone. "What's the number?" she asked.

Charles took a piece of paper out of his pocket and read from it. "Frobisher 2642."

There was a click and the operator in Cheltenham said "NUMBER PLEASE!" very loudly. There were two operators who usually worked the switchboard. Polly sighed when she realised it was the bad-tempered old man rather than the efficient younger woman who was working today. "Frobisher 2642," she said.

"WHAT?"

"Frobisher 2642," she repeated.

The old man was unaccustomed to connecting people to long-distance numbers. "FROBISHOP 2642? WHAT KIND OF A NUMBER IS THAT?"

"Just a moment."

"WHAT?"

"WILL YOU JUST WAIT A SECOND?" shouted Polly. "I'LL PASS THE TELEPHONE TO SOMEONE WHO CAN HELP YOU!"

"THERE'S NO NEED TO SHOUT!" shouted the man.

Polly gave the receiver to Charles. "He's deaf as a post, and he doesn't know where it is."

Charles took the telephone and said, in a normal voice. "It's a London number."

"WHAT?"

"IT'S A LONDON NUMBER!"

"LONDON??" The man sounded as if he was being asked to connect with the Emperor of China. There were clicking and mumbling sounds, and eventually Charles heard a telephone ringing.

"Frobisher 2642?" said a man.

"Uncle Ernest?" said Charles.

"Yes. Charles - is that you?"

"Yes, uncle."

"Thank goodness," said the man. "Why didn't you call earlier?"

Charles was puzzled. "Why didn't I do what?"

"I presume you got my letter?"

"Letter? No. Did you send me a letter?"

"I sent you two!"

"To my place in Hammersmith?"

"I sent it to the address you gave me. Anyway, it's just as well you called. The reading of the will is on Monday morning. You have to be here."

"The reading ... what?"

"Oh for goodness sake, Charles! Just get to my house by Monday morning!"

"Um ... can I come and stay tomorrow night? Sunday?"

"If that means you'll be here on Monday morning, yes," said Ernest. "Sorry, I'm rather busy. I have to go. Just make sure you're here on Monday. Otherwise, you could lose everything." He put down the phone.

"What was that all about?" asked Polly.

"I'm not sure. He said I have to be there on Monday for the reading of a will."

"Really? Who's died?"

"I don't know." Charles tried to think of someone apart from his father whose will he might expect to be mentioned in. He couldn't think of anyone. He wondered if he should tell Leonora.

"You're going to have trouble getting to London by Monday," said Polly. "You've missed today's train and there isn't one on a Sunday."

"Oh lord," said Charles. "What am I to do?"

372

"If I were you, I'd asked the doctor for a lift."

They walked back into the drawing room. Diana looked at them as they walked in and thought what an attractive couple they were. Not for the first time, she wondered if they were having an affair. Was that acceptable, or even legal, between stepbrother and sister? The two young residents of the house walked back over to the window where they had been talking earlier, and there was a sudden burst of sunlight that made Polly's hair shine. It reminded Diana of something she had always meant to ask Leonora.

"Polly's *very* blonde," she murmured, so as not to be overheard. "But you and Ronnie aren't. I mean, I know you do your hair these days, but you really *are* brunette, aren't you?"

"That's correct," said Leonora.

"And Ronnie has very dark features, sort of like a gypsy."

"You're right."

"Was it his wild look that attracted you in the first place?"

"Probably," replied Leonora. "It certainly wasn't his face."

They both chuckled quietly.

"But really," said Diana, "I've always wondered ... where did Polly get that blonde hair from?"

"Her father," said Leonora.

"What? Do you mean there's blonde somewhere on Ronnie's side of the family?"

"No."

"So what do you mean?"

"Work it out for yourself." Leonora held up her empty glass and wiggled it until Pickles came to refresh her drink.

Alexander had decided to approach Tarquin with a business proposition, so he walked over to the Duke's chair and crouched next to the arm. "Can I pick your brains about something?" he asked.

"Well, you may need a pair of tweezers," said Tarquin. "But feel free."

"Thank you." Alexander paused, deciding how best to start. "You may or may not be aware, but excessive use of alcohol is quite a problem these days."

"I *beg* your pardon?" Tarquin replied, looking offended. "Are you suggesting that I drink too much?"

"Oh goodness me, no!" Alexander looked horrified at the misinterpretation of his words. "No, the thing is ..." He turned to make sure that Diana wasn't listening. "Well, before I say anything else, I want to thank you for putting us up at such short notice."

"Don't mention it," said the Duke. He thought for a moment. "What exactly do you mean by 'such short notice'?"

"Well, obviously the only reason we're here is that the Viscountess and I happened to be passing Great Park when the prang took place."

"Prang?"

"Yes. Fact is, we were on our way back from a place near Cheltenham called The Hollies. Have you heard of it?"

Tarquin was confused. He'd been in bed when the two of them arrived, so he was unaware that Alexander and Diana had crashed their car on the main road. Nor did he know that Leonora had claimed to be Viscountess Grimbledon. He just assumed that Diana had decided to bring two guests with her.

"Did you say you were passing Great Park on your way somewhere else?"

"Yes, we were heading back to London from this Hollies place," replied Alexander. "A friend of hers is receiving treatment there."

"I'm not sure I understand."

"I'll explain," said Alexander. "But please don't tell Diana that I told you any of this. She doesn't want anyone to know the real reason she was out in this neck of the woods."

"Do continue," said the Duke. "I'm sure it will all make sense eventually."

"Right," said Alexander. "So ... The Hollies, it's a place just outside Prestbury."

"Yes, I know The Hollies," said Tarquin. "It used to belong to the Boddingtons, before they fell on hard times." Lord and Lady Boddington, people who used to hold the most lavish parties, had gone bankrupt a couple of years before and had to leave their ancestral home. They were now permanently resident at the Belmont Hotel in Lyme Regis, by coincidence the place where Leonora had first met Horace Goodgame. It was exactly this kind of fate Tarquin was trying to avoid.

"Well, the point is, it's a sanatorium now, run by an old chum of mine." Alexander chose not to add details of the 'old chum', who was another physician who had fallen foul of the system and had been forced to go into business on the outer fringes of the world of medicine. "They provide help for people with alcohol problems. The thing is, my friend can't cope with the demand. I mean, when we fetched up there with Diana's friend yesterday, two other new clients were arriving at the same time." He paused and looked around to make sure no one was listening. "There was a Member of Parliament there, I recognised him. Sir Burlington Fitzroy. His wife was starting treatment."

"I know Burlington," said Tarquin. "He's our MP. I actually invited him and Lady Fitzroy to the shoot." And now I know why they turned me down, he thought. "Mister Malleson, I'm not sure why you're telling me all this."

"What? Oh, right. I'm sorry. Well ... as I understand it..." Alexander paused, searching for the right way to make his offer, "you ... um ... you might need some financial assistance to keep Great Park ... um ... in its rightful place at the forefront of stately homes in the Cotswolds."

"Well...." said Tarquin.

"Oh, if I've got the wrong end of the stick, major apologies," said Alexander.

"No, no, please do go on," said the Duke.

"Well, the thing is ... there's clearly a need for more sanatoria, like the one at The Hollies. I would like to open one, and I think Great Park would be perfect for it."

The Duke's eyes opened wide with surprise, but he also smiled. "Let's discuss this more," he said. He stood up and showed Alexander out into the hall and led him down to the dining room. By the time lunch was ready to be served, the two men had shaken hands on a deal which would rescue Great Park.

Chapter 32
That was a bit rum

The surgeon who removed part of Godfrey Krumnagel's middle toe told him he would have to stay in hospital for at least a week, but the bank manager ignored his advice and discharged himself on Saturday morning. "Sorry, old chap," he said. "I simply don't have time. Too much to do." He asked for a pair of crutches and hopped the few hundred yards to his bank in The Strand.

Godfrey was determined to reunite Horace Goodgame with his inheritance, the money he now knew had been fraudulently withdrawn from the bank by Martha Goodgame and Emily Roebuck. Inspector Sparrow believed the story, but the police couldn't just present the loot to any Tom, Dick or Godfrey who claimed to know how the two women had amassed it. More investigation was necessary.

When he finally got to his office, he sent his secretary Avril to the Strand Cuppa Café for tea and bacon rolls with plenty of brown sauce and called Burgess the assistant manager into his office, where they compiled evidence of the last two years' activities relating to Horace's trust fund, including several dozen bank slips, all signed 'Martha Goodgame' in spidery handwriting.

At midday, Inspector Sparrow arrived with the suitcase containing the money. Like most people who spent any time with Godfrey, and despite the unfortunate incident at their original meeting, Sparrow had formed a positive opinion of the youngest member of the

Krumnagel banking dynasty. He had been persuaded that the money in the suitcase belonged to Horace Goodgame, and he was hoping that the bank would be able to provide some concrete evidence. Fortunately, some of the five-pound notes in the suitcase were brand new. When new currency arrived at the bank, the serial numbers were listed in a ledger, so if at least some of the stolen notes tallied with the bank's records, that should be sufficient proof to hand over the money.

Inspector Sparrow put the sky blue suitcase on the table and clicked the hasps. The top creaked open and the three men looked at the carefully packed bundles of ten-shilling, pound and five-pound notes, held together with elastic bands. Godfrey fished around until he found some white fivers that looked newer than the rest. He put on his reading glasses and looked at the serial number printed across the middle of the note at the top of the bundle.

"99456," he said. "Burgess?"

The assistant manager moved his finger slowly down a list of numbers in the ledger. His finger stopped and he breathed out. "99456," he repeated.

"Excellent," said Godfrey. "And the second one?"

"There's no need to do any more," said Sparrow. "I already thought that the money came into the possession of these two women in the way you indicated. I just wish we'd been able to charge them."

"Well, we know where they live," said Godfrey. "Shall we go down and arrest them again?" There was a pause. "I promise I won't take my shotgun this time."

Burgess coughed nervously, but both Sparrow and Godfrey laughed.

"That's a kind offer, Mister Krumnagel," said the inspector. "Unfortunately, to use your phrase, our birds have flown. Again."

"Really?"

"Yes. I sent officers to Peckham this morning to bring them in for more questioning, as is required by that confounded Habeas Corpus nonsense, but I'm afraid they weren't there. When we apprehended them on Wednesday, they were obviously planning to leave for pastures new."

"Pity," said Godfrey.

"Don't worry, we'll get them eventually."

"I'm sure you will, Inspector Sparrow. And it will give me great pleasure to testify against them in court, if required."

"Thank you, Mister Krumnagel."

"Don't mention it. Even so, this is an excellent outcome, and I'm very much looking forward to my next task, which is to inform Mister Goodgame of the good news. I'm going to call him right away."

"Do you mind if I stay and have a word with him?" asked Sparrow.

"Be my guest."

"Thank you."

"Do you like bacon rolls?" asked Godfrey.

"I certainly do."

"Tea with sugar?"

"Absolutely."

"In that case, I will send out for more refreshments, and then we can get down to business."

****

While Godfrey was making plans to return the money to Horace, the man himself was sitting in St Edmund's Church in Hunstanton at the funeral of postmaster Albert Looney. Almost the entire adult population of the town turned out for the service, an even bigger crowd than there had been for Martha Goodgame's funeral back in 1935, with the added attraction of a coffin containing a real body.

In the absence of immediate family to offer condolences to, people paid their respects to Mabel Pickersgill, whose parcel was on the scales when Albert succumbed to his fatal heart attack. The poor woman had been traumatised by witnessing the event, worrying that it was the weight of the books that had done for Albert. Now that people were commiserating with her, she felt doubly guilty. Trebly guilty, in fact. Not many people, and certainly not Mister Pickersgill, knew that the relationship between Mabel and Albert was closer than one might expect between a postmaster and a customer. As Albert was putting her parcel on the weighing machine, she had playfully suggested putting the CLOSED sign on the door so that they could spend a little time together. Albert's last utterance before he died was a string of taboo words, possibly because the idea of closing in the middle of the day was so outrageous. Or it was simply because he was having a heart attack. Mabel felt even worse because her rumpy-pumpy suggestion hadn't been entirely serious, as she had to rush off to see her mother, who had broken her false teeth and needed Mabel's assistance to glue them back together. Because of the dramatic turn of events, the teeth didn't get mended until the following day.

Esmond Hurd the vicar gave a eulogy which was slow, serious and, in the unanimous opinion of everyone present, excruciatingly dull. He listed the main events of Albert's life - his birth, his schooling, the year he started raising chickens, and the day he took possession of his faithful dog Gulliver. Most people in the church knew that the massive canine was actually called Goliath, but no one corrected him, because the good folk of Hunstanton didn't want the speech to go on any longer than was absolutely necessary.

The vicar made no reference at all to the postmaster's distinguished record in the Great War, possibly because he himself had avoided military service by signing up for ordination training in 1914. Albert had been a very brave soldier indeed, volunteering for the Royal Norfolk Battalion even though he was already thirty years old. He served with distinction on the Western Front and was decorated for bravery after the Battle of Mons. About all of this, not a dicky bird from Esmond Hurd.

Eventually, and in no way dramatically, the vicar reached the climax of his account of Albert's life story - the momentous day in 1929 when he took control of the Post Office, the latest in a long line of Looney postmasters. To the dismay of the congregation, Hurd felt it necessary to name them all. "First there was Ephraim Looney, who opened a shop offering postal services in 1881," he droned. "Ephraim was succeeded by his son, Jeremiah, who was the father of the third postmaster Abraham. And then ----"

"... Abraham begat Isaac, and Isaac begat Jacob," said a loud voice towards the back of the congregation. A ripple of laughter echoed around the church. The vicar glared over his half-frame glasses and scanned the congregation, hoping to work out where the remark had originated. The culprit must have been one of the farmers sitting at the back, but almost every face in that part of the church was looking downward, possibly in prayer, although several shoulders were shaking. All the vicar could see was a line of pale bald spots, which were usually hidden under flat caps but were getting a rare outing in public.

To the relief of all, the service ground to a conclusion and Albert's body was taken by carriage to its final resting place in the graveyard behind the church. The women of Hunstanton went back to their domestic chores, and all the men except Horace filed into the Wash and Tope public house. Horace didn't feel comfortable spending time where conversations became bawdy or obscene as more alcohol was despatched, so he agreed to Mrs Normington's suggestion to go back to Cliff Terrace for a cup of tea.

On the way, they passed the Post Office and Mrs Normington looked through the window. Nothing had moved, not even Mabel's parcel, which was still on the weighing machine. It was now five days since Albert's fatal encounter with Mabel's books, and the same question was on everyone's lips. When would the Post Office open again?

"Have you given it any more thought?" she asked.

"Have I given what any more thought?"

"Becoming the new postmaster."

Horace had forgotten that suggestion. He had been so embarrassed by his misinterpretation of Mrs Normington's idea - he had thought she was suggesting marriage - that he had wiped the memory of the whole episode from his mind.

"Can we talk about it over a cup of tea?" he asked, shelving the problem for a little longer. He walked up the pathway to the front door of 24 Cliff Terrace and slowly took a bunch of keys out of his pocket. There was a faint tinkling noise from inside the house. Horace didn't recognise it as the sound of a telephone because hardly anyone called him when he was in Hunstanton. In fact, he received very few telephone calls wherever he was. He continued to fiddle with the keys on his key ring.

"Shape up, Horace!" said Mrs Normington. "The telephone's ringing!"

"What?" Horace turned round, looked at her and wrinkled his nose.

"Oh, give me the flaming key!" She opened the door, ran into the hall, and picked up the telephone. "Hallo, who is it?" she asked, rather loudly. A voice at the other end asked her to hold the line.

Horace walked past her into the living room and lowered himself slowly into his favourite armchair. He kicked off his boots and put his stockinged feet on the metal rail round the fireplace, in front of the last embers of the fire.

Mrs Normington said "Hello?" again, and then ran into the room, holding the telephone receiver in one hand and the cradle in the other. The wire stretched taut behind her into the hall.

"Horace, get up!" she said.

"What?"

"Get up!"

"Why?"

"It's the man from Krumblies!"

"What?"

"The man from the bank in London! Horace! Get the telephone and talk to him!"

Horace stared at her. Mrs Normington groaned with annoyance and moved quickly towards him. The telephone cord vibrated behind her like the string of a cello. When she thrust the phone towards him, there was a tearing sound as the cord ripped out of the wall. She put the phone to her ear, said "Hello?" three times, sighed and put the receiver down. She carried the equipment back into the hall, and when she came back into the living room, she looked very angry.

"Horace, when are you going to stop behaving like a child?" she said. "That was the manager of the bank, Mister Krumble himself, and he said he had something very important to tell you. Now you've gone and missed it!"

"I'll call him back," said Horace.

'You can't!"

"Why not?"

"Because the telephone's buggered!" Horace was shocked to hear her use such a terrible word.

"Oh."

"Honestly, Horace!"

"Look," he said. "It's the twentieth of the month, the day I used to get my payment from the trust fund. He was probably calling to remind me that I won't be getting one this month. Or ever again." He sighed and looked at the dying fire.

"We could go to Mabel Pickersgill's and use her phone."

"No thanks."

Mrs Normington looked at the ceiling, tutted quietly to herself and went into the hall to put her coat on. Then she went into the kitchen and sifted through a pile of letters until she found the one she wanted. She walked past the door of the living room without saying anything to Horace, left the house and set off in the direction of Mabel Pickersgill's house.

*****

At Krumnagel's Bank in The Strand, Godfrey stared at his phone. "Well, that was a bit rum," he said. "A woman answered the phone, and when I spoke to her, she called out 'Horace! Get up!' Then the phone went dead."

Inspector Sparrow took the phone from Godfrey, put it to his ear, heard the disconnected tone and put the receiver down. "Very odd," he said.

Godfrey looked at his assistant manager, as if he expected him to provide an explanation. As usual, Burgess had nothing useful to offer. "I expect the telephone service is a bit temperamental in Norfolk," he said. He imagined East Anglia to be a place full of semi-feral people with beards who lived beside smelly marshes.

"Maybe." Godfrey hopped out into Avril's office and asked her to try Mister Goodgame's number again. She dialled the operator, who confirmed that the line wasn't connected. Godfrey sat down, leaned back and looked up at the ceiling, deep in thought. Burgess looked silently at the ceiling too, as usual unable to come up with anything when a decision had to be made, waiting for his boss to do something.

"Well, there's only one thing for it," said Godfrey. "We know where Mister Goodgame lives, so we'll just have to drive out there to tell him in person."

"What?" said Burgess. "Drive all the way to Norfolk?"

"Yes. And we're going today." He hopped back to the door of his office and opened it. "Avril?"

"Yes, Mister Krumnagel?"

"Find Bert Branch and tell him to have the car ready in fifteen minutes. He's to drive us to Norfolk."

"Yes, Mister Krumnagel."

"And then get off to the Post Office and send a telegram to Mister Horace Goodgame at 24 Cliff Terrace Hunstanton Norfolk and tell him to expect to see us later today."

"Yes, Mister Krumnagel."

"Burgess?"

"Yes, Mister Krumnagel?"

"I want you to find out exactly how much money is in that suitcase, put it through the system, and get it back into Mister Goodgame's trust fund."

"Yes, Mister Krumnagel."

"Then bring me the exact figure written on official bank stationery."

"Yes, Mister Krumnagel."

"I expect it on my desk in fifteen minutes."

"Yes, Mister --- what?"

"You heard me, Burgess. Jump to it."

"Yes, Mister Krumnagel." Burgess got up and moved quickly to the door and left the office,

"Burgess!"

Burgess put his head back through the door. "Yes, Mister Krumnagel?"

"You forgot the suitcase."

"Sorry, Mister Krumnagel."

After Burgess stumbled out of the room, Inspector Sparrow stood up and put on his cap. He walked to the door, then stopped and turned back. "Mister Krumnagel, can I ask you another favour?" asked Sparrow.

"Certainly, go ahead."

"Could I accompany you to East Anglia?"

"I would be absolutely delighted to have you on board, inspector."

"How long before you plan to leave?"

"Well, as soon as possible, really."

"Do I have time to get back to the Yard before we leave? I have a car outside. I can be back in about twenty minutes."

"Absolutely no problem."

"Marvellous," said Sparrow. "I'll be back as quickly as I can."

Preparations for the trip to Norfolk took a little longer than expected. Burgess actually managed to do what was required of him in the time available, Inspector Sparrow got back from Scotland Yard, and Bert Branch was ready and waiting in the Bentley at the front door of the bank. It was Godfrey who held things up, first by sending out to The Strand Cuppa Café for a basket full of sandwiches, then by trying to call his wife to tell her he would be late home that evening or might not even make it back to Surrey. Clarissa Krumnagel wasn't at home, nor was she in any of her favourite locations - the perfume department of Harrods, the restaurant at Harvey Nichols or the Mayfair emporium of celebrity hairdresser Raimondo Bessone. Godfrey rang them all, and many more, before eventually giving up.

Burgess managed to call his wife, who was at home near Tunbridge Wells. She wished him a pleasant journey, poured herself another glass of sherry and went back to her knitting.

Eventually, the party set off for East Anglia, Bert Branch driving, with Burgess in the front passenger seat, fretting, his clasped hands in his lap. Godfrey and Sparrow were in the spacious leather seats in the back of the car, the basket of sandwiches between them and Godfrey's crutches to one side. In the inside pocket of the manager's jacket was a piece of paper with the latest information about the Agatha Merchant Trust Fund, which indicated that Horace Goodgame was now five thousand, one hundred and twenty-four pounds and ten shillings better off.

Bert pointed the Bentley towards Aldgate, the starting point of the A11, a road he knew well from the times he had driven Godfrey to Newmarket racecourse. He had never driven beyond Newmarket, but he had an Ordnance Survey map of East Anglia, and it looked as if it would be plain sailing if he could just find his way to King's Lynn.

The Bentley breezed through the London suburbs and out into open country. An hour later, they passed a sign telling them they were entering 'Newmarket - The Home of Thoroughbred Horse Racing'. Bert drove down the High Street and pulled up outside the Hogshead pub, where a taxi was parked. The driver was smoking a cigarette and looking at the day's football fixtures in the *Daily Express,* comparing the score predictions of the paper's experts with the ones on his pools coupon.

"All right, guv'nor?" asked Bert. The man grunted a response. There wasn't much conversation to be had with Newmarket folk at the best of times, and the taxi driver was no exception. He didn't take kindly to people interrupting his meditations, particularly on a Saturday, when he was dreaming of what he would do with the hundred-pound jackpot if he managed to successfully predict eight draws.

"We're heading for Kings Lynn," said Bert. "Any recommendations?"

"Drink at the Duke's Head in Market Square," said the driver. "The beer's cheap." He looked at Bert and a smile creased his face. "And the barmaid's a bit of all right."

Bert laughed, but made a mental note to check out the barmaid if the chance presented itself. "No, I mean the route. What do you suggest?"

"Drive on down the High Street, turn left when you see the sign to Ely and follow that road. When you leave Ely, it's forward Little Downham, forward Littleport, forward Sothery, forward Downham Market, arrive King's Lynn."

Bert had driven a taxi before becoming Godfrey's chauffeur and enjoyed the way the local man had explained the journey. "How long should that take?" he asked.

"It's about forty miles." The local man looked over at the Bentley. "Put your foot down in that motor, you should be there in an hour."

"Thanks." Bert flipped a threepenny bit in the air, the driver caught it, grunted and went back to reading his newspaper. Back in the car, Bert told Godfrey that they would be in King's Lynn in an hour and after that, he would follow his Ordnance Survey map in the direction of Hunstanton.

"OK, let's press on," said Godfrey. "We can stop for something to eat when we get to Kings Lynn."

Burgess raised his eyebrows. With a little help from Inspector Sparrow, Godfrey had already hoovered his way through the Cuppa Café sandwiches, but he was still talking about food. Being a man who ate very little, the assistant manager couldn't understand his boss's constant need for refreshments. But then there was a lot about Burgess that Godfrey found incomprehensible as well.

It was beginning to get dark as Bert approached Kings Lynn and when he reached the town, he followed signs for the town centre, predicting correctly that he would end up in Market Square. He was delighted to see the lights of the Duke's Head, and he parked in the square in front of it. "The taxi driver in Newmarket recommended that place, sir," he said, pointing to the brightly lit windows of the hotel.

"Fine. Go and find out if they serve food," said Godfrey.

It was much colder than it had been when they set off, so Bert ran across the square to keep warm. Inside the hotel, it was warm but gloomy, and the bar was crowded, mainly with men. There were only two women customers, and they were sitting at a table near the fire. Bert glanced at them, did a double take and uttered an expletive.

It was Martha Donkin and Emily Roebuck.

He rushed out into the street and ran to the car.

"What's the verdict?" asked Godfrey.

"I didn't actually ask about food," said Bert.

"What? Really, Branch, I gave you a simple instruction, and I expect---"

Bert interrupted him. "Martha Donkin and Emily Roebuck are in there, sir!"

All three of the car's occupants looked at him in astonishment and Burgess made a low groaning sound.

"Are you sure?" asked Sparrow.

"Absolutely positive, sir," said Bert.

The inspector jumped out of the car and ran over to the pub. He took off his inspector's cap, looked through the window and saw the two women, both with pint glasses on the table in front of them. The one he remembered as Emily Roebuck was holding a piece of paper and talking animatedly to the other woman, who sat and nodded silently. Sparrow watched as she folded the piece of paper and put it into an envelope, which she then sealed by running her tongue along the flap.

Sparrow walked back to the Bentley. "I'm going to call the local police," he said, indicating a telephone box on the other side of the square.

"Oh yes," said Bert. "999, right?"

Sparrow nodded. "I need you to keep an eye on the two exits to the building while I'm doing it."

"Excellent idea," said Godfrey. "No problem."

Sparrow shook his head. "With the greatest respect, Mister Krumnagel, I think you should stay in the car. You aren't in any condition to help out if the women decide to make a run for it."

"Stuff and nonsense," said Godfrey. "I'll keep a watch on them through the window, Burgess will stand guard at one exit and Bert can look after the other. I'll sound the alarm if the women look as if they're planning to leave the building."

Neither of the bank employees were completely at ease with this plan but Godfrey was a difficult person to disagree with, so they both reluctantly walked towards the Duke's Head and took up their positions outside the entrances, while Godfrey hopped on his crutches to stand at the window between the two doors. Sparrow hurried across the square to make his 999 call.

The three of them had barely arrived at their posts when the two women stood up.

"Be alert!" shouted Godfrey. "They appear to be leaving!"

In fact, only one of them was planning to leave. Martha Goodgame walked towards the staircase which was next to the bar and disappeared upstairs. Emily Roebuck put on her coat, picked up the envelope and walked towards the door where Rupert Burgess was stationed. She walked out and went to pass him, but he stood in her path. When she tried to swerve past him, he moved in front of her again.

"What are you up to, you piss-pot?" she said.

Burgess put his hand on her shoulder.

"TAKE YOUR HANDS OFF ME!" she shouted.

He removed his hand as if he'd been stung. But instead of retreating from the confrontation, the assistant manager seemed emboldened by her aggressiveness. "Please lower your voice," he said, with a ring of authority he hardly recognised.

"I WILL DO NO SUCH BLOODY THING!" said the woman and made to walk past him.

Once more, Burgess moved to one side to block her path. "LISTEN!" he said. She stood still and, before his new-found courage deserted him, he said: "We have evidence to prove beyond all reasonable doubt that you and your co-conspirator have perpetrated a grand larceny viz-a-viz the embezzlement of funds from an account to which you should not have been privy." He realised he could have expressed this more simply and Emily Roebuck clearly agreed with him.

"What the devil are you on about?" she asked.

By this time, Godfrey had managed to hop up to a point behind her. "You're under arrest!" he shouted.

She turned and saw a large man on crutches. She kicked one of them away, which caused Godfrey to crash to the ground. Bert Branch ran up and confronted his Peckham neighbour. "Emily! The game's up!" he said, grabbing her arm.

"What the bloody hell are you doing here?" she yelled. She yanked her arm away from his grasp and smacked him across the head, knocking him to the ground. She then turned and punched Burgess on the nose, and he fell backwards onto the stone path, cracking his head.

She then saw a man in a police uniform running towards her. "Officer!" she shouted. "I'm being assaulted! I ----." She stopped when she recognised her Scotland Yard interrogator.

Sparrow stopped in front of her. "Emily ---" he began.

She punched him in the face, and he fell to the ground, but got up quickly and chased her into the square. Sparrow had been a good enough rugby player in his youth to represent the Metropolitan Police, and he tackled her as they were passing the Bentley. She thumped into the radiator and the inspector crashed into the headlamp. The flying B on the bonnet jammed into Emily's neck and she slithered to the ground, where Sparrow was also lying, knocked unconscious by the collision.

A police car raced into the square and four King's Lynn constables tumbled out and surveyed the scene. A woman and a police officer were lying unconscious in front of a fancy car and near the door to the pub there were three other men, two lying down and the third on his knees.

Standing at the window of her upstairs room, Martha Goodgame, aka Martha Donkin, saw that her friend's attempt to escape had failed, and she decided there was only one thing for it. She closed the window, walked downstairs and out into the street, where she waited until the police had sorted out who was who. Then she gave herself up.

Chapter 33
Horace Goodgame, you're daft as a brush

Saturday evening, The Duke's Head, King's Lynn -
brass monkey cold

The four heroes of the skirmish in the square sat in the bar of the Duke's Head, drinking and discussing the events of the day. Two of them, Inspector Sparrow and Rupert Burgess, had bandaged heads and the inspector also had his arm in a sling. All four could take great satisfaction from their roles in the apprehension and arrest of the two women who, later in the year when their trial began, would become known as The Trust Fund Tricksters. One of the accused was now sitting in a cell at the police station, which was less than half a mile away in St James's Street. The other was in a hospital ward in London Road, with two police officers in the corridor outside.

Everyone had sustained injuries in the mêlée, but Emily Roebuck had fared worse than the others. She broke three ribs when she collided with the grille of the Bentley and the Flying B on the bonnet had jagged into her neck. Her life had been saved first by an ambulance team, then by a surgeon who was sitting at home playing chess with his son when the hospital called. He jumped on his bicycle and was in the operating theatre a mere twenty minutes after receiving the call. In fact, his hands were still blue with cold as he stitched up the gash in her neck, after which he dealt with the less life-threatening cut on Inspector Sparrow's forehead.

At the Duke's Head, Godfrey was already drinking his third whisky and soda, and his three companions were also getting slowly sozzled. Bert Branch was drinking a pint of bitter, and Rupert Burgess was breaking the habit of a lifetime and doing the same. Inspector Sparrow felt a little uncomfortable to be seen drinking alcohol whilst in uniform, which under normal circumstances was banned by the Metropolitan Police code of practice. But given that the cut on his head had needed ten stitches and his dislocated shoulder had been yanked back into place at the hospital, he felt that the usual rules could be ignored for the evening. He was already on his second pint of cider.

Godfrey had decided they should all stay at the Duke's Head and press on to Hunstanton the next morning. The four rooms the hotel had available were booked and the men took it in turns to call their nearest and dearest on the telephone at the reception desk. Sparrow also called Scotland Yard, where he left orders for a Black Maria to drive out to King's Lynn the next morning to transport the two women back to London.

Burgess called his wife near Tunbridge Wells, and she expressed her concern that he was spending the night away from home without his ulcer medication. When she put the phone down, she opened another bottle of sherry to celebrate having an evening to herself.

Bert Branch's parents in Peckham didn't have a telephone, so he called the telephone box in the Old Kent Road, the one where he had dialled 999 just a few days before. As usual, he had to wait until a passer-by picked up the telephone and then trust that they would convey the message by walking up to the third floor of Emsworth Dwellings.

Godfrey called his house in Surrey and Jozintje the Belgian maid answered the phone, a sign that she was becoming more confident with her communication skills in English. "Can you tell my wife that I'm stuck in Norfolk for the night," he said. He repeated the message more slowly. "Stuck ... in ... Norfolk for the night. Do you understand?"

"Yes," said Jozintje, who understood the expression 'Do you understand?'

"Please write it down," said Godfrey.

When she put the phone down, Jozintje found a piece of paper and wrote down: *Your husband is stuck, has no fuck for the night.* She left the message on the kitchen table and went to bed.

*****

When the Krumnagel party set off for Hunstanton the following morning, the atmosphere in the car was much improved. The previous day, there had been a feeling that Rupert Burgess wasn't quite part of the team, saying very little and exhibiting anxiety throughout the journey from London to Kings Lynn. How different it was now. Everyone had witnessed the crucial role he played in delaying Emily Roebuck and getting himself a cracked head for his trouble. More important, he had managed to grab the letter she was carrying, which she was intending to post in the box on the other side of the square. The reason Inspector Sparrow was in such an ebullient mood was that the letter was a blackmail threat to a local man, who was clearly the next person they were planning to fleece of his savings. The letter would be a valuable piece of evidence against the Trust Fund Tricksters when they finally appeared in court.

However, the atmosphere at number 24 Cliff Terrace Hunstanton was even frostier on Sunday morning than it had been the previous afternoon. Mrs Normington was still annoyed with Horace after the incident of the broken telephone, although Horace pointed out that it was she who had done the damage by lurching forward and thrusting the implement at him.

She had gone to Mabel Pickersgill's house to use her telephone, giving the operator a number she found on a letter from Krumnagel's, but no one at the bank answered. In the short time between Godfrey's original call and her attempt to reply, it had closed, as it always did on a Saturday, at one o'clock sharp.

The Bentley drove into Hunstanton and eventually pulled up in front of Horace's house. Mrs Normington was in the kitchen and Horace was in the lounge, asleep in front of the fire with a cat on his lap. Goliath the dog was still in the back garden, occasionally barking like a mad thing whenever he heard an unusual noise. The sound of three Bentley doors being slammed at slightly different times was unusual enough to warrant an angry outburst, so he provided one. Mrs Normington went out and tried to calm him down by tickling his immense ears, which he enjoyed, but he felt it was important to keep barking, to indicate that strangers were approaching the house. The housekeeper's awpawpawing failed to stop him.

Bert Branch stayed in the car and the other three walked or hopped up the path to the front door. Godfrey leaned on one of his crutches and pulled the metal rod that should have activated a small bell in the hall. He wasn't to know that there was no actual bell, and there hadn't been one for more than thirty years. After a few seconds, he rapped on the door three times, which set

Goliath off again. Burgess heard the dog, and his anxiety antennae told him that they should beat a retreat. His boss was made of sterner stuff. He turned the doorknob and the door creaked open.

"Let's go in," he said.

Sparrow put the hand that wasn't in a sling on the bank manager's arm. "Technically," he said, "you'll be trespassing if you enter the premises without the permission of the owner."

Godfrey laughed. "Oh, I hardly think Goodgame will press charges," he said. "Particularly when he finds out that he's five thousand pounds better off than he thought he was." He opened the door and walked into the hall.

"Hello?" he shouted.

"Hrrmmuurthoo?" said a half-asleep Horace.

Godfrey looked into the room and saw that the source of the strange honking noise was a man sitting in front of the fire. He walked in and Sparrow followed him. Burgess stayed in the hall. Out in the garden, Goliath was aware that people had entered the house, even if Mrs Normington wasn't, and he decided that it was time to protect the occupants from insurgents. He yanked forward on his leash, and the hook that had restrained him for the past few days finally pulled out of the wall. Free at last, he raced into the house and through the kitchen. When he saw a thin stooped man with a bandage round his head standing in the hall, Goliath roared his loudest bark yet and ran towards him. Burgess looked in horror at the snarling beast, gave a loud groan and crashed to the floor in a dead faint. Goliath screeched to a halt, puzzled, and walked round his intended victim, sniffing at the man's clothes, his tail wagging slowly.

Mrs Normington came running into the hall and grabbed Goliath's leash, just as Godfrey and Inspector

Sparrow appeared from the lounge. The housekeeper looked suspiciously at the three men, one on crutches, one with a bandaged head and an arm in a sling, and the third lying on the floor. Her concern was only partially lessened when she saw that one of them was wearing a police uniform.

"Who are you and what are you doing here?" she asked. Goliath growled quietly and she held his leash tight. He was equally interested to discover the identity of the three strangers before he tried to detach a leg from one of them.

"We came in because no one answered when we rang the bell," said Godfrey.

"There is no bell," replied Mrs Normington.

"Well, that explains that then," said the bank manager, and took a step forward, intending to offer his hand to the woman. The sudden movement ended Goliath's temporary cessation of hostilities, and the massive dog leapt up onto Godfrey's chest, knocking him over. Mrs Normington yanked the dog back and shouted at him. Goliath retreated slightly, but his face remained defiant.

"Wait a minute," she said, and walked the dog back into the kitchen. She talked to him for a few moments, then closed the kitchen door and came back to confront the men. Godfrey was slowly getting up and Sparrow was on his knees, shaking Burgess, who eventually lifted himself onto one elbow. Once he had established that the dog was no longer in the hall, he stood up.

Godfrey apologised to Mrs Normington for surprising her and in a few words explained why they were there. "Did you get our telegram?" he asked.

"No, we didn't."

"That's a bit strange. I sent it yesterday."

"Ah!" said the housekeeper. "The Post Office is closed. Albert Looney died, you see."

Godfrey didn't see how the death of someone known as Albert the loony could affect the delivery of a telegram but decided that wasn't important right now. He pointed into the room behind him. "The gentleman in the chair," he said. "Is that Horace Goodgame?"

"Yes," said Mrs Normington.

"Yes," repeated Burgess, looking into the lounge. He recognised Horace as the man he had spoken to at the bank a few days before.

"Excellent," said Godfrey. "We have some good news for him."

Godfrey hopped on his crutches into the room and the others followed him.

"Mister Goodgame?" said Godfrey.

"Horace! Wake up!" said Mrs Normington.

Horace opened his eyes and looked woozily around. "Hanummph?" he said. He saw Mrs Normington and three men standing front of him, in shadow because the light from the window was behind them. The men all looked as if they had been in some kind of accident.

The one who was leaning on crutches spoke. "Mister Goodgame," he said. "My name is Godfrey Krumnagel, and I'm the manager of Krumnagel's Bank in London."

"What?" said Horace.

Godfrey repeated his introduction.

"You're from the bank? What do you want? A pound of flesh?"

"I'm sorry?"

"You've come all the way out here to tell me I have no money? For goodness sake, are you trying to take away the last vestiges of my self-respect? I *know* I have no money."

401

All four people started talking at once. Godfrey waved his arms and asked everyone to be quiet. "Mister Goodgame," he said. "On the contrary, we came to tell you that we have apprehended your wife Martha Goodgame and retrieved a large sum of money from her and her accomplice, Emily Roebuck. Money they fraudulently withdrew from your trust fund."

When she heard the names of the women she despised, Mrs Normington hissed quite loudly, enough to stop Godfrey in his tracks. He looked at her, then continued. "We have been able to put more than five thousand pounds back into your trust fund."

Horace listened to what Godfrey had to say, thought for a moment, then stood up. The cat, which had managed to sleep through the entire episode, including Goliath's noisy intervention, woke up when the lap she was sitting on suddenly went vertical, jumped elegantly onto the rug and went off in search of mice, of which there was a plentiful supply in the cellar.

"I'm sorry, I don't quite understand," said Horace.

Again, everyone started talking at the same time, and this time Mrs Normington shouted for everyone to shut up. When the visitors all finally went quiet, Goliath decided to start another fit of barking.

"Horace, listen, will you?" said Mrs Normington. "That nasty piece of horse-droppings Martha Donkin isn't dead, as we suspected she wasn't, and she's been taking money from your trust fund, but they got it back."

There was a moment's silence.

"I see," said Horace. He scratched his head. "All very interesting."

"I think everyone needs a cup of tea," said the housekeeper. "Follow me!"

402

When Mrs Normington opened the door to the kitchen, Goliath was remarkably calm. He'd worked out that the visitors were not burglars or any of the other unwelcome types that Albert Looney had trained him to frighten away, namely insurance salesmen, tax inspectors, Wilfred Pickersgill, or indeed anyone who looked like the angry husband of one of the Post Office's women customers.

Mrs Normington made some tea and put a plate of chocolate biscuits on the table. While they drank their tea, Goliath walked round the table, sniffing the clothes of the new arrivals, and occasionally pushing his nose onto the table with the intention of stealing one of the biscuits, something he continued to do even though Mrs Normington slapped his proboscis whenever he tried.

In spite of the good news that the London party had brought, Horace seemed subdued as the conversation swirled around him. The new arrivals gave details of the previous day's events in King's Lynn, the whole thing becoming more dramatic by the minute, but the man at the centre of the story sat quietly, looking at his mug and occasionally sipping the contents.

There was a lull in the conversation, which was what Horace had been waiting for. He stood up, cleared his throat and began to speak. "There's something I wish to say," he said. He paused for a few seconds to collect his thoughts.

"Well, go on then," said Mrs Normington. "Say it."

"I will. This money ... first of all, I want to thank you all, the police, the bank, my sincere thanks for your kind efforts to reconnect me with what was stolen from my dear Aunt Agatha's trust fund."

403

"You're most welcome," said Godfrey. "It has given me great satisfaction to be the bearer of such good tidings."

Thank you, sir," said Horace. "And I really and truly do appreciate it."

There were smiles and sounds of approval.

"The thing is ... I don't want the money."

"I beg your pardon?" said Godfrey.

"I don't want the money."

"But ... but it's yours!"

"Let me explain," said Horace. "Last year, I entered into a state of matrimony with a woman called Leonora Capstan, illegally I now realise, as my first wife Martha is still alive. Martha did not, as we were led to believe, drown in September two years ago. So, in actual fact, my second marriage to Mrs Capstan was bigamous and, as such, invalid. I'm still married to Martha."

"Horace! Stop!" said Mrs Normington. "You aren't planning to get back with that woman, are you? She's a witch!"

"Edna, please just wait a moment," said Horace. "Let me finish." He took a deep breath and continued. "In the eyes of the law, my marriage to Leonora Capstan is unlawful. In fact, as a bigamist, I could probably go to prison."

"Surely not," said Godfrey. "Inspector, what do you think?"

"Well, strictly speaking, Mister Goodgame is right. Bigamy is an offence which can carry a sentence of seven years' imprisonment." There were intakes of breath and other sounds of astonishment when Sparrow said this. "But given the circumstances," he added hastily, "I doubt there would be any chance of this happening. I mean, as I understand it, a death certificate was issued after your first wife went missing."

"Correct!" shouted Mrs Normington. "It's a flaming pity it turned out she's still alive!"

"If you will just let me say what I want to say, without interruption," said Horace, a hint of impatience in his voice.

The table went quiet. Horace wasn't used to having people's undivided attention like this, and for a moment, he hesitated. He took another deep breath and began again. "So, the situation is like this. My first wife, Martha Goodgame, is under arrest and will go on trial for embezzlement. Is that right?"

"Correct," said Inspector Sparrow.

"And what will happen if she's found guilty?"

"Well, she'll probably go to prison."

"For how long?"

"I'm not sure, but if memory serves, the maximum sentence would be ten years."

"Marvellous!" shouted Mrs Normington.

"In all probability, she'll get a custodial sentence of rather less than that."

"I see," said Horace. "Right ... so that brings me to my second wife, as it were. Leonora Capstan. I'm not actually married to her, is that right?"

"Well, yes," said Inspector Sparrow. "But as I said earlier, under the circumstances, the courts would take a favourable view of your situation. And given the deception wrought by your first wife with her disappearance, fabricating her own death, in fact, it seems to me that it would be a simple matter to divorce your first wife and re-marry, as it were, your second."

"I see," said Horace. "The fact of the matter is ... I don't want to be married to either of them."

Everyone was now staring at Horace, apart from Goliath, who took advantage of the moment to steal a biscuit.

"Let me explain what I want to do. But first, I have another question. How difficult would it be to get a divorce from my first wife?"

"Well, as it happens, there's a new bill going through parliament now," said Inspector Sparrow. "It will extend the grounds on which a divorce may be sought."

"New grounds? Really?" said Godfrey, suddenly hopeful that his wife's spending habits might allow him to divorce her. "What sort of thing?"

"I believe the new grounds are drunkenness, insanity and desertion," said the inspector.

"Well, Martha Donkin's guilty on all three counts!" said Mrs Normington, triumphantly.

Godfrey and Bert both laughed, but Sparrow ignored this interruption. "I suppose technically, her attempt to fake her own death could be interpreted as desertion," he said. "I'm no expert on these matters, but I imagine with a good lawyer, you would have no difficulty securing a permanent separation."

"Right," said Horace. "In that case, I want to divorce Martha Goodgame and annul my bigamous marriage to Leonora Capstan. I then want to divide the trust fund money into two and give half to Mrs Capstan, as I suppose she still is, and half to ---- "

Mrs Normington was on her feet. "Horace! No!" she shouted. "Don't even think about giving a brass ha'penny to that terrible woman!"

Horace finished his sentence. "... and the other half to my son, Charles."

"But Mister Goodgame," said Godfrey. "That will leave you with nothing!"

"That won't be a problem. I intend to take up gainful employment here in Hunstanton as the new postmaster."

Mrs Normington was still standing. "Well done, Horace!" she shouted and began to clap her hands.

Horace smiled. "And one more thing. When it's clear that both my marriages have been annulled ... I wish to get married again."

"Well, third time lucky, I suppose," said Godfrey. "And who's the fortunate lady this time?"

"Well, I haven't asked her yet," said Horace. "But if she'll accept me, I intend to ask Edna Normington to be my wife."

Everyone looked at Mrs Normington and there was a burst of applause.

"So, what's your answer, Mrs N?" asked Bert.

Mrs Normington sat down. She shook her head and looked at Horace, who was still standing. "Horace Goodgame," she said, "you're daft as a brush."

Chapter 34
It's time you made
an honest woman of her

Sunday, Great Park - early rain followed by glorious
sunshine

If they woke up early on Sunday morning, Great Park
residents with rooms facing south or west heard rain
pattering against their windows. If they looked out of
those windows, they saw the rain pock-marking the
snow all the way across the estate. By nine o'clock, the
clouds had drifted away, and the sky was a deeper blue
than it had been the previous day. It was as if the capture
of Ronnie Capstan had hastened the arrival of spring.

Charles's corner suite faced south and west, and the
panoramic view of fields and woodland bathed in
sunlight should have raised his spirits, but he still felt
anxious and confused. So many thoughts and questions.
His feelings about Polly, his worries about the future
and, the thing that was disturbing him most when he
woke up, the puzzling phone conversation with his uncle
Ernest the previous evening. Why had he been
summoned to London for the reading of a will? Was his
father dead? If so, why hadn't Ernest told him, instead of
saying he was busy and putting the phone down?

Alexander had agreed to drive Charles back to town
and deliver him to the door of his uncle's house in South
Kensington. His Bentley had been retrieved from the
ditch and was standing at the front door, and he asked his
passengers to be ready to leave by eleven o'clock.
Charles packed his battered suitcase and then went out
to the conservatory for his paint box and portfolio. He

looked through the window of Polly's office and saw her sitting with her chin in her hands, staring at the wall. He knocked gently on the window, and then a little harder. When Polly saw him, she waved a lethargic arm towards the door. He walked in and stood in front of her desk.

"Hello," he said.

"Hello."

"I think we're leaving at eleven."

"Oh well, safe journey."

"I have to go to town for this will thing. But I do want to come back if I'm allowed."

"Of course, you're allowed. You're welcome any time." Polly's voice lacked enthusiasm.

"I thought I could repair the painting."

"Oh, that." She made it sound like the least important thing in the world.

"It shouldn't take me long."

"Right."

"I could be in and out in two shakes of a lamb's tail."

"Yes."

There was a pause.

"Look," said Charles. "I don't know why you got so frosty with me when I said I wanted to go back to London, but the fact is, if I stay here --- "

He didn't finish the sentence. Someone knocked on the door. Charles turned and saw Diana leaning against the frame, a smile on her face. She looked as if she had been listening to their conversation and didn't want to witness anything more intimate. "I don't want to interrupt you two lovebirds," she said, winking at Polly, who opened her eyes wide and shook her head vigorously. This just made Diana smile even more. "Charles, are you ready?" she asked. "Alexander would like to get on the road sooner rather than later, in case the weather changes again."

"What? Oh yes, of course," Charles looked at Polly, who stood up and walked to the front of her desk. "Bye then," he said.

"Bye. Come back soon," she said, and held out her hand for him to shake.

Diana laughed. "You two are *so* funny," she said. "Anyway ... Polly, I was wondering if you'd seen your mother anywhere."

"My mother? Yes, she was here about twenty minutes ago."

"Oh really? Do you know where she went?"

"Well, she asked if Winstanley was available."

"Who's Winstanley?"

"The Duke's chauffeur."

"The chauffeur? What did she want with him?"

"She said she needed to go somewhere," said Polly.

"How bizarre. She knows we're leaving imminently."

"Sorry, it didn't occur to me to ask her where she wanted to go. I sent her off to the stable. Winstanley is usually there in the mornings, tinkering with the motors."

"I wonder what on earth she's up to," said Diana.

Leonora was indeed in the stable and Winstanley was tinkering with the Humber Pullman, as Polly had predicted. He had removed the wedges of snow in the engine and the wheel arches, and his head was now under the bonnet while he checked the spark plugs. He was so engrossed in his work that he didn't hear Leonora approach.

"Excuse me," she said. He didn't reply, so she pinched him hard on the nearest part of his anatomy, which happened to be the seat of his trousers. His head came up

411

quickly, hit the bonnet and dislodged the rod that was holding it open. The bonnet crashed down, and the chauffeur yelped and collapsed onto the engine.

Leonora stood horrified, then lifted the bonnet slowly. "Hello?" she said. Unsurprisingly, Winstanley didn't reply, as the massive bonnet had knocked him out.

"Oh God, this really isn't my day," she said. Not knowing what one did to hold the bonnet open, Leonora rested it on his back, then looked around the empty stable. "Can anyone help?"

A large man appeared at the door and walked towards the car. Leonora recognised him as the gardener who had tackled Ronnie when he was trying to escape.

"Hello! It's Gavin, isn't it?" she said.

"Garth," said the gardener. His voice reached maximum squeak when he had to talk to someone he didn't know well.

"I think I knocked this chap out by mistake," she said, pointing at the body lying half inside the engine.

Garth pulled up the bonnet, clicked the support rod in position and carefully lifted Winstanley's unconscious body. The chauffeur's head flopped forward, but he was breathing and there was no sign of a wound. The gardener turned to Leonora and asked if she could open the back door of the car, which she did.

"He isn't dead, is he?" she asked, as Winstanley flopped onto the seat.

"No, he should wake up in a few minutes."

"The thing is," said Leonora, looking at her watch. "I need to get to Stanford Saint Mary station. Can you drive?"

"I'm afraid I can't."

"Look, I've got an idea."

412

A few minutes later, the Humber Pullman was racing down the main drive, Leonora at the wheel with a very nervous Garth Prodgers in the passenger seat. In the back seat, Winstanley was slowly coming to his senses.

*****

Just after eleven o'clock, Alexander walked down the steps to where the Bentley was parked. Diana and Charles had already put their luggage in the boot, and Diana was smoking her first cigarette of the day.

"Did you find her anywhere?" she asked.

"No," replied Alexander. "I sent the boy to see if she was in her room, which she isn't, and I looked in the stable. No one there either, but I think one of the Duke's cars has gone. Someone could have driven Leonora off somewhere."

"But why would she go gallivanting when she knew we were leaving?"

"Search me." Alexander asked Diana if she wanted to wait longer, and Charles was relieved when she said she didn't. They had already said their goodbyes to the Duke and Pickles, so they got into the car and headed down the driveway. On the road towards Stanford Saint Mary, they passed the Humber Pullman travelling back towards Great Park, with Winstanley driving and the large gardener sitting next to him, but Alexander could see that there was no one in the back seat, so he continued in the direction of Oxford.

In fact, Leonora had driven the car to Stanford Saint Mary station, and once she was safely ensconced in Arnold McGurk's cottage, she said goodbye to Winstanley and Garth. The chauffeur had nothing more serious than bruises on the front and back of his head and his excitable conversation technique was unimpaired, so he spent the entire journey back to the house speculating about what Leonora and the stationmaster might be getting up to.

The Bentley breezed through Oxfordshire and Buckinghamshire, then the fields and villages gave way to clusters of suburban houses as they approached London. When they passed the Hoover Building in Perivale, Charles felt his spirits rise. Despite finding it difficult to make a living in the city, he was inspired by London - the noisy hubbub of people and traffic, the galleries, and museums, and particularly the spectacular architecture. He was also fond of the folk he rubbed shoulders with near his studio in Hammersmith - the Irish greengrocer in King Street, the old man who spent the day fishing off the bridge, and the eccentric woman who walked back and forth along the exposed riverbed at low tide, looking for coins that people had thrown for good luck as they crossed the river, of which she found many.

And of course, over in South Kensington was Veronica Stoodley, his favourite older person. He was also very fond of her dog Fish. He made a mental note to pop down Pelham Crescent to see them after the will business had been sorted out.

"We're almost there," said Alexander. They were on Fulham Road and about to turn into Pelham Crescent. "What number does your uncle live at?"

"You know, I can't actually remember," said Charles. "But I'll recognise it. There's a rowan tree in front of the house. It's a pity that you won't see the berries, they're really beautiful in late autumn. And it's too early to see the blossom."

"Sounds lovely," said Diana.

"And the back garden is a work of art," said Charles, his enthusiasm clear. "The flower beds are stunning in the spring, and there are some gorgeous bushes - azalea, forsythia, hydrangea, all sorts."

"Do you know about things like that?"

"Things like what?"

"Garden things. Are you good at gardening?"

"Well, yes I suppose I am. I used to love working in the garden when we lived in Norfolk." It was just as well I did, he thought. No one else in the house was the least bit interested.

"And you're an artist," said Diana. "Have you ever thought about combining the two skills?"

"In what way?"

"Well, I have a vast garden in Dorset. A man comes and plants things every spring, but what he does isn't very exciting. I was just wondering if I could employ you to, I don't know, jazz it up a bit."

"Jazz it up a bit?" repeated Alexander. "Where did you learn an expression like that?"

"I have no idea. From my friends who like American music, I suppose."

"There's so much I don't know about you."

"Well, there's plenty of time for you to find out."

They smiled at each other, and Charles feared that the offer of work had disappeared. He wondered if he should remind her before he lost the chance. After all, he had nothing else in the pipeline. "Um, we're here," he said. "This is the place."

The car pulled up in front of Ernest's house.

"Thanks awfully for driving me back."

"Don't mention it," said Alexander. "Do you need any help with your things?"

"No, I'll be fine."

He felt too embarrassed to remind Diana about her gardening suggestion, so he got out and opened the boot, and put his suitcase, box of paints and portfolio next to each other on the pavement.

"Just a second." Diana got out of the car, walked back and gave him a hug. When he leaned towards her, Charles wobbled and nearly fell over his luggage, and remembered doing the same thing when he arrived at Stanford Saint Mary station less than a week before.

"It's been awfully nice meeting you again," she said, "despite the rather unusual circumstances."

"It's been a real pleasure meeting you too, Lady Grimbledon."

"Oh, please don't call me that. Just call me Diana. Anyway, I might not be able to call myself Lady Grimbledon for much longer."

"Really? Why not?"

Diana looked back at Alexander, who was in the car and wasn't listening to their conversation. She smiled and said: "If I marry, I have to give up the title."

"Oh! Well, that's amazing!" said Charles.

"Yes, it might well be," she replied. "Talking of amazing, it's time you made an honest woman of her."

Charles looked at her, puzzled. "I'm sorry?"

"You know what I'm talking about, or rather *who* I'm talking about. If you don't do something soon, you're going to lose her."

"Are we talking about Polly?"

"Are we talking about Polly?" Diana mimicked the shock in his voice. "Of course, we're talking about Polly."

"And you think I'm going to lose her?"

"Absolutely. Strike while the iron's hot, I say."

"Oh no, you don't understand!" said Charles, and laughed nervously. "Polly isn't the least bit interested in me."

"Is that what you really think?"

"Yes, of course. I'm not nearly well off enough, plus I don't have anywhere to live." Or any prospects, he thought.

Diana shook her head and smiled. Then she opened her handbag and took out a visiting card. One on side, it had her Saint John's Wood address and on the other, there was information about her Dorset home. "Give me a call on the London number, sometime tomorrow. I'll take you out for lunch and we can talk about Harcombe Bottom."

"About what?"

"Harcombe Bottom. My place in Dorset. I want you to design my garden, remember?"

"I'd be delighted to do that. But I think you should know that I've never designed a garden before."

"There's a first time for everything." She kissed his cheek and walked back to the car. As she opened the passenger door, she turned and smiled. "Don't forget! Call me!"

"Of course. Um... before you go, there's something else you should know."

"What?" Diana waited for a moment, then walked back to where he was standing. "Something that can't wait until we have lunch?"

"Something that might mean you change your mind about inviting me to lunch."

"Really? What could possibly make me want to do that?"

"I need to tell you something," Charles paused. "Do you remember the painting that I sold you?"

417

"Yes. The Horace Tuck. What about it?"

"Well, that's the thing. It isn't a Horace Tuck."

"Really? Why did you tell me it was?"

"I didn't. I told you it was in the style of Horace Tuck."

"So, who painted it?"

"My father."

"Horace Goodgame painted it?" said Diana. "Oh, how amusing!" She laughed, but then her face turned serious. "Actually, that *is* a pity, because I was hoping to sell it. I'm glad you told me before I made a fool of myself with some art collector. Anyway, we have to get off. *Au revoir*!"

Charles shook his head in disbelief. "Aren't you angry with me?"

"Angry with you? Whatever for?"

"I mis-sold you a work of art."

"So what? It's only a painting." She walked back to the car and opened the door. Before she got in, she turned and smiled at Charles. "On the other hand, I *will* be angry with you if you don't call me tomorrow and arrange lunch."

"Of course I will."

"Goodbye, Charles."

"Goodbye, Lady ... um ... Diana."

Charles watched the car disappear round the crescent, and felt a warm glow spread through his body. He had confessed to something that he thought would ruin him if it ever came to light, and it had been dismissed as of no great consequence. He started laughing, a deep carefree noise he couldn't remember making since he was a student. He made a yelping noise which made a dog bark a few houses away, then he picked up his suitcase, portfolio and paints and walked up the steps of uncle Ernest's house.

He knocked on the door and when he turned to look at the bay window, he saw a red-faced man with white hair brushed back from his face looking back at him. The man disappeared and a few moments later, he opened the door.

"Oh hello," said Charles. "Er... I'm Charles Goodgame."

"Ernest's nephew, yes I know," said the man. "He told me to expect you. He'll be back in a few minutes. Come in." The man walked away from the door and into the front room.

Charles picked up his luggage and placed it in the hall at the bottom of the stairs. He wondered whether he should go directly out to the shed in the garden or wait in the house until his uncle returned. And if he waited in the house, should he follow the man with the red face into the front room? The man helped him decide by poking his head back through the door. "Sorry," he said, "I'm not being much of a host. Would you care for a drink?"

"Oh yes, rather," said Charles.

"Come on in." He turned and disappeared, and by the time Charles entered the room, he was standing at the walnut drinks cabinet. "What's your poison?"

"I'm sorry?"

"What can I get you to drink?"

"Um ... what is there to choose from?"

"Pretty much whatever you want. I won't offer you this ..." he said, holding up a bottle of rum, "... because Ernest gets it in specially for me and there's hardly any left. But there's just about anything else." He held up another bottle. "This brandy usually does the trick. Do you want some?"

Charles wasn't really a brandy drinker, but he was in such a buoyant mood that he accepted it and sat down on the sofa.

"Ernest told me that you paint portraits, is that right?" said the man, settling himself at the opposite end of the sofa.

"Yes, indeed," replied Charles, sipping the brandy, which was delicious.

"In that case, we're in the same line of work."

"Really? You're a portrait artist?" Charles took a longer sip of the brandy, which warmed his mouth and throat. He was enjoying the effect immensely.

"Yes."

"I say, that's marvellous. Do you make a living out of it?"

"I get by."

"How wonderful." Charles drained the last of the brandy and rolled the liquid around his mouth. "May I ask your name?"

"Washbrook," said the man. "Walter Washbrook."

Charles exhaled like a burst tyre. Brandy spurted out of his mouth and hit the older man full in the face. There was a moment's silence, and Walter Washbrook took a handkerchief out of his pocket and dabbed his forehead. "Actually, I'm happy just drinking the rum," he said, and laughed a deep throaty laugh.

"I'm most terribly sorry!" gurgled Charles, suddenly feeling very tipsy. "I ... I don't know what came over me."

"Not a problem," said Walter. "By the way, you look very familiar. Haven't we met before?"

"I don't think so."

"I'm sure we have. I remember you from somewhere." Walter frowned and looked at the ceiling. "Yes! Ernest

420

was throwing a dinner party a year or so ago, and you popped your head into the room." He smiled a rather oily smile. "I remember thinking what a charming young man you were."

"Ah." Charles remembered what Polly had told him about Walter Washbrook and began to feel a little uncomfortable. "Yes, I used to live in the shed in the garden. But ... "

"Yes?"

"Well, the thing is, I've come to London to look for somewhere to live because .... er ... I'm getting married."

"Really?" said Walter, looking a little disappointed. "Who's the lucky girl?"

"My sister," said Charles.

"What?"

"Well, no. Not my actual sister. I --- "

"Charles! Thank goodness you're here!" Ernest was standing at the door of the lounge. "I hope Walter has been a good host, although it would be a first if he has."

"No, he's been absolutely wonderful," said Charles.

"Your nephew tells me he's going to marry his sister," said Walter.

"What?"

"He's going to marry his sister."

"Don't talk rot," said Ernest. "He doesn't have a sister. He's an only child."

Walter looked at Charles, disappointment on his blotchy face. "Why did you tell me you wanted to marry your sister?" he asked.

Charles was always intimidated by Uncle Ernest, a much more powerful presence than his brother Horace. But he realised that he needed to say something quickly to make sense of his first statement. "She isn't my real sister," he said. "She's my stepsister."

421

"You're going to marry your stepsister?" asked Walter. "Is that legal?"

Ernest interrupted the conversation. "Walter, will you stop wittering on? I need to talk to Charles. So make yourself useful and fix me a gin and tonic."

"Certainly, squire." Walter eased himself up from the sofa and walked slowly back to the drinks cabinet, groaning slightly because of the arthritic pain in his knees.

Ernest sat down in the place that Walter had vacated. "Charles," he said, with the quiet authority in his voice that stopped conversations whenever he spoke. "I have to say it was a complete surprise when they told me you were a beneficiary, but I gather if you aren't at the reading of the will, you might have to forfeit your claim."

"I see," said Charles, suddenly feeling miserable again. "Is it ... my father?"

Ernest looked at him, puzzled. "Is what your father?"

"Is my father ... has he passed away?"

"Horace? No, of course he hasn't! What on earth made you think that?"

Charles always felt like an ignorant or naughty schoolboy when he was with his uncle and now, he felt like both. "Well," he said, his face flushing with embarrassment. "When you said I had to come back for the reading of the will, I couldn't think of anyone else who might have left me something. Sorry."

"I see what you mean," said Ernest. "You're quite right, I should have apprised you of the situation when you called. Many apologies."

"Room for a little one in the middle?" Walter hovered over the conversation, holding Ernest's gin and tonic in his hand.

"No," said Ernest, taking the drink. "This is an important conversation. Go and make yourself useful in the kitchen."

"Doing what?" asked the artist.

"There are some peeled potatoes next to the stove. Put them in a pan of water and boil them," said Ernest.

Walter grumbled under his breath, but hobbled out of the lounge.

When they were finally alone, Ernest repeated his apology. "Thinking back, it was quite wrong of me to be so brusque with you on the phone. I suppose the main reason was that I was rather annoyed that you hadn't replied to my letters. I wrote two of them," he added to further increase Charles's sense of guilt.

"I didn't get them, so I apologise for causing you so much concern."

"Apology accepted."

"So ..." said Charles, afraid of another rebuke. "Who .... why did I get mentioned in a will?"

"Oh, right," said Ernest. "I'm not being clear at all, am I? It's Veronica Stoodley."

"Oh no!" said Charles. "Miss Stoodley died? I'm so sorry!"

"Well, she was about ninety, so she had a good innings."

Charles realised the probable reason that he was mentioned in the will.

"Is it Fish?" he asked.

"Is it what?"

"Fish. The dog. Has she left me her dog?"

"Well, yes, I imagine she has," said Ernest.

"Right," said Charles. He wondered how on earth he could look after a dog when he had nowhere to live.

Asking Ernest if he could put it in the shed in the garden didn't seem a viable option.

"More to the point," said his uncle, "and the reason why you had to be here, is that she has left you rather more than the dog."

Oh dear, thought Charles. She's probably left me that huge stone kennel in the back garden, too. He simply wasn't in a position to take on so much responsibility. "Is it the kennel as well?" he asked.

Ernest laughed a loud, deep laugh. "You really are very funny, Charles," he said. "Have you thought about a career in the music halls?"

"I'm sorry?"

"I don't seem to be getting my message across to you terribly well," said Ernest. "Veronica Stoodley had no children and no siblings. She has decided to leave you not only her dog and its kennel, she's left you her entire house."

When he was asked later to describe what happened when he heard this news, Charles was unable to give details. The next thing he could recall was lying on the floor next to the sofa. When he opened his eyes, Ernest and Walter were staring down at him.

"Give him more brandy," said Walter.

"I think water might be more advisable," answered Ernest.

When Charles was finally compos mentis, the three of them ate dinner in Ernest's spacious kitchen, and they managed to drain two bottles of red wine while they were doing it. When the meal was finished, they went back into the front room and Ernest poured everyone a brandy. Charles was feeling woozy and excited and hardly able to think straight. He was suddenly aware that his uncle was speaking.

"Did you hear what I said?"

"Sorry, no."

"I said there's something important I need to ask you," said Ernest.

"Fire away," said Charles.

"I think it's curious that Veronica decided to leave the property to someone she hardly knew. It's a decision that might arouse suspicion. So I have to ask you - did you at any time put any pressure on her to do it?"

"What? Goodness me, no!" said Charles, spilling brandy on his shirt.

"Good. They may ask you about it, that's all."

"I thought you said she was an only child who never married," said Walter. "Who would think they had a right to her stuff?"

"Oh Walter, you do live in cloud cuckoo land," said Ernest.

"Do I? I thought it was *clown* cuckoo land. Isn't it?"

"Oh for goodness sake, no it isn't. It's *cloud* cuckoo land. You can't even speak English!"

"I don't give a tuppenny fuck what kind of cuckoos live there. Answer my question. If she's an only child, and she never married, who could possibly have dibs on her house?"

Ernest shook his head. "Look," he said. "Houses in this street are worth a fortune and the prices are shooting up all the time. One sold for more than seven thousand pounds just last month."

"Good Lord!" said Charles.

"So previously unknown family members - great aunts in Greenwich, cousins twice removed in Canterbury, nephews of her grandparents in Nottingham - may well come crawling out of the woodwork."

There was a moment of silence while they all considered this. Charles made what he thought was a valid point. "Can we really expect a visit from a great aunt?" he asked. "Miss Stoodley was nearly ninety."

Ernest looked at him and shook his head. "Honestly, Charles, for an artistic type, you are terribly literal-minded. 'Great aunts in Greenwich' is just a figure of speech."

Walter chuckled. "Ah, right!" he said. "Like 'around the rugged rocks the ragged rascals ran'. Or is it ragged rocks and rugged rascals?"

"What ARE you blithering on about?"

"I was giving an example of a figure of speech. I remember learning about them at school. What I just said was ... um ... alliteration."

Ernest sighed loudly. "I think this evening has run its course. You're talking nonsense, like a baboon."

"Ah! Talking nonsense like a baboon. Now that's a simile," said Walter.

"Oh do shut UP!" said Ernest. "And go home. The boy and I have to get some sleep to be ready for the morning."

Walter slowly drained the last of his rum.

"Come on! Get your coat on and leave," said Ernest.

"All right, all right, calm down. I'm on my way."

"You can get a taxi on the Brompton Road."

"I think I'll walk," said Walter. "The fresh air will do me good."

When Walter finally stumbled out of the house, Charles and Ernest sat in silence for a while in the front room.

"I now understand that you didn't answer my letters because you weren't in London," said Ernest. "Where were you?"

426

"Well... " Charles decided that what he had been doing might impress his uncle. "Actually, I've been at a country house in Gloucestershire. Painting a portrait of a Duke."

"Really?" said Ernest. He looked quizzically at Charles. "Painting a portrait of a Duke? In Gloucestershire?"

"Yes indeed," said Charles.

"What was the name of the Duke?"

"Well, it's spelt Bur-faught-on-leigh, but it's pronounced Burley."

"Well, well, well. Tell me something."

"Yes?"

"While you were there, did you meet someone called Bernard Delgado?"

Chapter 35
Are you threatening me, Mister Goodgame?

Monday morning, South Kensington - forecast for thunderstorms

A loud clap of thunder woke Charles up. He sat up in bed, groaned and rubbed his head. Too much wine and brandy had been consumed the night before, and he was feeling like death. After crawling in and out of a hot bath, he felt slightly less like death and stumbled downstairs to join his uncle in the kitchen. Ernest seemed totally unaffected by the large amount he had drunk the night before and walked purposefully from stove to larder, preparing eggs and bacon, making toast and coffee and feeding peeled oranges into a large metal machine on the wooden dresser.

"What *is* that thing?" asked Charles, blinking and trying to focus.

"This machine? It's a Norwalk Juicer. Apparently, it's healthier to just drink the juice of oranges. Juicing them brings out the vitamins. When you get to my age and your powers start to wane, you look for anything to give you a bit of an edge."

Charles was astonished to hear his uncle say this. As far as he could see, Ernest's powers weren't waning at all - he was muscular, healthy and confident, the complete opposite of his brother Horace. Charles munched away at the enormous breakfast, while Ernest drank a black coffee and smoked a cigarette.

"So, do you remember what I told you last night?"

Charles paused, a fork full of runny egg halfway to his mouth. The egg slowly dripped back onto the plate as he tried to remember what Ernest might be referring to. "About what in particular?" he asked.

His uncle twisted his mouth, his way of expressing annoyance. "I told you to be ready to leave by ten o'clock. That's when a solicitor will be fetching up at Veronica's house."

Charles looked at his watch. It was a quarter past nine. "Right."

"So can you change into your smartest clothes, please?"

"My smartest clothes?"

"Yes."

"These *are* my smartest clothes."

"Good heavens, really?"

Even after the Great Park staff had repaired the holes in the sleeve and the back, Charles's cream suit still looked old and shabby.

"I'm afraid so."

"Well, you're about the same height as me. Go and root around in my wardrobe and find a decent suit and shirt."

"Right ho."

"And even artists are required to wear ties at times like this."

"Oh yes. Of course."

There were more than a dozen suits in Ernest's wardrobe. Charles chose a black one and also a pale blue shirt from the fifty or so that were hanging there. He completed the transformation by putting on a black necktie with a diagonal blue stripe. He looked at himself in one of several mirrors in Ernest's bedroom and couldn't believe the transformation, but when he put his scuffed brown shoes back on, they spoiled the effect.

Ernest was standing at the door. "Ready?" he asked. He saw the shoes and did the twisty thing with his mouth again. He opened a door that led into a small dressing room that contained dozens of pairs of shoes, laid out on racks from floor to ceiling. "Have a look in there," he said. "But be quick about it."

There was another loud thunderclap as the Messrs Goodgame walked the few yards down Pelham Crescent, and rain was falling quite heavily by the time they reached Veronica Stoodley's house. They ran up the path and to the top of the steps, where a short, red-faced man in a tight-fitting suit and a black trilby was waiting for them.

"Mister Goodgame?" asked the man.

"Yes," said Charles and Ernest at the same time.

"Which one of you is Mr Goodgame?"

"Both of us," answered Ernest.

The man looked perplexed. He took a piece of paper out of his pocket, read it and re-phrased his question. "Which one of you is *Charles* Goodgame?"

"It is I," said Charles, and then thought that sounded rather pompous. "It is me," he added.

"I see," said the man. He looked at them both and, like many people before him, felt immediately intimidated by Ernest. "Well, I'm Sebastian Kugelhorn, from Kugelhorn, Kugelhorn, Gummy and Schütz of Temple Bar, London EC4. I have been instructed to carry out probate for the estate of Mrs Sturdley."

"The name is Stoodley," said Ernest. "And it's Miss, not Mrs."

The man stared at Ernest. He wasn't in a position to confirm or contest this piece of information without opening his briefcase, which he wasn't going to do in front of total strangers. He decided it was best not to say any more until he had the relevant papers in front of him. For Ernest, the man's inability to get the name of the deceased right was a warning signal. He resolved to listen very carefully to everything this Kugelhorn character said. Charles could feel the hostility building between the two of them.

The solicitor was about to say something else when he noticed Charles's tie. "Ah!" he said, his fat face bursting into a beaming smile. "I'm delighted to see that we were at the same school, Mister Goodgame."

"Were we?" asked Charles. "Did you go to Hunstanton Boys' Academy?"

The solicitor looked puzzled. "No, of course not. I was at Eton."

"Were you? I wasn't," said Charles.

"But you're wearing an old Etonian tie," said Kugelhorn, looking affronted.

Ernest looked at the tie. "That belongs to me," he said. "My nephew didn't have a tie, so I lent him one of mine."

The rain was falling even more intensely now.

"Can we talk inside?" said Ernest. "The two of us are getting soaked."

Kugelhorn turned and put the key in the door, pushed it open and walked inside.

"I didn't know you were at Eton," said Charles quietly, as they followed him into the house. "I thought you and papa went to the local place in Fakenham."

"We did," whispered Ernest. "The tie must belong to one of my guests. But don't tell him that."

The solicitor stood in the hall, then looked into the nearest room. "Is there anywhere with a table where I can spread out the documents?" he asked.

432

"The kitchen," said Charles. "Follow me."

When they were seated, Kugelhorn opened his briefcase and took out a copy of *The Times* newspaper, followed by three manila files and a large brown envelope, which he put neatly next to each other on the kitchen table. He then put the newspaper back in his briefcase, closed it and put it on the side of the table. The first file contained only one four-page document, held together at the corner with a piece of string. He scanned the document, then looked at the two men suspiciously. "I have to say that this is an extremely unusual situation," he said. "One that I haven't encountered in twenty years working on probate issues."

"What exactly do you mean?" asked Ernest.

"It would appear that Mrs..." he glanced at the name at the top of the document, "Stoodley..."

"Miss Stoodley," said Ernest, sighing with annoyance.

"Miss or Mrs ... the fact remains that she's left her property to someone who is no relation to her and whom she hardly knew."

"That isn't true," said Ernest. "Veronica knew Charles very well. Indeed, she was aware of my nephew's burgeoning reputation in the art world even before she invited him to paint a portrait of her pet."

"Paint a what?"

"If you knew anything about the world of modern art," he continued, "you would know that the name Charles Goodgame ranks up there with the best of the new wave of English watercolourists."

Charles stared at Ernest and decided not to tell him that he wouldn't know what to do with watercolours if his life depended on it. But Ernest had gambled correctly that Kugelhorn knew nothing about art and wasn't able to dispute anything he said.

"Speaking of animals," said the solicitor, desperate to move the conversation back to the will, "there is an animal involved in the legacy."

"Ah yes, that'll be Fish," said Charles.

"No, I believe the creature in question is a dog," said Kugelhorn. "Fishwick Braccorian Wellington Saint Leger," he read from the document he was holding. "A Bichon Frise, whatever that is."

"Yes, Fishwick et cetera et cetera," said Charles. "Known to friends and family as 'Fish'."

Kugelhorn shook his head, then opened the second file, which contained a sheaf of correspondence. He took out a letter and read it quickly. "Apparently the animal is in the care of one Gisèle Lemarchand, who lives in the basement of the property."

Gisèle, Miss Stoodley's maid. Charles felt alarmed when he heard her name. She had never taken to him, regarding it as an imposition when she had to provide food and drink for him on his dog-sitting visits. What if she suggested that he had coerced Veronica Stoodley into giving him her house?

"I have asked Miss Lemarchand to join us here for the reading of the will."

As if on cue, they heard the front door open.

"We're in the kitchen!" the solicitor shouted.

All three men stood up as Gisèle walked in, Fish the dog trotting reluctantly behind her. Woman and dog were clearly not the best of friends and were making strenuous efforts not to look at each other.

"Fish!" shouted Charles. He was really pleased to see his canine friend and the feeling was mutual. Fish's eyes opened wide with delight as he raced across the kitchen floor and tried to jump into Charles's arms. He didn't quite make it and his small but powerful paws smacked forcefully into his human pal's scrotum, causing him to groan and his knees to buckle. His fall to the ground was halted by Gisèle, who rushed forward and caught him.

"Errrrr nerrrr, Monsieur Gerdgermmmm!" she said, holding Charles in a tight embrace. Even though she looked old enough to be his grandmother, they looked like lovers meeting after a long separation. The bony Gisèle held Charles upright until the searing pain in his groin subsided. They looked at each other, and through the tears that was blurring his sight, he saw that she was smiling.

"Monsieur Gerdgerm, it is serrr guurd to see yerrr," she said.

"Good to see you too, Gisèle," said Charles, when his ability to speak returned. Why on earth was she being so nice to him, he wondered? Then he realised that he was her employer now, and she presumably thought that she needed to be nice to him to keep her job.

Gisèle and Ernest managed to get Charles back to his chair, and Fish wandered off and started noisily lapping water from a dish.

"I think you will agree that the dog and the maid are both well acquainted with my nephew," said Ernest, seizing the moment to make a point.

Kugelhorn ignored the remark. "Now that all interested parties are here," he said, "I will get straight to the nexus of the matter." He looked at them all triumphantly, imagining that none of them knew what 'nexus' meant. He wasn't sure either, but it was a word that tended to draw people's attention when he needed it.

"Vota nostra sumus nexus," said Ernest.

Kugelhorn blinked several times rapidly. "I'm sorry?" he said.

"We are all the centre, or nexus if you will, of our own desires," said Ernest. "Ovid, Metamorphoses, Book 12, I think. The first example of the word 'nexus' being used in the sense of central or focal point, as I believe you intend it to mean. Before that, it was only used in the sense of a connection or a series of connections linking two things. Which the Romans were terribly keen on discovering, as you doubtless know."

Like an inner tube with a puncture, Kugelhorn was visibly deflating. However, he had yet to reveal his trump card, so he decided to ignore Ernest and press on with his plan. He picked up the large envelope lying to the right of the manila files and emptied the contents onto the table. There were about a dozen letters in envelopes addressed to Sebastian Kugelhorn, c/o Kugelhorn, Kugelhorn, Gummy and Schütz, Temple Bar, London EC4.

He picked up one of the letters and took it out of its envelope. "I have here in my hand one of several letters..." he paused and indicated the others on the table in front of him, "which have arrived at our office since the sad demise of Veronica Stoodley. Each and every one of them contains a claim to Miss Stoodley's estate, and it would be extremely remiss if we at Kugelhorn, Kugelhorn, Gummy and Schütz failed to examine them and decide if they're authentic or not."

"What on earth do you mean?" asked Ernest.

"Miss Stur ... Stoodley first deposited the will with our company two years ago. Then suddenly last month, she called the office to ask for it back. We delivered the document to her and a week later, the document was returned to us, much revised."

"And ...?"

"We have to keep an open mind about its validity."

"Open mind, my arse!" said Ernest.

"Please, Mister Goodgame, let's try to control our language here. There's a lady present."

"There's also a charlatan present." Ernest's eyes were blazing now. "Answer me this. How did all these people find out about Miss Stoodley's death?"

"I'm not at liberty ----"

Ernest stood up and reached over for Kugelhorn's briefcase. The solicitor grabbed it, but Ernest snatched it from him. He opened it and pulled out the newspaper that he had seen earlier. It was a copy of *The Times*, dated Friday 12th February.

"I noticed this when you took it out earlier," he said. "I was wondering why you were carrying a newspaper around that's more than a week old. Let's see what's in it."

He didn't have far to look. On the front page, along with other classified advertisements, was a boxed announcement of Miss Stoodley's death, including an estimate that her estate was worth ten thousand pounds. Anyone who believed they may have a connection with the deceased were encouraged to write to Sebastian Kugelhorn, c/o Kugelhorn, Kugelhorn, Gummy and Schütz, Temple Bar, London EC4.

"Do you people have no shame?" asked Ernest. "I know what your seedy little trick is. You follow up each of these enquiries, charging a small fortune for every letter you write. By the time you've finished, you decide the will is genuine, but you land the recipient of the inheritance, in this case my nephew Charles Goodgame, with a bill for your so-called *services*, which by this time is probably five hundred guineas or more!"

"We are following due process when there's suspicion about the authenticity of a will," said Kugelhorn.

"But there *is* no suspicion. You're creating a problem where there isn't one. Do you believe the signatures on the will to be authentic?"

"Miss Stoodley's signature seems to be authentic, but we're keeping an open mind about the witnesses."

"Well, you can bloody well close your mind right this minute," said Ernest. "If you'd bothered to check, you would have seen that one of the witnesses is me. And it would be a good idea if you check out the name of the second one, as well."

Kugelhorn glanced down at the names of the two witnesses. The name Ernest Goodgame was clearly recognisable from the handwriting. He tried to work out the staccato signature of the second witness before reading the person's name typed below it. When he read the name, his eyes opened wide.

"Good, now we're getting somewhere," said Ernest. "You can see that I have friends in *very* high places."

"Indeed," said Kugelhorn.

"That man is one of my closest friends, and he has the power to bring prosecutions against anyone he likes, including solicitors who are illegally trying to contest the authenticity of a will."

"Now, now, Mr Goodgame. You used the word 'illegally', that's slander!"

"I say again - I am confident I can persuade my friend to view this as an illegal attempt to contest the authenticity of a will."

"Are you threatening me, Mister Goodgame?"

"Yes, I am," replied Ernest. "And you'd better take it seriously." He picked up the third manila file, the one that Kugelhorn had so far not opened.

"Mister Goodgame! That file is the property of Kugelhorn ----"

438

"Oh do shut up, you pathetic little man!" Ernest examined the documents in the file. As he expected, the deeds to the house were there, and a whole series of other documents relating to stocks and shares owned by Miss Stoodley. Ernest flicked through the sheets of paper, doing a quick calculation as he looked at each one. He then picked up the will and checked if there were any provisions for anyone other than Charles. No. Everything, property, possessions, stocks, shares, dog - all bequeathed to Charles Goodgame.

"Mr Kugelschreiber, I think your business here is done," said Ernest. "So, you can give us the keys to the house and clear off."

Kugelhorn ignored the deliberate mispronunciation of his name. "I have no intention of parting with the keys so easily," he said.

"Fair enough," said Ernest. "If you're going to be juvenile about this, we'll use Gisèle's keys for the time being to get in and out, and we'll change the locks. And I will be in touch with my friend at the House of Lords regarding your company's improper conduct."

The four people at the table stared at each other. A flash of lightning lit up the kitchen, and there was the loudest crack of thunder so far. The rain that had been pattering against the window increased to monsoon proportions.

Kugelhorn replaced the letters from the bogus claimants into the brown envelope and put them and the manila file containing other correspondence into his briefcase. Ernest was still holding the will and he had the file with the house deeds and stocks and shares in front of him. The solicitor thought about trying to get them back but decided against it. He put his hand in his pocket, tossed the keys to the house onto the table and walked out of the kitchen. The house shook slightly as the large front door slammed behind him. Fish ran into the hallway and barked loudly.

"What a pity he hasn't got an umbrella," said Ernest. "And he seems to have forgotten his hat."

Chapter 36
Flesh and blood and whatnot

Ernest and Charles stayed in the kitchen until the rain stopped. Gisèle scuttled about tidying up, even though there was nothing to tidy up.

"Durrrrs on wernt a curp erf tea?" she asked as soon as Kugelhorn was out of the house.

"Tea? Oh, yes please, Gisèle," said Charles.

"Moi, je préfèrais café, s'il te plaît," said Ernest.

"Aaaaahh! Vous parlez français!" she said.

"Un petit peu seulement," he replied, modestly.

Gisèle bustled about the kitchen, opening and closing cupboards, moving empty flower vases a few inches to the left or right and then back to their original position, all the time chatting with Ernest, who responded with the occasional "Oui!", the less occasional "C'est vrai!" and a single "Pffft!". Charles looked at his uncle with even more respect than before. In addition to all his other talents, he was a linguist.

"Uncle Ernest, I'm very impressed," he said. "Your French is excellent. Where did you learn it?"

"Oh here and there," said Ernest, trying not to look too pleased about the compliment. "I can't actually do much more than order food or drink. And people think you're fluent in French if you know when to say pffft!"

"Pffft!" agreed Gisèle. She served them tea and coffee, apologising that there was no milk in the house, and apologising even more when she accidentally poured scalding tea into Charles's lap, making him groan almost as loudly as when Fish had caught him middle stump with his outstretched paws. It became clear that her anxiety was making her clumsy, so Charles and Ernest reassured her in a mixture of French and English that her position as housekeeper was safe.

The rain stopped rattling against the windows, and they got up to leave. Charles pocketed the key that Kugelhorn had thrown onto the table and told Gisèle he would move in just as soon as he could work out how to bring his few possessions over from Hammersmith. Once they had established that she was prepared to look after Fish by herself for a couple of days, the Goodgames made their way back to Ernest's house.

Before getting down to business in his office, Ernest poured out two large brandies. Charles happily accepted one, even though it wasn't even midday, and he didn't normally drink until the evening. He wondered if getting blotto in the morning was going to be a feature of his new life.

Ernest spread the various documents over his large desk. "You're going to need a good solicitor to make sure the transition of ownership goes smoothly," he said. "Someone who isn't a lying toad like that Kugelhorn worm. I know exactly the person."

"Thank you, uncle Ernest. I can't begin to tell you how much I appreciate what you've done for me."

Charles had the innocent look that Ernest had always found annoying in his brother Horace, but the previous week, Horace had said: "Why on earth would I blackmail you? You're my brother. Flesh and blood and whatnot." It had made an impression on the more jaundiced older sibling, and now he saw that Horace's son suffered from the same simple attitude to life.

"You're family," said Ernest. "Flesh and blood and whatnot. And when I'm down on my luck and walking the streets, I will come knocking on your door for a roof over my head."

Charles laughed, finding it hard to imagine his uncle ever being down on his luck.

Ernest was reminded of something he had meant to ask. "This place of yours in Hammersmith, why didn't you go there when you came back to London?"

"I owe the landlady some rent."

"How much?"

"Up to now, about five weeks."

"And do you have funds to pay it?"

"I'm afraid not."

"How much do you owe her?"

Charles calculated that he was about seven pounds twelve shillings in debt.

"Right. And she will probably want another month's rent when you tell her you're leaving," said Ernest. "I'll stump up the money to tide you over, but I expect to get every penny back."

"Of course. And once again, thank you very much." Charles thought that things could not possibly get any better than this, but they were about to do just that.

The telephone on the table rang, Ernest picked it up, spoke to someone, then passed the phone to Charles. "It's for you," he said.

Charles looked puzzled as he took the phone. "Hello?" he said.

"Is that Mister Charles Goodgame?" said a voice.

"Yes."

"Marvellous! My name's Godfrey Krumnagel, and I'm the executive manager of the Strand branch of Krumnagel's Bank. We look after the Agatha Merchant Trust Fund on behalf of your father, Horace Goodgame. It was he who suggested I try this number to locate your whereabouts, and I'm delighted to have found you."

443

Charles spent the next five minutes with his eyes and mouth wide open as he listened to Godfrey Krumnagel telling him his father's plan. When the bank manager almost casually mentioned that his mother Martha was still alive, Charles gasped out loud.

"What did you just say about my mother?" he asked.

"Your mother?" repeated Godfrey.

"You just said that my mother is still alive and has been fraudulently withdrawing money from my father's trust fund."

"Oh, yes, Martha Goodgame is your mother," said Godfrey. "I'm ... I'm terribly sorry that you didn't know about that."

Charles took a deep breath, paused for a moment, then tried to process the main part of the manager's message. "Let me get this right," he said. "My father wants me to have part of his trust fund, and he plans to work as a postmaster in Hunstanton?"

"That's pretty much the crux of it, yes," said Godfrey.

"I can't let him do that," said Charles. "I'll give him a call and tell him."

"I'm afraid you won't be able to do that. Your father's telephone is out of action at the moment." Godfrey explained that it would also be impossible to send a telegram because no one would be *in situ* running the Hunstanton Post Office until Horace had completed his training course in Norwich.

"OK, I'll write him a letter. Please leave the money where it is until I've sorted something out."

"Right you are," said Godfrey. "And don't hesitate to contact me or my assistant manager Mister Burgess if you need any further assistance." He said goodbye and put the phone down, thinking what an odd family the Goodgames were. All this money and no one wanted it.

444

*****

Charles paid his landlady Mrs O'Riordan the money he owed her, plus the extra month's rent that Ernest had predicted she would demand. He organised a horse and cart to take his possessions to Pelham Crescent and finally moved into Veronica Stoodley's house. He opened an account at Krumnagel's Bank, after which he had a rather unusual lunch with Godfrey Krumnagel at the Strand Cuppa Café, which consisted of several bacon rolls and cups of tea. Godfrey insisted that Charles accept an interest-free loan of two hundred pounds to tide him over while he sorted out payments from his stocks and shares. Once he had a cheque book, Charles headed to Savile Row, where he had three suits made. He bought a dozen shirts in Jermyn Street and, remembering Polly's comment that he clearly didn't buy his underwear at Harrods, he purchased the finest undergarments, garters and socks that the Knightsbridge emporium stocked.

On a sunny Friday morning at the end of February, he took the train to Hunstanton and spent the day with his father and Edna Normington. After much argument, Charles persuaded Horace to keep the trust fund money where it was. He did this by threatening to give it away if Horace refused to keep it.

"But I want to give something to you," said Horace. "You're my only child, and I don't imagine I'll have anymore. Children that is, not money." Edna's eyebrows raised sharply when she heard this. "I feel as if I've neglected you over the years. I just wanted to do something good for a change."

445

"You haven't neglected me, papa," said Charles, although when he thought about it later, he decided there was quite a lot of truth in the assertion. "And I have money of my own now." He told them that dividends from Miss Stoodley's massive portfolio of stocks and shares were going to amount to more than a hundred pounds a month, more than enough for his needs.

Charles went back to London, took a train to Lyme Regis and spent the next five days working in Diana Bagshot's Garden at Harcombe Bottom. Alexander Malleson was there, taking a break from his work at the new Malleson Sanatorium at Great Park, so Charles asked him for a lift back to Gloucestershire, apologising for using him like a taxi service again.

Great Park had been completely transformed in the few weeks since his last visit. The Malleson Sanatorium seemed to be a quiet, well-organised place, and there were already a large number of patients being treated for alcohol-related ailments.

Polly was surprised to see Charles, but there was tension in the air when they met. He explained that he had only come back to repair the damage to the Duke's portrait and wouldn't outstay his welcome. Polly told him the painting had been moved to the conservatory, so he took his box of oils and brushes out of the back of the house and spent the rest of the day alone with his work.

In the evening, Polly walked into the room and sat on the chaise longue. They remained in silence for a while, and eventually, she spoke.

"Are you angry with me?" she asked.

Charles stopped what he was doing and looked around the easel at her. "Angry with you? Why would I be angry with you?"

"I don't know. You went all cold on me before you went back to London. You didn't even give me a hug."

"If I remember rightly, you held out your hand for me to shake."

"You didn't have to shake it."

Charles sighed. Polly always managed to be the one who was right in any argument they had. "I'm absolutely not angry with you," he said. "Things just seemed to be ... I don't know ... strange when it was time for me to leave last time."

She stood up and approached the easel and put her arms round his neck. "I do love you," she said. "At least, I think I do."

"And I think I love you, too," he replied.

"Let's ..."

"What?"

"Let's see if there's anything for dinner."

Back in London, Charles signed up for driving lessons and after a small amount of actual practice, he passed his test in uncle Ernest's Daimler. The test was not very demanding - he was required to drive from one end of Fulham Road to the other without crashing the gears or hitting an old lady, which he managed to do. The next day, he bought a secondhand MG for a hundred and twenty pounds.

And so his new life began. He was a man of means, often seen walking his white Bichon Frise in Kensington Gardens, or driving to Richmond Park with the dog in the passenger seat.

One evening a few weeks later, he was sitting in his front room, smoking a cigar and drinking a glass of brandy, when there was a knock at the front door. He wasn't expecting anyone, so he peered round the curtain to see who it was.

It was Polly. He stumbled quickly out of the room and opened the front door.

"Hullo, Chas."

"Hullo, Pol."

"The Duke has gone off on a grand tour," she said.

"Really?"

"Yes. Rome, Florence, that sort of thing. He told me to take some time off, so I thought I'd mooch around in London for a few days."

"I see."

"Any chance that I can stay here while I do my mooching?"

"Stay here?"

"Yes."

"You mean in this house?"

"Yes."

"I suppose so."

"Are you going to let me in then?"

"Yes."

Postscript

The inclement weather that caused the cancellation of the Great Park shooting weekend in February continued into March, and parts of southern England experienced their heaviest snowfalls since records began. Then April was warm and pleasant and, as spring progressed, this is what happened to our principal characters...

Horace Goodgame divorced his wife Martha on the grounds of desertion, and his bigamous marriage to Leonora Goodgame was annulled. In accordance with his wishes, Leonora received half the money that had been recovered from the Trust Fund Tricksters, a total of two thousand, five hundred and sixty-two pounds and five shillings, minus solicitor's fees and bank charges, which came to twenty-two guineas. His son Charles refused to take the rest of the money, so it remained at Krumnagel's Bank and accrued interest. After a short training course, Horace became the new Hunstanton postmaster and after a slightly longer courtship, he married Edna Normington.

Martha Goodgame was convicted of faking her own death, which was considered a crime because it was done with the intention to defraud. She was also found guilty of the illegal withdrawal of funds from the Agatha Merchant Trust Fund and was sentenced to three years' imprisonment at His Majesty's Pleasure in Holloway Prison.

Emily Roebuck was convicted of the same crime of fraud and of assaulting two people, namely a police officer, Inspector G Sparrow Esquire, and a member of the public, R Burgess Esquire, and was sentenced to five years AHMP. It was decided that she should be separated from her partner in crime, so she was scheduled to be incarcerated at Manchester's Strangeways Prison. A Black Maria van set off to transport her to that smoky dark city in the north, but the guard who was supposed to sit with her in the back of the van found her so frightening to look at that he decided to sit in the front of the van with the driver. When the van reached the Staffordshire village of Leek, the driver stopped to urinate against a wall - the other guard was asleep while he was doing this - and Roebuck escaped. The two prison officers didn't notice that she was gone until they drove through the gates at Strangeways, parked the van and pulled open the back doors.

Both were dismissed for negligence, and the driver was also fined five shillings for gross indecency. The wall in Leek he had urinated against belonged to the vicarage of St Edward the Confessor Church, and his long and noisy piss (he had prostrate problems, so he always groaned when urinating) was witnessed by the vicar's wife and three of her friends who were taking tea at the window of the sitting room.

A year later, in Miami Florida, Roebuck had the misfortune to bump into **Inspector Sparrow**, who was attending an international conference for police officers in the city. She literally collided with him when she came out of a store and he recognised her voice when she called him a 'piss-pot', the same expression she had used when Rupert Burgess the assistant bank manager had tried to stop her leaving the Duke's Head Hotel in Kings Lynn. American lawyers then spent weeks trying to save her from extradition until her funds ran out, they lost interest and she was taken back to England to serve her sentence at Strangeways.

Leonora Capstan discovered that she was not legally married to Horace and was also informed of his generosity with the recovered funds. Even though she was the author of seven novels under the name Leonora Capstan, she had no wish to continue to be nominally linked to her former husband. In order to recall the one time in her life when she was deliriously happy (even though it lasted barely three months), she changed her name to Leonora Petworth, which recognised that her husband's Argentinian business partner was her one true love, and indeed the father of her daughter Polly. Before the end of the year, under her new pen name, she had written and published *She Never Forgot*, the story of a woman who takes revenge against her unfaithful husband by clubbing him to death with an artist's easel, which she then burns in a fireplace underneath a portrait painted by Vincent Van Gogh. It was the first of several best-selling Leonora Petworth murder mysteries. She continued to live at the apartment in Earls Court, and enjoyed occasional visits to Stanford Saint Mary for a spot of rumpy-pumpy with **Arnold McGurk** the stationmaster.

When her former husband **Ronnie Capstan** appeared before magistrates in Cheltenham on the Monday after his arrest at Great Park, the authorities decided not to bring charges against him for the attempted theft of a work of art, and convicted him merely of attempting to steal a police vehicle. He was fined two pounds and ten shillings. His request to the presiding magistrate to pay by cheque was refused and he spent another night in a cold cell at the police station. When he woke up in the morning, he was told that someone had paid the fine, and he was free to go. He asked who it was and was told the person had asked to remain anonymous. Ronnie took the first train to London, and made it back to Hampstead in time to see his sister **Cornelia Wickham-Thynne** standing on the doorstep of 47 Well Walk with her husband **Sir Arthur** and a woman Ronnie recognised as the barmaid from the Flask, **Betty Burton.**

Sir Arthur had admitted adultery with Betty and took full responsibility for the breakdown of his marriage to Cornelia, who accepted that their relationship was over, but demanded to continue living in the house. Arthur agreed, but told her that he and Betty would also be living there. By the time Ronnie arrived on the doorstep, Cornelia had re-focussed her demands and was heading for Claridge's, where she would stay until Arthur found her somewhere suitable to live. Ronnie asked if he could tag along, and the two of them shared a suite for a month, until Arthur bought them an apartment in Saint John's Wood. A few months later, Ronnie was shot dead by a business associate. Cornelia continued to live in the apartment which was, by complete chance, next door to the former Viscountess Grimbledon, now known merely as **Diana Malleson,** after she relinquished her title when she married **Alexander Malleson.** The ceremony took place at Chelsea Register Office, where Horace Goodgame and Leonora Capstan had got hitched, the event which kick-started this whole saga. Three days after her wedding, Diana discovered she was pregnant. An immediate success, you might say, as was Alexander's new business venture, the sanatorium at Great Park.

Alexander was also the anonymous person who paid Ronnie Capstan's fine in Cheltenham. He felt it best for everyone if the man whose eyes were too close together left the area as soon as possible.

The Duke of Burfaughtonleigh was saved from financial disaster by the injection of funds provided by the Malleson Sanatorium. He embarked on a Grand Tour to Venice, Florence and Rome, accompanied by **Montmorency Pickles** the butler.

And what of **Gilbert Woolnough** and **Lawrence Kimberley-Waugh?** On the night that Ronnie Capstan was caught red-handed trying to steal the portrait of Robert Louis Stevenson, the two failed art thieves drove through the night to London. Kimberley-Waugh went to his flat in Upper Montagu Street W1 and sat there with the curtains closed for three days, expecting a knock on the door from the Old Bill. Gilbert headed back to the house in Pimlico where he rented a room from another Marquis, who was also waiting impatiently for his father to pop his clogs.

Gilbert scrounged some money off his housemate and went to Paris with more of his mother's jewellery. Unfortunately, he tried to sell a very unusual emerald and pearl necklace to Margaritte, Duchesse d'Alençon, who lived in a grand apartment on the edge of the Bois de Boulogne. La Duchesse was a good friend of his mother and knew perfectly well that the necklace had never belonged to Queen Victoria, so while Gilbert was noisily slurping down a glass of wine in her drawing room, she went into her boudoir and called the gendarmes. On his way of out the building, Gilbert was arrested. By the end of the day, he was under lock and key in a dingy cell at the Place du Marché police station in Saint-Honoré, with surly guards who didn't speak English and responded to his angry barking by hitting him on the head with their batons until he shut up. When he finally made it back home, he was arrested by Sergeant Conway and Constable Prodgers, after Gilbert's mother Florence told them that he had stolen jewellery from her worth hundreds of pounds. He ended up in

Wormwood Scrubs, sharing a cell with **Billy the Badger.**

After his three days in hiding, Lawrence Kimberley-Waugh went back to Sotheby's, where he was summoned to the boss's office and dismissed, with no explanation given. In fact, one of his married woman conquests had complained to the company about him, claiming that he had encouraged her to pay over the odds for a painting. This was true, it was something he often did to increase his commission, but what had really incensed her was the fact that he told her he was bored with her and didn't want to see her again. Her husband was a major shareholder at Sotheby's, and this carried enough weight for Kimberley-Waugh to be sacked. The following week, he started work in the men's underwear and hosiery department at Harrods, where Charles Goodgame was his first customer.

There's one final event to relate.

The morning after Polly turned up at Charles's house in Pelham Crescent, they put a portfolio into the back of the MG and set off to Gloucestershire. They knew exactly what time they wanted to arrive at Great Park, so they stopped for lunch at the Dog and Ferret, then got back into the MG and drove out of Stanford Saint Mary.

A few minutes later, they arrived at the gate to the property, where the old weather-beaten sign that said EAT ARK had been replaced by a brand new one that said MALLESON SANATORIUM. Charles drove up the main drive towards the house and parked at the foot of the steps leading up to the double-door entrance. It was deathly quiet as they entered, Polly having timed their arrival to coincide with the inmates taking their enforced afternoon nap and the staff having tea and biscuits in the kitchen downstairs. They walked down

454

the corridor and into the blue drawing room, where they were alarmed to see two of the residents asleep in armchairs. Fortunately, both were snoring loudly and seemed dead to the world.

Charles walked over to the fireplace, climbed onto the table, and took down the portrait of Robert Louis Stevenson and carefully removed it from its frame. He then opened his portfolio, and took out another version of the same painting, placed it in the frame and put it back over the fireplace. He put the first painting in the portfolio, and they left the room. They saw no one from the house as they made their way to the front door.

They drove down the driveway in silence. When Charles turned into the road towards Stanford Saint Mary, he turned quickly to look at Polly. "We've done the right thing, you know," he said. "We were never cut out to be international art thieves. It's best that we took it back."

"If you say so," she replied. "What are you going to do with the copy?"

"I think I'll hang it over the mantelpiece in the lounge. See if anyone thinks it's a real Van Gogh."

Polly laughed.

"OK ... let's head back to the smoke," said Charles.

"Actually, I'm a bit tired," said Polly. "Do you mind if we don't go straight back? Can we see if there's a room at the Dog and Ferret?"

"Are you sure?"

"Positive."

Charles put his foot down and accelerated towards the village.

"Careful," she said. "Let's make sure we get there in one piece."